# THE GRANVILLE LEGACY

## Una-Mary Parker

This first world edition published in Great Britain 2006 by
SEVERN HOUSE PUBLISHERS LTD of
9–15 High Street, Sutton, Surrey SM1 1DF.
This first world edition published in the USA 2007 by
SEVERN HOUSE PUBLISHERS INC of
595 Madison Avenue, New York, N.Y. 10022.

British Library Cataloguing in Publication Data

Parker,   Una-Mary
    The Granville legacy
    1.   Granville family  (Fictitious characters)  -  Fiction
    2.   Upper class – England  -  Fiction
    3.   Great Britain  -  Social conditions  -  1945  -  Fiction
    4.   Domestic fiction
    I.   Title
    823.9'14 [F]

    ISBN-13:  978-0-7278-6412-3   (cased)
    ISBN-10:  0-7278-6412-2       (cased)
    ISBN-13:  978-0-7278-9187-7   (paper)
    ISBN-10:  0-7278-9187-1       (paper)

*All Severn House titles are printed on acid-free paper.*

Typeset by Palimpsest Book Production Ltd.,
Grangemouth, Stirlingshire, Scotland.
Printed and bound in Great Britain by
MPG Books Ltd., Bodmin, Cornwall.

# Part One

# New Beginnings

# 1946–1947

# One

'I can't believe this is really happening,' Juliet said in a hushed voice, as the Daimler drew up outside Caxton Hall.

'Too good to be true?' Henry Granville teased, smiling fondly.

'Oh God, Dads, much too good to be true.' She turned to him and her eyes looked dazed as if she were half-blinded by happiness. 'I've been in love with Daniel for eight years . . .'

Years of gut-wrenching desire and longing, frustration and despair; years when she didn't care whether she survived the Blitz or not. Sometimes the thought of dying had seemed more like a promise than a threat, especially when she'd lost the baby daughter he'd known nothing about. Daniel Lawrence, the thirty-six-year-old divorcee, whose strong personality and good looks gave him such presence that when he entered a crowded room, everyone else seemed to fade into insignificance. Daniel Lawrence, who had overshadowed any other men in her life, and who, at last, was about to become her second husband. He'd be waiting for her now in the registry office, tall and broad shouldered, wearing an immaculate suit, his dark eyes glittering, his mouth turned up at the corners in the quirky smile that still sent her heart thudding after all these years.

'Here we are,' Henry said, as the chauffeur opened the car door and Juliet stepped on to the pavement. There was a barrage of flashing bulbs as a group of photographers and journalists pressed closer; Fleet Street were out in force to take pictures of the famous society beauty who had grabbed their attention ever since she'd exploded on to the stage of London society as a debutante. Now, as the ex-Duchess of Kincardine stood before them, slim and glamorous in a champagne coloured satin suit and a hat trimmed with matching osprey feathers, they saw she'd lost none of her allure, in fact she'd never been seen looking so radiant.

Juliet felt a hand cupping her elbow. 'Time we went in, darling,' Henry suggested. She nodded and turned to enter the building, holding her bouquet of orchids in her left hand.

'Happy ever after, this time,' he whispered, grinning.

Impulsively she turned and flung her other arm around his neck. 'Oh Dads, I love you!' she exclaimed, a tremor in her voice.

Henry's eyes were extra bright as they entered the simple formal room where the marriage was to take place. It flashed through his mind how different this scene was from the last time he'd given her away in the magnificent setting of Westminster Abbey, which had been festooned with thousands of white roses. How different things would have been if they'd been aware then that Cameron Kincardine was homosexual, which meant he could never be a full husband to Juliet.

'Darling, you look ravishing,' Liza Granville greeted her daughter in a whisper, as if they were in a church and Juliet flashed a smile around the room, but she only truly saw Daniel, standing by the registry table, behind which stood a beaming Registrar.

Daniel's eyes looked deeply into hers as he mouthed, 'Hello.'

'Would everyone like to be seated?' the Registrar requested.

There was a refined kind of shuffling as Henry's mother, Lady Anne – looking more like Queen Mary than ever – took a seat beside her daughter Candida, who was with her new husband, Colonel Andrew Pemberton, while Juliet's four sisters filled the row behind; Rosie with her American fiancé, Salton Webb; Louise, glowingly pregnant, accompanied by her husband, Dr Shane Hunter; Amanda, who'd refused to get 'dressed up like a dog's dinner' for the occasion; and Charlotte who, at fifteen, promised to be the greatest beauty of all the sisters. Cousins and close friends filled the other rows of seats.

Juliet stood beside Daniel and for a long moment they gazed at each other. There was no need for words. The long hard road they'd both travelled to reach this moment was over. Daniel was remembering that night in 1936, when he'd seen a girl with slanting aquamarine eyes through a haze of cigarette smoke in a Soho jazz club, and knew in that instant that he'd met his destiny, forgetting in that same instant he was a married man.

Juliet was remembering a weekend in Paris three weeks

later and how that first encounter had turned her from a dizzy debutante into a sensual woman who knew what she wanted.

Back at Juliet's magnificent Park Lane house, for which she would always be grateful to Cameron for having made it part of her divorce settlement, the indomitable Dudley, an elderly ex-army batman who had acted as her butler throughout the Blitz, when he wasn't a fire watcher, was preparing a buffet lunch for the wedding party. Having called upon all his black market contacts to help him procure a feast of almost pre-war standard, he'd managed to get hold of lobsters, York ham, and smoked salmon. He'd even acquired several cases of champagne.

There was only one thing he regretted about the occasion and that was he'd no longer be able to address Juliet as 'Your Grace', a formality that had greatly impressed his contacts, and had given him a sense of self-importance, too.

But old habits die hard, and when Juliet and Daniel hurried, hand in hand, up the front door steps of the house, Dudley swung open the front door with a flourish and exclaimed in greeting, 'Your Grace, may I offer you my warmest congratulations . . . I mean . . .' His small pixie face flushed a deep red and his eyes showed his mortification. 'I b-beg your pardon,' he stammered. 'I mean madam, and sir, may I wish you every happiness in the future.'

Juliet burst out laughing. 'You're forgiven if you get me a glass of champagne this instant!'

'And one for me, too,' Daniel quipped. He slipped his arm around Juliet's waist. 'Come on, darling.' He led her away from the drawing room, where they were to gather for drinks before luncheon. 'Take off that silly hat so I can kiss you properly.'

'It's a beautiful hat!' she protested, giggling.

'What's beneath it is more beautiful,' he whispered, as he pushed her gently into their bedroom. Then he lifted the concoction of cream silk and feathers off her head and threw it to one side. 'Hello, Mrs Lawrence,' he said softly, looking deep into her eyes as he pulled her close.

Juliet felt herself melting and her heart started hammering. 'Hello, Mr Lawrence,' she breathed as a wave of sudden desire swept through her.

'God, I want you so badly,' Daniel groaned, burying his face in her neck, clutching her tightly as if he could never bear to let her go.

'You've got me for the rest of our lives.' She took his face in her hands and reaching up, kissed him deeply.

'Juliet? Your guests are arriving, darling,' trilled Liza from the landing outside the door. 'Come along, sweetheart. Everyone's expecting you to receive them.'

'I'll be there in a moment, Mother,' Juliet shouted crossly. Then she gazed into Daniel's eyes. 'At least we'll be on our own for the next two weeks.'

Daniel stepped back, a look of resignation on his face. 'You have such a *large* family,' he said lightly.

As Juliet quickly powdered her nose she felt a tiny pang of alarm. Although he'd made light of the fact that his family had refused to attend the wedding, it had obviously hurt him more than she'd realized, so wrapped up had she been in her own happiness.

'Too large sometimes,' she said with equal lightness, as if it was a joke.

There was already a hubbub of chatter in the white and silver art nouveau drawing room, as waiters hired for the day moved around with trays of champagne, Juliet went straight over to Lady Anne, who was sitting in regal splendour in a deep rose-pink outfit.

'Granny, how wonderful you look!' she exclaimed, kissing her on both cheeks. 'That colour really suits you.'

'My darling girl, you're the one that looks wonderful.' Lady Anne held her hand for a moment. 'And where's that nice looking young man of yours?'

Daniel had overheard her. He stepped forward and kissed her, too. 'Lady Anne, I can see where Juliet gets her good looks from.'

Juliet turned to talk to other guests and found Liza at her elbow. 'Don't you like my outfit?' her mother queried, looking hurt. 'Norman Hartnell managed to dig out this velvet; it's pre-war, you know.' Her voice dropped to a whisper. 'He let me have it without having to give any coupons! Don't let Daddy or Granny know.' Liza's eyes roamed the room enviously. 'I do wish Daddy would let us move back to London.'

It was an old refrain and the last thing Juliet wanted to

listen to on her wedding day. Although Liza had promised Henry she'd be content to live in the country after their Green Street house had been demolished by a bomb and he'd nearly been killed when Hammerton's Bank, of which he was Chairman, had been hit, she'd soon forgotten her promise. The lure of London drew her like a pin to a magnet. There was nothing about the countryside she liked; in her mind it was bleak and boring. And she desperately missed the opportunity to wear glamorous clothes and totteringly high heels.

Juliet tried to hide her impatience. 'Mother, Dads is worn out. He's exhausted. The stress of the last five years had taken its toll, you know. He needs the peace and quiet of Hartley.'

Liza, her looks faded now and her brow puckered with discontent, sighed deeply. 'But we haven't even got the Campden Hill flat any more.'

Juliet moved away. 'Listen, I've got to talk to everyone. We can't discuss this now.'

At that moment Amanda bounced over. At eighteen, she was a big girl, blonde and blue eyed like her father but, to Liza's horror, had the large busted figure of her Aunt Candida.

'I never thought we'd get in!' she was telling someone robustly. She clapped her hands together, spilling some of her champagne down the front of her shabby tweed jacket and grey flannel skirt. Her strong legs were encased in thick woollen stockings and on her feet were stout walking shoes.

'Darling, I do wish you'd made an effort today with your appearance,' Liza nagged in a slightly whining voice.

'Oh, tommyrot!' Amanda scoffed.

'What are you talking about – we've got in?' Juliet asked her.

Her sister looked at Juliet as if she were mentally deficient. 'The General Election last year, of course. When we got rid of the Conservatives! Now that Clement Attlee is the Prime Minister the Labour party will get things done.'

Henry, listening to Amanda, frowned in anxiety. 'I think the way this country has repaid Winston Churchill is utterly disgraceful,' he said sternly. 'If it hadn't been for him we'd have lost the war, so you don't know what you're talking about, Amanda. Having a Labour government is a disaster, as it always is, in the end.'

7

She flushed. Her father was usually sympathetic to her views although he didn't agree with them. 'Churchill's an old man, Dad. We need new blood to get this country up and running again. We need to look after the poor, give them houses, schools, and we should provide free medical care for *everyone*,' she said hotly.

Henry turned away, not trusting himself to contain his anger. In his opinion many people in the country, including the overseas armed forces, had been foolishly allowed to think that even if they voted Labour, Churchill would still be the PM, because he'd been head of a coalition government throughout the war. Then he remembered that Amanda was still young and what did they say? If you're not a socialist when you're eighteen you have no heart, and if you're still a socialist at forty, you have no head. He made his way through the now crowded room towards Louise.

'How are you, darling?' He kissed his pretty gentle daughter and shook hands with Shane, his new son-in-law. 'You're both looking very well. How are you liking being pregnant?'

She spoke brightly and cheerfully but at the back of her mind she was thinking; it wasn't like this when I was expecting Rupert. Swiftly she banished those bitter sweet memories of that other baby, her first baby that she hadn't been allowed to keep, because she'd been fifteen and her boyfriend, Jack, had not been considered 'suitable' for her to marry.

'I love it,' she replied simply.

Henry spotted the shadow that had fallen across her face. 'And how's the new house getting on?' he asked to distract her.

'We've joined the twentieth century!' Shane quipped. 'We've actually had electricity installed . . .'

'Talk about *Fanny by Gaslight*,' Louise cut in. 'We actually had gas mantles which we had to light every evening!'

'Not to mention an outside loo in the backyard, and a bath which was a big metal tub.'

'I think the lack of amenities was reflected in the price, wasn't it?'

Shane nodded. 'I paid three hundred pounds for the freehold, because it's in Fulham. Chelsea was too expensive. The great thing is I can walk to St Stephen's Hospital in ten minutes. By the time we've done it up it could be worth five hundred.'

'Not that I'm moving again,' Louise pointed out, proud of

her first home. 'Three bedrooms should be enough for us. We won't be having more than a couple of children.'

Henry and Shane looked doubtful, but said nothing. Her father could see the pain at the back of her eyes that would never leave her, no matter how many children she had with Shane. Henry had always felt a deep sense of guilt that they'd sent Louise away to Liza's aunt in Wales when she'd been pregnant, as if they'd been ashamed of her.

'You must invite me to dinner one night,' Henry said, as if there was nothing in the world he'd like better.

'Are you sure you want to risk my cooking?' Louise laughed.

'At least I'll know, if I'm poisoned, that you didn't intend to bump me off deliberately!' Henry joked, patting her arm.

Shane was moved by the bond between the father and daughter. In fact since he'd married into the family what struck him most was the closeness between the five sisters, in spite of their disagreements and quarrels. Strangely, the only one who didn't seem to really *belong* was Liza. Even Amanda was a true Granville and very similar to Henry's sister.

At that moment Rosie came up to join the group. Her deep blue eyes widened as she looked at Louise's swollen stomach. 'Lucky you!' she said. Then she turned to Salton. 'As soon as we're married we're going to have a baby, aren't we?'

Salton, a laid-back and relaxed lawyer from Washington, who was now working for the American Embassy in Grosvenor Square, smiled indulgently, taking the remark in his stride as he did everything with Rosie.

'Sure, honey. As many as you want.'

Rosie glowed, her hand to her throat so everyone could see the enormous sapphire and diamond engagement ring he'd given her.

'Have you decided when you're getting married?' Shane asked.

'As soon as possible,' Rosie cut in swiftly. 'Now we've got your wedding out of the way, Juliet, we can get on with planning ours.'

Juliet raised her plucked eyebrows in amused surprise. 'I wasn't aware I was holding you up?'

'Oh, you know what I mean,' Rosie replied carelessly. 'Juliet may be younger than me but she always has to have her way, first!' she said to Salton.

'Not always,' Juliet replied quietly. Shane looked embarrassed. He was never sure how meaningful these spats were between Rosie and Juliet, for they maintained a solid front to defend each other if needed, and Rosie had told him that without Juliet she'd never have survived the death of her husband, Charles, in the London bombing.

Over by the fireplace, Daniel was still talking to Lady Anne.

'I'm so glad she's found happiness with you at last,' she told him. 'The darling girl's had the most wretched time; and I don't know how she got through the Blitz, working on an ambulance as a nurse. The sights she must have seen! I can hardly bear to think what it must have been like. And she never complained, you know. She's the bravest girl I've ever met.'

And your favourite grandchild, Daniel thought, smiling. He could see that this magnificent old lady and he were going to get on like a house on fire.

Dudley popped up from nowhere and refilled their glasses.

'M'lady, can I offer you a foie gras canapé?'

'Foie gras, Dudley? Goodness, where on earth did you get foie gras?'

Goodness had nothing to do with it, he reflected, quickly saying he'd saved a pre-war supply which he'd kept for a special occasion. 'And they don't come more special than today, m'lady,' he added.

'Quite right, Dudley.' Lady Anne smiled, not believing a word he'd said. 'I hope you'll be staying on here to take care of my granddaughter?'

He bowed his head and pursed his lips primly. 'Her Grace . . . I mean, Mrs Lawrence, has done me the honour of asking me to stay on.'

'I'm sure they couldn't do without you, Dudley.'

The little man turned red with gratification, and bustled off to get the foie gras.

'What a find,' Lady Anne remarked, shaking her head. 'I think his assiduous care of Juliet during the past six years has kept her sane.'

'And well fed,' Daniel remarked with a knowing look.

'Well . . .' She made a little grimace and shrugged. 'I think he can be forgiven.'

10

'What are you two plotting?' Juliet asked, laughing as she joined them on the sofa.

Daniel caught her hand and held it fast. 'We're praising the efforts of Dudley,' he told her.

'He's a natural. The second most important man in my life now,' she teased.

The room was packed, filled with the laughter and chatter that typified Juliet, who sparkled with vivacity as she and Daniel mingled with everyone, moving as one, in perfect unity and harmony, his hand constantly holding hers, or stroking her back or arm, or clasping her to his side as if he could never bear to let her go. And from time to time Juliet looked up into his face, as if wanting to imprint this moment, the memory of him standing beside her, into her mind for the rest of her life.

The only person who rivalled her in beauty, but a very different type of beauty, was her youngest sister, Charlotte. At fifteen she was breathtakingly exquisite, with silvery blonde hair, small perfect features, and enormous blue eyes fringed with dark lashes. Altogether petite, she reminded her mother of a perfect little doll, with her tiny waist and slim legs; a creation you'd expect to find on the counter of Harrods' toy department, Liza reflected proudly.

What was to become of Charlotte? Everyone in the family had their own vision of her future, from a Hollywood film star, to marriage to a Marquess, or in Liza's case, a foreign prince. Only Lady Anne felt apprehensive, and suggested they should all let the poor child be.

'For goodness sake, she's only fifteen,' her grandmother pointed out. 'Let her decide for herself, when she's older.'

But Charlotte lived in a dream world and had no idea what was to become of her. Get married and have babies, she supposed vaguely; that's what all young women from her background did, except for Amanda.

Henry came up to Juliet and Daniel. 'I think it's time we drank to your health, don't you?'

'And we've got to cut the cake!' Juliet said. 'It was made specially. God knows how Dudley managed to get enough sugar to ice it.'

Standing close together they made the first careful cut amid cheers and a chorus of 'Good show!'

Then there was silence as Henry stood beside them to speak.

'As the father of the bride . . .' he began, knowing that would give everyone a laugh, 'I'd just like to say how delighted Liza and I are to welcome Daniel into the family.' More cheering and a cry of 'Here, here!' was heard. 'I needn't say how proud I am of Juliet and how we, as a family, admire the way she was out in the Blitz, night after night, helping the injured, the frightened, the lost and the shell-shocked citizens of this city. And she dragged her own sister, Rosie, from the ruins of the Café de Paris, when it received a direct hit, putting herself in danger from falling masonry. Meanwhile, although the details must remain hush-hush and will do so for some time, Daniel, I know, did a magnificent and highly dangerous job in SOE, which Mr Churchill himself confirmed helped shorten the war by at least a year.'

Everyone started clapping and while Juliet blushed and her eyes brimmed at the tribute her father had paid her, Daniel looked down at the floor, deeply embarrassed and at the same time remembering those colleagues of his who had not been lucky enough to survive their efforts of sabotage behind the German lines.

'Thank God,' Henry continued, 'these two magnificent young people, who love each other so much, are able to enjoy a richly deserved happy ending, together at last. Everyone, I give you Juliet and Daniel, and God bless them.'

Glasses were raised and there was a roar of 'Juliet and Daniel' as the guests toasted them. Juliet immediately hugged her father, while Daniel shook his hand.

'It's so beautiful,' Liza wept emotionally, dabbing her eyes.

Rosie sipped her champagne and hoped her father would make as moving a speech about her at her forthcoming wedding. Was it likely? she wondered. What could he say about her? Stayed in the country for the duration. Looked after her two children. Had an affair with a wounded airman. Then Charles was killed at the Café de Paris the night they dined there . . . then what? Met and got engaged to a rich American lawyer? It was hardly a heroic war story.

It was late in the afternoon before all the guests had departed. Alone at last, Juliet and Daniel looked at each other.

'Well, Mrs Lawrence?' he asked, catching both her hands and staring steadily into her eyes.

'Well, Mr Lawrence?' she replied, suddenly tremulous. She was reminded of that first night in Paris, when, as a virgin, she'd allowed Daniel to take her again and again, changing her life forever.

'Are you ready to go?' he asked, his voice husky.

She nodded. 'Dudley's already put the cases in the car.'

There was no going to Paris this time. Europe was still suffering chaos in the aftermath of war. Tonight they would stay at Claridge's and tomorrow Daniel was taking her to Ireland, which she'd never been to before.

He stooped to kiss her, gently and lovingly. 'Let's go then.'

Dudley was waiting in the hall below as they came down the stairs. There was a white envelope in his hand. 'This has just come for you, sir,' he said, handing it to Daniel. 'I found it on the doormat a few minutes ago.'

Daniel frowned, taking the envelope and ripping it open.

'Who's it from?' Juliet asked, peering over his shoulder as he scanned the handwritten note.

With a grunt of anger he crushed it in his hand, grinding it into a small ball which he flung on the floor.

Juliet started with surprise. 'What is it?'

His mouth was grim, his voice harsh. 'Nothing for you to worry about, darling. Come on. Let's go.'

He pushed her almost roughly towards the front door.

Juliet hesitated, turning to Dudley. 'Thank you for arranging everything so perfectly today,' she told him. Dudley could see the bewilderment in her eyes, and for a moment remembered how strained she used to look when she returned from the First Aid Post. 'Have a rest while we're away,' she continued, 'and we'll be back on the 27th.'

'I'll have everything ready for your return, Your ... madame.' Dudley's small dark button eyes held the adoration and loyalty of an old and devoted dog.

Juliet flashed him one of her ravishing smiles. 'I know you will. I'm depending on it, Dudley.'

'Come along, darling,' Daniel said, grabbing her hand, impatient to be off.

With a flurry they hurried down the front steps into Juliet's Rolls Royce.

Dudley watched them go with a lump in his throat. He wouldn't spend the next fortnight resting, he'd spring clean the house, turn out all the cupboards, arrange to have flowers in all the main rooms ready for the return of the young woman he worshipped from afar, watching over her like a guardian angel as he'd done for the past six years.

Closing the front door, he stopped to pick up the crumpled letter and envelope from the white marble floor. Then seated at the kitchen table, he carefully smoothed out the creases with the heel of his hand, so he could read it.

It didn't take long, and as he sat there, alone in the great house that he'd come to love as if it were his own, his lean shoulders sagged, and his pixie face paled and grew lined and lumpy, as if he'd aged in the last few minutes.

He stayed like that for quite a while, praying to God that the content of the letter wasn't true.

# Two

'Oh dear, back to real life,' Liza grumbled mournfully as Henry drove up the drive of Hartley Hall. The Georgian family home stood welcoming as it had done for the Granvilles for the past hundred and twenty years; its soft pink brickwork bathed in an autumn sunset, its symmetrical windows, surrounded by climbing roses and wisteria.

Henry's two young black Labradors, Rufus and Nelson, lay by the white front door, instinctively knowing he was about to return home.

Seeing them, Henry remarked mildly, 'I think Real Life is rather pleasant myself.'

'Mrs Dobbs said she was going to make toad-in-the-hole and treacle pudding for dinner,' Lady Anne volunteered, thankful to be home after a long and emotional day.

'I couldn't eat a *thing*,' Liza protested, pulling off her gloves and dropping them carelessly on to the floor of the car.

Henry glanced at his discontented wife. Juliet's wedding party had unsettled Liza, reminding her of how their lives used to be, but were unlikely ever to be again. For one thing, food rationing had become worse since the end of the war because what resources there were had been diverted to feed the starving people of Europe. And although they'd advertised for more staff to help run Hartley and the large garden surrounding it, no one wanted to go into service any more. Especially not women.

'The girls who are being demobbed want to work in shops and offices now they've known what independence is like,' the head of a London agency told him. 'No one wants to be a servant any more.'

The grim reality of maintaining a ten-bedroom house, with outbuildings and land worried Henry greatly. He was no longer as rich as he'd been in 1939, something that Liza was failing to comprehend. She still expected to be able to spend hundreds of pounds a year on clothes, and she was forever going on about entertaining, and how they should be giving weekend house parties; a life he could no longer afford except on a small scale. He was also tired, suffering a deep weariness of bone and brain that a few good nights sleep no longer assuaged. He planned to retire in three years, and then nothing on God's earth was going to take him away from Hartley. Nothing, he swore to himself, except the occasional day in London to see his daughters.

'I do wish Juliet knew some *really* intelligent people,' Amanda remarked as she and Charlotte climbed out of the car. 'There wasn't a single person at the reception who was remotely interested in politics. What do these people *do* with their lives? Apart from going to parties?'

'I expect they are interested, Amanda, but a wedding is neither the time nor the place for you to extol the virtues of Clement Attlee, to a room full of people who voted for Winston Churchill,' Henry told her.

'I suppose they were all Conservatives,' she said in disgust. 'You'd have thought the war would have opened their eyes to how poor people suffer hardship though, wouldn't you?'

Lady Anne paused at the door of her private sitting room. She gave her granddaughter one of her serene I-know-what-you're-feeling-but-don't-make-such-a-fuss smiles. 'Times *are* changing, my dear girl. Try not to be too impatient. Rome wasn't built in a day.'

Amanda stomped up the stairs to her bedroom. 'I'm going to change into some comfortable old clothes.'

As she disappeared round the bend in the stairs, Liza observed with asperity, 'I thought she was already wearing her comfortable old clothes.'

Henry and his mother exchanged amused looks.

'I'm going for a walk, Mama.'

'Good idea, Henry.'

'Can I come with you, Daddy?' Charlotte asked.

'Yes, but you'd better put on some sensible shoes, darling.'

'OK. I shan't be a sec.' She ran up the stairs, taking them two at a time, her silvery hair, which to Henry's regret Liza had had cut short because it was 'more fashionable', bouncing with hot-tongued curls.

16

'When you get back, perhaps you'd like to join me for a glass of sherry?' Lady Anne suggested.

Henry nodded, reading the subtext of what she was saying. 'Thanks, Mama.'

Walking through the rose garden, which Lady Anne had created when she'd first married his father, Henry felt the beneficent peace of Hartley enfold him in a cocoon of tranquillity. His cares seemed to fall away. The lush grass beneath his feet was soft, the air about him fresh and clean, heady like wine after the smoke-laden atmosphere of London.

With Charlotte by his side, and Rufus and Nelson lolloping happily around them as they walked in companionable silence, Henry wished his life could always be like this. The war was over and he felt a great sense of peace and thankfulness that all of them, with the exception of Rosie's husband, had survived. Now a feeling of great contentment swept over him as he trod the earth of his beloved home; a home that would provide a haven for his family and their descendents, even after he'd gone. Hartley was his legacy to his daughters and grandchildren, and it gave him a feeling of solace to think that in another fifty, or a hundred years the Granvilles would still be treading the rich soil of this beloved place.

'Juliet looked very happy today, didn't she, Daddy?' Charlotte remarked, tying her silk scarf under her chin, as her steps matched his.

'Very happy,' he agreed. 'I like Daniel very much. I think he's good for her.'

'Why did none of his family come to the wedding?'

'Well, he's Jewish, darling, and his religion doesn't really allow him to marry a Christian.'

Charlotte looked thoughtful. 'Then he must love Juliet a lot.'

'They've loved each other for a very long time.'

'I think,' she said solemnly, 'that religion gets in the way sometimes, don't you? After all, there's only one God, so why doesn't everyone get together and worship Him in the same way?'

Henry smiled at the simplicity of the reasoning of the young. 'If only they did,' he said fervently, thinking of the recent terrible discoveries of Belsen, where thousands of Jews had perished at the hands of the Nazis.

'Do you think Daniel's family will ever want to meet Juliet?' she asked curiously.

Henry thought about Daniel's three children, whom Juliet had told him were now aged ten, twelve and fourteen years old. 'They're still very young, Charlotte, and it's not really up to them, but perhaps in time . . .' His voice drifted away. Their mother had fallen in love with someone else during the war and it had been her choice to ask Daniel for a divorce so why should she prevent the children seeing their father?

'Perhaps they were too young to come to the wedding?' Charlotte suggested hopefully.

'I expect you're right.' But Henry felt uneasy. Daniel's parents were dead, but what about his sister? Surely she'd have wanted him to be happy?

In their suite at Claridge's, Juliet lay beside Daniel on the vast bed, a pulsating mass of emotional desire, wanting him again and again as if she could never have enough of him. As if she'd only dreamed they were together at last and needed to be reassured they were lovers once more, as they'd been on that weekend in Paris, so long ago. As they'd been in his Chelsea cottage when the air-raid siren had sounded and she'd conceived their baby. And as they'd been the day, earlier this year, when he'd returned to her as she sat in her bedroom over looking Hyde Park, believing her life was over and wishing herself dead.

Now, for the first time in her life, her sense of psychological self-protective reserve had been broken, and she was giving the whole of herself to him, not just physically, but heart, mind, and soul. She'd stripped herself of all pretence and artifice and the woman now in his arms had come a long way from the flirtatious virgin he'd first known.

'I love you, Juliet.' He spoke with a depths of passion she'd never heard before. His eyes were boring into hers with a profoundness that made her shiver; it was as if he was making a vow before God. 'Now I've found you again I'm never going to let you go.'

'And I'll never let you go,' she echoed feverishly. 'I want to spend every moment of the rest of my life with you.' She wrapped her arms and legs around his strong body. 'I want all of you . . . I want your baby . . .'

18

He buried his face in the fragile hollow of her neck. 'My darling . . . My darling . . . All the babies you want . . .'

But a sad little voice in her head reminded her of the little girl she'd lost, the baby daughter she and Daniel had never known.

'Come in, my dear,' Lady Anne greeted Henry as he entered her private chintzy inner sanctum when he returned from his walk. 'Help yourself to sherry and you can pour one for me, too.'

Henry went over to the side table on which Warwick, creaky, ancient and suffering from bad feet, had placed a silver tray with glasses and a decanter. He'd been Lady Anne's butler for nearly fifty years, having come to Hartley Hall as a boot boy when he'd been a seventeen-year-old orphan. Devoted to the family, he still struggled through each day without complaint. The Granvilles were the only family he'd ever had, and Hartley his only home and he clung on to his position because his greatest fear was that one day someone should suggest he retire.

'Are you all right, Henry?' his mother asked, as he took the chair opposite her by the smouldering log fire that gave out little heat.

'I'm fine, Mama.'

'You're worried about Liza pining for London, aren't you?'

He took a deep breath. 'She needs to have something to keep her occupied,' he replied loyally.

Lady Anne remained silent. Hartley was screaming out for another pair of hands to darn worn-out bed linen, mend frayed chair covers and curtains, spring clean rooms and shampoo carpets, turn out cupboards and get to grips with cleaning the silver. She did what she could, but she couldn't do the heavy work any more, and neither could Warwick. Even Mrs Dobbs was struggling, at seventy-seven, to do all the cooking, single-handed. And now Rosie was engaged and living in London, she was no longer able to help as she'd done during the war.

And what did Liza do? Lady Anne asked herself. She wandered down at nine o'clock to get Mrs Dobbs to make her some tea and toast (breakfast on a tray in her room was a thing of the past much to her dismay), and then she spent the next three hours getting dressed and doing her face, writing letters, making phone calls and asking what was for luncheon. She never walked Rufus and Nelson, never collected vegetables or fruit from the garden, never lifted a duster or a dustpan and brush. Those jobs, along with looking after the hens, ducks and rabbits, were done by Amanda and Charlotte, for the time being. But what was going to happen when Amanda went to Oxford?

'Perhaps it was a pity she gave up being in the WVS when the war ended?' Lady Anne suggested generously.

'She wasn't interested in belonging to the Guildford branch; it was London or nothing, she said. And I've no intention of moving back to London,' he added stubbornly.

'The daily journey is a lot for you though, my dear. In the winter you leave Hartley in the dark, and you return at night in the dark. You don't think . . .?'

'Mama, I'd settle for a tiny flat in London during the week, but what I don't want is to go out every night. I can't do it any more, but if we were to return that's what Liza would want. London itself isn't the attraction, it's the merry-go-round of people.'

'Henry,' she said dismayed, 'you sound quite overwrought. Just be firm, my dear. Say it's too much for you these days.'

He smiled sheepishly. 'You're right, Mama.'

'I think you should have a check-up with your doctor. You've had a tough five years, and you could probably do with some vitamins or something. Everyone's run down, and the fact that food rationing has got worse is too depressing for words. Sometimes it feels as if we've *lost* the war, instead of won it.'

He sighed again, and took a large sip of his sherry. 'One thing is certain, we've lost the peace. Britain is bankrupt, for a start. Did you know we're ten billion in debt? It will take us a decade or more to recover. And just when we should all be rejoicing, morale is very low in the country. The price of peace has been heavy.'

Too heavy for some, Lady Anne reflected, looking at her son. Henry was only fifty-seven but the last five years had taken their toll, and the last thing he needed was the nightly nagging from Liza when he returned to Hartley.

'I don't think Mr Attlee is getting on top of things the way

Winston did in 1940,' she observed. 'One can only thank God Attlee wasn't our PM then. He's a nice little man, I suppose, but he's got about as much charisma as one of our hens.'

Good old Ma, Henry thought, brightening. She was the one who had kept Hartley going when all had seemed lost. She was the one who gently chastized Liza and Rosie when they complained they couldn't get make-up, shampoo, nail varnish or silk stockings. She was the one who told everyone to wear more clothes to keep warm when they ran out of fuel for the boiler. She was the one who assured the household that it wasn't the end of the world when soap and floor polish was scarce, and when towels wore out and saucepans couldn't be replaced. 'It won't last forever,' she'd tell them all. Well, it hadn't lasted forever, but the peace seemed to be proving almost more challenging than the war, and she was worried about her son. How much longer could he stand the strain of a marriage in deep trouble?

Four months later, the whole Granville family were gathered together again, this time for Rosie and Salton's wedding, delayed so that his family could come over from America for the occasion.

His widowed mother, Mary-Beth Webb, arrived at the Savoy Hotel, where Salton was putting up his whole family, in a flurry of excitement. With her came her sons, Hank and Clint, with their respective wives, Donna and Lee, her daughter and son-in-law, June and Ronald Keating, and several nieces and nephews of assorted sexes.

'It'll cost you a *fortune*, darling,' Rosie had pointed out, but Salton had smiled in his usual laid-back way and said, 'Gee, honey, I can afford it and I want to give Mom and the others a good time. Remember we used to live in a trailer park when I was a kid. I kinda want them to see how far I've come; and this is the only wedding day I'll ever have.'

Rosie, very touched, had kissed him warmly. He was really the most amazing man she'd ever met and she was longing to meet his family.

She was also desperate to impress them.

Juliet had offered to lend her house for the reception, but Rosie was having none of it. Nothing but the ballroom of the

21

Dorchester would do, following the service at St Paul's, Knightsbridge.

'I don't need to get married at Caxton Hall, like Juliet, because I've not been divorced,' she added with a touch of smug malice when anyone expressed surprise that she was having what amounted to another white wedding.

'How many people are you planning to invite?' Henry asked nervously, seeing Liza's fingerprints all over these plans.

Rosie shrugged her elegant shoulders. She and her mother had made a list of all their old friends, some of whom they hadn't seen since before the war. 'This is a way of getting back *in*,' Liza had pointed out.

'I suppose around four hundred,' she told her father casually, then seeing his expression added quickly, 'Salton has to ask so many people from the embassy, you know.'

'Four hundred?' he repeated in dismay.

'We don't want to look penny-pinching in front of his relatives,' she said defensively. 'After all they're flying all the way over from America to be with us. And Salton is putting them all up at the Savoy!'

Liza's excitement bordered on hysteria as the acceptances flowed in; Lady Diana Cooper, Chips Channon, Lady Violet Bonham-Carter, Countess Mountbatten. The King's brother, the Duke of Gloucester and his wife . . . everyone who was anyone had accepted because to go to a lavish party these days was a treat in itself. Cecil Beaton was booked to take the photographs and Rosie went to Molyneux to get him to make her a long cream brocade dress and matching coat.

There was no doubt about it; the Webb family from Phoenix were going to be impressed out of their minds! Liza reflected with ecstasy.

She and Henry had been out of the limelight for far too long, but wasn't it marvellous that they clearly hadn't been forgotten? The thought spurred her on to *insist* that once the wedding was over, she and Henry simply *must* get another town house, where they could entertain in style.

Rosie became alarmed at her mother's excitement. 'For goodness sake, don't patronize the Webbs,' she implored. 'It's one thing to impress them but another to show off.'

Liza looked hurt. 'I've never patronized anyone in my life,'

22

she protested. 'I merely want to assure them that their son has found a suitable wife.'

At that moment, Rosie realized with a pang of horror that she was very like her mother; something Juliet had taunted her about for years.

Two days before the wedding Salton held a dinner party in a private room at the Hyde Park Hotel for the Granvilles to meet his family. A long table for eighteen guests and another table for nine – mainly for the kids, namely Salton's nieces and nephews – had been set up in the elegant reception room overlooking the lush greenery of the park. Great vases of flowers had been arranged in the four corners, and smaller arrangements had been placed on the tables which were lit by tall white candles. The scene was set for a memorable evening and Salton had gone to great trouble to make sure every detail from the setting to the wine and menu was perfect.

Liza and Henry were the last to arrive and the moment she walked into the room she knew she was overdressed. Salton had stipulated it would be a black tie affair, and all the women, including his mother, sister and two sisters-in-law, not to mention Rosie, Juliet, Louise, Charlotte and Lady Anne were in simple classical dinner dresses with sleeves, and their jewellery was tasteful and discreet. Even Amanda looked half-decent in a long dark skirt and white silk blouse. But Liza had really gone to town, and even she didn't quite know why, except that she was feeling insecure that night, and felt it necessary to make an impact on the assembled company.

In a swirl of off-the-shoulder gold satin with a slight train, and a blaze of emeralds and diamonds, she swept through the opened double doors and then stood uncertainly, like an actress who has mistaken her cue to go on stage and forgotten her lines.

Salton stepped swiftly forward, graciously presenting his mother as he did so.

'How do you do, Mrs Webb,' Liza extended her hand grandly.

'Oh, please call me Mary-Beth.' A pretty grey haired woman with a gentle expression and sincere eyes, clasped Liza's hand in both of hers. 'It's great to meet you and we're just so thrilled that Rosie is going to become part of our family,' she continued earnestly. Her face was sweet and friendly, and her expression

23

was warm. 'Come and meet my daughter, June, and her husband, Ronald, and these are my beautiful daughters-in-law, Donna and Lee, with my sons, Hank and Clint.' Then she waved her hand in the direction of a clutch of children between the ages of eleven and fifteen who were standing staring at Liza as if she was like someone from a travelling show. 'These are my grandkids, but I won't confuse you with all their names right now.'

'And have you met . . .?' Liza began, indicating her daughters with a sweep of her hand.

'Sure.' Mary-Beth sounded as if she thought Liza needed comforting. 'Salton's been a great host, and I just think you've got the most beautiful family. You must be very proud of them all.'

Liza blinked rapidly. Her eyes were suddenly pricking with the most unexpected and unwelcome tears. She looked around wildly for a moment and to her great relief a waiter stepped forward and offered her a glass of champagne. 'Thank you,' she said, grandly again, and took a swift gulp.

'So . . . how are you enjoying London?' she asked in her social voice.

Henry was engaged in easy conversation with Hank and Clint and their wives, and for a moment she felt betrayed. Why wasn't he being supportive? She knew she looked overdone and vulgar and desperately nouveau riche, but she'd only wanted to impress these Americans, and now they were the ones who were looking and behaving like the aristocracy. For a moment she felt furious with Henry, especially when she saw Juliet's eyes sweep over her gold evening dress with astonishment.

Rosie joined them at that moment in an obvious attempt to help things along. 'Mummy, you look so glamorous,' she said brightly, but there was pity in her deep blue eyes that cut Liza to the quick. 'Look what Mrs Webb has given me; isn't it beautiful?' She held out her wrist, showing a fine gold chain bracelet. 'It belonged to Salton's grandmother.'

'It's beautiful, darling,' Liza said in a choked voice. Tears were gathering in a rush now and she was hit by a wave of panic. To cry? In public? It was the most shaming thing she'd ever done, and why? Why?

Mary-Beth smiled understandingly, and taking Liza's arm

24

drew her gently aside. 'It's *such* an emotional time, isn't it, when one's children get married? I have to admit I howled like a dog when Salton told me he was engaged; I was just so happy for him, and he and Rosie are perfect for each other, aren't they? And it's not the best time for us is it – what with the Change and all that? If I'm not weeping I'm having hot flushes and palpitations!' She laughed gaily as if it was all a part of *This Wonderful Life*. 'At least they're going to be living in London, so you'll get to see your girl all the time,' she continued consolingly.

Liza took an instant dislike to Mary-Beth for being kind to her.

Much later, in bed that night, Liza reflected she'd never had such a horrible evening. To be reminded that she was ending one cycle of her life, the *best* cycle, and from now on she'd be getting steadily older, was the final straw. The next two hours of that dinner party had been agonizing, as she tried to be bright and cheerful when she felt like dissolving into a puddle on the thick carpet of the Hyde Park Hotel. She'd drunk too much wine, but what the hell! At least she was rich enough, thanks to Henry, to be miserable in comfort.

By the day of the wedding, Liza had recovered some of her self-confidence, having taken Juliet's advice on what to wear.

'Not too big a hat, either,' Juliet had warned. 'We're not in Westminster Abbey this time around.'

In the end everything went very smoothly, and Liza gloried in her day of being back where she considered she belonged. As she and Henry stood with Rosie, Salton and Mary-Beth, receiving their illustrious friends in the ballroom of the Dorchester she felt as if she 'arrived' all over again, just as she'd felt when she and Henry set up house in London.

But alas, if, as she'd hoped, the Webb family were knocked sideways by the calibre of her guests they certainly didn't show it. In fact they seemed utterly underwhelmed by the cream of Debrett's peerage.

Instead, rather to her annoyance, they seemed to concentrate their approval on the religious part of the proceedings, praising the choice of heartfelt prayers, appropriate readings and stirring music. They were also entranced by Rosie's two children, Jonathan, who was now eight, and nine-year-old

Sophia, who clutched Nanny Granville's hand throughout the service and never said a word.

'I don't think they even *noticed* the flower arrangements,' Liza remarked mystified, as they changed into evening dress that night. They were staying with Juliet and Daniel, and she'd invited the Webb family to dinner.

'Rosie's very lucky to have such nice in-laws, isn't she?' Henry remarked, doing up his mother-of-pearl and sapphire cufflinks.

'Very nice.' Liza didn't really want to talk about the Webbs. They were so damn *nice* it was sickening. Christian, do-gooding, deeply moral and really very unexciting. She wondered what they thought of Juliet? A divorcee married to another divorcee? And what if they found out Louise had become pregnant when she'd been fifteen?

'Wasn't it great seeing so many of our friends today, darling?' she asked instead, preferring to dwell on more pleasant matters.

Henry mumbled something about being glad it was all over bar the shouting, and she realized this was *not* the moment to suggest they return to town permanently.

In the master bedroom Juliet looked across at Daniel as he stood, feet apart and with his hands dug deeply into the trousers of his dinner jacket, looking out at Hyde Park in brooding silence. He'd been in a strange mood all day, ever since he'd opened his mail while they'd breakfasted.

'Is everything all right, my darling?' she said softly, coming up behind him and slipping her slim arms around his waist. He stiffened and glancing at his profile, she saw the angry line of his jaw.

'What's wrong?' she asked immediately, moving round so she could look into his face.

He seemed to be watching the heavy traffic moving below, creeping along Park Lane. 'Nothing for you to worry about,' he said shortly.

'You would tell me . . . if you could, wouldn't you?'

She knew his job at MI5 forbade him to talk about his work; the end of the war hadn't changed that and never would, and sometimes she hated the fact that there were important parts of his life he could never share with her. It isolated him, forbidding him from taking her into his confidence. His gaze shifted to her face, and she could tell he was making an effort to appear light-hearted.

'I sometimes wish we could get away from here.'

'Away?' she echoed in surprise. 'What do you mean? Away to another country? Are Salton's family making you wish you lived in America?'

He shook his head. 'No, nothing like that.' Then he leaned forward and kissed her very tenderly on the lips. 'I just want to be wherever you are, sweetheart, and wherever you are is fine by me.'

Juliet kissed him hungrily. 'Let's hope we can get to bed early. I want you to make love to me all night.' She pressed herself against him. 'Oh, God,' she groaned as she felt his arousal. 'Can we . . .?' she begged.

'But you're all dressed . . .'

'So are you! So what?' She backed him playfully towards her maharaja's silver bed, and then pushed him down on to the purple velvet coverlet. A moment later she slipped out of her black satin evening dress. 'Please, darling . . .' she whispered seductively. 'Make love to me now or I shall die.'

'Juliet and Daniel should be down by now, the Webbs will be here in a minute,' Liza fretted, pacing around Juliet's drawing room, adjusting the black velvet cushions that Dudley had already pumped up on the white sofas. 'Are you feeling all right, Louise?'

Louise was sitting down and looked pale. 'I'm just tired, Mummy. I was standing at the reception for over two hours and now my back's killing me.'

'Thank God this is the last night of all this stupid socializing,' Amanda exclaimed. 'I can't imagine what it's cost you, Daddy, but I bet it's enough to have kept a hundred families in food for a year.'

'You're going to want Daddy to give you just as good a wedding, when *you* get married,' Liza told her crisply.

'No, I won't! It's a complete waste of money. At least Juliet had her reception here, and not in some swish hotel! Anyway, I've no intention of ever getting married; it would get fearfully in the way of my political career.'

Liza looked nervous. Was Amanda going to be one of those

women . . . who *preferred* other women? How would she explain that to her friends?

Lady Anne merely smiled. She'd heard it all before and when Amanda found the right man, she'd want all the trimmings, just like her sisters.

They heard the doorbell ring.

'They're here!' Liza said, 'Oh, it's so rude of Juliet not to be down to greet them. What on *earth* can she be doing?'

But at that moment Juliet swanned into the drawing room, her neck covered with red blotches and her eyes glowing. 'Hello, everyone. Sorry I'm late, my zip stuck and I couldn't do up my dress! Never mind, I've made it just in time.'

'What's that rash?' Charlotte asked in alarm. 'You haven't got measles, have you?'

They could hear Mary-Beth's voice as the Webb family came up the stairs, before anyone had a chance to tell Charlotte to shut up. Mary-Beth was saying, 'What a perfect example of art deco!'

Juliet was at the drawing-room door to greet her.

'My dear, this is all exquisite!' Mary-Beth said, kissing her on the cheek. 'You're too young to have been inspired by the *Exposition Des Arts Décoratifs* in Paris in 1925, but you've obviously studied the period to perfection!'

'Thank you.' Juliet smiled with pleasure. 'I must show you my bedroom after dinner. It's the real pièce de résistance of the place.'

Liza was staring at Mary-Beth, a jealous gleam in her eyes. How was it that this woman was so cultured? She frowned with irritation. Unless she exerted herself she was the one who was going to look as if she came from Hicksville, not Mary-Beth.

Within moments Lady Anne and Salton's mother were greeting each other like old friends. In fact, everyone was getting on famously, with Charlotte talking to the teenage nephews and nieces, and Henry and Daniel discussing with Hank, Clint and Ronald how well the wedding had gone, while Juliet and the young American wives were discussing the London shops. In desperation Liza found herself trying to make conversation with Amanda who was in no mood for small talk.

'I hope it's not going to be a late night,' Amanda grumbled. 'I should be at college, studying.'

For a moment Liza wished that Rosie had stayed for this dinner instead of going on honeymoon. Her precious first-born was always so supportive and the sudden longing for Rosie's presence made her eyes sting. Damn, she thought, reaching for another glass of champagne. I'll have to get something from the doctor if the Change is going to make me weepy all the time. Maybe a prescription for Bromide? That's what they'd given Rosie when Charles was killed.

# Three

'You and Daniel must come for dinner,' Rosie suggested, phoning Juliet one morning. 'When are you free?'

She must have finished decorating their new house, Juliet reflected, reaching for her diary. 'We're pretty tied up for the next couple of weeks; Daniel is trying to make a date to see his children. Is May 9th any good?'

'That would be fine,' Rosie agreed. 'So are his family coming round to him being married to you?'

'I don't think so; we think his ex has been trying to turn the children against him, but legally, he's supposed to be able to see them whenever he wants.'

'Perhaps she'd hoped he'd always yearn for her and it was a shock when he remarried?'

'Seeing she fell in love and married this artist, and didn't even know about me until last year, I can't see why she's being so difficult. She's got no cause for complaint as far as I can see.'

'Some women are very possessive, Juliet. They want to have their cake and eat it!'

'Well done, Rosie!' Juliet exclaimed. 'At last you're becoming a realist.'

Rosie spoke indignantly. 'I've always been a realist!'

'Oh yes? You used to fall for every man who looked at you because you believed everything they said. Then you got upset when you found out what they were really like.'

'That's not true,' Rosie protested hotly. 'Salton's everything I could have hoped for.'

'Yes, thank God, and remember I introduced you to him. But what about Alastair Slaidburn who dumped you for me and then jumped off a building because I'd found out he was a gold-digger? What about poor penniless Charles, who you actually *married* because he promised you a house in Mayfair, which turned out to be rented, and you ended up paying the

30

rent out of your dress allowance? What about that wounded airman, Freddie Something? You had an affair with him, and then he left you a note to say he was off to get married? You used to be hopeless at judging men,' Juliet added teasingly.

'Well,' Rosie retorted, sounding like Liza, 'at least I didn't marry someone who was homosexual without *knowing* it!'

'No, but he was a very rich duke, who gave me a fantastic divorce settlement.' Juliet paused for a moment. 'So, are we still invited to dinner on the 9th of May?' she added good humouredly.

'I suppose so.'

'Cheer up, Rosie. I'm dying to see your new house. Did you do the drawing room *Eau de Nile* after all? I sometimes wish I'd chosen that colour . . .' Juliet chattered on, knowing she'd been unkind to tease Rosie, but sometimes her sister really asked for it. She was maddeningly smug at times and took herself so seriously, it was good for her to be ribbed.

Later that morning Juliet got a call from Shane. 'Louise is in hospital.'

He sounded worried.

'What? Is the baby arriving?'

'No, she's not well. Losing Rupert has been preying on her mind for the past month or so. She has been having dreadful nightmares, about giving him up. I'm afraid having this baby has brought it all back to her.'

'Is she actually ill? Or upset and depressed?'

'Her blood pressure's too high. I know she'd love you to drop in and see her; she's in Queen Charlotte's Hospital.' He sounded tired and strained.

'Of course I will. Is there anything else I can do, Shane? Do you want to stay here, while she's in hospital? At least we can feed you?'

'Thanks, but I've got impossible shifts at the hospital right now, so I'm sleeping at odd hours.'

'Then I'll go and see Louise this afternoon. Does she need anything? Spare nighties? Or bed-jackets? Or maybe books and magazines?'

'I think just mainly your company for the moment, Juliet. She's a bit lonely when I'm working.'

\*     \*     \*

31

'Sweetheart, I know you can no more forget Rupert than I can forget my baby daughter, but you should be concentrating on this new baby, if only for Shane's sake,' Juliet remonstrated gently, as she sat by Louise's bed. 'After all, it's *his* first baby and you should both be excited right now, instead of which he's worried sick about you.'

Louise looked thoughtful. 'To be honest, I don't think I'd feel as bad about Rupert as I do, if he *had* died. I know that sounds dreadful but death is so final, which in a way makes it easier to accept, because there's no alternative. Knowing Rupert's in Wales, running around, learning to talk, calling another woman 'Mummy', that is what really hurts, Juliet. There's this great gap in my life, and I can't help feeling it's disloyal of me to be having another baby which I'm allowed to keep, when I had to give him away!'

'It wasn't your fault and you mustn't blame yourself,' Juliet scolded gently, gripping her sister's hand.

'It wasn't *his* fault he was born either. It was mine and Jack's, and yet he's being deprived of having his real mother bring him up.' Her voice broke, and she clapped her hand over her mouth to suppress her sobs.

'Oh, darling.' Juliet put her arms around her sister and hugged her. 'I *do* understand how you feel, but are you being fair to this baby, by not wanting to give him the biggest welcome in the world? By feeling guilty about loving him too?'

'I suppose not,' Louise murmured reluctantly. 'I suppose I'm being selfish, wallowing in my own misery, when Shane is such a wonderful husband and I'm so lucky to have him.'

'Shane's one in a million, alongside Daniel,' Juliet agreed. 'We're both jolly lucky.'

'Did I tell you we've painted the little room next to ours pale yellow? With Mickey Mouse curtains?' Louise gave a watery grin. 'And darling Bella is going to be sleeping with us, instead of in the kitchen; I don't want her to be jealous!'

'Do you remember how angry you were when I gave you Bella? Accusing me of thinking a little dog would help you get over losing Rupert?'

'Sorry about that! You can see how touchy I am on the subject, can't you? Shane's thinking of getting a pair of blue budgerigars and hanging their cage where the baby can see them from his cot! He says you must stimulate a baby's mind from the beginning.'

Juliet raised her fine eyebrows. 'I wonder what Nanny would think of that? A dog in the bedroom and birds in the nursery? She'd have a fit and go on about germs and it being unhealthy, wouldn't she?'

'I'm never going to have a nanny,' Louise said firmly. 'Do you remember how we only saw Mummy and Daddy for an hour, after tea? We were stuck up in the nursery all the time, except when we were taken for a sedate walk in the park.'

Juliet nodded, remembering how they were dressed in party frocks, with white silk ankle socks and red shoes with a strap, to be brought down to the drawing room every afternoon. 'But when Daniel and I have children I'm definitely going to get someone to help, Louise. I want to be there for Daniel whenever he needs me, and be able to go out in the evenings with him.'

'But I want to look after my baby, myself. I don't want another woman in the house, getting under my feet,' Louise protested.

'People are getting foreign au pairs instead of old-fashioned nannies, these days, why don't you get one of those? You only pay them three pounds a week, plus board and keep, and they do all the boring stuff, like the washing and ironing, and then they baby-sit when you go out at night,' Juliet explained.

Louise smiled. 'Shane and I don't go out that much, he's usually exhausted at the end of the day. I can't see you with some Swiss eighteen-year-old looking after your children,' she chided gently. 'You'll get a smart Norland Nanny in that brown uniform they wear, who'll expect to live in luxury in Park Lane, and your children will look like we did; all polished and partyfied! Actually, when are you going to start a family?'

Juliet flashed her wicked scarlet-mouth smile. 'I don't know, but we're having great fun trying.'

When she returned home, Juliet found Daniel in a dangerous mood. Her heart sank. It wasn't the first time since they'd married that he'd seemed angry about something and when he was like this, he shut her out, refusing to say what was wrong. He was coming down the stairs when she arrived, and without looking at her he stalked past her and into the ground-floor library, which had become his study, his face flushed, his eyes dark with fury. He slammed the heavy door shut behind him.

Dudley, hovering in the hall, looked strained, his face closed and his button mouth prim.

'Everything all right, Dudley?' Juliet asked casually, taking off her hat and gloves and shrugging off her coat.

'Yes, madam,' he said, his expression remote.

'Right. I think I'll have some tea; could you bring it up to the drawing room, please? And ask Mr Lawrence if he'd like some, too.'

'Yes, madam.' He turned and left on silent feet, as if the white marble floor had been snow. Juliet went thoughtfully up the black carpeted stairs, her hand trailing on the silvery banister rail. Hurt by Daniel's behaviour, she wondered what had upset him? Had his ex-wife made more trouble between him and his children? For eight years their relationship had been passion driven, consisting of exciting secret meetings, whilst forbidden feelings had consumed them to the point of madness. Up until the time they'd got married they'd never spent time together doing ordinary things, like other couples. They'd never gone to the theatre or cinema together, or had walks in the park or spent lazy Sunday afternoons reading the newspapers, because they'd always been overwhelmed by lust, preferring to stay in bed. That burning desire for each other was still as strong as ever, but so was the ordinary banality of real life and domesticity and maybe that was the rub.

She sat alone, drinking her tea, but Daniel did not come upstairs to join her. What could she do to please him? To distract him? To excite him? She was sure Dudley knew what was wrong, but she could hardly embroil the butler in a domestic situation. Since she'd got married, the unspoken understanding and sense of camaraderie that she and Dudley had shared, such as when they'd sheltered in the basement together during the Blitz, had gone. His devotion to her and the way he'd managed to get little treats for her on the black market had now merged into his dutiful attendance on both herself and Daniel, which was perfectly correct and as it should be. But she sometimes missed the old days and close alliance between them which was never openly expressed.

Right now she'd have liked to have gone down to the kitchen and asked him if he knew what had upset her husband. But of course she couldn't. Granny always said you must never put servants in an awkward position and you must never show your emotions in front of them, because to do so would embarrass them.

Juliet shrugged and reached for a cigarette, determined not to let her imagination run away with her. Daniel was probably only worried about something to do with his work which he couldn't talk about. Or could his problems be financial? He'd be too proud to admit it, if they were. And if she offered to lend him money, or suggest they have a joint bank account she knew it would be the worst thing she could do. Daniel was such an independent man who liked to be in control of a situation, and that was what had first attracted her to him. What was it he had said to her that first time in Paris, melting her with his potentness when she moved her hips provocatively against him as they danced at Maxim's? *I do the leading in this relationship.*

Juliet was awoken by the telephone on the bedside table. Beside her Daniel turned restlessly, grunting at being disturbed.

She picked up the receiver. 'Hello?' Night calls scared her. They rarely brought good news.

'This is Shane. Louise has gone into labour . . .'

'Oh my God . . . So soon? She's not due for another seven weeks.'

'I thought you'd want to know. There are complications because of eclampsia . . .'

'Oh, Jesus! I'll be there as soon as I can!' Juliet exclaimed. 'Tell her to hang in there, tell her I'm on my way.'

'How is she?' Juliet demanded, her heart lurching with fear, when she saw Shane standing disconsolately outside the delivery room.

Shane turned to look at her. Without make-up and with her blonde hair ruffled wildly around her delicately featured face, there was a stark dignity about her beauty he'd never noticed before. Her slightly slanted aquamarine eyes were looking beseechingly into his, her sensual lips parted.

He took a deep breath and in an effort to control his emotions, spoke like a doctor rather than a husband and father.

'The baby's heartbeat is rather faint and it's a breech birth. They're trying to get the baby out quickly with forceps. The

35

problem is the placenta is breaking away from the wall of the uterus so Louise is haemorrhaging. They're doing their best to stabilize her, but with her blood pressure so high, it's not easy.'

Juliet nodded. More than once she'd had to help deliver a baby during the Blitz, once in a bombed building and twice in a shelter. 'Is she conscious?'

'They're giving her gas, but I'm afraid she's having a bad time.'

'At least she's here, Shane, in the best hospital in the country for childbirth, and not some run down cottage in the wilds of the Welsh mountains, like she was last time.'

In the darkness of their car, Henry and Liza sat in silence as he concentrated on the road ahead. There was hardly any traffic at this hour and they were making good time but it would be another half hour before they reached the hospital.

Henry was thankful for the silence; it gave him time to mull over Daniel's words again and again, trying to analyze by his tone just how serious the situation was. Obviously Daniel hadn't wanted to alarm them too much, yet he *had* admitted Juliet had asked him to phone right away. In turn, Henry didn't want to frighten Liza; time enough when they got to the hospital to find out exactly what was happening.

But Liza had guessed at once that the baby might not survive. 'They sometimes only weigh two or three pounds at seven months,' she told Henry, but so far it had not struck her that Louise might be in danger.

Henry pressed down harder on the accelerator. It was the not knowing which he found hard to bear. The road stretched ahead like a flat black snake in the darkness and he started praying.

Half an hour later a door opened, and Juliet, Daniel and Rosie spun round as Shane emerged from the delivery room. His cheeks were wet with tears and he looked exhausted.

Not daring to ask, their hopes suspended in a moment of apprehension, they braced themselves.

He ran his hand across his forehead in utter weariness. 'We've got a beautiful little girl and they think there's a good chance she'll pull through,' he croaked.

Juliet's heart hammered in her ears. 'And Louise?'

'Very tired and weak, but she'll be OK.' He sank on to a wooden bench as if his legs could no longer support him. 'She needs to rest, though. Her gynaecologist says she's not to have any visitors for the moment.'

Juliet rushed forward to embrace him. 'Oh, Shane. Thank God they're both all right. Have they put the baby in an incubator?'

'Yes. They've taken Daisy into the intensive care nursery. She's beautiful –' his face broke into a tired smile – 'even if she does resemble a skinned rabbit at the moment.'

'Daisy?' Rosie exclaimed. 'What a sweet name.'

Daniel shook Shane by the hand. 'Congratulations, old chap! You must be done in. Are you on duty tomorrow?'

''Fraid so.' He took a deep breath but with each passing moment he seemed to be reviving as if he couldn't believe that everything was all right after all. This had been the worst night of his life. As a paediatrician he spent most of his time assuring parents that their offspring would be all right, that everything was being done and that they were not to worry. Now, for the first time he realized with profound shock what it was like to actually be a parent himself, with his own child in mortal danger.

Footsteps coming towards them made them all turn to see Henry and Liza, white faced and anxious, hurrying towards them.

Daniel met them with outstretched arms. 'Everything's all right. I'm so sorry my call got you out in the middle of the night . . .'

'That was my fault,' Juliet said, kissing her mother on the cheek and hugging her father. 'We didn't want to scare you, but things went very wrong for a while, and they're both only out of danger now.'

Shane greeted them, smiling broadly now. Quickly he outlined what had happened.

'And Louise is really all right?' Liza insisted. 'Can I see her?'

'She needs to rest right now. She's lost a lot of blood, but you can visit her in the morning.'

'Why don't we all go back to Park Lane?' Juliet suggested. She looked at her parents. 'You'll stay with us for a few days, won't you? Wait to see Louise and Daisy properly?'

Liza needed no persuading. 'Of *course* we will! I'll have to nip down to Surrey tomorrow to fetch some clothes, but otherwise . . .'

Juliet and Rosie exchanged amused glances. Daisy's arrival in the family was a perfect excuse for their mother to catch up with her London friends, and do a bit of serious socializing.

# Four

'Why don't we invite your children to stay for a few days?' Juliet suggested. It was the end of July and London was teeming with children who had broken up for the summer holidays, paying routine visits with their mothers to dentists and oculists, and getting kitted out with new cricket pads and tennis rackets. So far she'd failed to get pregnant, and the longing she felt for children was making it hard for her to see Louise and Daisy, who was now three months old.

'I don't think their mother will let me bring them here. She's quite bitter that I've found such happiness with you.' Daniel reached out to stroke the back of her hand as she relaxed on a chaise longue in their bedroom.

'Even though she was the one who wanted the divorce? And now she's happily remarried?' Juliet queried.

Daniel frowned, as he studied the carpet at his feet. 'It's not as straight-forward as that. My sister has been making mischief.'

Juliet raised her eyebrows. 'Your *sister*? What's it got to do with her?'

'You've never met Esther.' His deep voice was harsh. 'She's seven years older than me and she's always been eaten up with jealousy. She's even jealous of people she doesn't know. Public figures like the Queen, for whom she hasn't got a good word to say.'

'Are you being serious?' Juliet asked incredulously.

Daniel nodded. 'Deadly serious. She's not an attractive woman and she's never married, or even had a boyfriend. When she sees other women who are successful and happy, it seems to *do* something to her. She remembered seeing photographs of you in magazines when you married Cameron, pictures of you as a rich and beautiful young duchess living in a castle and . . . I'm afraid, sweetheart, that was that. When she heard you and I were going to marry she went crazy.'

'Was it she who was responsible for stopping the rest of your family coming to our wedding?'

He nodded again, averting his eyes.

'Daniel – ' she was on her feet now – 'what did she say? What *could* she have said to keep them away, for God's sake? Why didn't you tell me about her lies before?'

'Darling, I didn't want to upset you, and I didn't want anything to spoil the best day of our lives; the day we'd both wanted for so long,' he added, softly.

Juliet reached for a cigarette. 'I don't believe this.' She felt astounded. And hurt, too. Not because Daniel's sister apparently didn't like her, but because Daniel had kept something as important as this from her.

'Has she been writing to you?' she asked suddenly, her eyes narrowing.

'Yes.' He raised his head. 'How did you know?'

She shrugged and placed the cigarette in her long jade holder, lighting it with a silver table lighter. Her hands were shaking slightly.

'Darling.' He reached for her again, but she moved away beyond his reach. 'Why do her letters make you so angry?' she asked.

'Because she says unforgivable things about us.'

'Such as . . .?'

Daniel shook his head. 'They're not worth repeating.'

'Not *worth* . . .? Although they keep you from having your children to stay? And they cause you distress when you receive them – no, don't argue, Daniel. And don't take me for a fool either. Where are these letters?'

'D'you think I'd keep them? They're scurrilous, Juliet.' He was flushed with anger, his fists clenched. 'I throw them away and do my best to forget about them.'

'That's not going to stop her writing,' Juliet protested, angry now. 'Daniel, I didn't think we kept things from each other now we're married? Look at what happened the last time we stopped communicating? Do you want this to come between us? – You're going about it the right way if you do.'

Daniel rose and started prowling around their bedroom, picking little ornaments up and putting them down again. 'You are incredibly rich though, aren't you?' he said, almost bitterly.

She stood quite still, her back to the fireplace, which was laid ready to be lit if it got chilly in the evenings.

'What's that got to do with it?' Her voice was dangerously soft.

Daniel shrugged and looked away. 'My sister is spreading a tissue of lies and she's convinced the rest of the family that you're a bad lot, and I'm a gold-digging monster.' He paused, then continued. 'Seeing that we're living in a ten bedroom mansion in Mayfair, they believe her. Let's face it, I could never provide a home like this on my income, especially as I give Ruth money to support the children.'

Juliet snorted in disgust. 'So they think you're a kept man? That's the most ridiculous thing I've ever heard. Not only is it insulting to both of us, but anyone knowing me would know I can spot a fortune hunter a mile away because I've been pursued by them since I was seventeen. Why don't you tell your sister it's a damn lie?'

His eyes met hers levelly. 'I've told her until I'm blue in the face, but she refuses to listen. I happen to have ended up with everything *she* wanted in life, and now she's determined to try and ruin my happiness. The twisted lies she's told Ruth have even ruined the basic goodwill I had with Ruth when we got divorced.'

Juliet's troubled eyes searched his. 'Does she know we were lovers nine years ago?'

'She does now, thanks to Esther. According to her, Ruth was forced to build a new life for herself when she found out about us, and that's why she found someone else to marry. The worst part is the children's minds have been poisoned, and they too believe that I deserted their mother when the war started.'

'How ironic, because that's when we actually broke up . . . thanks to my stupidity,' Juliet pointed out regretfully. 'God, what a mess. We've got to sort it out, though. Your children are missing out by not seeing you. And we must put a stop to what your sister has been saying about us.'

His voice raised with impatience. 'Do you think I haven't *tried*? How do you think it makes *me* feel being referred to as a whore? Don't you realize that no matter how hard I deny

41

it the fact is I'm living in this bloody great house, with a Rolls Royce parked in front, a butler to answer the door and a wife who is a millionairess!'

Juliet flushed and then the colour drained from her face. 'Is that what you feel?'

Daniel remained silent, as he stared broodingly out of the window.

'*Is* that how you feel?' she repeated sharply. 'Times have changed, Daniel. Women found independence during the war. It's no longer a question of the man being the provider, while the little wifey stays at home, doing the housework. Women are never going to go back to that again. My mother has been a "kept woman", if you want to use that phrase, all her life; the wives of her generation expected to be supported financially by their husbands, but my generation isn't like that. If I didn't have any money, I'd get a job; I wouldn't expect you to keep me.'

He frowned, his eyes like cold flint, his manner withdrawn. 'Right now people despise me and I'm not used to that.'

She felt a faint stab of fear which she hid by saying, loftily, 'I'm the one who should be angry; it makes *me* look like an ugly woman who could only capture a husband by dangling a great fat cheque book under his nose. I think you'd better get your sister to shut up, and if you don't, I will.'

With that, she turned and walked swiftly out of the room, terribly afraid that no matter how much they loved each other, her wealth might come between them, because, in truth, she *was* the one who owned the house, paid the staff and all the outgoings. Even the Rolls that was parked outside was hers.

A little while later, as she sat in the drawing room trying to concentrate on a new novel, she heard Daniel slam out of the house. It was the first fight they'd had since they'd been married, but that wasn't the point. There was a serious issue between them now, and she had to think of a way of solving it.

'We're missing out on *so* much, Henry,' Liza wailed, when he returned from London that evening. Heaped on his desk in the library, like ammunition with which she intended to assault him, was a pile of expensive looking invitations, with copper plate printing on stiff white cards.

'*Look* at all the parties we've been invited to,' she said accusingly. 'What was the point of asking everyone to Rosie and Salton's wedding if we didn't intend to accept the invitations that were bound to follow?'

'Darling, I never wanted to ask that number of people in the first place,' he said mildly, sinking into the worn leather captain's chair behind his desk.

'But we *did*,' she countered irrationally, 'and Rosie and Salton are going to *everything*, while we're stuck down here. I can't ask Juliet if we can stay with her again; she'll think we're using her house like a hotel. And unfortunately Rosie doesn't have a spare room, which I think is quite ridiculous for a town house.'

Or extremely sensible, Henry thought privately. Salton had bought them a charming four bedroom house in Halsey Place near Marble Arch, (the wrong side of the park, Liza had sniffed) and Sophia, Jonathan and their nanny each had their own room.

'We've got to get a house, Henry. Get all our lovely stuff out of storage. Establish ourselves in London once more,' Liza insisted.

Henry looked at his once pretty wife, whose mouth had been so permanently turned down at the corners that two deep wrinkles had formed. 'Have you forgotten your promise?'

Liza looked flustered. 'That . . . that was in the middle of the Blitz . . . and we *have* stayed down here for eight years; *eight* years, Henry! And you know how I hate the country.' Her voice was tinged with desperation. There were tears in her eyes. 'Just because I want to return to London doesn't mean I don't love you,' she pleaded. 'I want both of us to have some fun. We deserve it. The last few years have been so terribly dreary.'

'The trouble is, I know the sort of house you'd like, and we simply can't afford it; we couldn't get the staff nowadays, either.'

Liza said sulkily, 'Juliet seems to manage all right and she's got an enormous place.'

'Juliet's rich, and contrary to appearances, she and Daniel don't entertain on a grand scale. Half the rooms are never used. And she mostly has daily help, apart from Dudley. You'd want a cook, a scullery maid, housemaids and parlour maids, a butler . . .' Henry's voice trailed off, weary at the very thought of going back to the sort of life they'd lived before the war.

'But Henry . . .' she burst out, exasperated by his attitude, and frustrated that she was being denied the life she so craved. 'I'm so unhappy here. I want to *see* people again, I want to go dining and dancing. I want to wear my pretty clothes and my jewels . . . and all that's happening is I'm wasting away in the company of your mother and . . . and –' she looked wildly out of the library window at the distant fields beyond the garden – 'and a lot of *cows*!' She jumped to her feet and rushed out of the room, sobbing.

'I think, my dear,' Lady Anne said to Henry later that evening as they dined on their own, as Liza had excused herself with a headache, 'that maybe a compromise could be reached.'

Henry raised his eyebrows. 'What are you suggesting, Mama?'

'A flat, my dear, a small but nice flat in a good area. There's a block of flats in the Brompton Road, opposite Harrods, which are not expensive to rent. You'd probably get one for between three and four hundred pounds a year, and I know, because I have a friend who lives in one of them, that heating and hot water is included in the rent. Wouldn't that perhaps be the answer? The close proximity of Harrods would surely compensate Liza for not having a house?' she added drily.

Henry smiled. 'You heard our little *contra temps* earlier, then?'

Lady Anne looked him straight in the eye. 'I think the whole village probably heard it. Liza's not happy down here, my dear. She was never a country girl, you know. Why not let her have three nights a week in town? It would save you travelling up and down every day, too.'

'I read the newspapers and work on my papers so I hardly notice the journey,' he protested.

'It's a tiring journey, though, Henry. I think the block is called Princes Court. If you like I'll ask my friend if any flats are available?'

He sighed inwardly. There seemed no escape, but he knew his mother was right, if he wanted a peaceful life. 'That would be most kind, Mama. And please don't mention it to Liza until we know if it's possible. Then hopefully, I can present it to her as a *fait accompli*, ruling out the possibility of getting a house.'

Lady Anne gave a roguish smile. 'I'd love to be a fly on the wall when you tell her!'

Juliet awoke with a start as she felt his naked body pressed close to hers, while his arms enfolded her. His face was buried in her neck and the familiar smell of him sent her senses quickening.

'Hello,' she said throatily, placing her hands on either side of his face.

'I'm sorry, so sorry about being rotten to you.' His voice was muffled. Then he found her mouth and started kissing her, deeply and thirstily, while she clung to him, wrapping herself around him, wanting to take him inside her so he could assuage her instant burning desire.

'I love you,' she whispered, through parted lips, as she arched her back. 'I want you . . . I want you now.'

'Oh, my darling, you can have all of me. I want to fill you with my love,' Daniel groaned as he started to make love to her with a feverish intensity. 'You're my all . . . you're everything I ever wanted.'

Juliet felt herself burning up, flames shimmering through her body as she gave herself to him with abandon. Letting him weave the magic she'd experienced when he'd first made love to her all those years ago, when she'd still been a virgin. It was Daniel who had shown her how wonderful lovemaking could be, and his touch was still as tender and exciting. Surrendering to the way his lips and hands were setting her on fire, he brought her slowly and exquisitely to a climax that had her crying out with pleasure. Only then did he lose control, riding her almost roughly, his breath ragged, his thrusts more and more urgent until he suddenly collapsed on top of her with a roar of wonder. It was then that she held him tightly within her as they lay still and breathless, locked in a love so deep Juliet shuddered again and again.

They made love twice more that night, and when she finally got out of bed and drew back the curtains as dawn was breaking, the moon, like a thin wafer of mother-of-pearl was floating above the trees in Hyde Park.

She returned to the silver bed and sat naked on the side, and looked at Daniel, who lay with his hands behind his head, unable to take his eyes off her.

'We must never lose sight of the fact that we're together because we're in love,' Juliet said softly. 'Damn other people. Damn what they say. We know the truth and that's all that matters.'

He nodded, taking her hands in both of his. 'That *is* all that matters, and I shall love you for as long as I live.' Then he dropped back against the pillows, his eyes hardening. 'I just wish my sister would mind her own bloody business.'

'How about coming up to join me in London next Wednesday?' Henry suggested amiably, as he and Liza had a glass of sherry before dinner.

'What for?' she asked suspiciously.

'I thought you'd enjoy it? We could have lunch at Claridge's if you like, and then perhaps a trip to Harrods to do a little shopping?'

A smile was spreading across her face as if she was a child who'd been promised a treat. Nevertheless, Henry had been so difficult recently, she viewed his offer with mistrust.

'What's brought this on, Henry?'

'I realize you're very bored down here, so I thought a little trip to town might cheer you up?'

Liza nodded. 'That would be lovely. I must get my hair done.' She said no more though, frightened of pushing Henry when he seemed to be in a good mood. If Wednesday went well, she might be able to build on it, letting him see how much fun they could have in town. It was obvious that being stuck at Hammerton's, day after day, with no light relief, had given him a jaundiced outlook.

She started to pin her hopes on the trip: maybe after a cocktail in the bar at Claridge's, followed by a delicious lunch, (they were bound to bump into a few friends!) Henry would realize she was right; they *were* missing out, stuck down at Hartley during the week. It also occurred to Liza that after they'd shopped at Harrods, and Henry had returned to work, she might just drop into a couple of estate agents, before catching the train home. There was no harm in seeing what they had on their books, was there?

\* \* \*

46

After Daniel had left for his office at Millbank, Juliet went to his study, determined to find his sister's address. She had to put a stop to Esther's letters once and for all and although she felt guilty about going through his papers, she was not going to let this woman sour their relationship. When he'd said he'd destroyed all her letters, he'd been truthful. All that Juliet could find were the usual bank statements, receipts, the deeds of his Chelsea house which had been bombed, several insurance policies, and receipts from his tailor. There was also a file containing correspondence from his solicitor referring to his divorce and financial obligation to support Sarah, Susan and Leo.

Then she spotted an old address book. Opening the index at the Ls, she quickly found that both Ruth and Esther Lawrence were listed but there was no way of knowing whether Esther's London address and phone number were still relevant? When had the entry been made? Ruth's address in Devon was certainly out of date, because Juliet knew she'd moved to Hertfordshire since she'd remarried.

Having copied down Esther's details, Juliet slipped out of the room, shutting the door quietly behind her. It wouldn't do for Dudley to catch her going through Daniel's things. Hurrying up to her dressing room she touched up her make-up and added a glossy layer of scarlet lipstick to her voluptuous mouth. Then she put on a dark-red coat and a small red hat with a veil.

It was time she paid Esther Lawrence a visit, and she just hoped to God the bitch was at the same address.


After luncheon at Claridge's, Henry and Liza stepped into a taxi hailed by the commissionaire of the hotel.

'Brompton Road, please, just opposite Harrods,' Henry told the driver.

'Why opposite Harrods?' Liza queried. 'It means we'll have to cross the road?'

He spoke casually. 'There's something I want to show you.'

Liza vaguely wondered what shops were opposite Harrods. A dress shop, perhaps? A jeweller?

When they stepped out of the cab, she looked up and down the street while Henry paid the fare.

'Where are we going?' she asked.

He took her by the elbow and led her to a twenties style doorway set under an art deco canopy. Without saying a word, he pushed open the glass door which led to a large lobby, with lifts at the far end.

'What *is* this place, Henry? A new store?'

He looked pleased with himself as they stepped into the lift, and he pressed the third floor button. 'No, it's not a store.'

'Then what . . .? What's this?' she asked in bewilderment as he took a front door key from his pocket and handed it to her.

'It's the key to number 17, Princes Court; your new London home,' he said, unable to quench his delight.

'My . . .! Oh, my God! Henry! Do you mean it?' Her hands were shaking as she took the key, and her face had flushed red, her eyes brimming with emotional tears. 'Truly, Henry. Truly?'

'Truly, darling. Come along, it's just here.' As they stepped out of the lift, he turned left along a wide luxuriously carpeted corridor. Number 17 was the first door on the left.

'I can't believe it,' Liza kept saying, as he showed her around. There was a master bedroom and drawing room leading off a small square hall, and along the corridor, a beige marble bathroom, a dining room, another bedroom, and a kitchen, with its own back door for putting out the rubbish.

'What do you think?' he asked. 'The rooms could do with a coat of paint . . . that is if we can find anyone to do it, but I think once we get some of our stuff out of storage, it'll be all right as a pied-a-terre, don't you?'

Liza clapped her hands together. It wasn't a grand house, it wasn't even remotely a grand flat, but the location was fine and that was more important than anything. They could at least have fifteen to twenty people to drinks in the square drawing room, which led on to a miniscule balcony, facing Harrods, and she was sure she could squeeze in eight people for dinner parties. Liza was also relieved to see there was a separate staff lavatory beyond the kitchen.

Henry had obviously made a great effort to get them a place in town and it *was* a start. Gradually she was sure he'd agree to somewhere bigger. She hadn't mentioned it yet, but she was determined that Charlotte should come out in two years time and then they'd definitely need a much bigger place.

'It's perfect darling!' she exclaimed, and in a way it was only a small lie. 'We can make it very cosy, and give intimate parties, which are always *so* nice.' She turned to kiss him with gratitude and Henry held her close for a moment, glad she was pleased.

'Right, then,' he replied, smiling. 'Keep the keys so you can get on with planning how you want the place to look.'

Liza held them with reverence as if they'd been the keys to paradise itself. 'Thank you Henry,' she said solemnly, desperate to tell Rosie and Juliet the exciting news.

'I'd better be getting back to the bank,' Henry said, picking up his bowler hat, gloves and umbrella, which he'd left on a shelf in the hallway.

'Will you be all right getting to Victoria?'

Liza spoke sturdily. 'Don't worry about me, darling, I'll be absolutely fine.'

Henry was no sooner out the door than she was going from room to room again, making lists with a slim gold pencil in her tiny diary. The thrill of having somewhere to live in London made her hands tremble and her brain buzz with excitement. After eight years of being incarcerated in the country, she was at last about to return to her rightful place at the centre of high society.

The face that stared at her with undisguised hostility was long and narrow, like a keyhole. Dark hooded eyes glittered maliciously and the lips of her thin mouth were pressed together in a hard line.

'Miss Lawrence?' Juliet asked unnecessarily, as she stood on the doorstop of an ordinary looking red brick house near the Edgware Road.

She noticed the mean looking windows were heavily-veiled in lace, giving the building an old-fashioned closed-up look.

'What do you want?' Esther asked in a harsh voice, her drab black clothes hanging from her bony body like a dusty carapace.

Juliet's gaze was steady. 'I think it's time we talked.'

'I have nothing to say to you.' She started to close the door.

Juliet swiftly placed the flat of her hand on the black painted

49

door, forcing it to remain open. 'But I have a lot to say to you.' Then using her shoulder, she pushed her way past Esther and strode into the narrow hall, and once inside, swung round to face her sister-in-law.

'Why are you against us?' she demanded. 'Why did you stop Daniel's family from coming to our wedding?'

Esther raised her chin arrogantly. 'Daniel has brought shame on the Lawrence family. Until he met you he was a loyal husband and father. Since you *bought* him with your stinking wealth, he's deserted the Jewish faith and he cares nothing for his family, so it's only natural we don't want to have anything more to do with him.'

'That's not true!' Juliet shot back. 'He adores his children. He wants them to come and stay with us, he . . .'

'Their mother won't allow them to enter the house of a godless gentile and a rich whore!' Esther retorted, her face flushed in rage. 'Haven't you done enough harm? You've ruined one man's life by marrying him for his dukedom, only to use the fortune he settled on you to destroy Daniel's life. Have you no shame?'

Juliet blinked, stunned for a moment. 'You'd better be careful what you say, and what you put in your letters to Daniel, because I shall have you up for slander, libel and defamation of character.'

Esther's mouth twisted in a sneer. 'Oh, no doubt you can afford the best lawyers to try and ruin my life too, but you won't succeed. Every word I've said is true! I read the newspapers, you know,' she added slyly.

Juliet flashed back, 'And if you believe what you read you're more stupid than I thought.' Her aquamarine eyes blazed. 'Do you really believe that Daniel is the type of man who can be *bought*?'

Esther didn't flinch. 'I know he's married a scheming adulteress, who's been involved with more men than he's got fingers on his hands! I know that his children are hurting, and are ashamed of him. It's my duty to open his eyes to how he's been manipulated, seduced into living off the spoils of your first husband. It's disgusting. You're ruining his life, and destroying his family. Now get out of my house.' She flung open the front door and a gust of wind whirled in from the street.

'You'll be hearing from my lawyer,' Juliet said coldly as she swept past the older woman and walked down the front steps.

As she drove home, she felt deeply shaken. Esther had obviously been reading all about her for years, and she knew too much. Juliet felt uneasy. She was never going to be able to defend herself over leaving Cameron Kincardine because it would mean revealing his homosexuality; his over generous divorce settlement had been to buy her silence. As to the other men in her life, they'd been casual affairs, apart from her engagement to Edward Courtney who'd been killed in action.

Casual affairs, she reflected, that looked degenerate in peace time. That even shocked her now, thinking back to those torrid nights of the Blitz when, on her nights off, she slept with various boyfriends. But at the time, when every minute could be your last, when she and Daniel were totally estranged and she thought she'd never see him again, when she was frightened and lonely . . . yes, there *had* been a lot of men in her life then, but she'd long since forgiven herself for her sins and as long as Daniel never found out . . .

She clutched the steering wheel tightly, feeling a frisson of nerves.

God knows how, but Esther seemed to have found out what even Juliet's family didn't know; the frantic lifestyle she'd had with Richard, Hugh, Andrew, Steve, Peter . . . Oh Christ, she couldn't even remember all their names now. They'd get drunk, have a line of coke, go back to her silver bed as the bombs were dropping all around and the nights were shaking with explosions, passion and the fear of imminent death.

A great weight of guilt suddenly settled on Juliet. She'd told Daniel about getting engaged to poor Edward who'd then been killed; he hadn't liked it but he'd understood. But he wouldn't understand about the others.

But had Esther already told him about the others? Was that why he'd been so angry when he'd got her letters? Surely he'd have said something if he'd known? Juliet parked the car round the corner in Green Street and sat for a few minutes, feeling too weak with anxiety to walk the hundred yards back to her house. She was churning inside with shame and misery, terrified of Daniel's reaction if his sister told him everything.

51

She'd say it wasn't true, of course. She'd deny everything, saying how could Esther possibly know how she spent her time off? Anyway, there was nothing wrong in going out to dine and dance with her men friends, was there? Esther had probably seen photographs of her in *Tatler* and *Bystander*, with someone in uniform dining at the Dorchester or the Savoy . . . but they were just friends, weren't they? Nothing more! Juliet rehearsed in her head what she'd say if Daniel questioned her. What would be the point in confessing? Those mindless liaisons had meant nothing, anyway. She'd always been attractive to men and she'd been desperately lonely at the time with all her family down in the country, and so she'd accepted every invitation, going out with whoever asked her. None of them were like Daniel, for whom she'd pined. None of them did more than offer her lust and that was all she'd wanted from them.

And that had been *then*, when she'd never in her wildest dreams expected Daniel to come back into her life. When she no longer cared whether she lived or died. When she'd lost her baby daughter and, it seemed, Daniel too.

But this is *now* and I'm a different person, she reflected, as waves of panic flowed through her, making her legs feel as if they were weighed down by lead, while her heart raced so that she felt sick. Daniel was the only man she'd ever loved and the only man she'd ever wanted. They were so close that when they lay together she could never be sure whether she could feel her heart beating or his. She would do anything to keep him and nothing on God's earth was going to take him away from her now.

She'd wish Esther dead before that happened, she thought with passion.

She let herself into the empty hall and stood taking off her hat when, with a start, she realized Daniel was standing at the top of the staircase, looking down at her.

The power of his presence was like a body blow and for a moment his black glittering eyes were the eyes of Esther and the grim line of his mouth was like his sister's mouth. Then he spoke. And his deep voice was like rolling thunder plundering the silence of the house.

'I hear you've been to see my sister.'

\*    \*    \*

'I just *had* to come and tell you,' Liza gushed, plumping herself down on the sofa in Rosie's drawing room. 'Isn't it exciting?'

'I never thought Daddy would move back to London,' Rosie agreed. 'It'll be wonderful having you up here. You'll be able to baby-sit for me sometimes, won't you? When Nanny has her day off?'

Their old nanny had needed no persuasion to return to life in the city. Rosie's small house was a far cry from the opulence of Green Street, with its many living-in servants, including a nursery maid, but Nanny was desperate to leave Hartley, where she'd complained how she'd hankered for the Odeon Cinema, Lyons Corner House, Selfridges, Woolworths and good solid pavements to walk on instead of twenty acres of mud. Now that Sophia was nine and Jonathan eight, they both went to school, so she didn't have to work too hard, because Rosie also employed a 'daily' as they were called, who did the 'rough' work.

Liza looked taken aback by Rosie's presumption. She certainly wasn't returning to London in order to help with the grandchildren.

'Daddy will want me to do things with him,' she said firmly. 'You and Salton must come to dinner as soon as we move in. I can't wait to start entertaining again. Just like in the old days.'

Rosie nodded without enthusiasm and said nothing.

Liza frowned. 'Is everything all right, darling?'

'I don't seem to be able to get pregnant,' Rosie burst out fretfully.

'But you've only been married seven months. That's nothing. Don't you think it's good for you and Salton to have some time together before you start a family?'

'Why? I've known him for nearly two years now. We've had plenty of time to settle down.'

'Well, I'm sure it will happen,' Liza pointed out. 'You'll just have to be patient.'

Rosie's eyes brimmed and a tear slid down her cheek. 'I got pregnant easily enough with Charles, and I do so want another baby.' She rubbed her cheek with the back of her hand. ' I don't know why it hasn't happened.'

Liza spoke reassuringly. 'Don't worry about it. The more

53

you worry the less likely you are to get pregnant. Salton isn't worried, is he?'

'He's never worried about *anything*,' Rosie remarked flatly, reaching for her handbag and taking out her gold powder compact. 'They may call it laid back in the States, but I call it positively laid out. Nothing bothers him,' she added with a touch of petulance.

'But that's nice, isn't it? You don't want rows. You don't want someone who argues with you. I think you're rather lucky.'

Rosie peered into the little round mirror in the lid, and dabbed her reddened nose with a velvet powder puff. 'Mummy, it can be quite boring when someone just says "fine" or "great" about *everything*!' she complained, looking at the faint bags under her eyes with dissatisfaction.

Liza looked at her anxiously. Rosie couldn't afford to have another unhappy marriage. Salton was very comfortably off, unlike Charles, and he'd provided a lovely home for Rosie and her children. It crossed Liza's mind that her daughter had spent the past ten years of her life grumbling about everyone and everything, but then she quickly banished the thought, because she preferred not to know about the unpleasant things in life. It would be *too* inconvenient for things to go wrong again, she reflected. After all, if one was going to be honest, it was only the death of poor Charlie Padworth that had saved Rosie from eventually getting a divorce. And now that Juliet was happily settled, at last, and so was Louise, that only left Amanda and Charlotte to worry about. Which was quite enough.

'Why don't you and Salton go away for a nice weekend somewhere?' she asked brightly.

'I don't see how that's going to help?' Rosie remarked peevishly. 'Do you want some tea?'

'Just a quick cup perhaps, darling. Then I must catch my train home. Just think! The next time I come to see you "home" for me will be opposite Harrods!'

'Very convenient,' Rosie remarked drily as she rose like a weary middle-aged woman.

Liza watched her receding backview with unease. Rosie's shoulders were slumped forward and she was too thin again. The way she'd looked when she was married to Charles. Comforting herself with the thought that perhaps Rosie was only depressed because she'd failed to conceive, Liza fished in her handbag for a tiny gilt box.

The doctor had prescribed some darling little purple heart-shaped pills to help her through 'difficult' moments that were 'connected to her age', as he'd delicately described it. She popped one into her mouth now, and swallowed a couple of times. There! Within moments she felt much better. In fact they worked so well she had a good mind to keep on taking them for as long as she could.

Juliet gazed up at Daniel, shocked by the strength of his compelling dominance, as he stood looking down at her with barely suppressed fury. His tall broad-shouldered frame seemed overpowering, his furious dark eyes making her momentarily speechless. She knew she should run up the stairs to face him, but she hesitated. It was as if she were in the grip of his powerful presence and couldn't move. The silence between them lengthened as he continued to glower down at her. At last she could stand it no more.

'I wanted to stop your sister making mischief,' she said in desperation.

'I don't need you to fight my battles for me,' he stormed, his great voice reverberating in the empty hall.

'But I thought . . .?'

'You *didn't* think, Juliet. You rushed off in your usual fashion, wanting to take control, as you always do, without thinking of the consequences.'

She'd never seen him so angry, so bitterly passionate about anything before. With an effort she quickly gathered herself together in defence of her actions. 'Esther has to be stopped from spreading lies and trying to stop you seeing your family,' she said, taking off her coat and flinging it on the hall chair.

'*My* family,' he roared, 'are *my* business! I won't have you interfering with *my* affairs.'

Suddenly she felt a burst of rage equal to his. Storming up the stairs she reached his side and glared at him, her eyes glinting dangerously.

'Don't you dare talk to me like that,' she said in a low voice. 'I was only trying to get her to stop making trouble. Don't you want to be able to see your children? Why are you letting a bitter old maid ruin everything for you?'

Daniel scowled and gave her a black look. 'Because it's got nothing to do with you. That's why.'

'It has *everything* to do with me!' she exclaimed, gesticulating with her slim hands, her scarlet painted nails flashing. 'It's me she hates. Not you. She thinks I'm ruining your life. She blames me for everything. I *have* to defend myself and I have to stop her trying to drive a wedge between you and the rest of your family.' *And I have to stop her telling you how badly I behaved when we were estranged . . .*

'Don't be such a fool!' Daniel fumed. 'Can't you see you're playing into her hands? By charging round there today you've added fuel to the fire?'

Juliet turned angrily away and walked swiftly through the double doors into the drawing room. 'By going to see her today I've been able to warn her that if she writes any more vile letters I shall sue for slander, libel and defamation of character.' She strode to a side table, and helped herself to a cigarette. Without bothering to put it in a holder, she lit it with shaking hands.

Daniel groaned as if he were in pain. 'Are you mad?'

'Not at all,' she said loftily, raising her chin. 'I don't know why you haven't already taken out an injunction, stopping her from contacting you in the first place? Why have you been letting her get away with it?'

'For God's sake . . .! Do you want our dirty linen washed in public?'

Juliet drew her breath in sharply, and quickly placed her cigarette between her lips again. 'What dirty linen?' she asked carefully.

Daniel was staring at her. 'Think about it,' he said sternly.

'I don't know what you mean?'

He spoke impatiently. 'I told you the other day. She thinks I married you for your money. She thinks you were the cause of my divorce. She thinks you're a bad lot because you left your first husband . . . and we can't let *that* get out because you promised Cameron you'd never reveal the truth,' he added bitterly.

Juliet flushed with relief that that was all Esther seemed to have told him about her.

Daniel continued, 'You've got to leave Esther to me. I forbid you to go anywhere near her again.'

56

'Forbid me?' Juliet cut in, incensed.

'Yes, forbid you, you stupid fool . . .' he began harshly, then stopped as he saw the pain in her eyes, and ran his hand through his thick dark hair in a gesture of desperation. 'Oh, God, darling . . . I'm sorry . . .'

The next moment she was in his arms, and he was holding her so close she could hardly breathe. She clung to him, loving him so much she felt sick with misery at the thought that they'd been fighting.

She gave a dry sob. 'I didn't mean to upset you . . . I love you, Daniel.'

He raised his head and looked up as if asking forgiveness from some deity. Then his mouth sought hers, crushing her to him as he kissed her with feverish intensity.

'I love you, too. I love you, too,' he kept repeating, between kisses. 'I love you more than anything on earth.'

'I don't want us to fight,' she whispered, reaching up and holding his face in the palms of her hands. 'I'm sorry I made you so angry.' She started returning his kisses hungrily, until their legs seemed to give way and they were kneeling on the floor, facing each other, swept away on an incoming tide of all consuming desire. Then Daniel was pulling at her skirt, and she was tugging off his jacket and undoing the buttons down the front of his trousers until they were lying on the floor, unable to wait, oblivious of everything around them, wanting only to be joined together as one, as they were always meant to have been, from the beginning.

# Five

'Ugh! Who would want to go to university?' Rosie remarked, as they sat down to Sunday lunch at Hartley on a pleasantly sunlit October day. The whole family had gathered together for the weekend to celebrate Henry's fifty-eighth birthday, and Amanda was about to take a place at Somerville College, Oxford.

'Anyone with more than two brain cells,' Amanda snapped acerbically.

Lady Anne looked at her fourth granddaughter with pride. 'Well, I think it's wonderful and you're to be congratulated. So you're off this month?'

Amanda nodded, pushing her glasses up her nose with her forefinger.

'There aren't enough women taking higher education,' Shane said. 'I wish we had more women doctors and even surgeons.'

Smiling genially and ignoring Rosie's remark, Salton turned to Amanda, who was looking radiant in spite of her thick glasses and dowdy clothes. 'It's what you've always wanted, isn't it, honey?'

Ignoring the 'honey' which she found patronizing, as if he thought men were superior to women, she smiled briefly. 'If one's going to be taken seriously in politics, it's essential to have a university background.'

'So you still want to be a parliamentary secretary, old thing?' her Aunt Candida observed. 'Good show! No prizes for guessing which party you'll join, I suppose,' she added with cheerful philosophy.

'Absolutely none,' Amanda affirmed. 'I'm reading politics, and as soon as I have an MA I'll get a job in Whitehall.'

Liza, in an effort to make the best of it, said hopefully, 'I *suppose* you could end up as a great political hostess, like

Nancy Astor? Wasn't she the first woman to take a seat in the House of Commons, Henry?'

'She was, darling, in 1919,' Henry replied smoothly. Seeing Amanda was about to scoff at the ridiculousness of the idea, he added almost defensively, 'Lady Astor was particularly interested in women's rights. She's an excellent example of how far we've come since women got the vote.'

Rosie shifted restlessly in her seat, and looked glumly at the cold slice of spam on her plate, wishing it was hot roast beef.

'How much longer is this rationing going to last?' she asked no one in particular. 'The war's been over for ages, for God's sake!'

'Some time yet,' Salton said easily. 'Britain is having to share what we've got with the starving people in Europe.'

Rosie snorted impatiently. 'Oh, damn *them*!' Another month had passed and she still hadn't got pregnant, and she blamed the lack of good nutritional food. 'I don't know why you can't get extra stuff through your contacts at the American Embassy, Salton.'

'We're all having enough to eat, honey, we're just bored by the lack of variety, that's all.'

'I don't suppose you're suffering,' she sniped at Juliet, who was picking at her lunch. 'With Dudley to cater to your every whim on the black market, you're probably both living off the fat of the land.'

'You're wrong there,' Juliet replied, putting down her knife and fork.

'Well, he got you anything you wanted during the war,' Rosie persisted.

'Even Dudley's contacts can't create miracles these days.'

'Probably because they've all been sent to prison by now!'

Henry looked coldly at Rosie. 'That's enough. This is supposed to be a happy occasion, and I don't want any back-biting.'

Rosie shrugged and made a face. Salton looked embarrassed. Everyone else dug silently into their spam and Liza wished they'd ignored Charlotte's wishes, and killed a couple of the rabbits for lunch.

Daniel leaned towards Henry, smiling darkly. 'Juliet has something to tell you that will cheer you up.'

Henry's tired blue eyes lit up and he turned to his daughter with an expression of affection mixed with hope. 'Have you, darling?'

Juliet took a sip of water and smiled and nodded almost shyly.

'We're going to have a baby.'

A chorus of delight went up around the long table. Lady Anne's eyes brimmed with emotion, remembering how devastated Juliet had been when her first baby had died at birth. Liza clapped her hands, glad that Henry hadn't been the first to know what Juliet was up to this time. Daniel beamed proudly and received glances of congratulations from the other men. Louise gave Juliet a knowing smile of understanding; when it came to having babies they shared a special closeness. Everyone had something to say, especially Candida.

'Good show, old girl. I always knew Daniel was a stallion!'

Everyone laughed, and few people noticed Rosie leaving the table and dashing out of the dining room door, her hand clasped over her mouth and tears streaming down her cheeks. It was too, too unfair, she thought, sobbing as she ran up to her bedroom, the room that had been her haven since she'd been a small child. She flung herself on the bed, forgetting that Nanny was giving lunch to Sophia and Jonathan on the floor above in the nursery and might hear her. Not that she cared. She craved a little baby. Her whole body ached to have another child. The very thought of Juliet having a baby made her feel ill with longing.

God damn and blast Juliet, she thought, wretched with self-pity. Juliet always got everything she wanted. Always landed on her feet as if she was blessed by the gods. Ever since she could remember Juliet seemed to have been the favoured child in the family; none of them had been as lucky or successful as Juliet . . . and was she grateful? Like hell she was! Rosie fumed as she searched frantically for a handkerchief in her chest of drawers.

'What's the matter, Rosie?' asked a sweet soft voice in the doorway. Rosie looked up resentfully at Charlotte who was standing there, exquisite in a delicate ethereal way, with her silvery hair, which she'd grown long again, held back by combs on either side of her face. She was wearing a white jumper and a pale blue linen skirt that showed her long slim tanned legs.

'I want another baby,' Rosie explained resentfully, 'and it doesn't seem to be happening.' She eyed her young sister with envy. Charlotte wasn't only the most beautiful of them all, she also had the rest of her life to look forward to and Rosie wondered if she appreciated that fact.

She was now twenty-nine, nearly thirty, and she was already feeling old and past her best, and she didn't even have a new baby to look forward to. She started crying again, muttering, 'It isn't fair. It's not asking for much.'

'Hey, you guys! What's this all about?' Salton asked cheerfully as he came into the room. Not that he didn't know. He was disappointed himself that Rosie had failed to get pregnant and it was obvious Juliet's news had upset her.

Charlotte looked sympathetically at them both. 'I'll leave you,' she said diplomatically, slipping out of the room. She couldn't imagine what it was like to actually *want* a baby; not that babies weren't sweet and she loved helping Louise with Daisy, but she did think Rosie's attitude to Juliet's pregnancy was strange. After all, Rosie already had two beautiful children which she didn't seem in the least interested in these days, and that, Charlotte thought, really was odd.

Back in the dining room everyone was talking and carrying on as usual and as Charlotte took her own seat again, she saw the family had closed in around the table, filling the gaps left by Rosie and Salton as if nothing had happened.

Candida was holding forth on her latest acquisition, a three-year-old bay hunter. 'She's a beautiful mare. Wonderful stamina, and she'll jump anything! She goes like the clappers!'

Andrew Pemberton, a retired Major-General who Candida had married two years before, nodded in agreement. He didn't hunt himself but he admired Candida's amazing courage in the field, especially over high fences. 'Clover's a fine animal, and she's still young. I think she'll get even better as she matures,' he observed.

'Good for you, Candida,' Henry said encouragingly. His sister was the only one in the family who had inherited their father's love of hunting.

'You're both coming for Christmas, aren't you?' Henry reminded them. 'And you'll be bringing Sebastian and Marina with you, I hope?'

'They're looking forward to it. Goodness, how many of us does that make?' Candida turned to Liza and her mother. 'Have you really got room for us all? We could easily come for the day . . .' she began, but Henry raised his hand. He wanted this to be a real family Christmas with all of them together, just like it used to be before the war. They'd decorate the house with branches of holly from the garden, and he'd buy a big tree to stand in the hall. When he and Candida had been children they'd always had the tree in the hall, and it was only in the past twenty years that Liza had insisted it should be in the drawing room. All the old traditions must be adhered to he decided, not knowing why it seemed so important to him this year, but quickly dismissed from his mind the thought that his mother wasn't getting any younger and that that could be the reason he wanted the celebrations to be perfect.

'Liza and I are going to try and make it as much like a pre-war Christmas as we can,' he announced stoutly. 'We've been promised a goose from a local farmer, and Mrs Dobbs has been hoarding sugar and dried fruit for months, so we should be able to rustle up some kind of Christmas pudding.'

'Splendid, old boy,' Candida said fondly. 'We'll bring a bottle of port, won't we, Andrew? And we've probably got a drop of brandy for the pudding.'

After coffee in the drawing room, Juliet and her father went for a stroll in the gardens, whilst the others lounged around talking or reading the weekend newspapers.

It was a sunny October afternoon with a cloudless blue sky, but the trees were shedding their golden leaves and the heat had gone out of the sun. Nature was winding down, preparing for the cold and damp of another English winter, and there was a melancholy atmosphere as plants began to retreat into themselves, having stored up their energy to lie fallow until next spring.

Now that she was pregnant, Juliet was beginning to feel an affinity with nature that she'd never felt before. The magical cycle of life from birth to death, the constant replacement and new growth that replaced the old, had awakened her senses to the miracle of nature.

'Look at all these berries, Dads!' she exclaimed as they walked past a heavily-laden crab apple tree.

Henry raised his eyebrows judiciously. 'Sign we can expect a hard winter,' he pointed out.

'We could decorate the house at Christmas with leaves and berries, couldn't we?'

'Darling, the birds will have eaten all of them long before Christmas,' he laughed. 'You've been living in town, too long!'

She smiled. 'Sometimes I think I'd like to live down here, permanently.' She stopped and turned to look back at the mellow dusky-pink brick walls of Hartley Hall, with its wide-awake windows framed in white. It was a perfectly proportioned George II house, with a grey slate roof, set in beautiful grounds that had grown around it, like loving and protective arms shielding it from the elements.

'You'd miss London and the bright lights. Remember how you hated living in Scotland?'

Juliet looked at him in astonishment. 'That was because I was married to Cameron, and that old witch of a mother of his was driving me mad.'

'I know, but I still think you're a townie, sweetheart. But maybe, when you're older it would suit you more than now.'

'And for our children,' she affirmed. 'Dads, I'm warning you, I'll be coming every weekend when we have children. I want them to know and love this place like I do.'

Touched, Henry put his arm around her slim shoulders. 'I'm looking forward to that more than I can say,' he said softly. There had always been a special closeness between him and Juliet, like a golden thread that was tied from her heart to somewhere tender in the middle of his chest; and he cared for her so much that when she suffered, the thread tugged at him as if the pain was his. He knew Liza was jealous of their special relationship and the way Juliet confided in him rather than her mother, but that was the way it was. And as far as he was concerned the way it always would be.

A gust of wind came sweeping across the kitchen garden, tossing the branches of the trees, so the leaves whirled past them as if it was Juliet and Henry who were moving fast, and not the leaves. Juliet shivered.

'Are you cold?' Henry asked anxiously. She shook her head.

'No,' she said without conviction.

'Let's go back. It is getting quite chilly.' He turned to retrace his footsteps. Juliet stood still, indecisively. Then she followed him slowly.

'What is it?' he asked.

'Dads, do you know a really good lawyer? Or barrister?'

Startled, he stopped and looked at her inquiringly. 'I expect so, but what do you need a lawyer for?'

She stepped to his side and slipped her arm through his. 'Don't tell anyone and don't tell Daniel I've talked to you about this, but I may be forced to sue his sister,' she said in a serious voice.

'Daniel's sister?'

Juliet nodded. 'She's got it into her head he's married me for my money . . . Cameron's money, actually,' she pointed out ironically, 'and she's angry I'm not Jewish, and she's said a lot of dreadful things about me. If she carries on like this I've got to put a stop to it.'

Henry looked mystified. 'How did you find out about this?'

'She's been writing to Daniel; the first letter arrived on our wedding day. So I went to see her . . . and she does know an awful lot about me, Dads.' Juliet's voice dropped. 'She knows about things in my life. Things that even Daniel doesn't know. Things that happened after we'd split up and I thought I'd never see him again.'

Henry could guess what Juliet was referring to, but he didn't feel judgemental. That's what war and danger and fear did to people; made them grab the moment, squeezing every ounce of fun out of it because there might be no tomorrow; and for thousands there hadn't been.

'Has this woman any proof to back up her accusations?'

Juliet's eyebrows were drawn together in concentration. 'I don't see how she can have. Except what she's read in the newspapers.'

'Which Daniel already knows about?'

'He knows about Eddie, of course,' she replied, evading the question. They were silent as they retraced their steps and were once again near the house. 'But how can she know about people I went, well, out dining and dancing with?' she added falteringly.

Henry made no comment. Juliet was a beautiful red-blooded young woman; even he wouldn't have expected her to sit at home alone throughout the war, when there must

64

have been dozens of men who would have been attracted to her.

'This woman is probably just trying to make mischief, Juliet. You could take out an injunction against her to stop her talking, but do you really want to go to court? If she's as vengeful as you say, she'll try and accuse you of all sorts of things, and even though none of it might be true, remember, mud sticks. You don't want the suicide of Alastair Slaidburn brought up again, do you? Or your divorce from Cameron? Especially as you can't say *why* you left him.'

She hung her head, scuffing the fallen leaves with her feet as they stood in the drive. 'I know,' she said in a subdued voice. 'That's the rub. So what shall I do?'

'Can't Daniel get her to stop?'

'I don't think she'll pay any attention. She seems to think I bewitched him and he's beyond redemption. I had thought of going to see Ruth and talking to her, but Daniel would kill me if he found out.'

Henry spoke firmly. 'You mustn't get embroiled with his family, Juliet. He'd have every right to think you were interfering. Why don't you just sit tight? His sister is bound to get bored with trying to make trouble if you ignore her. Concentrate on having this new baby of yours, my darling. It's the best thing that could have happened for you.'

She raised her head to look at him. 'It *is* marvellous, isn't it?' She smiled. 'It's what we both want so much.' But she couldn't stop thinking about Esther, and how she could ruin everything for them. What effect would it have on Daniel if he were to find out about the lovers she'd had? What if Esther was able to prove it was true? At one level London was a small place and Juliet was a well known figure on the social scene. People talked. Once started, gossip became rife.

'Let's go back to the house, Dads,' she said suddenly, tugging his arm.

When they got back to join the others they found Salton had taken Rosie and the children back to London.

'She was upset,' Louise whispered to Juliet. 'She's desperate for a baby, you know, and finding out you were pregnant . . . well, you know Rosie.'

'But she'll have one soon,' Juliet protested, annoyed that it seemed to be her fault that Rosie was unhappy.

Louise lifted Daisy out of the old family pram they kept at Hartley. 'I've got to change her.'

'I'll come with you.' They climbed the stairs, walking side by side, until they reached the top-floor nursery. 'She's so adorable and good tempered, isn't she?' Juliet observed.

'Umm.' Louise carried the baby in her arms like a bundle of washing, not even looking at her.

'What's the matter? Are you very tired?'

She turned to Juliet, her expression blank. She spoke in a low voice so no one would overhear. 'I'm not bonding with her,' she said flatly.

Juliet looked shocked. 'What does that mean? You don't love her?'

'I feel *nothing*. When she was born, and she was handed to me, it felt no more wonderful than if I'd been handed the morning newspapers. I mean, I don't *dislike* her or anything, it's just that she means nothing to me.'

They paused on the landing, out of earshot of the rest of the family.

'You had such a bad time having her, you're probably still in shock,' Juliet whispered comfortingly.

Louise shook her head. 'It's not shock, it's not baby blues. I thought I was excited before she arrived, but when she did . . .' Her lips suddenly trembled and she looked beseechingly at Juliet, desperate to be understood. 'I thought,' she said brokenly, 'that she'd take over in my life where Rupert had left off? I thought she'd sort of replace him. I thought I'd recognize her because I'd carried her for nine months and I thought she'd look just like him. I thought it was going to be like getting Rupert back!' She put her hand over her mouth to quell her sobs. Juliet took Daisy from her very gently, and held her close.

'But she's not a bit like Rupert!' Louise continued feverishly. 'She's got Shane's grey eyes and brown hair and she's small and . . . Oh, God, I can't help resenting her because she's *not* Rupert.' She leaned against the landing wall, her arms crossed defensively across her chest.

'Have you told Shane all this?'

'How can I? He's so thrilled and proud, and it's his first baby; but she's not *my* first baby.'

'I think you should talk to someone, Louise. Lots of mothers reject their babies at first, you know. Stop blaming yourself. You may not think you've got the baby blues, but you probably have. Don't they call it post-natal depression or some new fangled name these days?'

Louise sighed. 'I don't know,' she said wearily. 'All I know is I love Bella more than Daisy. Isn't that shameful?'

Juliet smiled sorrowfully. Louise was still so young and childlike herself and her honesty was touching. 'Well, Bella is a darling little dog. I'm sure you'll soon feel as loving towards Daisy. Why don't you come with me to see my gynaecologist? I can understand you'd find it difficult to talk to one of the doctors Shane works with.'

'What good will that do? I can't change how I feel.'

'A specialist will help you feel differently about Daisy. Let's go one day this week.' Juliet strode into the nursery, and placed the baby on the old sofa. 'Now, will you teach me how to change a nappy? I haven't a clue, and it's time I learned.'

Down in the drawing room Liza found herself unwittingly embroiled in an argument with Henry and his sister, about Charlotte's future. Now that they were installed in their flat in Princes Court, Liza was determined to launch Charlotte as a debutante when she became seventeen.

'We can give a cocktail party and later on a coming out ball at the Hyde Park Hotel because it's just round the corner,' Liza said decisively.

'Coming out ball?' Candida exclaimed incredulously.

Henry remained silent, eyes downcast. Lady Anne picked up her knitting.

Liza continued defiantly, 'Why not? *Hundreds* of girls are going to be debutantes next year. My friend, Lady Mackenzie, is determined Susan will do the Season, and as Rosie and Juliet did it, we must do the same for Charlotte! I've found out there's going to be an informal presentation at Buckingham Palace, so it will be low-key compared to before the war, nevertheless . . .' She'd run out of breath in her fervent protestations.

'But does Charlotte want to do it?' Candida asked, glancing at Henry, who was studying the carpet.

'She'll regret it if she doesn't,' Liza snapped back. 'It's like having a white wedding; you can only do it once in your life. And things are back to normal now. Mrs Clive Arbuthnott is already planning Priscilla's coming out party, and so is Laura Nepean. She plans to give a dance for Mary at 23, Knightsbridge, which is a house you can hire for parties and receptions these days. Of course Charlotte must do it. Look how many friends Rosie and Juliet made?'

Amanda looked up from the newspaper she was reading. 'Charlotte's too scared to refuse. She fears the wrath of God will descend on her if she says "no" and that she'll end up on the shelf as an old maid, according to you.'

'Nonsense!' retorted Liza, flushing. 'She doesn't feel like that at all.'

Everyone in the room seemed to be looking at her; particularly Henry. 'Well, she doesn't!' Liza continued. 'She's looking forward to it. All young girls want to go to parties and wear pretty clothes.'

Amanda rose, putting down the newspaper with a flourish. 'That's a total generalization, Ma. The majority of young women in this country have to get a job at sixteen and they're lucky if they're taken down to the pub for a pint when they're eighteen! Have you the foggiest what *real* young women want? Or get? Do you imagine that in the Welsh mining communities, or the factories in Sheffield, or for that matter in the slums of Hackney, seventeen-year-old girls are planning their debutante season?'

'That's enough, Amanda,' Henry said severely. 'There's no need to be rude to your mother.'

She turned to look at him, her pale face earnest. 'But Dad, people like us form only four per cent of the whole population! And Mummy talks as if it's compulsory for every girl in the country to be a deb! As if the daughters of miners in Merthyr Tydvil, factory workers in Skegness, and dockers in Deptford, are planning their coming out parties! I don't think even many daughters of dukes are going through this rigmarole any more. Society has been wiped away in one fell swoop by the war. And about time, too. Especially now we've got a Labour Government. It's time the workers had a chance.'

Out of earshot, Candida leaned towards her mother, murmuring, 'The girl's got it in her to be a top-hole Labour MP, hasn't she? She certainly knows how to make a case for what she believes in.'

'That's how she may well end up,' Lady Anne agreed. 'She's

right about one thing. The war has changed everything. Can you get servants any longer?'

'No, damnit, I can't!' Candida laughed. 'Mama. I think we're about to become the under-privileged nouveau pauvre!'

'I thought we already were!'

Amid their good humoured banter and laughter Liza slipped from the room and went upstairs. Lady Anne and Candida shared something, a sort of *understanding*, that always eluded her and made her feel like an outsider. She had a sneaking feeling Henry was a part of their secret world of jokes, too, but he was too kind to let it show when she was there. No doubt he was joining in their badinage right now, as she sat at her dressing table, powdering her nose and putting on some more lipstick. Then she reached into one of the drawers and withdrew the little box containing her pretty little purple heart-shaped pills. She popped one into her mouth and within moments a warm comfortable feeling spread through her body, leaving her quite cheerful.

Knowing that she was returning to their nice new flat tomorrow was a relief. Once in London she could telephone her friends, do some shopping, and perhaps fix a luncheon party, without being under the critical gaze of Henry's family.

# Part Two

# Times of Turbulence

# 1948–1950

# Six

Charlotte stepped lightly along Bond Street in her high heels, the long full skirt of her Dior 'New Look' outfit swirling around her slim legs. Oblivious of admiring glances from passers-by at her tiny nipped-in waist and small round breasts, she glanced into the shop windows with interest. Staying with Juliet for the past week had been a revelation and she'd been encouraged to buy all sorts of clothes her mother would think were too old, too sophisticated and too theatrical for her coming out.

'What's Mummy going to say?' Charlotte asked, after their first day shopping in Knightsbridge. In the spare room of 99, Park Lane, her bed was piled high with chic off-the-shoulder cocktail dresses, wasp-waisted suits, little flower or feather hats, and high-heeled shoes with platform soles and ankle straps that she couldn't stop gazing at.

'They're so divine!' she crowed ecstatically.

'As Mummy's stuck down at Hartley with a broken ankle, she can't say anything.' Juliet grinned. 'Anyway, she can't complain because Princess Elizabeth and Princess Margaret wear clothes exactly like these; and even the Queen's wearing platform shoes. They're the latest thing.'

'Thank God for Dior,' Charlotte breathed. 'I feel like a film star in all this stuff. Was it terribly expensive?' she added anxiously.

'Call it my early present to you for your birthday, darling.' Juliet stood up. 'How about a new hairstyle to go with your new wardrobe?' she suggested.

'What do you suggest?' Charlotte asked, looking at herself in the big mirror that hung on the wall between the two windows.

'Let's go through *Vogue* for some ideas.'

Juliet had continued to take Charlotte around for the rest of the week, buying more clothes, and taking her to Elizabeth Arden's salon to have her hair cut in a short stylish fashion.

Now, as she continued her perambulations along Bond Street, while Juliet was having a manicure and pedicure, Charlotte paused to look in the window of Asprey's. There was a magnificent display of jewellery and her eyes marvelled at the size of some of the stones. She was just thinking how she'd give anything to wear the aquamarine and diamond necklace and matching earrings that lay on a black velvet cushion, when she heard a discreet clearing of the throat just behind her.

Turning, she saw a slim young man, dressed as if for the country in grey flannel trousers and a tweed jacket. His hair was untidy, but his smile was warm and wide.

'Excuse me,' he said diffidently, 'but I couldn't help seeing you walking along the street just now. Are you a model?'

Charlotte raised her eyebrows and blushed. 'A *model*?' she repeated.

He nodded. 'I'm a fashion photographer. My name's Simon Franks. I work on *Vogue* magazine and I wondered if you'd posed for any fashion shots?'

'No-no. You've got the wrong person!' she stammered, feeling slightly alarmed. She moved to walk on, but he stepped in front of her, his eyes exploring her face as if he was examining a rare work of art.

'You've got the most exquisite features,' he said dreamily. 'I've never seen such perfect bone structure. Surely you've been photographed?'

'No, really . . .!' she protested. All her mother's warnings about talking to strange men came flooding back. She wished Juliet was with her; she'd know how to get rid of this strange but pleasant looking young man, whose accent was almost cockney but not quite.

He started searching in his pockets, producing bits of paper some of which dropped to the pavement. 'Here!' he said at last. Triumphantly he showed her a slightly battered business card.

*Simon Franks*, she read. Underneath it said *Photographer*. Printed in one corner was his address. Charlotte caught the word Chelsea, and remembered her mother saying no one lived in Chelsea. It was full of artists and the like and was not really a respectable area.

'Take this,' he urged, thrusting the card into her hand.

'No, really . . .' she said again, not wanting to be rude but anxious to get away.

He started scribbling a telephone number on the back of the card. 'Listen, ring this number.' He sounded agitated. 'Why don't you speak to the fashion editor of *Vogue*. Tell her I've seen you and I think you'd be perfect for the June issue. We're doing evening dresses by Mainbocher, Schiaparelli and Molyneux . . .'

He gabbled on while Charlotte stood, no longer taking in what he said so bemused was she by his offer. She'd always secretly hankered to be a film star, but it had been a dream, one which started when a friend of Mummy had said she'd end up in Hollywood, and she'd never considered it seriously. But now . . .?

'What's your name?' she heard him ask.

'Charlotte,' she answered automatically, without thinking.

He repeated her name almost reverently. 'Charlotte. It's a beautiful name. Have you heard of Barbara Goalen?'

'No.'

He looked surprised. 'Oh! Well, anyway, you're going to be bigger than Barbara Goalen. You're going to be the face of the decade. Believe me, Charlotte, I know what I'm talking about. What's your phone number?'

She drew back nervously. 'I, umm, I'm staying with my sister, I don't remember her number. Now, I really must go.' At that moment an empty taxi drove up Bond Street, and she hailed it and, jumping in quickly, gave the driver Juliet's address.

As it drew away from the kerb she sneaked a look out of the back window; Simon what-ever-he-was-called was watching the receding cab, and at the same time writing something down. Charlotte turned her head quickly away, blushing at being caught looking at him.

When she got back to Park Lane, Juliet was still out, so she went to the table where the magazines were kept in the drawing room, and started flipping through the pages of the latest *Vogue*. Sure enough, under the most stunning photographs of models in a feature headed 'Spring Wardrobe' there was the name Simon Franks. So he really was a bona fide photographer and not some serial rapist!

When Juliet returned, ordering Dudley to bring them tea, Charlotte spoke with studied casualness. 'Have you heard of someone called Barbara Goalen?'

'Have I heard of Barbara Goalen?' Juliet asked incredulously. 'Everyone's heard of her. She's the most marvellous model. What a face! What a figure! I believe her waist really is only eighteen inches, and she wears incredible clothes and terrifically high heels. Why?'

Charlotte drew a deep breath and handed her Simon Franks' card.

'He stopped me in the street today. He said he wanted to photograph me for *Vogue*.'

'*What*?' Juliet sat upright, her hand clasping her swollen stomach.

'What did you say?'

'I told him I wasn't a model.'

'Are you crazy?'

'Well, Mummy wouldn't let me, would she?'

Juliet waved her hand airily. 'Don't worry about Mummy. I'll talk to her. You *must* do it, darling. It's a tremendous compliment, you know. Tell me exactly what he said?'

Charlotte gave a little giggle of embarrassment. 'He said I was going to be bigger than Barbara Goalen. He said I was going to be the face of the decade. Do you think he meant it? I mean he only saw me walking along . . .'

'Charlotte, this could be your future,' Juliet said, her voice serious. 'It's the most marvellous opportunity. Don't you realize what it means? You'll become a famous beauty. Your picture will be everywhere. You'll get to wear the most wonderful clothes . . . you'll travel and be treated like royalty, and you'll make a lot of money. Your own money; not just a dress allowance from Mummy and Daddy.' She was walking two and fro now, up and down the black carpet of the drawing room, gesticulating excitedly.

'But Mummy has always talked about models as if they were no better than . . . than prostitutes!' Charlotte burst out anxiously. 'She'll go mad!'

Juliet came and sat down again beside her sister.

'Listen, Mummy's talking about the Dark Ages. Barbara Goalen has made modelling utterly acceptable and is genuinely admired and invited everywhere. She's a lady from a good background; I believe her husband was killed in the war. If this photographer thinks you're *half* as good as her, then you're made. Believe me, I would stop you doing this if I thought it would ruin your reputation,' she added forcefully.

'So what shall I do?' Charlotte asked, bewildered. Everything seemed to have gone skew-whiff in the last few minutes, like shaking a kaleidoscope and seeing all the coloured patterns change. 'What about my being a deb?' she asked in a small voice.

'Do both,' Juliet advised. '*Vogue* would love that. "Clothes modelled by a debutante who is also a great beauty." Darling, I'm so proud of you. Ring him up right away. Say you'll do it. I'll go with you to the studio the first time if you're nervous. And it means you can stay here, with Daniel and me; won't that be fun?'

Charlotte started laughing as she hugged her sister. 'It's all madness!' she exclaimed. 'Promise me you'll be the one to tell Mummy?'

Liza took the news like a tragedy queen being told her daughter was doomed.

'How could you let this happen?' she raged accusingly at Juliet, who had taken the precaution of breaking the news over the telephone. 'I had such high hopes for Charlotte, but who will want her now? No decent girl becomes a model . . .'

'Mummy . . .'

'She'll be looked upon as a tart . . .'

'Please listen . . .'

'Plastered in make-up like a street walker—'

'*Mama!*' Juliet shouted, exasperated. 'Things have changed.'

'Being an actress is bad enough, but a *model*!'

'She'll only model couture clothes, for God's sake!'

'She'll be *ruined* if she does this. I should never have let her stay with you and all your raffish friends,' Liza exploded.

'Charlotte can be a deb *and* a model,' Juliet replied angrily. 'It's not like it used to be. Barbara Goalen has changed the face of modelling; it's now a respectable and much admired profession, so for goodness sake calm down. Do you think I want Charlotte to get a bad reputation? I look upon this as a wonderful opportunity and she can stay with me and—'

Liza cut in furiously, 'She'll stay with *me*, in Princes Court. At least *I'll* be able to keep an eye on her. If she stays with you and Daniel, God knows what will become of her.'

Juliet's tone was cold. 'I resent that. You know perfectly well I would never let her come to any harm.'

'You'll be too busy with your baby, anyway,' Liza remarked sourly, knowing perfectly well that Charlotte would prefer to stay at Juliet's, where the house was lively with the coming and going of their friends.

'Thank heavens Mummy's still at Hartley,' Charlotte said to Juliet the following week. She'd been told to arrive at Simon Franks' studio in Elm Park Gardens at ten o'clock, and Juliet had promised to accompany her.

'Come as you are,' Simon had said. 'You'll have your hair and make-up done when you arrive, so you needn't bring anything.'

Juliet smiled. 'Mama's furious she still can't walk on her ankle. I think she'll be staying down at Hartley for several weeks yet.'

Charlotte gave a little shudder. 'I'm scared enough as it is, but if she were with me, with all her embarrassing remarks, it would be ghastly!'

'Don't worry, darling. You'll be fine. Before you know it, you'll be rushing off on your own, being photographed on locations all over the place and your picture will be in every glossy magazine.'

When they entered the basement studio, it was as if a reception party had been formed to greet them. The fashion editor of *Vogue* and two of her assistants had arrived, with armfuls of ball gowns, boxes of jewellery and bags of high-heeled gold and silver kid evening shoes. In a corner a hair-dresser and a make-up artist had laid out all their paraphernalia on a table and there was a high stool waiting for her to sit on.

Simon Franks greeted her as if she was an old friend, and immediately introduced his assistants to her. Charlotte's face became transformed, her skin glowing and her eyes wide and bright with delight. It was as if she'd accidentally found what she'd always been searching for. This was where I really belong, she thought in wonder. Everyone was looking at her rapt expression, and Simon Franks was grinning from ear to ear, knowing a 'natural' when he saw one.

She felt a rush of confidence. 'Isn't this fun?' Her light voice was childish in its enthusiasm. In the last few minutes she'd found a new, loving family, who were ready to embrace and make a fuss of her as if she was precious to them. 'This is my sister, Juliet Lawrence,' she explained.

Simon shook Juliet's hand. 'How do you do, Mrs Lawrence? I know you from the many photographs I've seen of you in magazines and newspapers.' He smiled at them both. 'My goodness, beauty really does run in your family, doesn't it? Come and sit down. There's a chair over here,' he suggested.

Juliet looked at Charlotte. 'I've only come to drop her off,' she began, realizing her sister did not need to be chaperoned now she'd seen the set-up.

'Oh, do stay for a bit,' Charlotte said, but she also relaxed, showing that she knew she was going to be fine.

'Yes, do stay and watch,' Simon coaxed. 'Can we get you a cup of coffee? Or tea?'

Juliet chose tea, and settled in the comfortable chair to watch, fascinated, as Charlotte was transformed from a lovely unspoilt seventeen-year-old girl from the country into a stunningly exquisite young beauty, groomed, chic and poised. When she appeared from the changing room wearing a pale pink silk crinoline, with a drift of fine chiffon around her bare shoulders and a jewelled belt clinching her tiny waist, there was an audible gasp from the fashion editor.

Charlotte glided forward, a playful smile hovering on her lips and a glint of pure happiness in her blue eyes. It was obvious she was enjoying herself and pleased with the way she looked.

Juliet beamed and nodded in approval.

For a moment Simon looked as if he'd been hypnotized. His eyes were wide and his mouth gaped in sheer amazement. Stunned, he turned to his assistants. 'Let's get on with it, then,' he told them, his voice shaking.

As Juliet watched, she saw Charlotte really was a natural. She moved so easily from position to position, taking Simon's directing as if she'd done it all her life. She was as graceful as a ballet dancer, or like a living figure from a Fragonard painting. The atmosphere in the studio was electrifying.

The whole session lasted several hours, as Charlotte put on dress after dress, most of them inspired by Dior's version of the romantic 1880s. Some were in fine white lace threaded with blue satin ribbon, others were in taffeta or satin which lay over a froth of tulle petticoats. All had tiny waistlines, huge crinoline style skirts, and bodices that revealed her smooth white shoulders.

At last they were finished, and everyone was exhausted except for Charlotte, who seemed to have been energized by the whole experience.

With his face white and drawn with exhaustion, Simon thanked her solemnly. 'I'll see you very soon,' he said quietly as the sisters left.

The fashion editor and her assistants said the same thing in gushing voices, and the make-up artist and hairdresser gave her their business cards and told her to ring them when ever she wanted.

'Was it really all right?' Charlotte whispered to Juliet, as they got into the car.

'Darling, you were bloody marvellous,' Juliet said succinctly. 'You enjoyed yourself, didn't you?'

Charlotte clasped her hands together. 'I *adored* it!' she breathed ecstatically. 'When do you think they'll want me again?'

That night Juliet went into labour early. 'It's all the excitement,' she gasped between the contractions which were rapidly escalating.

Daniel, sitting by her bed in St George's Hospital, held her hand tenderly. 'You're so brave, my darling. I wish they'd let me stay with you so I could share some of the pain.'

She squeezed his hand. 'I'm glad it's not allowed.' Another wave of pain took her breath away. 'Having a baby is not exactly dignified.' She had to stop again, biting her bottom lip before she could continue. 'I wouldn't want you to see me looking a mess.'

'I'll be waiting outside the door,' he promised. 'And the minute it's over, I'll be right back beside you.'

'That'll be lovely.' She screwed up her eyes with agony,

and the midwife who had been hovering for the past two hours stepped up to the bed.

'Come along now, Mr Lawrence,' she said in a kindly voice. 'Your wife's going to be very busy for the next hour or so, so go and get yourself a cup of tea and we'll let you know as soon as the baby arrives.'

Daniel kissed Juliet, reluctant to leave her, wishing that doctors allowed fathers to stay.

But when he'd gone Juliet was relieved. He'd have hated to see her suffer, and she intended to be sitting up in bed, looking pretty in a new nightdress and bed jacket with the baby in her arms, when he eventually came back into the room. But it was wonderful to know that he'd be waiting outside, she reflected. Memories of the last time she'd been here in this very hospital when she'd lost their baby and she didn't know where Daniel was, or if she'd ever see him again, still haunted her.

'You're doing fine, Mrs Lawrence,' the midwife announced, after examining her. 'This is not your first baby, is it?'

Tears slid down Juliet's cheeks. 'No,' she whispered throatily, turning her face to the wall. How old would their daughter have been by now? Eight years old. A little girl, going to her school, having dancing lessons, playing in the garden of Hartley.

'Could I have something . . . for the pain?' Juliet wept. But it wasn't the pain of childbirth she wanted to banish; it was the pain in her heart.

Three hours later Juliet was delivered of a healthy little boy weighing seven pounds and two ounces. And as she'd promised herself, she'd had a bed bath and was dressed in a pale blue satin nightgown and a blue chiffon bed jacket, trimmed with white marabou feathers when Daniel was ushered back into the room. His face was radiant and he went straight to her and folded his arms around her.

'My darling girl,' he kept whispering, as he covered her face in kisses. 'Are you all right?'

She lay back contentedly. 'I'm fine. Isn't he beautiful?'

'He's wonderful. And quite big, too. Did you have a dreadful time, darling?' He gazed anxiously into her eyes.

'Actually, it was overshadowed by the excitement of his

arrival,' she replied candidly. And it was true. The pain had paled to nothing once she'd seen their baby son. Then she giggled. 'He looks just like you, doesn't he? Lucky boy!'

'So . . . it's Tristan Lawrence?'

Juliet nodded happily. They'd already decided if it was a boy they'd call him Tristan, and if it had been a girl, Madeline.

Daniel kissed her again, gently and lovingly. 'You get some sleep now, sweetheart. I'll phone *The Times* and the *Telegraph* to announce he's arrived, then I'll ring round the rest of the family.'

As Juliet drifted off to sleep she thought about her baby, and for the first time in years a sense of completeness swept over her. Now she had the beginnings of her own family, and it was a wonderfully secure feeling.

Rosie and Salton had recently moved into a much bigger house, in Chapel Street, Belgravia. 'We're going to need more space,' she told everyone, 'for when we have a baby.'

Sadly, there was still no sign of a baby, and as month after month passed, and Jonathan and Sophia grew bigger, Rosie's frustration was reaching a fever pitch. It was all she could think about. All she could talk about. Her disappointment every month was crushing. Her medical bill, as she went from one Harley Street doctor to another, was beginning to alarm Salton. He'd already taken a test to make sure it wasn't his fault, and they'd shown he was fertile. The problem lay with Rosie, but nobody seemed to know what it was.

When she heard Juliet's baby had been born she took to her bed, swamped by feelings of defeat. What was the use? she asked herself. It was hard enough that Charlotte now had a career as a model who everyone was talking about, and Louise now had Daisy to replace Rupert and even Amanda was having a wonderful time at Oxford. It all made it harder to accept that her own life was so blighted. Rosie began to feel that she was jinxed.

From the moment she'd made her debut in 1935 everything had gone wrong. Her memory trawled over all the young men she'd known; only Alastair had fallen for her, until Juliet stole him away. Charles had married her for her money, and Freddie had left her for a fiancée she didn't even know about. She's also had to bring up Sophia and Jonathan on her own, and although Salton was wonderful with them, he too wanted them to have their own baby.

So deep was Rosie's despair, she couldn't even find pleasure in her beautiful new home. Even though Salton had got them a cook and they already had two daily cleaners, as well as Nanny, she felt herself burdened by life.

Knowing she should be more grateful to Salton for providing her with everything she'd asked for, she couldn't help despising him at times, for being so easily manipulated. His easy going nature maddened her. She could twist him around her little finger and then twist him some more. Then she'd feel terribly guilty and spent days fearful that he might leave her.

'I wish I could be *happy*,' she confided to one of the specialists she consulted. He'd previously suggested her failure to get pregnant was being caused by her state of anxiety and that if she relaxed there was no medical reason why she shouldn't have another baby.

'What are you unhappy about, specifically?' he enquired, looking at her face, thinking how her prettiness was spoiled by her discontented expression.

'Nothing's *ever* as good as I think it's going to be,' she admitted tearfully. 'Mummy always said I'd have a marvellous life, make a brilliant marriage, be a great society beauty, and have anything I wanted . . . and it hasn't happened.'

'Maybe your mother gave you too great a sense of expectation?' he suggested carefully. 'Are any of your sisters unhappy?'

'None of them,' she said swiftly, her voice full of resentment.

The specialist had advised her to get a hobby, some interest that would take her mind off her worries, and then sent her on her way.

'Such rubbish!' Rosie scoffed afterwards. 'As if some hobby could be a magic wand that could change everything.'

Nanny knocked on her bedroom door as she lay there feeling sorry for herself, and then barged in before Rosie had time to say anything.

'Do you intend to spend the whole day in bed?' Nanny asked, as if Rosie had still been a small child. 'Jonathan wants to go to the zoo this afternoon, and Sophia's dying to see Juliet's baby. I'll take him to the zoo, but why don't you go with Sophia to see Tristan?'

'I don't feel well,' Rosie complained.

'Nonsense,' Nanny snapped. 'You're just wallowing in self pity. It's time you stopped behaving like a spoilt child and started looking after your husband and children.'

Rosie sat up in bed angrily. 'You can't speak to me like that!'

'I can and I will, because it's for your own good,' Nanny retorted. 'I've looked after you since you were born and mark my words I'm not going to let you get away with laziness. You're letting yourself go, and it's not fair on the children. Count your blessings for once, Rosie. You've got a really nice husband who you don't appreciate, and this lovely big house, and I'll grant you, another baby would be lovely, but if it doesn't happen, it doesn't happen. Some women can *never* have children, but they don't mope all over the place! Jonathan is a fine little fellow, and he'll keep the Padmore title going, and Sophia is a gem! What more do you want?' She stood in her navy blue uniform with a white apron, and a belt with a silver buckle, glaring down at Rosie's recumbent figure aggressively.

Rosie wilted against the pillows under Nanny's onslaught.

Nanny had one more card to play. 'No matter what happened, you'd never find Lady Anne lounging about, feeling sorry for herself, would you?'

Rosie blushed. 'No,' she said in a small voice.

Nanny's booming voice filled the room. 'Then get up and get on! I'll have Sophia nicely dressed and ready to go with you to see Juliet and the baby at half past two.' With that she strode out of the bedroom, and closed the door noisily behind her.

Shortly before three o'clock Rosie and Sophia arrived at St George's Hospital bearing a large bouquet of flowers and a little white teddy bear for Tristan.

Surprised, Juliet exclaimed, 'How lovely to see you! You look good, Rosie. I love your outfit.'

Rosie had made a great effort with her make-up and had put on a new coral and white silk dress over which she wore a fine wool coral coloured coat. As a finishing touch she'd put on a small hat covered in white and coral flowers.

Sophia, holding her mother's hand shyly, had been dressed

by Nanny in exactly the same way she'd dressed all the Granville girls when they'd been small before the war. She didn't approve of the new 'casual' style of children's clothes so Sophia was wearing a pale blue linen coat under which she wore a cream Viyella hand smocked dress and a blue ribbon bow holding her long blonde hair back.

'Hello, darling,' Juliet greeted the child affectionately. 'Have you come to see your little cousin?'

Sophia, who was the image of Rosie, nodded. 'We've brought him a present from Harrods,' she whispered.

'That is so kind. Thank you very much. And flowers, too.'

'Coals to Newcastle,' Rosie observed, glancing around at the bouquets that stood on every surface and all along the floor down one side of the room.

'Do you want to hold Tristan?' Juliet asked with studied casualness, knowing how painful this moment must be for Rosie.

Tristan lay in a cot by the side of Juliet's bed, wrapped in a Shetland shawl. His soft black hair was a fluffy halo and his rosebud mouth worked as he dreamed of sucking milk.

'He's asleep. I don't think we should disturb him, do you?' There was something about Rosie's voice that was as brittle as dried flowers.

'Maybe later then.' Juliet lay back, longing for her afternoon nap. 'How's the new house? Is it nicer than the other one? You didn't stay more than five minutes there, did you?'

Rosie spoke dismissively. 'It was too small. We should never have taken it. When you're up and about you must come and see it.'

'Right now I'm so tired I don't think I'll ever move again.' Juliet chuckled. 'It's the night feeds that are such a killer, coming on top of actually giving birth. I still feel as if I've been shifting boulders!'

'You don't have to feed him yourself.' Rosie kept looking at the baby surreptitiously, pretending all the while she wasn't that interested, but her whole body was wrenched with such longing she felt sick.

'But I want to. At least for the first few months.'

'Mummy never fed any of us herself, did she?'

Juliet gave an amused smile. 'It would have got terribly in

the way of her social life. You can't very well take a baby with you to Buckingham Palace, and then start breast feeding him in the middle of a court ball, can you?'

'Mummy misses those days,' Rosie said thoughtfully. 'She and Daddy have never become friends with this King and Queen, as they did with the old King and Queen. They were always being invited to the Palace then, weren't they?'

'Mummy wearing every bit of jewellery she'd ever possessed.'

Rosie smiled, remembering how she and Juliet had watched from the nursery landing their parents setting off to various royal functions. Those had been such happy days! Safe and cosy, protected from outside forces and with the rest of their lives before them. If she'd known then how things would turn out and what deep disappointments she'd have to cope with, she wouldn't have wanted to grow up, she reflected bitterly.

At that moment, a buxom young junior nurse came into the room, bearing two large bunches of flowers.

'These have just arrived for you, Mrs Lawrence. You'll soon be able to start a florist's shop, won't you?' she added, laughing. 'You should be having your rest, you know. Tristan is going to wake up in an hour or so, and then there'll be no rest for the wicked!' With a saucy waggle of her forefinger she plonked the bouquets on Juliet's feet and bounced out of the room again.

'Oh, God! I'm going to have so many thank-you letters to write, aren't I?' Juliet reached for the nearest bouquet and plucked from it the tiny envelope containing a card. 'Open the other one for me, will you, Rosie? It's all getting a bit too much. Oh, these are from Candida and Andrew! How kind.' Juliet lay down again. 'Who are the red roses from? They're a bit flamboyant, aren't they?' she giggled weakly.

Rosie, having glanced at the other card, stuffed it back into the bunch of crimson roses, and carried it to the side table just inside the doorway. She pushed the other vases to one side to make more room, so the roses made a magnificent central arrangement.

'I can't make out the writing. Something about "many congratulations" and a squiggly signature.' She came back to Juliet's bedside. 'Sophia and I ought to be off now so you can get some sleep. Come along, darling.' She took Sophia's hand.

'Do we have to go? I want to see Tristan when he's awake.'

'We've got people coming to dinner tonight, and there's still a lot to do.'

'Then come to tea when I'm home again,' Juliet suggested. 'That would be fun, wouldn't it?' She smiled at Sophia. 'Perhaps you could help me bathe Tristan?'

Sophia's small chest heaved with delight. 'Could I really? Mummy, Aunty Juliet says I can . . .'

'Yes, darling,' Rosie replied evenly. 'Bye now, Juliet. Have a good sleep. You need to keep up your strength.'

'Thanks.'

After they'd gone, Juliet curled up on her side and quickly sank into a deep untroubled sleep. It was to be the last time she'd speak to Rosie for over two years.

# Seven

Daniel's anger was almost palpable. Ashen faced, he paced around Juliet's hospital bed, exuding a sense of danger, his black eyes glinting with fury, his footsteps on the linoleum heavy and dragging, as if he was becoming paralysed.

For a moment he looked down at the small white card in his hand, almost as if he didn't believe the words he read. But it was written clearly, four lines carried out in blue ink, penned by a man with small handwriting. Daniel would have given anything at that moment to believe he was mistaken. That this was a joke in bad taste. Only it wasn't. It was a vengeful card, sent to make mischief, and worst of all, confirming what Esther had said about Juliet.

Juliet, lying still and watchful, knew something was terribly wrong as soon as Daniel stopped to read the card tucked into the bouquet of dark red roses.

'What is it?' she asked guardedly, remembering Rosie had been unable to make out the writing.

His voice was laced with venom. 'Who is Peter Osborne?'

Juliet felt as if her body had been plunged into freezing water, and that tiny shards of ice were flowing through her veins.

'Peter Osborne?' she echoed hollowly. Her mind worked fast. The last time she'd seen him had been about three or four years ago when she'd refused to sleep with him, because she'd become engaged to Edward Courtney and he'd been enraged, taunting her for being a cock tease, before storming off into the night. This moment could be her worst fears coming true, she thought in panic, the moment when Daniel finds out she'd slept with other men, lots of them. The moment when all that Esther had said about her would be confirmed.

But surely Peter Osborne couldn't be seeking revenge for having been turned down after all these years?

Juliet's mind was spinning in ever tighter circles of terror and she knew she was expected to say something.

'Who *is* this man?' Daniel insisted harshly. 'What was he to you?'

'I knew Peter Osborne during the war,' she replied vaguely, somehow managing to keep her voice steady. 'Why? Did he send those flowers? Rosie said she didn't know who they were from because she couldn't make out the writing.'

His eyes widened with incredulity. 'Couldn't make out the writing? What are you talking about? It's practically written in block capitals!' He flung the card on the bed where it lay, small, white and deadly. 'Read it for yourself!'

Taking a deep breath Juliet reached for the card. Daniel was right.

A child could have deciphered the neatly written lines, and the signature, at the bottom right hand corner.

It took her seconds to read it, seconds that shamed her, seconds that could end her happiness forever. Like a tolling bell each word shuddered through her body, pounding her to the core of her being, leaving her defenceless.

Congratulations, Juliet. Fancy you being a respectable married woman these days. And now a mother. Remember our nights together? That is when you weren't in bed with the rest of the gang. Love, Peter (Osborne, in case you've forgotten!)

Agonizingly she felt her face beginning to burn and she broke out in a sticky sweat. Her hands were shaking as she tore up the card.

'He's joking,' she said trying to sound amused and blasé. She *had* to lie. It was instinctive because the rest of her life depended on how she handled this situation and she couldn't afford to admit there was a word of truth in what Peter had said, and worse, had implied. 'It's all rubbish and it's meant to be a joke, I presume. I hardly knew him at all!'

She gave Daniel a little twisted smile and her eyes looked at him brazenly. 'You don't believe him, do you? He always was a tease.'

The small white room was silent for a moment, except for the sweet snuffling sound of Tristan waking up.

'Don't lie to me, Juliet.' Daniel spoke with icy coldness. He stood at the foot of her bed, a powerful figure in a dark suit, compelling her to speak the truth. 'He was your lover, wasn't he? And the others . . .? The Gang? Did you . . . did you sleep with other men, *too*?'

His voice broke and the hurt in his eyes was like a knife plunging into her heart. Something in her head snapped and she threw caution recklessly to the wind without thinking of the consequences, deciding attack was the best means of defence.

'It was during the war!' she said with emphasis. 'No one knew if they'd be alive the next morning. Everyone was sleeping around, and drinking too much, but it meant nothing! You know that. Don't tell me you got through the whole war without having sex with anyone? Your wife was in Wales, you'd cut me out of your life, and if you've forgotten it was *you* who didn't want to have anything to do with me. I owed you absolutely nothing, Daniel. I was divorced from Cameron and a single woman, so don't start accusing *me* of being unfaithful. How many girls did you go to bed with during the war?'

'It's quite different for men,' he retorted harshly, his face flushed, his hands gripping the white frame of the bed as if he wanted to shake it and her in it.

Juliet glared at him. 'That's utter rubbish. What did you think I was doing when I was off duty? Knitting? Like Granny?'

He turned away as if the sight of her disgusted him. 'I didn't think you'd behave like a tart.'

'I did not behave like a tart! One man, whom I haven't seen for years, sends me a jokey card and you go off the deep end. Why should I have been faithful to you, anyway?' By now she'd worked herself up into a rage and she spoke with deep anger. 'You were out of my life at that time, Daniel. You were still a married man, and I was a free woman. I could do as I liked, for God's sake.'

'And you chose to act like a gutter-snipe!' he taunted, beside himself with anger and hurt. He started wandering around her small hospital room, dazed, as if he were drunk. 'So my sister was right!' he said suddenly, swinging round to glare at her.

'Was she?' Juliet lashed out, rashly. 'So you *did* marry me for my money then?'

'That's not what I meant.'

'Oh, surely it is? If she's right about my past, then she must be right about your intentions when you married me, too,' she said sarcastically.

Tristan woke up as if he'd been startled by their quarrelling and started crying. Juliet could feel her breasts tingling with milk. She turned to her baby swiftly, with the same love with which she'd turned to Daniel until everything had changed a moment ago.

'I must feed him,' she said, picking the baby out of his cot, and holding him tenderly in her arms. When she looked up, Daniel had gone.

Juliet's sense of betrayal was so deep she could not bring herself to speak to Rosie. When Louise came to visit her the next day she found Juliet distraught and unable to stop crying.

'Baby blues?' Louise asked gently, as she hugged her sister.

'Much worse. Much, much worse.' She wiped her eyes and blew her nose. 'I don't know how Rosie could have done this to me.' Then she told Louise what had happened.

'You mean she read what was on the card, but pretended the writing was so bad she couldn't make it out? Surely she couldn't have left it there on purpose? For Daniel to see as soon as he walked in the door?' Louise asked incredulously.

Juliet nodded. She glanced at the dark-red roses. They reminded her of large blobs of blood, like evil-bearing clots impaled on long straight stems. Not for a moment did she doubt Peter Osborne's motive in sending them; his male pride had been wounded by her refusal to have sex with him on that last occasion. But why wait until now to get his revenge? Worst of all, how could Rosie have lied about the writing on the card? Only to leave it where Daniel was bound to see it?

Juliet's beautiful face was awash with tears and her eyes red and swollen. 'I was so tired when Rosie was here I could hardly keep awake, and so I wasn't paying attention,' she explained. 'I've had so many flowers in the past three days and this was just one more bunch as far as I was concerned. And then Daniel found it . . .' She choked and she started sobbing. 'He was so angry. And it's not as if we'd been together

91

when I knew Peter. And now his sister . . .' She stopped, unable to continue. 'Get them out of here, Louise. I can't bear the sight of them.'

Louise jumped to her feet and hurried over to the table. Once in the corridor, she carried the offending flowers to the general ward and plonked them on a central table. Then she went back to Juliet's room, and resumed her seat by the bedside. 'What were you saying about Daniel's sister?'

Pulling herself together with an effort, Juliet described what had happened. 'She's an evil woman who hasn't only got it in for me, but Daniel, too. He's driven mad by her accusation that he married me for my money, as if he were a gigolo. She's accused me too, of being a tart. I wanted to sue her, but Dads advised against it. And now this.' She looked at Louise in anguish. 'Daniel said last night that he thought Esther had been right about me all along.'

'Oh, darling.' Louise grabbed her hand and held it fast. 'You mustn't let yourself get so upset. You'll make yourself ill and you've got to think about Tristan.'

'I know.' Juliet nodded dejectedly. 'I had hardly any milk this morning. The nurse had to give him a bottle as a supplement.' She heaved herself into a sitting position. 'I've got to get out of here. Daniel hasn't been to see me today and I've got to talk to him.'

'I expect he's busy. He'll probably be along this evening.'

Juliet fiddled with her thin platinum wedding ring, turning it round and round on her finger. 'He usually pops in on the way to his office in the morning, but he hasn't even phoned me today. I must try to make him understand that Peter never meant anything to me. Nor did any of the others,' she admitted dropping her voice.

'Others?' Louise raised her eyebrows.

'Yes, others.' She looked at her sister directly. 'You don't know what it was like. I was burning up and demented with longing for Daniel. He was the only man I loved and wanted, and because I couldn't have him . . . I just went with anyone else who did want me. It sounds dreadful and I'm terribly ashamed at the way I behaved then, but it was the only way I knew how to ease the pain I felt. I became grateful that someone, *anyone*, wanted me, even if Daniel didn't.'

Louise spoke softly. 'Poor you. I never suspected a thing.'

'I managed to keep it from you when you came to live with me by going to hotels. My life then was a mess. Somehow Esther has found out, and of course she's told Daniel. That's why I've got to explain it all and make him understand it was only him I wanted.'

'Wouldn't it be better to let him cool down first?' Louise suggested. 'You've both got fiery tempers. You might end up saying things you'll regret.'

'I can't leave things as they are!' Juliet ran her hands through her hair in a gesture of desperation. 'I'd die if I lost Daniel now.'

When Louise left St George's Hospital, she decided to walk back to her home in Fulham, glad of the fresh air and a chance to think. She'd always known Juliet had lots of boyfriends before she married Daniel, but she'd assumed they were mere flirtations. Not that she felt judgemental of her sister's behaviour now. In a way she could even understand how Juliet had felt. She'd been under enormous strain throughout the war, facing death every night she was on duty; and she believed then she'd lost the one man she loved.

The real tragedy seemed to be that Rosie had purposely left Peter Osborne's card where Daniel would see it.

Louise started to feel deeply angry as her feet pounded down Grosvenor Crescent. Jealousy between sisters was one thing, but Rosie had gone too far. Of all her sisters, it was Juliet who had supported her, through thick and thin, in practical and emotional ways.

Now was the time to stand by her.

Louise turned left along Grosvenor Square and left again into Chapel Street. Rosie and Salton's house was the fourth one along on the left.

Its white stucco frontage gleamed like icing sugar and the window boxes, overflowing with red geraniums, looked prosperous and cheerful. Louise pressed the brass front door bell and after a moment an elderly char woman opened the dark green door.

'I've come to see Mrs Webb,' Louise announced. 'Is she in?'

'Yes, but I don't think she's expecting visitors,' the woman said reluctantly.

'I'm not a visitor, I'm her sister,' Louise said politely, and then walked past her into the prettily decorated hall and up the red carpeted stairs which led to the first-floor drawing room.

She found Rosie sitting at her desk, writing letters. She looked thin and there were hollows in her cheeks. Her lipstick made a straight strong scarlet line on her pale face.

'Louise?' she said surprised. 'What are you doing here?'

'I've come to see you,' Louise replied bluntly, sitting down on a chair that faced Rosie.

'Oh! Would you like some tea?'

'No thanks. I've just come from seeing Juliet. You were there yesterday afternoon, weren't you?'

Rosie suddenly looked wary. 'Sophia and I dropped in for a few minutes to see her, yes.'

'And she asked you to open the note that came with some flowers?'

'Umm . . .' Rosie glanced around her elegantly furnished room as if seeking inspiration. 'I can't remember,' she said vaguely. 'I know some flowers arrived while we were there.'

Louise spoke sharply. 'Come on, Rosie. You opened a card, and then you told her it was so badly written you couldn't make it out.'

Her sister smiled, as if remembering. 'Oh, yes. It was a scrawl. Something about "congratulations" but the rest was indecipherable.'

'So why did you put the card back in among the flowers? Why didn't you give it to her? *She* would have been able to read it.'

'What is this?' Rosie asked imperiously. 'You come barging in here, and start cross examining me about some wretched flowers and who sent them? I don't know what you're talking about.'

Louise rose and stood over Rosie. 'You know damn well they were from an old friend of Juliet's, and that the card was written in clear block capitals. Juliet got to read it herself . . . after Daniel had found it.'

Rosie remained silent, her cheeks flushed, her mouth sulky. 'Well, so what?' she said at last. 'Everyone thinks Juliet is God's gift to the world. Everyone praises her and says she is so wonderful. And she's got everything she ever wanted, hasn't she?' Her voice was bitter and angry. 'Juliet has spent her entire life scheming to get what she wanted; money, a man she loved, and now a baby. It won't do her any harm for people to realize she has feet of clay.'

'And if it breaks up her marriage to Daniel . . . do you want that on your conscience?' Louise asked harshly.

'Daniel already knew what she was like when she was seventeen and he seduced her just like *that*, in Paris.'

Louise stared at Rosie, shocked. 'Do you really hate her that much?'

Rosie shrugged. 'When you think of all the things she's done to me over the years . . . why should I care? Anyway, she's got a baby to occupy herself with now, so why should a note from an old lover upset her? God knows, she's had a lot of *those*. If they all sent her bouquets her room would look like Constance Spry's flower shop.'

Juliet had installed herself back in her silver four poster Maharaja's bed by the time Daniel returned from his office. Tristan was up in the new nursery with the monthly nurse she'd taken on, and a worried looking Dudley was trying to eke out what food he could from the ever tight rationing, in order to make her tempting little dishes.

Earlier, when she'd arrived she'd asked him nonchalantly, 'Is there any post for me, Dudley? Or for Mr Lawrence?'

'Here are your letters, madam.' He indicated the silver salver on the hall table. 'Shall I bring them up to you?'

'Yes, please. Are there none for Mr Lawrence? Or has he already collected his post?'

Dudley looked straight at her. The silence between them was heavy with unspoken understanding. Then he cleared his throat.

'Mr Lawrence doesn't seem to get as much post as he used to.'

Juliet paused for a moment. 'Really?' she said lightly.

'Hardly any, madam,' he said formally.

At half past six she heard the front-door slam shut. She lay listening to Daniel's footsteps. Would he go to his study? Or come up to the drawing room? Dinner wouldn't be served until eight o'clock, so maybe he'd get himself a drink.

Anger had replaced heartache in the past few hours and she

was determined to stand up for herself. She would not let him make her feel guilty about something that had happened years ago, when she'd believed they'd never see each other again; more than that, when she'd thought he'd been killed in an air raid.

Sitting up in her grand bed, she surveyed the exotic room with its rich furnishings and soft lighting. Flowers stood on every surface and Dudley had lit a fire of apple wood, the aroma mixed in a heady fashion with the perfume of lilies and roses. She took a deep breath, wishing she was in a position to seduce him once she'd had her say, but then thought that maybe that was just as well; to have him wanting her and unable to have her, would surely make him desire her even more.

Suddenly the bedroom door was flung open, taking her unaware.

Daniel stood in the doorway staring at her. His expression was defiant. As always the powerful sexuality he exuded took her breath away and left her with a pounding heart. Then he spoke, and his deep vibrant voice almost crumbled her resolve to be strong and resolute.

'Where's the baby?'

'How did you know I was home?' she asked.

'I could smell your perfume. Anyway, I'm only here to pack a few things and then when I've seen Tristan I'll be out of your way,' he said brusquely, turning towards his dressing room.

Alarm shot through her veins like icy particles. 'What do you mean?'

Her carefully made-up face was ashen and she could hear the fear in her own voice.

'I'm surprised you find it necessary to ask.'

'Daniel, for God's sake! Sit down and talk to me. I've come home against doctors' orders so we can talk and sort out this nonsense.'

He spoke dismissively over his shoulder as he disappeared into his dressing room. 'There's nothing to talk about. You've made it perfectly clear that you believe Esther when she says I married you for your money. You're just going to have to make do in future with the rest of the staff you employ.'

'What the hell . . .?' She could hear cupboard doors being

opened and drawers being slammed shut. 'Daniel, you're deliberately twisting what I said. You told me that your sister was right after all about my being a tart. What I said was; if you believe *that*, then she must also be right about you being a gold-digger! You know Esther's letters are poison.'

'We both know now that you slept with Tom, Dick and Harry during the war,' he shouted back. There was a thud as he pulled a heavy leather suitcase down from the top of the wardrobe and it crashed to the floor.

'Don't worry, I'm not going off with the silver,' he added harshly.

Juliet struggled to sit upright, and then carefully swung her feet to the floor. Every move hurt, but she had to stop this craziness. Gripping one of the silver bed posts she pulled herself up until she was standing, swaying weakly but determined to walk the short distance to the dressing room.

'Get back to bed,' he said when he saw her leaning against the door lintel. 'It's finished, Juliet. I can no longer stand being pointed at, and have people at the club sniggering at me for having married money. Admit it, I'm a kept man. We live in this bloody great mansion, funded by your fortune. You pay for everything; the servants, the food and drink, the car, our entertaining . . . you should have married a man of equal means if you intended to maintain your previous life style.' He closed the case with a snap of the locks and then picked it up. As he stalked out of the room he turned to give her a final look. 'Go back to your ways of having men dancing attention on you, while you pick up the bills,' he growled. Then he was gone, slamming the bedroom door after him.

She could hear his footsteps hurrying down the stairs, and then the final crash of the front door closing.

Unable to speak, Juliet sank to her knees, sobs wracking her body as the full magnitude of Daniel's last words hammered through her head. She stayed like that, curled up on the floor for several minutes, unable to move. Then slowly and painfully she started to crawl towards her bed, too weak to stand up again, and too anguished to think straight.

All she knew was that she seemed to have lost Daniel again, and this time it really hadn't been her fault.

# Eight

Their suite over looked the Mediterranean, which stretched like a sea of sapphires, glittering and twinkling to the distant horizon. Smart yachts were moored in the harbour, protected from storms by two long jetties that stretched across the water like embracing arms, leaving only a gap, with a lighthouse on the right hand jetty, through which boats could slip to safety.

Rosie stood in the open French window of their *petit salon* looking out to sea, as she drank her coffee. Wearing a peach satin dressing gown over her matching nightdress, and with white feathered mules on her feet, she resembled a beautiful Hollywood film heroine, waiting for her hero to arrive.

In truth, she was a discontented thirty-year-old housewife, wishing she didn't feel so dejected. She'd been miserable, it seemed, for such ages that she'd almost forgotten what it was like to feel happy.

She'd thought marriage to Salton would bring her joy and the sort of life she'd always wanted . . . well, *almost* wanted. Marriage to a man with a title, and a country estate would have been preferable, but Salton was kind, and comfortably off, and yet her dissatisfaction was profound. And if she was bitterly disappointed she wasn't pregnant, she also knew that her life was somehow desperately dull.

There was a dreadful sameness about every blessed day, and a laborious repetition in their thrice weekly love-making. If Salton asked her one more time if she was 'all right' after he'd rolled off her and returned to his side of the bed, she'd scream.

His kindly blandness, his unruffled personality, even his generosity in letting her have whatever she wanted, was getting on her nerves.

98

She knew she ought to be jolly grateful; not every man would land himself with a war widow who had two children and no money. She also counted her blessings; he didn't chase women, drink or gamble. He was a good steady man, honest and dutiful. But he bored her to death.

'What would you like to do today?' she heard him ask, as he joined her in the window. 'Looks like good weather.' He glanced up at a peerless clear sky.

'It's *always* good weather in the South of France,' she retorted peevishly. 'I suppose we could go for a drive, or something.'

'Good idea, honey. Maybe we could find a nice restaurant for lunch?'

She nodded. 'I'm going to have a bath now. And I need to buy some shoes for the beach.'

'Well, we could go shopping first and then drive along the coast to Nice and swim there?' He slid his arm around her waist affectionately and gave her a little hug. 'I thought we might go to the casino tonight? Have a little flutter?'

Rosie gave him a little smile and slid out of his embrace. 'How lovely!' Her voice was clipped.

Neither of them had mentioned Juliet's name since they'd arrived, as if a change of scenery had removed them from the seat of the action. As if Juliet belonged to another life and another world. Yet Salton realized Rosie was unhappy, though she wouldn't admit it, and he was worried about her. But what more did she want than the life they'd chosen to share together? He'd bent over backwards to please her because he loved her deeply, but sometimes it seemed she didn't really want to be happy. His mother had said something very wise when she'd written to him after he'd sought her advice.

> . . . It could be that Rosie is using Juliet as a whipping boy in order to have someone to blame for her own inner discontent . . . try to be patient, honey . . . if you can't make her happy, then no one can.

Salton still hoped he could turn things around and that was why he'd brought her to this sophisticated French paradise, hoping it might prove to be a second honeymoon for them. Maybe they should get acquainted with some of the other hotel guests and set up a few interesting excursions or even some dinner parties. Rosie had a lot of her mother in her, he reflected and he was quite prepared to sacrifice the peaceful holiday he'd planned if a spot of socializing would cheer her up.

Maybe he could even make her pregnant.

That evening they sat at one of the little tables in the glamorous foyer of the Hôtel de Paris enjoying cocktails before dinner. In one corner of the marble and mirrored area, which had leafy aspidistras growing in large pots at intervals along the walls, a string quartet played *The Blue Danube*, as well dressed couples took their seats, greeting their friends and waving to new arrivals as they entered through the glass doors. The atmosphere was festive and merry, as if everyone had something to celebrate. Salton decided this was a good way to start their evenings.

At that moment a well dressed elderly lady hovered by their table. She was looking at Rosie in a puzzled fashion.

Salton smiled up at her, eyebrows raised, as she obviously wanted to speak to them. 'Good evening?' he said.

She stepped forward. 'Good evening, monsieur.'

She had a French accent and he guessed she was in her seventies, but well preserved, her face immaculately made up, her white hair beautifully coiffured under a little black hat. She was wearing a stylish black dress embroidered with jet beads and he noticed, under her sable wrap, ropes of pearls and a large diamond brooch.

Smiling gaily, she raised a gloved hand and spoke to Rosie. 'Excusez-moi, madame, but I believe I recognize you? Your papa is Henry Granville, is he not?'

Rosie preened prettily. 'Yes. I'm his eldest daughter, Rosie.'

The old lady clasped her hands together in a gesture of joy. 'Your papa was a great friend of my late husband, Walter Fulsham. When we lived in England we banked at Hammerton's.'

'Really?' Rosie exclaimed.

'I remember seeing so many pictures of you when you made your debut. You were quite the debutante of the year, weren't you? Such an English beauty!'

Rosie flushed with pleasure. 'Thank you. Won't you join us for a drink?'

'Well . . . I'm supposed to be meeting my nephew. He's late, as usual.'

She stood, small boned and dainty, like an elegant bird, her long neck turning this way and that as she looked around the ever more crowded foyer. A moment later a waiter came hurrying over to her at that moment.

'M'lady, I have a message for you from Baron Guerin. He has been delayed but he will be with you very soon.'

'Merci.' She shrugged.

Salton, standing, brought forward a chair. 'Do please join us?'

She threw up her hands in mock surrender, and laughed. 'You're very kind. Philibert has only one fault; he's late for everything.'

'Are you staying in the hotel, too?' Rosie asked.

'I live here,' the old lady replied quietly.

'You *live* . . . in the hotel?'

'*Mais oui!* I moved back here when my husband died two years ago.'

In the last few minutes Rosie had fallen in love with the glamour of Monte Carlo, the sheer luxury of the famous Hôtel de Paris with its romantic music in the background and the bowing and scraping of the waiters. Everyone looked so chic and elegant in their perfect clothes. It was as if being stylish came naturally to the French.

For a moment Rosie remembered what London had been like before the war. How exciting and glittering everything had been then. And how drab and grey and sort of defeated everyone at home seemed now. The people were tired, everything was shabby, rationing was worse than it had ever been, and morale seemed at its lowest. For the first time in her life Rosie wished she still lived at Hartley, where the countryside renewed itself every spring, bringing a feeling of hope to everyone.

Salton had ordered more drinks, Lady Fulsham opting to have a Pernod, while Rosie asked for a gin and lime.

Their new acquaintance was speaking earnestly. 'Once a Labour government got in, I knew I had to leave England and come here. I have no children so I felt free to return to my homeland. My nephew lives in Digne-Les-Bains, although he seems to spend most of his time here in Monte Carlo.' She caught Rosie's eye and smiled mischievously. 'He's young like you, and likes the bright lights.'

Rosie sipped her second drink, feeling better by the moment. 'We thought we'd go over to the casino after dinner,' she said.

A faint shadow flashed across Lady Fulsham's eyes but was gone as quickly as it came. 'The casino is *tres amusant*!' she said lightly.

'So, you have a suite here?' Salton asked conversationally.

'Two suites, actually. One for myself, and Philibert if he wants to stay for the night, and the one next door for my own servants. It is very convenient. If I want to entertain, I use the restaurant. Otherwise we use room service and my maids serve it to me in my *petit salon*. The food here is excellent.'

Rosie leaned back in her chair and knew that this was the life she wanted. When the children were older and she was free from responsibility. What could be more marvellous than living in this perfect climate, in the most glamorous hotel in the world, with your own private staff to look after you, and a restaurant at your disposal for when you wanted to entertain?

She tried to catch Salton's eye, sure he'd be thinking the same thing, longing to say to him, 'Let's do that, too, one day,' but he was deep in conversation with Lady Fulsham who was nodding in agreement with what ever he was saying.

Then she saw him, walking quickly across the foyer towards them. Tall, slim, tanned with blond hair, this young man resembled a Greek god . . . with sexy eyes and a charming smile.

'Ah! At last!' Lady Fulsham held up her hands when she saw him. 'How are you, *mon chérie*?'

Philibert bent down to kiss her on both cheeks, '*Pardon. Je suis* . . .' Then he realized she wasn't alone.

She introduced Rosie and Salton. He shook their hands warmly and made direct eye contact, especially with Rosie, his gaze lingering on her face a fraction too long for good manners.

'Did you say you were dining here, tonight?' Lady Fulsham

asked Salton. 'Then you must be my guests. It is so nice to have English people to talk to for a change.' She turned to Philibert. 'They're also going to the casino tonight. Maybe they will bring us luck?' Her laugh was gay and girlish.

'I do hope so,' he replied, his wide smile showing perfect teeth and his eyes still fixed on Rosie.

When they arrived at the casino it was obvious to Salton that Lady Fulsham was a regular and so was her nephew. The staff hovered around them as if they were royalty, escorting Lady Fulsham to a roulette table where the minimum stake was so high, Salton drew in his breath in horror. He'd planned that he and Rosie would gamble very modestly, just for the fun of it, but Rosie was looking entranced at the green baize table and its markings. The rattle of the little white ball as it spun around on the roulette wheel seemed to hypnotize her, and when Lady Fulsham tossed a handful of French notes to the croupier, who then pushed a high pile of chips in her direction, Rosie sat down on the empty chair beside her, enthralled.

'Rosie,' he said urgently, 'we can't play at this table. Look at the stakes!'

She frowned, annoyed that he seemed to be showing her up, behaving like an unsophisticated American. 'Why not?' she asked imperiously.

'Because we were only allowed to take seventy-five pounds, each, out of England. You know it's a new government regulation,' he reminded her.

'Can't you give a cheque or something?'

Salton chuckled. 'Don't be silly, darling. It's against the law.'

Lady Fulsham looked at Rosie sympathetically. 'Your husband's right. All the British tourists going abroad are limited to that amount.'

Rosie stood up again. 'Oh, how boring,' she said petulantly. 'There's not much point in our being here, is there?' She looked at Salton as if it was all his fault.

Philibert spoke. 'I'm not in a great mood for gambling myself, tonight,' he said smiling at Rosie and Salton, 'Why don't I take you to Le Chat Noir? It's an amusing leetle club where we can have a drink?'

'That would be fun,' Rosie replied.

Salton hesitated. 'Why don't you go ahead, darling?' he told Rosie. 'I think I'll stay and keep Lady Fulsham company for a bit.' His tone indicated it would not be polite to leave her as she'd given them dinner.

Rosie pretended to be reluctant. 'Of course . . . Perhaps I'd better . . .'

'Salton, why don't you join us in a while?' Philibert suggested.

'I might do that.'

Rosie tucked her gold beaded evening bag under her arm. 'See you later then.'

When she and Philibert had left, Salton turned to stand behind Lady Fulsham's chair and watched with a sickening feeling of horror as she continued to place bets of the equivalent of fifty pounds on each spin of the wheel. Thanking God that his reason for not gambling was genuine, he could only conclude that she must be a millionairess. And as she lost again and again until she was several hundred pounds down, he suddenly remembered a conversation he'd had with Louise the previous week, which highlighted the vast differences between the rich and the poor.

Louise had recently taken a part-time job in the Red Cross Hospital Library in Grosvenor Crescent. 'It's really good, I work three mornings a week and they pay me two pounds, ten shillings,' she'd said proudly, 'which is a great help. I can feed us on ten shillings a week, quite comfortably, and that leaves two pounds for the gas, electricity, and things for Daisy, while Shane pays the mortgage and everything else on his salary.'

'All done?' Salton said after a while, watching Lady Fulsham fiddling with her evening bag as she watched the wheel turning and the little white ball plopping into one of the grooves. Her face was very white now and she looked much older than he'd first thought. It was possible she was even in her eighties.

She looked up at him, her eye sockets were hollow and her expression blank.

'*Oui*,' she said in a thready voice. 'I think it is time to retire for the night.' She struggled to her feet, as if she was stiff and her joints hurt. 'It is quite late, *n'est ce pas*?'

'It's half eleven,' he said easily. 'Shall I escort you back to the hotel? Or do you want to join your nephew and Rosie?'

'Oh, I think it's time for my bed. Perhaps if you are so kind . . .'

'It would be my pleasure.' Suddenly Salton felt very sorry for this frail old lady who earlier in the evening had put on such a show of vibrant vivacity and strength, as if she'd been no older than his mother.

He took her arm and together they walked the short distance back to the Hôtel de Paris. At the bottom of the wide steep entrance steps she paused and pointed up the street.

'If you take the second turning on the left you will find Le Chat Noir on your right, a little way along.'

'Thank you, but first, allow me to take you as far as your suite,' he said swiftly, 'and I'll check that Rosie hasn't already returned.'

But Rosie wasn't in their suite. Having left Lady Fulsham in the care of her personal maids, he walked briskly and had no trouble in finding the black and white striped awning which led to the basement of a building from which loud music emanated. It was so dark and smoky inside that at first Salton couldn't spot Rosie amongst the crowd who sat drinking at little tables or shuffling around, clinging to each other, on a tiny floor.

At last, feeling out of place and rather too old for this sort of thing, he found them seated on a banquette in a corner, deep in conversation and drinking champagne.

'*Darling!*' Rosie greeted him effusively. 'We're having such a *marvellous* time! This is the most *amazing* place; isn't the music divine?'

'It's certainly loud.' Salton chuckled. He squeezed himself on the end of the banquette. He realized she was a bit tipsy; Rosie was never this high-spirited when sober. He leaned towards Philibert. 'Can one get a bourbon here? On the rocks?' he shouted above the din.

'He means American whisky,' Rosie giggled. '*We're* drinking champagne,' she added unnecessarily.

'So I can see.' Salton's voice was dry. Later, as he sipped his drink and watched Rosie have a last dance with Philibert before they went back to the hotel, he realized that to keep

Rosie happy was to keep her amused. Just like her mother. He made up his mind that when they returned to London he'd encourage her to socialize again, and suggest they do some entertaining. It wasn't what he enjoyed doing and he realized he and Henry had more in common than he'd thought, but like Henry, he loved his wife and he considered it his duty to keep her content.

Juliet somehow got through each day, though despair stalked her every moment, and the darkness in her soul was bleak and without a glimmer of hope. She was certain that Daniel's damned pride was keeping them apart, but so, she had to admit, was her own anger at him for twisting her words. She'd never for a moment thought he was a gold-digger, nor had she ever accused him of being after her money.

But one mischievous card from an old lover had opened Pandora's box and her past had come whirling out, destroying everything. How could Peter have done something so vengeful? Angry he might have been, most men hated being rejected, but to have sent that note, knowing she'd just had a baby, had shocked her deeply. Peter had been an affable man, kind and generous and with a great sense of humour . . . until that last encounter.

And now Daniel had walked out, denying her the chance to explain. If only he'd been prepared to listen, if only she hadn't snapped back at him, more in fear than anger at that moment, if only . . .

Juliet paced her bedroom in the solitude of the night, holding Tristan to her breast, as if they could comfort each other by clinging fast together.

She looked down into his sleeping face, recognizing his likeness to Daniel and felt more love for the little scrap of humanity than she could ever have imagined.

She should be sharing these precious moments with Daniel, but she didn't even know where he was. Henry had phoned his office on her behalf, asking to speak to him, but the very nature of his work at MI5 had caused his department chief to be evasive. 'Unavailable at present' and 'not at his desk' were the only answers Henry got, although he insisted he wanted to speak to Mr Lawrence on an urgent family matter.

Juliet had even asked her father to contact Daniel's ex-wife and Esther, pretending to be Daniel's bank manager, but both women had told him politely they had no idea where he was.

'His sister may have suspected I was ringing on your behalf,' Henry told Juliet, 'but Ruth Lawrence sounded very surprised, and explained they were no longer married and she hadn't heard from him for ages.'

'What can I do, Dads?' Juliet asked, as she lunched with him in the city the next day.

Henry looked at his favourite daughter with concern. She looked thin and her face was drained of colour.

Only her aquamarine eyes still flashed with passion and a determination to carry on whatever happened.

'Do I just sit and wait?' she demanded. 'I cannot believe he's being so pig-headed!'

'You've asked all your friends if they've seen him lately, I presume?' Henry ventured.

'No, Dads. I don't want anyone to know what's happened. I'm using Tristan as an excuse for staying at home for the time being. And I don't want the whole of London hearing about that wretched bouquet from Peter Osborne! Since I married Daniel I've put my past completely behind me, or so I thought. I don't even know what possessed Peter to do such a thing. I haven't even seen him for four years, for God's sake! The strange thing is I thought he wasn't the sort of man to harbour a grudge.'

Henry gave a deep sigh, and looked disconsolately at his plate of spam and salad as if its unappealing coldness was symbolic of life today. 'Do you have his address?'

'I don't think I ever knew where he lived. I mean, we were ships that passed in the night, that's all. He'd phone me and say he'd be off duty that night and did I want to go dining and dancing . . .' Her voice trailed away with shame.

'I'm so sorry, sweetheart. I really thought you'd be happy with Daniel.'

'So did I, Dads,' she said sadly. 'People think money can make you happy, that it's important and that as long as you're rich, you've got everything that matters. It's not true, is it? Louise and Shane are utterly happy on twopence a week, and Amanda doesn't care a fig about cash, does she? I bet the dress allowance you give her is sitting in the bank untouched, and she's earning huge interest on it!' She gave a wry smile.

'And there are you, worth several million pounds . . .' He spoke with irony.

'That's life, isn't it? Oh Christ, Dads, I miss him so much.'

'I know you do, darling.'

'And he's missing these first precious weeks with Tristan.' She raised her head and looked into her father's eyes. The heartbreak in her face wrenched him with pity. 'What can I do?' she asked helplessly.

'He'll come back, sweetheart. I know he will, but promise me something.'

Juliet looked surprised. 'What?'

'When he does . . . don't get on your high horse. Don't let pride get in your way. Don't fly off the handle and blame him for everything. It seems to me,' Henry said with more force than usual, 'that you're going to have to handle your marriage with more diplomacy than passion. He's obviously a proud man, and frankly, most men don't like their wives to be richer than they are. It can emasculate a man, Juliet.' He paused for effect. 'When he comes back, I think you should seriously consider selling your house. Why not buy a much smaller and less grand place?'

Shocked, Juliet stared at him. How could she bear to get rid of her pride and joy? She'd designed every inch of 99, Park Lane, and she'd chosen every piece of furniture to create a perfect art deco setting for her life as a beautiful young duchess. Only she wasn't a duchess any more. She was married to a civil servant, who was paid an ordinary salary by the government, added to which he had three children to support.

'But . . . but it's so *useful* to have so many spare rooms,' she protested in panic, as if she was standing alone on a beach, and the tide was sweeping everything she cared for out to sea. The house had always been like a refuge where she knew she'd be safe, no matter what. It had sheltered her in heart-break and horror, in sickness and in health, in happiness and in the throes of passion.

Henry watched her closely, seeing her emotions rise to the surface.

She spoke defensively. 'The family can stay with me at any time. In the past it's been a haven for Rosie, when Charles was killed, and Louise after she'd had Rupert. Charlotte can come and stay if you give up the flat in Princes Court . . . I *need* to keep the house, Dads.'

Henry shrugged and smiled at her affectionately. 'I didn't mean to upset you, darling, it was just a suggestion.'

She bit her bottom lip. 'Yes, but Daniel said the same thing some time ago,' she admitted miserably.

'I see.'

'I *love* that house,' she continued vigorously.

'More than you love him?'

'What . . .? No, of course not.' She hesitated. 'But a house can never let you down, can it? It's always there for you, no matter what.'

'Then let's hope he doesn't make you choose which you want most,' Henry told her seriously.

The telephone rang while Rosie and Salton were still enjoying their coffee and croissants with apricot confiture, in their suite. She reached eagerly for the instrument, as if she was expecting a call. Her cheeks were prettily flushed.

'Oh! Hello, Philibert!' she exclaimed, pretending to sound surprised. 'How are you today? Yes, we're fine. It was *such* fun last night. I adored that night club. Yes?' She paused to listen and her expression became more ecstatic by the moment. 'Oh, we'd *love* to,' she gushed. 'Right. We'll meet you in the foyer at eleven o'clock. *Au revoir!*'

She returned the phone to its cradle and turned triumphantly to Salton.

'That was Philibert,' she told him unnecessarily. 'He's invited us on to a yacht for lunch. We're to meet him downstairs. Isn't that exciting? He said we might potter down the coast and have a swim.'

She was already on her feet, hurrying into the bedroom where she started pulling swim suits and wraps out of the cupboard, and a sun hat and a smart beach bag. 'I think I'll wear my pale blue linen slacks and a white top,' she said with relish, sounding like a little girl going to her first party.

'How kind of him to invite us,' Salton said wonderingly. 'Is Lady Fulsham coming, too?'

'I shouldn't think so,' Rosie replied vaguely. 'She's a bit old for that sort of thing, isn't she?'

He remembered the frail looking woman with the pale drawn face and haunted eyes whom he'd escorted back to her suite from the casino. 'Maybe.'

'Come on, Salton. Hurry up. We don't want to keep Philibert waiting.'

'We've plenty of time, honey.' Salton lit a cigarette and went to stand at the French window, gazing out over the magnificent view. 'Do you remember anything about Lady Fulsham's late husband?'

Rosie brushed her blonde curls, newly permed, into a halo around her head. 'Philibert told me that he was his aunt's heir, and that his uncle had made a fortune in steel. Apparently they had a huge estate in Yorkshire, which she sold when he died. One day Philibert is going to be exceedingly rich.'

Salton looked serious. 'Providing she doesn't lose money at the rate she did last night.'

Rosie gave an impatient little snort. 'You're too cautious, Salton. One's got to live a little, you know. Don't you think we should take them out to dinner tonight? Maybe the concierge could recommend a good restaurant?'

'Let's think about that later, shall we?' he suggested affably.

Philibert, looking more like a Greek god than ever in white trousers and a navy blue blazer, with his blond hair as smooth as silk, was waiting in the foyer when they stepped out of the lift. He bowed and taking Rosie's hand, brushed it with his lips.

'Good morning, Rosie. Good morning, Salton.' He shook Salton's hand firmly. 'I have the car, and we'll drive to where the *Marie Clare* is docked. Have you everything you need?' With a charming smile that encompassed both of them, he asked, 'I have most things on board, including dark glasses and sun oil; you have your swimsuits?'

Deeply impressed, Rosie nodded.

'Excellent, then let us go, *mes amis!*'


'Can you meet me for lunch today?' Henry asked when he phoned Juliet a few days later.

'Yes, Dads, but why? We've only just had one of our luncheons.' she queried. There was something urgent about his tone, and she dreaded hearing bad news about Daniel.

'I have something to tell you,' Henry said shortly. 'I can't talk now, I'm about to have a meeting, but meet me at the Savoy Grill at twelve thirty, will you?'

'Yes, Dads,' she said again. Her mind spun with the dreadful thought that he'd heard Daniel had . . . what? Gone to live abroad? Met someone else? Been to see a lawyer about divorce? 'Oh, God,' she muttered to herself, feeling panicked. She looked at her wrist watch. It was eleven o'clock. Somehow she had to get through the next hour and a half before she found out what her father had to say.

Feeling sick, she occupied herself by writing more thank-you letters to all the people who had sent flowers and gifts for Tristan. Then she changed into a royal blue suit from Dior, and a small matching hat.

'Call me a taxi, will you, Dudley?' she asked the butler. Her hands were shaking too much for her to dare drive the Rolls.

'Certainly, madam.' He noted her white face and anxious eyes but said nothing.

The traffic in Trafalgar Square was heavy, and she sat feeling desperate with frustration, as the cab inched its way past the National Gallery. It was twenty minutes past twelve; would they get along the Strand to the Savoy in five minutes? She doubted it. She bit her lower lip, forcing her mind to reject her worst fears. What her father had to say must be serious, or he'd never have summoned her at such short notice.

At last, they drew up outside the hotel, and she hurriedly thrust two shillings into the driver's hand. 'Keep the change,' she murmured distractedly.

'Thank you, madam!' he said astonished.

Henry was waiting for her at a corner table.

'Dads. I'm sorry I'm late.' As soon as she was seated, she leaned across the table towards him. 'What's happened?' she asked urgently. 'Why did you want to see me?'

Henry looked concerned at her agitation. 'Darling, it's all right. It's not bad news. Sorry, I should have said . . .' He looked exhausted and there were bags under his eyes. 'We're frantic at the bank and I was so rushed when I spoke to you.'

'So what is it?' She felt as if a fist was squeezing her heart.

'I phoned the Air Ministry. I don't know why it didn't occur to me before.'

'The Air Ministry?' For a moment she felt confused. 'Oh! Oh, my God!' she exclaimed with dawning realization.

'Yes.' Henry nodded, and took a sip of his whisky and soda. 'I asked if they knew the present whereabouts of Flight Lieutenant Peter Osborne. I thought it was time we asked him what the hell he was playing at, Juliet, so I told the Ministry he was an old friend, and I'd lost his address.'

'And . . .?' She leaned back, weak with relief that her father didn't have bad news about Daniel to impart.

'When was it you last saw him?'

Juliet looked surprised. 'About four years ago. I'd just got engaged to Eddie.'

Henry nodded again. 'That's what I thought.' He paused and looked straight into her eyes. 'Those flowers and that note couldn't have been from him, because the Ministry informed me he'd died two and a half years ago.'

Juliet started, with shock. '*Died!*' she repeated incredulously.

'He was invalided out of the Air Force because he'd contracted cancer.'

Her hands flew to her cheeks and she gazed at Henry, appalled. 'How dreadful! Then that means . . .?' Her mind was scrabbling to take in the news. 'Then that means . . .?' she repeated, her eyes widening. '*Esther!*'

'I think you're probably right,' Henry said heavily. 'Didn't Daniel say that she'd worked at the Air Ministry during the war? I'm sure I remember him mentioning it.' Henry rubbed a weary hand over his eyes.

'Dads, are you all right?' she asked suddenly.

He smiled immediately. 'Just tired, darling. There's a lot on. Anyway, I'm sure this will make a difference, won't it?' he asked hopefully. 'Daniel can hardly mind about those wretched flowers now, as the man who's supposed to have sent them is dead?'

Juliet looked thoughtful. If Esther had known Peter during the war, and perhaps they'd worked in the same office, he might have talked about who he was seeing and who he was going out with.

No wonder Esther seemed to know so much about her private life!

'Dads, I can't thank you enough,' she told Henry gratefully. 'I should have contacted the Air Ministry myself, but I was so devastated by Daniel's reaction, I just felt like curling up and dying.'

'That's not like you, sweetheart.'

She smiled weakly. 'I know. But I felt betrayed by Rosie, and Peter, who I couldn't believe had written that note, and then by Daniel when he twisted my words and walked out.'

When they'd had lunch, Henry escorted her out of the Savoy, where there was a line of waiting taxis. The commissionaire raised his gloved hand, and a cab came swiftly towards them.

'Thank you for everything, Dads,' Juliet said, kissing him on both cheeks. 'You've no idea how grateful I am.'

'Let me know how everything works out, sweetheart.'

'I will. And take care of yourself, Dads.'

Henry smiled, and spoke to the taxi driver. 'Park Lane, please.'

'Yes, sir.'

Juliet waited until the cab had turned round into the Strand and she'd given a final wave to Henry. 'I've changed my mind,' she told the driver. 'I'd like to go to the Edgware Road, please.'

Dudley was in the hall, arranging flowers that he'd already arranged that morning, when Juliet let herself into the house late that afternoon.

His button eyes looked into hers pointedly and he pursed his mouth as if to say 'Shh . . .' Then he nodded his head towards the closed study door, before darting back to his quarters in the basement.

Juliet stood still, her heart pounding and the blood raging in her ears. Her legs weakened as if she was ill and she thought she was going to faint. Whatever was said and whatever was done in the next few minutes would determine the rest of her life.

She paused, trying to steady her breathing. Then gathering her strength she clenched her hands until her red nails dug into her palms, and strode forward. For a second she hesitated before the mahogany double door before gripping the handles. A moment later she flung open the doors and found

Daniel sitting behind his desk. He looked up as she entered, stunning her with his looks as he'd done the first time they'd met. His strong featured face and dark hair, his almost black eyes and seductive full-lipped mouth, melted all her inner feelings; defiance turned to supplication, resistance to reconciliation, and anger to an overpowering love for him.

'Hello,' she said in a small voice.

His mine-shaft deep voice washed over her like a tolling bell. 'I came to see Tristan,' he said coldly.

Hurt, she tried not to flinch. 'He's asleep in the nursery.'

'I know.'

Juliet looked at him searchingly. Had he only come to see their baby? There were a thousand questions she wanted to ask, but she was too afraid of what his answers might be.

'How are you?' she said eventually, wishing he would come forward and take her in his arms. 'Where have you been?'

He shuffled the papers in front of him. 'Away.'

'And now you're . . . back?'

He gave her a black look, his mouth tight. 'I don't know.' There was a finality to his tone, forbidding further questions.

'I have something to tell you.'

'And what would that be?' he asked, disinterested.

'I've had a long talk with Esther.'

He jumped to his feet, red in the face with fury. 'I told you to keep away from my family . . .!' he stormed. 'Don't you ever do as you're bloody well told?'

'It was Esther who sent me those red roses and wrote that note,' Juliet said as calmly as she could.

'What are you talking about?' he demanded savagely.

'I've been to see her again. She's just admitted it. Peter Osborne died of cancer two and a half years ago. Esther worked alongside him during the war. She was in love with him, Daniel, and he wasn't interested. Apparently he talked a lot about me.' Juliet was careful not to repeat how Peter had apparently told Esther that he was 'crazy about Juliet' and eventually 'wanted to marry her'.

She looked Daniel straight in the eye. '*That's* why she hates me. Not because you married me, not because she thought you were after my money. She hates me because she saw me

114

as a rival for Peter's affections. And she admitted that she hoped she could get her revenge and make my life a living hell by writing that card.'

Daniel sat down again but remained silent.

'And she succeeded, didn't she?' Juliet demanded. 'Knowing you as well as she does, she knew you'd go off the deep end.'

'This changes nothing,' he said at length.

'How can you say that?'

'It doesn't alter the fact that people think I married you for your money.'

Something hardened in Juliet's heart at that moment. It was a feeling of her own self-worth. If Daniel really loved her, why did he so despise all that was hers? Why wasn't he happy that at least Cameron had done all he could to recompense her for having tricked her into a sham of a marriage?

'Really?' she lashed back, continuing sarcastically. 'So I'm supposed to suffer alone in my lavish house? With my Rolls Royce at the door? A fortune in my bank account? And a box full of jewels? Is that what's getting you? It's what you accused me of last time, as if being rich was a sin. I can't *help* having all this money Cameron made over to me. Why are you punishing me because of it?'

Daniel continued to look at his papers, but he remained silent.

'Don't you think you're being absurd?' she challenged angrily.

He flushed deeply, and his eyes flashed dangerously. 'For once this isn't all about you, Juliet!' he retorted. 'It might not have occurred to you, but I happen to miss my children very much. Do you ever consider my feelings as you sail blithely through your elitist life?'

Juliet looked at him as if he'd slapped her across the face. 'Of *course* I do, I think of nothing else,' she said shocked. 'How can you say that to me? How can you call me elitist? You know I want them to come and stay here. I want to get to know them. It's hardly my fault that their mother won't let them come here and see you.'

His voice was harsh. 'Esther has poisoned her mind. Ruth says she won't allow them to stay in the house of a whore.'

Juliet looked stricken, and her hand flew to her mouth. 'And you let her say that about me?' she whispered, horrified. She sank on to a chair by the side of his desk, feeling sick. Her stupid, reckless past, when her loss of Daniel had driven her to a life of decadence, was catching up on her now. And he seemed ready to believe every word of Esther's venom.

His voice was icy and laden with innuendo. 'Esther seems to know rather more about you than I do.'

'She knows *nothing* about me, the real me,' she whispered defensively. 'She only knows what Peter Osborne told her and he didn't really know me. Whatever she may say, you're the only man I've ever really loved. From the beginning, from the moment we met, it was only you I wanted . . .' Her voice broke, and she covered her face with her hands. 'And I believe, by the time we'd finished talking this afternoon, that Esther believes that, too. She's bitter, Daniel, because Peter was the love of her life. And she can't forgive me for, as she sees it, taking him away from her.'

'I'm not a fool, Juliet,' he said harshly. 'Esther isn't the only person who's mentioned your past.'

'I did go a bit wild for a while,' she admitted. 'I'd lost our baby, and you seemed to hate me . . . and with all the bombs and everything I didn't care what happened to me, but I never, *ever*, for one single moment, stoped loving you. You're my life, Daniel . . .' She was crying so hard now she could hardly breathe, all the fight knocked out of her, washed away by a torrent of grief and regret.

She heard the sound of a chair being pushed back and the next moment Daniel was by her side, his strong arms pulling her close, his hand pressing her head against his cheek. 'I know, I know, my darling,' he said fervently. 'Forgive me . . . I love you more than life . . . and I never want to lose you.'

Juliet clung to him until her sobs subsided, then she looked at him, tilting her head back so she could see into his eyes. 'I can't bear it when we quarrel.'

'Neither can I,' he said, sounding exhausted. He lead her over to a deep buttoned brown leather sofa which stood facing the fireplace, where logs from Hartley glowed warmly. 'I shouldn't care what people say, but I can't help thinking that if the war hadn't changed everything, your family would never have allowed you to marry me.'

'What do you mean?'

'Think about it, sweetheart! A Jewish divorcee, with not much money and three children. I'm hardly what your mother would consider "suitable". In peacetime I wouldn't have stood a chance in hell with your parents.'

Juliet wriggled from the crook of his arm and sat upright, her normal assertiveness returning. 'Listen, Daniel, I married who I wanted to marry, and I love who I wanted to love, and no one would ever be able to stop me, least of all Dads, whose opinion I do respect. It was only Mummy who wanted Rosie and I to make what she calls brilliant matches – and look what happened when we did!'

Daniel pulled her close again. 'Do you think I'll ever get used to people thinking I married you for your money?'

'I look upon it as Cameron's money and so should you. I didn't inherit it, nor did I earn it! Just forget about it and let's have a lovely life,' she said, desperate to end this power struggle that existed between them. 'To hell with what people think! And frankly, to hell with your bloody sister for stirring up trouble.'

'She's so jealous of you and now we know why. I've refused to have anything more to do with her and that still stands. To send you those red roses with a card that purported to come from an old flame, is unforgivable.' He paused, looking thoughtful. 'Now I've got to tell Ruth what happened and try and persuade her to let me see the children.'

Juliet looked up into his face. 'Why were you so ready to believe really bad things about me? And let Ruth believe I'm a whore?'

His eyes drilled hers and he spoke bluntly. 'Jealousy. Terrible searing bloody jealousy at the thought of your being with anyone else.' His voice dropped and he looked away, pained. 'Look, darling, I don't expect you to have stayed at home all alone on your nights off and you certainly had no reason in the world to be faithful to me. I behaved like a swine because I was so jealous of you marrying Cameron. That's when it all started to go wrong between us. I wanted you for myself, although I was married. From the moment I set eyes on you, I knew you were the only woman I wanted.'

Juliet reached for his hand and held it in both of hers. Her expression was trusting and she spoke with honesty. 'What ever I did during the war, including getting engaged to poor Eddie, meant nothing to me, compared to what we've always had.'

Daniel held her tightly, as if he could never bear to let her go. 'The whole world was gripped by madness for five years,' he said thoughtfully. 'None of us should be judged on what we did during that time.'

'The main thing is we're together now.'

'Will you ever forgive me for being such an utter fool and such a jealous swine?'

Juliet knew how much it cost a proud dominant man like Daniel to make such an admission and to ask such a question. His sudden humbleness touched her deeply. And she was so exhausted now, she wanted an end to their quarrelling.

She kissed him gently on the lips, a kiss of love and commitment, a kiss of pure devotion. 'Of course,' she murmured, her voice low and throaty. 'There's nothing to forgive.'

# Nine

B ronzed and glowing, Rosie entered the grand dining room of the Hôtel de Paris wearing a white halter neck evening dress, cut on flowing Grecian lines with a cascade of pearls around her neck. Heads turned as she swayed her way to one of the tables in the window, followed by Salton, to where Lady Fulsham and Philibert were sitting, drinking champagne.

'I'm so sorry we've kept you waiting,' Rosie trilled, 'Salton had a business call from London which I thought would *never* end!'

Ten days in the South of France had changed Rosie from a pale discontented housewife into a dazzling beauty, brimming with confidence and *joie de vivre*. As she took her seat she accepted Philibert's offer of champagne with a prettily coquettish tilt of her head and a radiant smile.

Sitting quietly beside her, Salton felt a painful mixture of pride and hurt. Rosie had never been like this before. Even when they got engaged and then married, and he'd bought her the house she wanted, she'd never fizzled and sparkled and been merry and laughing like this. It was as if a switch had been turned on in her head and instead of finding the world a grey bleak place in which she was unhappy, she'd discovered this sunny paradise, where she could shine, unchallenged. There was no Juliet to steal the limelight, and no Charlotte who had been tipped as an up-and-coming fashion model of outstanding beauty. He couldn't help feeling hurt and inadequate because he was perfectly well aware that *he* wasn't the cause of her new-found happiness. And he knew in his heart now that he never would be.

Rosie, like Liza, thrived on the admiration of strangers. Like an actress her stage was the world of socializing, on a grand scale. Unless of course ... the change in her was so remarkable he was struck by a sudden suspicion, could it be . . .? He started counting how many days they'd been away as he pretended to study the menu. It was just possible, he reckoned, that she'd become pregnant in the past ten days. It would account for the vibrant joy that emanated from her. Pregnancy was supposed to make women feel special and contented, wasn't it? With mounting secret excitement he started counting the days again. He was sure he hadn't got the dates wrong; goodness knows they'd spent time every month since they'd been married, counting the days since . . . It *was* possible! he thought with a wave of exultation. He looked across the table at Rosie, watching her as she chatted to Philibert and his aunt. Her eyes blazed with excitement and her skin gleamed with well-being. She *must* be pregnant!

Salton felt his eyes prick with emotion and a huge sense of relief swept over him. At that moment he wished they'd been alone, so great was his desire to take her in his arms and tell her how much he loved her. Darling Rosie, he thought tenderly. He adored her so much. Now they were going to be a real family, after all, with Sophia and Jonathan whom he'd also grown to love. Sipping his champagne, he silently thanked God he'd brought her on this trip. The warm weather, relaxed atmosphere, plenty of good food and wine and the sea air had worked their magic, and their dearest wish was about to be granted.

'So when do you have to return to England?' he heard Lady Fulsham ask him. 'We shall miss you very much when you leave here.'

Salton beamed at the elderly lady of whom he'd grown quite fond. 'In a couple of days, I'm afraid,' he replied genially. 'We've had the best time ever, but, alas, I have to get back to work.'

'Such a pity.' Her tone was wistful, as she spread her hands in a gesture of appeal, her heavy rings almost slipping from her thin fingers.

'Philibert is planning a big trip on the *Marie Clare*. We're going to go across the Tyrrhenian Sea to Palermo and then on to Catania and Valletta and end up in Gozo. It would have been such a lovely trip for you both if you could have stayed longer.'

'It sounds wonderful but we really do have to get back,' Salton said, with genuine regret. 'And you're going, too?'

'*Certainement*. Philibert thinks I need to get away for a rest.' Her voice was frail and tinged with sadness. 'But I have too much rest as it is. I miss Walter so terribly. That's my problem. We were so devoted and when he died, it seemed as if he'd taken the rest of my life with him.'

'Perhaps,' Salton suggested gently, 'Philibert just thinks a change of scene would be good for you?'

Lady Fulsham shrugged and spoke simply. 'My broken heart goes with me where ever I am.'

A burst of laughter from Rosie and Philibert interrupted their conversation and the mood became lighter as they dined on exquisitely cooked roast fillet of beef garnished with *foie gras*, and *soufflé glace amardine* to follow.

Rosie continued to chatter gaily and the evening passed swiftly, with Salton and Philibert engaged in amusing badinage, while Lady Fulsham watched them all and wished she was still young.

Salton awoke in the early hours of the next morning and heard Rosie in the bathroom of their suite, moaning and swearing in equal measure.

'Bloody hell! Oh, damnation! For God's sake . . .!' she wailed shrilly.

He slid rapidly from the bed and rushed to her side, guessing what had happened. She was sitting on the loo and the tears were rolling down her angry face.

'A thousand fucks!' she exploded forcefully when she saw him standing helplessly in his pyjamas. 'What the hell's wrong? I got pregnant at the drop of a hat with Charles,' she added accusingly. 'And this time I was so *sure*.'

'Oh, honey, I'm so sorry.' He stepped forward to put his arms around her.

'Get off me,' she shrieked furiously, raising her arms as if she might strike him. 'This is the last fucking straw. I really thought that this time . . .' She shook her head in furious grief. 'It's so unfair!'

Salton had never felt so useless in his life. Words of comfort weren't going to be any use this time; he'd offered the usual banalities too often now for them to be of any comfort to her. Every month her disappointment grew greater and more anguished. Instead he went to the drinks cabinet in their suite and poured her a glass of brandy.

'Here, honey, have this,' he suggested, handing it to her.

She pushed it away. 'I don't *want* a bloody drink. Why can't I have a baby? That's all I want. Why doesn't it happen? Month after month I live in hope, but it never happens.'

Salton rinsed one of the hotel's face flannels in cold water and tried to dab her brow with it, but she rose, and turned angrily away.

'For God's sake, leave me alone, Salton,' she shouted. 'Why the hell can't you just leave me alone?' Then she grabbed a large towel from the heated rail and wrapping it around herself, stomped back to their bedroom.

Salton lay carefully down beside her, but he couldn't sleep. There was no dealing with Rosie when she was in this mood and he prayed that by the morning she'd be in a better frame of mind. For the rest of the night she lay as far away from him as she could in the large double bed, and in the morning she was up early, washing her hair and making up her face with particular care.

'What would you like to do today, honey?' Salton asked as he joined her for their *petit déjeuner* which a waiter had put on a table on the balcony, overlooking the sea.

Her profile was stubborn as she gazed at the ink blue line of the horizon. 'I want to stay on here a bit longer,' she said evenly.

Salton looked appalled. 'But I have to be back at the Embassy on Monday.'

Her tone was impatient as if she thought him stupid. 'I *know* that,' she snapped. 'They want us to go on that cruise with them, you know,' she continued, as if it was obvious who she was talking about. 'Lady Fulsham's quite frail, and she said last night how she wished I was accompanying them, so I could keep her company.'

'But they'll be away for weeks,' Salton protested. 'They're going all over . . .'

'I know,' she snapped again, 'and I think I'll join them. Nanny can stay on with the children at Hartley and you'll be all right on your own in town, won't you? It's ages since I've had a really good time, and I've never travelled anywhere. We were always sent to Bembridge or Frinton with Nanny when we were children, and frankly, I've only had seaside holidays like that. This would be a marvellous opportunity to see a bit of the world. And in luxury, too.'

'But we've hardly any money left. You couldn't stay here.'

Rosie turned to face him. 'God, you do look on the black side of things, don't you? When Philibert first mentioned the cruise he said we could always leave our things in the suite with Lady Fulsham's servants. All I need is my fare home and I'm sure they'd lend me some money for spending, I could repay them next time they're in England.'

Salton's eyebrows were raised in disquiet. 'You've got it all worked out, haven't you?'

'Yes, because you're such a stick-in-the-mud! I knew you'd raise every objection you could think of,' she retorted.

'So you've made up your mind?'

'Yes.' As she spoke, she rose, tying the sash of her pink satin dressing gown firmly. 'If you refuse to stay then I will, and go with them on my own.'

'Rosie, you know I'd like to stay . . .' he began, but she'd swept off to the bathroom, and shut the door behind her.

Two days later Salton cut a lonely figure as he climbed into the *auto-taxi* to take him to Nice aerodrome. Rosie was standing on the top steps of the Hôtel de Paris waving him goodbye and he raised his soft brown trilby in acknowledgement. There was an excitement about her that slightly puzzled him, in view of her recent crashing disappointment. Then he saw she was waving to someone else, a dashing male figure who was crossing the road and making for the hotel.

Suddenly it occurred to Salton, in a heart-thudding stab of impending doom, that maybe going on a cruise wasn't the only thing that was making Rosie smile so radiantly and wave with such relentless anticipation.


Rosie sat on the deck of the *Marie Clare* gazing enraptured at the dark star-lit waters of the Mediterranean as they headed towards Naples, its harbour outlined with pin-pricks of light. A balmy breeze ruffled her hair and tickled the warm skin of her bare shoulders. She couldn't remember a time when she'd felt so deliciously happy.

Lady Fulsham had retired to her cabin after dinner, and Philibert was on the bridge, discussing with the captain the navigational route for tomorrow, and deciding whether to drop anchor at Capri for a couple of days or not.

'Heaven,' Rosie whispered to herself, thankful there were

only the three of them on board plus a very discreet crew who managed to remain in the background most of the time. The yacht had been built in 1929, and it rode the water as smoothly as a knife cutting through butter. The atmosphere seemed to be charged with romance, a setting for a Hollywood film or an Ivor Novello musical. Rosie breathed deeply and felt a great sweeping desire to be loved. She was in a fairy tale setting and it seemed a waste to be alone, here, on a night like this.

Philibert suddenly appeared out of the darkness, walked silently on deck towards her, a tall slender figure in white, with a glass of champagne in each hand.

'There you are!' he said, making her wonder where else he thought she might be. 'I've brought us a nightcap.'

Rosie was bowled over. There was something so intimate about the way he'd said 'us.' And the night was warm and the gentle breeze smelled of roses and pine

'How lovely!' She took the glass from him, aware of his fingers touching hers. Then he sat down beside her on the basket-weave sofa, so close his hip pressed into hers. She sipped the ice cold pungent wine and instantly felt dizzy. Desire now ripped through her leaving a fiery trail, hot with a deep sense of longing.

It flashed through her mind that Charles had never made her feel like this, that Freddie had, but only at the beginning of their affair, and that Salton never had and never could cause this scorching feeling inside.

She looked up and realized Philibert was watching her.

'You're looking very beautiful tonight, Rosie,' he said, his French accent making the words sound so much sexier than if they'd been spoken by an Englishman. 'How you say . . .? A penny for your thoughts?'

'They're not worth that!' She giggled flirtatiously and somewhat nervously.

'You're right.' His voice was serious. 'Everything about you is more valuable than a penny. You're pure gold, Rosie. All the way through.'

She felt his hand stroke her back. She could feel the heat of his skin and the warmth of his breath on her cheek as he leaned towards her.

'No, I . . . I c-can't,' she said, averting her face. There was little protest in her voice, though.

'You can, Rosie, you can,' he persisted, closing his arm around her waist. 'A beautiful woman like you needs to be loved. To be adored and looked after and cherished. The moment I first saw you I thought, *mon Dieu*! I have found the woman of my dreams! Rosie, *mon chérie*, don't deny me my dreams.'

The starlight, the gentle swell of the sea that rocked the boat, the champagne and the passionate ardour of Philibert as he pressed himself against her, melted away any thoughts of loyalty to Salton, and turning to face him again, she allowed him to cover her face with butterfly kisses before he latched on to her mouth with a hungry intensity.

His hands were everywhere, touching, stroking, feeling and searching for all her secret places.

'We shouldn't,' she whimpered as she clung around his neck.

'But we *must*,' he insisted. 'I must have you. I want to give myself to you, *chérie*. I must make you mine or I shall die.'

With a swift movement he stood, and picking her up in his arms he carried her across the deck and into his stateroom, where a shaded lamp stood by the large bed. Dazed and wondering if this was really happening, Rosie allowed him to wrench off her pretty dinner dress and underclothes, and all the while he was murmuring softly to her, telling her how exquisite she was, how silky her skin felt, how beautiful her breasts felt in his hands, how sweet her mouth and how glorious her golden hair.

As in a dream, Rosie let him do what he liked with her, as he brought her to a rushing frenzied climax, only to start making love to her all over again a little while later. Breathless and exultant, crying out for more, yet begging him to stop as he plunged her depths again and again, Philibert made her feel like a love goddess for the first time in her life.

She lay back and revelled in every brush of his hand and every touch of his mouth.

This is what love is all about, she reflected hazily, and for a split moment imagined this was what Juliet and Daniel must share. Well, she was going to have it, too. That's what she needed in her life; an exciting man who made love to her on a romantic yacht in the middle of the Mediterranean, who plied her with champagne and compliments, a man with whom

125

she could share the sunshine of the South of France, the divine food and wine and the luxury of living in a place that hadn't been decimated by five years of war.

This is what she needed and this is what she would take, like a greedy child who has long been denied sweets.

'She's gone mad!' Juliet exclaimed, shocked, when Salton came round to Park Lane two weeks later, to tell her what had happened. 'This man's turned her head!'

He'd aged since he'd received Rosie's rambling letter, which was written on Hôtel de Paris writing paper. Grey, and with dark shadows under his eyes as if he'd been punched in the face, he sat in one of Juliet's black drawing-room armchairs which suddenly looked too large for him.

'Oh, Salton, I'm so, so sorry,' Juliet said with genuine sympathy, her heart going out to him. She'd introduced him to her sister, thinking he might cheer Rosie up, and all that had happened was that, as Juliet had feared and suspected all along, Rosie had married him mainly because she liked being married, but also because he was 'a man of substance' as Granny would have said.

'Rosie is behaving atrociously,' she continued. 'You've been so good to her, giving her everything she wanted and now she does this to you. I think it's appalling.'

Salton's expression was wintry as he nursed a tumbler of whisky and soda with both hands. 'Maybe it's because she wanted a baby so badly and it hasn't happened.'

Juliet looked indignant. 'That's no excuse! Bad behaviour is bad behaviour, whatever the cause. Has she told Mummy and Dads?'

He shook his head. 'I don't know. I've only told you because I want to keep it quiet for the time being in case . . . in case she changes her mind and comes back,' he added, his voice dropping to a hoarse whisper. 'You never know. She might change her mind and come back.'

Juliet hadn't the heart to tell him it was unlikely. Rosie was obviously having the time of her life on the Riviera, quite apart from having fallen in love. 'Well, I won't be putting out the welcome home mat for her, if she does,' she retorted acerbically. 'What about Sophia and Johnny? How can she bear to leave them behind?'

'Her letter did say she'd send for them in due course.' He was making a great effort to be loyal but as the magnitude of what Rosie had done sank in, he was finding it more and more difficult. 'I wish I hadn't bought such a big house now. I'm rattling around in it; we've even decorated the top floor as a nursery suite . . . quite apart from Sophia's and Johnny's rooms.'

'Oh, Salton . . .!' She reached out and laid her hand on his arm. 'Why don't you come and stay with us for a bit? You don't want to be on your own in that great house at a time like this. And Daniel would love your company.'

Salton took a gulp of whisky to quench feelings of the pain and disappointment that threatened to engulf him. Juliet was an angel, but he didn't think he could bear to be in the company of a happily married couple, with a new baby, right now.

'You're more than kind, honey, but I'd better stay at home.' The word 'home' hung hollowly in the air between them. There was an awkward silence.

'At least you'll stay for dinner. I insist,' she said robustly.

She took his empty tumbler gently from him. 'Let me get you the other half.' She felt so angry with Rosie at that moment she could hardly trust herself to speak. Salton was a thoroughly decent fellow who came from a lovely family, and she felt ashamed at her sister for treating him so badly.

The next morning Juliet phoned her mother to ask if she'd heard from Rosie.

Liza, fussing around their modern flat trying to make it look aristocratic by decking it out with crimson brocade furnishings, sounded vexed. She was having a bad morning. The rooms were too square and boxy with low ceilings and metal window frames to allow her to achieve the grand look she wanted.

'Yes, I've heard from her,' she snapped. 'It's a great pity, but at least she hasn't gone off with a French waiter or something. This young man is a baron . . .'

'Nearly *all* the upper-class young men on the Continent are Barons or Counts . . . that is if they aren't Princes!' Juliet retorted, dumbfounded by the extraordinary set of values her mother clung to, as if it was still the beginning of the century instead of halfway through it. 'Who the hell cares *what* he is!' she exploded. 'Rosie has ditched her husband and her children for some foreign charmer who she's known for five minutes, and I think it's disgraceful.'

'Well, there's nothing we can do about it,' Liza fretted, wondering if the walls of the drawing room would look better with the red brocade if they were painted silvery grey. 'Rosie's a grown woman and I'm sure she'll want Sophia and Jonathan to join her as soon as she's settled.'

'But how is she going to live? She's only got her dress allowance and she can't even get hold of that with the present restrictions.'

'Her young man is probably rich.'

'Oh, really, Mother. The whole thing is madness and don't expect me to pick up the pieces when it all falls apart, as it most surely will.'

'Juliet, you're so cynical,' Liza said plaintively.

'I'm just sorry for Salton.'

'Yes, well.' Her mother sighed. 'These things happen.'


'Things happen if you let them,' Louise pointed out when the family gossip finally reached her ears. 'Mummy, I hope you've told Rosie to come straight home.'

'How can I? She wouldn't listen to me,' Liza wailed. 'Why is everyone blaming me for her running off like this?'

'Because you've got more influence over her than anyone else. How can she leave her children, for one thing?'

In her own little house, which Juliet once described as 'a place of happy chaos', Louise was appalled by her sister's disregard for Sophia and Johnnie. There wasn't a day when she didn't think about her own little boy, torn from her side at birth because of the shame of being an unmarried mother. And looking at Daisy now, who was sitting up in her highchair, giving her mother a wide gummy smile, Louise's heart melted at the sweetness of her baby, and the joy she'd brought into their lives. It made her realize she'd rather lie down and die than desert Daisy, as Rosie was deserting her own children.

Taking her in her arms, Louise held Daisy close, as if she could never bear to let her go, and kissed the warm little head which was covered with fine blonde curls.

'My precious little girl,' she whispered, sitting down in the untidy kitchen, where two blue budgerigars trilled happily in a cage, Bella stood on her hind legs with her paws on Louise's knee, wanting to be patted, and the latest addition to the family, a small tortoiseshell kitten slept curled up in a basket.

Louise's eyes brimmed with emotion, part angry, part grateful, as she looked around her. She was doing her best to create a home full of creatures to love. Shane affectionately called it 'nesting', and she thanked God for giving her this opportunity to give to others, even if they were only animals, the love she should have been able to give to Rupert.

She knew their house was shambolic; untidy piles of clothes lay about, the washing-up never seemed to get done and the smell of warm country cooking permeated the atmosphere in a way that horrified the rest of the family, but she didn't care. And neither did Shane. Between them they were creating a real home, unpretentious, comfortable and welcoming. And most important, filled with love.

Oh, Rosie, you don't know what you're doing. You don't know the pain you're causing, she thought.

'You must both stay with me, at the Hôtel de Paris,' Lady Fulsham had told Rosie and Philibert when they returned from their cruise. 'I'll have a word with the management.'

Rosie had beamed. It was so wonderful to be taken care of by this rich aunt and her nephew, who lived the most idyllic life of luxury, lunching and dining in various restaurants every day, taking drives along the Corniches, with their magnificent coastal views, or motoring up into the mountains of Grasse where the flowers were gathered for the famous perfumes produced in France. And if Lady Fulsham had been shocked when they'd told her they were lovers and that Rosie was seeking a divorce, she didn't show it.

Sometimes she and Philibert went along the coast to Larvotto, to lie on the artificially created beach, with sand imported from the east, while Lady Fulsham rested after a late night at the casino. Other days they shopped, Rosie using the money from her dress allowance which her mother mailed to her, disguised by being wrapped up in woollen scarves or gloves in a big envelope.

Rosie hadn't only fallen deeply in love with Philibert, but with the glamour of the Côte d'Azur and Monte Carlo in particular, a haven for the elite, the rich and the decadent. It was a paradise beyond her wildest dreams, and she shuddered when she thought back to the days when she'd been married to Charles, living in a poky village cottage, peeling potatoes in cold water, while Sophia ran about, getting into everything, and Johnnie screamed from his cot. How had she endured it? For that matter, how had she endured the boredom of being married to the worthy Salton? Probably because she'd at least felt financially secure with him, and now she wondered if she'd only wanted a baby because it would justify her marriage and give her something new and amusing to think about?

She wasn't quite sure how she was going to look after Sophia and Johnnie in this dazzling new life, but right now, having fun was everything. Perhaps she and Philibert could rent a villa, and Nanny could come to look after them?

This wasn't the moment to mention it, though. Their affair was still so new and exciting and she felt so drugged by sex, that she wanted Philibert all the time as if she could never be satisfied, no matter how often he made love to her.

Anyway, the children were perfectly safe and happy at Hartley with Nanny and Granny and her parents going down every weekend. In fact, she thought they'd probably be terribly bored if they came to Monte Carlo; it wasn't exactly a place for children.

'We're having guests to stay for the weekend at the end of next month,' Daniel told Juliet when he got home one evening. There was suppressed excitement in his manner and his eyes glowed with anticipation.

She looked up sharply from the book she was reading. 'Guests?' she repeated. 'You mean . . .?'

He nodded, sitting quickly down beside her on the sofa, and taking her hand. 'Ruth has relented. I will pick up Sarah, Susan and Leo on the Friday evening and they'll stay until Sunday.' The triumph in his voice, mingled with relief, filled the room.

'Oh, darling, I'm glad.' Juliet flung her arms around his neck. 'That's wonderful news. Are they happy to be coming?' she added anxiously.

'Hard to tell with children, but apparently they didn't put up any resistance.' He chuckled.

'We must plan lovely things for them to do; perhaps we could get seats for a matinee?'

Daniel grinned boyishly. 'They're no longer *small* children, you know, sweetheart. Sarah's sixteen, Susan's fourteen and Leo's twelve. I imagine some heavy shopping in Bond Street is what the girls will want to do, and maybe a trip to the Science Museum for Leo.'

'Then we must take them out to a nice restaurant and perhaps go to a show on Saturday evening? Ivor Novello is still on in *The Dancing Years*, isn't he?' Juliet's head was spinning with plans. For Daniel's sake she desperately wanted this first visit to be so successful they'd want to come often. 'I'm scared, Daniel,' she said suddenly. 'I know how much having them to stay means to you; supposing they don't like me?'

'Don't be ridiculous, darling, of course they'll like you. Remember, it wasn't you who broke up my marriage. Ruth did that on her own.'

'But we were lovers while you were still married to her. And I did have your baby,' she added painfully.

Daniel silenced her by kissing her firmly on the mouth. 'That's in the past, sweetheart, never to be talked about unless we're alone.'

'I know. I know,' she said nodding. It would still be there in her mind, though, she thought. A guilty secret knowledge that between them they had deceived Ruth. 'What made Ruth change her mind about them coming here?'

'Apparently Esther has had a breakdown. She confessed to Ruth that she'd deliberately made mischief in order to try to break us up. She also admitted to having been insane with jealousy over you and Peter Osborne.'

Juliet's face was compassionate. 'Poor woman!' she exclaimed, genuinely shocked. 'She must have suffered so, to behave in the way she did. I feel quite sorry for her.'

'It doesn't excuse her for turning my ex-wife against me so that I wasn't allowed to see my children. Thank God we can all get together now, and I'm sure they're going to love you, darling.'

Juliet felt the great weight which had hung over her for a long time slip away, leaving her feeling light and clean, her vision of the future clear at last. She and Daniel were going to make it in spite of the problems they'd had which had lain between them at times like a great impenetrable barrier.

He kissed her again, as one of his hands tenderly stroked the rim of her left ear with his fingertips, and her pearl drop earring quivered at his touch. 'How can they not love someone who makes me so happy?'

'How are the newspapers allowed to write about people like this?' Henry exclaimed, as he sat down to breakfast in the small dining room of their flat. 'It's much worse than it was before the war. When Alastair Slaidburn killed himself over Juliet I thought that was bad enough, but it was nothing compared to this.'

Liza sat opposite him, while their daily, Mrs Pinner, brought in a pot of coffee and a rack of fresh toast which she placed on the table. When she trotted back to the kitchen, Liza leaned towards Henry and spoke in a stage whisper. 'Hide the papers. We don't want her reading them.'

Henry looked up. '*Hide* them?' he repeated incredulously. 'Every newsstand in London, if not in the whole of Britain is going to see the *Daily Mail* with its front-page story of Rosie leaving Salton,' he thundered. 'They've turned her affair into the scandal of the week, for God's sake! Just *look* at this, Liza.' He thrust the newspaper across the table into her hands. 'I must write to Lord Rothermere to complain, and to Lord Beaverbrook,' he added, catching the headline of the *Daily Express* which lay on the side table. 'Why do you buy these rags? I won't have them in the house in future. Who ever wrote this article about Rosie ought to be shot!'

Liza's hands trembled as she read:

> The former Rosie Granville, a one-time debutante who has left her second husband for a well known French 'charmer', Baron Philibert Guerin, who has been linked in the past with rich and titled young women including the heiress, Comtesse Sarita Contini . . .

'Maybe he thinks Rosie is an heiress . . .' Liza began weakly.

'Maybe he's forgotten she's a married woman with two

132

children,' Henry snapped, getting up from the table, and storming out of the room and along the corridor to the front door.

'Henry . . .! Your breakfast . . .?'

'I'm going to make that girl see sense and bring her back to England if I have to drag her by her hair,' he shouted over his shoulder, before crashing out of the flat.

'Everything all right, then, Mrs Granville?' Mrs Pinner asked cheerily as she came out of the kitchen.

'No, this flat is too *small*!' Liza wailed, rushing to her bedroom. There was no privacy. The servants . . . well, the one daily, could hear everything that was going on, and she fervently wished once again that they still had the elegant spacious rooms they'd once occupied in Green Street, not to mention Parsons, the perfect butler who'd managed to shield her from any unpleasantness.

The trouble was, Liza was missing Rosie, the one child who was her soulmate, and the one who shared her interests, aims and ambitions. When she came up from Hartley, Rosie was the first person she went to see, and they'd go out to have morning coffee at Harrods, before embarking on a few days together that included shopping in Bond Street, going to the cinema, and giving dinner parties. She never had the same fun with Juliet. There was always that feeling at the back of her mind that Juliet rather despised her. As for Louise, she was so wrapped up in her domestic life that she never wanted to go anywhere.

At that moment Charlotte tapped on her bedroom door.

'Mummy, I'm just off,' she said, coming into the room, glowing with good health and a newly acquired self-confidence. 'I don't know when I'll be back because we're going on location,' she added importantly.

Liza turned to look at her youngest and most beautiful daughter with mixed feelings. Her modelling career was taking off and she had an agent now, who was taking fashion bookings for her from all the top fashion photographers, including Norman Parkinson. Today they were going to Richmond Park, hoping to get shots of Charlotte in a tweed and fur winter range of Dior's New Look against a background of grazing deer.

Proud that her child was considered beautiful enough to

appear in all the best magazines, it still wasn't what Liza had wanted for Charlotte. Surely being a photographic model was only a step away from being an actress? Where would it lead? All the other girls of her age were taking the debutante Season seriously, meeting eligible young men night after night at a variety of wonderful parties. And what was Charlotte doing?

Spending her time with the most unsuitable people like make-up artists, dress designers and hairdressers.

If Liza was worried about Rosie, she was privately far more worried about Charlotte.

In the end Henry decided it was pointless going to Monte Carlo to bring Rosie back. He'd managed to get hold of her on a long distance telephone call, pleading with her to return to her children, if not Salton, but she was adamant she wouldn't leave Philibert.

'Daddy, I'm truly happy for the first time in my whole life. It isn't only Philibert,' she assured him. 'It's this place. I feel as if I've come home and that I belong here. I'm speaking French, which I thought I'd forgotten. I love the people, the weather, the countryside, everything about this place. It's as if I'm really French at heart. I simply can't come back to England.'

'What about Sophia and Jonathan?' her father asked stiffly. The sadness and hurt he felt was like a physical pain in his chest. There was no doubt that Rosie sounded ecstatic, as if all her dreams had come true, but he couldn't bear to think of the children, going to bed in tears some nights because she hadn't returned. 'You can't leave the children at Hartley forever, you know.'

'As soon as I get a divorce, Philibert and I will get married,' she said confidently. 'Then we'll buy a villa out here with a big garden and the children will adore it. Don't worry, Daddy. Philibert's aunt is a multi-millionairess, and he's her only heir. We're going to be fine. You and Mummy must fly over and meet both Philibert and Lady Fulsham. You'll love them . . .'

Rosie prattled on, sounding more and more like Liza; too full of her own thoughts to listen to what anyone else was saying.

'Everything's fine at home,' Rosie assured Philibert blithely, when he emerged from the beige marble bathroom that led off from their bedroom, with a small white towel slung loosely around his hips.

'Excellent!' He smiled at her as he let the towel fall to the ground. Then he walked slowly towards where she sat by the phone on the edge of the bed, with the natural animal grace of a panther. As she reached out to touch him, he instantly became aroused, and stooping forward, kissed her on the mouth as if he'd been parted from her for days.

'*Mon chérie . . .*' he murmured between kisses, 'look what you do to me?' He glanced down at himself with a lazy smile. 'I want you all the time . . . and I must have you all the time.'

Rosie lay back as he tore open her negligee and made love to her again, as the warm morning sunshine streamed through the window, and outside the blue Mediterranean shimmered like sapphires under a cloudless sky.

'Juliet!'

She jumped to her feet, her heart lurching nervously, the blood draining momentarily from her head. Then hurrying across the drawing room she came out on to the landing at the top of the stairs, and looked down into the hall.

They were all standing there looking up at her, Daniel with an eager smile and Sarah, Susan and Leo with guarded expressions, each one a replica of their father, with his olive skin, dark hair, black eyes and strong classical features.

'Hello!' Juliet called back, clutching the silver banister as she stepped lightly in her high heels down the black carpet. 'How lovely to see you.'

She stretched out her hand to Sarah first, who shook her hand with polite graveness and penetrating eyes. She was a well developed sixteen year old, a young woman more than a child, and she looked as if she had a mind of her own. Then Susan stepped forward smiling Daniel's warm smile and Juliet wanted to kiss her on the spot, but knew it was too soon. The fourteen year old was adorable, with sparkly eyes and Juliet knew at once they'd get on.

'How do you do! What are we supposed to call you?' Susan asked in a gentle voice.

Leo gave Susan a dirty look and nudged her crossly. 'We're not going to call her Mother.'

'Don't be rude, Leo,' Daniel said in a firm quiet voice.

'We've already discussed this and Juliet would like you all to call her by her Christian name.'

'Just . . . Juliet?' Susan queried in surprise. 'Not Aunt Juliet or anything?'

'Just Juliet,' Juliet affirmed cheerfully. 'I was made to call people who weren't related to me "aunt" or "uncle" when I was young, and I thought it was silly then. It's so old fashioned, isn't it?' Then she turned to Leo, her hand outstretched. 'How do you do, Leo? It's very nice to meet you. Why don't we go upstairs and have tea?'

Dudley, who had been hovering in the background, all agog to see what Daniel's children were like, nodded to Juliet. 'I'll bring it up right away, madam.'

'Who's he?' Leo asked loudly and suspiciously.

'Dudley looks after this house and everything in it,' Juliet explained smoothly, catching Daniel's amused expression. 'He saved my life during the war with his cooking and cleaning.'

Leo raised his chin arrogantly. 'Why wasn't he doing war work?'

'He used to be in the army as a batman, but he'd retired, so when the Blitz started he became a fire warden, and he looked after this place during the day.' Juliet suppressed her irritation at constantly having to defend the fact that she had a butler.

Daniel spoke warmly. 'I don't know what we'd do without Dudley, he's worth ten of the others.'

Juliet smiled at him gratefully. It wasn't so long ago that Dudley had been a source of contention between them.

Sarah looked sharply at her father. 'How many servants have you got, then?'

He laughed. 'I lose count!' he joked. 'Actually, we only have a cook, and the rest are dailies.'

Sarah tossed her head in silent disapproval.

'Come and sit down,' Juliet said, leading the way into the drawing room. She spread her arms wide. 'Sit anywhere you like.'

Susan stood stock still in the doorway, pushing her long black hair behind her ears as she stared around the room in amazement. The black carpet, white sofas and chairs and art deco furniture, some of it mirrored, seemed to hold her spellbound. Mirrors and vases of white flowers added to the dramatic effect and from the large windows, the view over Hyde Park looked as if they were in the middle of the country.

'This is the most beautiful room I've ever seen,' she whispered awestruck. She caught her father's hand with a sweet childlike gesture. 'Daddy, isn't it wonderful?'

'Juliet designed the whole thing herself,' he said proudly. 'In fact, she designed the interior of the whole house herself.'

Susan turned to Juliet. 'That's what I'd like to do when I grow up,' she said shyly.

'You'll never be rich enough,' Leo said scornfully.

'Why not?'

'You'd have to get hold of an *exceedingly* large amount of money to do up a place like this.'

There was a moment's awkward silence and Juliet sensed Daniel was giving Leo a warning scowl, so she seated herself by a low round tea table which was covered by a white tablecloth and on which Dudley had arranged the tea things.

Juliet spoke lightly. 'Why don't you all grab a chair? I always think afternoon tea is the best meal of the day, don't you? Now, help yourselves. There are cucumber or Patem Perparium sandwiches, biscuits, scones and jam and Dundee cake. Ah! And here's Dudley with the tea.'

As she spoke, the butler entered with a heavy silver tray, on which was a silver teapot and hot water jug. These he placed deftly in front of Juliet.

'Tea, everyone?' she asked brightly, grabbing the teapot and thinking this was indeed going to be a very long weekend.

'Are you all right, sweetheart?' Daniel asked sympathetically as he got into bed beside her that night.

Juliet chuckled. 'I'm fine,' she assured him. 'I think it's going to be all right, don't you? Sarah seemed to relent towards me a bit when she realized I'd given her the best spare room, and Susan is a little angel, isn't she? I adore her, Daniel, and we're getting on fine.'

Daniel had wrapped his arms around her and held her close.

'She's always been the easiest of the three, and she loves Tristan already, which is great. I was afraid there might be some jealousy there, but they all seemed to take to him, didn't they?'

137

She snuggled her head into the curve of his neck. 'I think everyone loves a baby who just lies there gurgling with happiness, don't you? Leo is the one I'm worried about.'

'Sons are always protective of their mothers, darling. He may be afraid of appearing to desert Ruth, for you. He may be feeling guilty because he actually likes you.'

'You can see he's resentful at my having money though, can't you?' She moved restlessly in the bed. 'At times I honestly feel Cameron's settlement has been more of a curse than anything else, and I obviously can't explain to anyone that the money was more a form of compensation, can I?'

'Give Leo time, darling. Once he realizes you're not a rich bitch he'll come around. The great thing is we've got them to agree to come and stay and I don't think you'll have any trouble with the girls.'

Juliet reached up and wound her arms around his neck. 'I so want them to like it here, darling, and to like me. I feel like buying them all lots of lovely presents tomorrow, but I suppose that would be taken as trying to buy their approval, wouldn't it?' she asked wistfully.

Daniel smiled at her well known sense of generosity. 'It would be all right to buy them maybe one thoughtful present,' he said carefully. 'Susan would love you to buy her a book on interior design, for instance. She's mad about this house. And Sarah . . .' He thought for a moment, 'I'm not sure about Sarah. Girls like her, who are on the cusp of womanhood, can change overnight. She's too young for make-up, and she might think you were criticizing her clothes if you bought her something to wear; how about giving her a book, too? Maybe a suitable novel? Books always make a safe present. And I'll take Leo off to the Science Museum and get him a book. too.'

Juliet burst out laughing. 'Are we making heavy weather of this? Terrified of doing the wrong thing?'

Daniel pulled her closer. 'Probably, but it's so nice to have them here and thank you for being so patient, darling.'

Juliet silenced him with a kiss, and they became so engrossed in each other there was no more conversation that night.

'What sort of books do you like reading, Sarah?' Juliet asked, as they perused the bookshelves in Hatchards, Piccadilly. 'Novels or Biographies?'

'Novels I suppose, as long as they're not soppy,' Sarah replied decisively.

'Have you read *Rebecca*? Or *Jamaica Inn*? It has smugglers in it. Daphne du Maurier wrote them before the war and they're the most marvellous stories.'

Sarah shook her head and asked critically, 'They're not about unrequited love, are they?'

Juliet grinned. 'Definitely not, but what's wrong with unrequited love in a book? We wouldn't have had the story of Romeo and Juliet if the ending had been happy.'

Susan started giggling. 'She's thinking of Aunt Esther, who's always going on about what she calls "the love of her life", but he loved someone else and not her.' As she spoke she clutched the book on interior design she'd chosen.

Juliet kept her expression non-committal. 'It's always sad not to be loved in return,' she replied carefully, as she busied herself looking at travel books.

'She drives us all mad, though,' Sarah agreed. 'He was younger than her, and Mummy met him once, and described him as a dashing pilot; no wonder he wasn't interested in Aunt Esther. The book you mentioned about smugglers sounds fun.'

Juliet nodded. 'Let's get it then.'

Both Sarah and Leo politely thanked her for 'a lovely time' when they said goodbye at the end of their stay, shaking her hand gravely as they'd done when they'd arrived, but Susan reached up and kissed Juliet on the cheek, her pretty face glowing with gratitude.

'Can we come again, soon?' she asked with childish simplicity, reminding Juliet of how Louise had been at that age.

'Of course you can. As often as you like. It's been wonderful having you here,' she added with sincerity. It was true. By Saturday evening, after they'd been to the theatre followed by supper at Quo Vadis in Soho, Leo was behaving more like a normal boy of twelve, rather than a hostile teenager, and the girls were laughing as Daniel translated the Italian menu for them.

Juliet gave a deep sigh of relief. The weekend had been a success and now she was determined to build on it. She'd have to go carefully, though. There must never be too great a show of wealth or indulgence, and Daniel must always be the head of the family, even if the wealth wasn't his. Happily his children had taken to Tristan and had shown no signs of jealousy, and Juliet vowed that there would be no favouritism when they were around. These were her step-children and they would be treated in exactly the same way as her own children.

# Part Three

# Destructive Forces

# 1950–1951

# Ten

Liza was sitting up in bed, sipping her morning tea when the phone on her bedside table rang.

'Hello?' she asked brightly. She had almost recovered from the scandal caused by Rosie leaving Salton the previous year. 'Oh, hello! How are you?'

Henry, coming out of the bathroom, raised his eyebrows enquiringly. She waved him away and shook her head, smilingly. But as she listened to what the caller was saying, her expression changed and she looked horrified.

'No, absolutely not!' she exclaimed. 'On no account must she be told. She's happily married and settled now and we can't risk rocking the boat.'

'What's happened?' Henry asked, walking to the side of the bed. 'Who are you talking to?'

Liza covered the mouthpiece with her hand. 'It's nothing, Henry,' she insisted. 'I'm . . . it's just gossip, darling. Nothing for you to worry about.'

'I insist on knowing, Liza,' he said sternly. He could always tell when she was lying. Who was the 'she' who mustn't be told?

'It's only Aunt Tegan . . .' she began, her blue eyes reproachful.

'And . . .? What's happened?'

'Oh, Henry, it's best we should keep out of it. There's nothing we can do . . .'

Deeply perturbed he seized the phone from her hand. 'Aunt Tegan? This is Henry; what's happened?'

Her Welsh accent was strong and she sounded upset. 'There was an accident last night,' she told him bluntly. 'It was a bad car crash near my cottage. I'm afraid both Tostig's ma and da were killed and the police, knowing they'd adopted the boy through me, brought him to me. He's not hurt, but he needs a home, and as I'm too old to be doing with a nine-year-old child, I thought Louise might like to have him, now she's got a husband and all.'

Henry, ignoring Liza's frantic gesticulations, spoke without hesitation. 'I know there's nothing she'd like better. I'll get on to her right away. The poor little chap must be terribly shaken.'

'He is that,' Aunt Tegan confided, dropping her voice. 'It's a miracle he wasn't killed. I'm keeping him in bed today, because of the shock. It's a dreadful tragedy. They loved that boy like he was their own.'

Henry thanked her for all she was doing and when he'd hung up he turned to Liza. 'What the hell were you thinking of?' he thundered.

Liza shrank visibly under the bedclothes. She'd never seen Henry as angry as this in all the thirty-six years they'd been married.

'But Shane . . . and Daisy!' she said weakly.

'Do you honestly think Shane is going to turn against Louise's first baby?' he asked incredulously. 'And that Daisy won't be thrilled to have a half-brother? And as for Louise herself . . .' Henry's eyes suddenly stung with unshed tears.

Turning away from his wife he dressed hurriedly and left the flat, without saying goodbye. Then he hailed a passing taxi and gave him Louise's address.

'Daddy!' she squealed with delight, when she opened the front door to him twenty minutes later. Daisy was balanced on her hip, her small mouth grubby with porridge. 'Come in! Would you like a cup of tea?'

Shane came forward to shake his hand, while Bella hopped around, barking excitedly.

This, Henry thought, almost wistfully, it what family life should be like.

'I've got some news for you both,' he said without preamble, 'but maybe you should sit down first, Louise.'

'What is it, Daddy? Has something happened to Rosie?'

Henry shook his head. 'This is bad news but it's also, I believe, good news.' He looked at Shane and then at Louise again. 'How would you feel, both of you, about Rupert coming to live with you?'

Louise gave a shocked cry and her hand flew to her mouth. Her eyes were instantly awash and Shane put his arm protectively around her shoulder.

'Why? Why, Daddy? How can I get him back?'

Gently, Henry told them what had happened. 'Aunt Tegan is looking after him at the moment. He's obviously dreadfully shocked, but the great thing is he escaped the accident without a scratch.'

'Of course we'll have him,' Shane said at once.

Louise was sobbing now. 'I can't b-believe it. Oh my God! Little Rupert, after all these years.' She hugged Daisy. 'A big brother for you, my darling! Isn't that extraordinary, Shane?'

He stooped to kiss her. 'It looks like fate to me, darling. We were meant to have him after all.'

'What does Mummy say?' Louise asked, wiping her eyes with her fingertips.

'I think we're both in shock,' Henry replied lightly from his chair. 'I'll leave it to you to tell the rest of the family. Now, I'd better get off to the bank. I think I've had enough excitement for one day.'

'Let's go and fetch him today,' Louise said excitedly, when she and Shane were on their own again.

Shane took her hand. 'Will you allow me, as a doctor, to give you a bit of advice?' He smiled tenderly into her tear drenched eyes.

'Of course I will.' She settled herself at the kitchen table with Daisy on her lap.

'Both physically and mentally this will have shattered the boy. He'll be grieving for his parents, or the couple he's always looked upon as his parents. At least he knows your great-aunt, and he's in familiar surroundings. If we go rushing in, calling him Rupert when he thinks his name is Tostig, he'll be terrified. He doesn't know you and he'll be scared at the idea of our taking him away from the people he does know.'

Louise nodded in understanding, but it hurt to realize she couldn't just sweep him up and take him home and expect him not to mind.

'So . . .' Shane continued carefully, 'we're going to have to plan, in easy stages, how we're going to bring him up to London. He's probably never left Wales. We're also going to have to introduce ourselves to him, as his real mother and step-father.

That's going to be the biggest shock of all, unless he's already been told he's adopted.'

'You're right. I'd have gone rushing up there like a bull in a china shop.' She paused, her brow puckered with apprehension. 'What if he doesn't accept me? What if he wants to stay in Wales?'

'Let's take it a step at a time, darling. Children are more resilient than you think.'

The next day they took the train to Llandrindod Wells, and as soon as she saw the Black Mountains, Louise felt a sick sensation of dread in her stomach. She'd made this same journey on her own ten years ago, as a pregnant fifteen year old, who had brought shame to her family, and was having to give away the baby she was expecting. Her heart was already broken because she knew she'd never be with Jack again, the sweet boy she'd loved and to whom she'd willingly given herself. Everyone had referred to him as 'that East End evacuee in the village', but to her he would always be Jack, the boy who reminded her of Rupert Brooke. Confined to her aunt's tiny cottage, seven months of misery had lain ahead of her before she gave birth to 'an unwanted baby'.

How terrifying the future had been then, when she'd looked at those Black Mountains, as she was looking at them now. And how frightening it was now, to be faced with having to return to the place where she'd been more unhappy than she'd known was possible.

She glanced at Shane, seated opposite her, and knew she'd never be able to put into words, even to him, how deeply desperate she'd been, living with Aunt Tegan, wanting the baby to arrive, but at the same time hoping he wouldn't, just yet, because every day he stayed inside her, was an extra day to have him with her.

Louise held Daisy tightly in her arms, remembering the anguish when Rupert was ripped from her side three days after he'd been born.

'I never thought I'd get over losing him,' she suddenly said aloud, her eyes brimming at the memory. Aunt Tegan had just picked him out of his wooden rocking cot, and whisked him out of the little room under the eaves of her cottage where he'd been born, and carried him down the narrow stairs, where at the bottom the local farmer and his wife, waited to receive him.

Shane reached for her hand and squeezed it. 'God moves in mysterious ways and you were obviously destined to have Rupert back one day.'

'Do you think it's going to be all right?' she asked brokenly. 'I couldn't bear it if . . .' She was shaking now, terrified at the thought he might reject her.

Shane continued to reassure her and comfort her but he couldn't help being anxious. If the boy had been two or three years old, it wouldn't have been so bad. Even if he'd been six or seven, he'd have been able to adjust to a completely new way of life, going from being a penniless farmer's lad, to a boy from an upper class family who would be expected to go to Eton and Oxford and have a privileged life.

But a boy who was nine, nearly ten, already set in the ways of a simple farm life in the depths of Wales, was an entirely different matter.

'I want me ma!' Rupert screamed at Louise, when she'd suggested she take him back to London, even though she'd stayed down in Wales for a couple of weeks, trying to build a relationship with him. 'You're not me ma! And that man's not me da!' he added, referring to Shane who'd been forced to return home, because of his work at the hospital. Then he'd said something in Welsh to Aunt Tegan which Louise hadn't understood.

Aunt Tegan scolded him angrily, cuffed him lightly about the head and sent him into the backyard.

'What did he say?' Louise asked.

She pursed her lips, and for a moment Louise was reminded of how her mother looked when she was shocked.

'He said you were what we call lady dogs,' she said primly. 'He's going to need a firm hand is that one, mark my words! He's used to the belt so it won't do him any harm.'

'He was whipped?' Louise asked horrified.

'Children are like puppies, Louise. A quick spank and they soon learn what's what. Don't you go spoiling him now. He's lucky to have you and that husband of yours, not to mention the life of Riley to look forward to.'

But Louise felt like weeping for the heartbroken little boy

147

who was the image of Jack, and who was missing his 'ma' and 'da', and was also terrified of being whisked away from the only life he'd ever known.

She could see him now through the small kitchen window of the cottage, kicking pebbles around the yard. His shoulders drooped sadly in the cheap jumper he wore, and his small mouth was turned down at the corners. But it was the sight of the back of his small neck, so pale and vulnerable, that made Louise's tears rise uncontrollably to the surface.

Jack's neck had been like that, with the same fair curls nestling in the nape, and although Jack had been a big boy, his neck had been the neck of a child; inexplicably, she'd always been touched by the sight of it.

Suddenly, the memory was too painful and powerful, reminding her of how much she'd loved Jack in that last summer of her youth, before the dark clouds had gathered in her life.

For a mad moment she wanted to rush into the yard and gather Rupert up in her arms and tell him how much she'd always loved him, and how much she'd loved his father, and how she wanted him to be happy and how she would *make* him happy now. But she held back, scared by the strength of her own emotions, knowing she would scare him too, if he saw her grief and her guilt.

Instead, she dried her eyes, and picking up Daisy carried her into the yard, where she sat on a low stone wall watching Rupert messing around with an old wooden beer crate. He appeared not to notice her.

'If you came with us to London, Tostig,' she said forcing herself to call him by his Welsh name, while trying to sound matter-of-fact, 'we could take Daisy to the zoo to see the animals. She's never been and it would be a chance for you to show her what elephants and lions and tigers look like. I believe,' she continued swiftly, realizing he'd stopped playing to listen to her, 'they have penguins and monkeys and even giraffes at the zoo. I remember going when I was small but I haven't been since.'

He stared at her with Jack's blue eyes and for a heart-stopping moment she felt as if he were about to accept her into his life, but then he looked away, the resolute expression of hostility back once more.

'I'm not going anywhere with you,' he said rudely. 'Me ma told me never to go with strangers.'

'I'm not really a stranger, Tostig. I gave birth to you,' she said very gently.

He turned away, his expression stubborn. 'Me ma was me mother.'

'You were born here, in this cottage. In Aunt Tegan's top bedroom,' Louise persisted quietly. 'I nursed you for three days. I loved you then, and I love you now . . .'

He swung round angrily. 'Then why did you get rid me? Me ma an' da said you'd never wanted me! But they wanted me. They took me in 'cos I'd be an extra pair of hands when I was big. I don't want you here! You're not a real ma!' he yelled accusingly, kicking the wooden crate across the yard.

Stricken, Louise blanched, unable to conceal her anguish. 'It wasn't like that,' she protested. 'Didn't Aunt Tegan explain I was only just sixteen when you were born? Seven years older than you are now. I *wanted* to keep you, more than anything, but I wasn't allowed to. They sent me away from home, and . . . and . . . Oh, Tostig, I've missed you every day since the day you were born,' she wept. 'And I'm sorry, so sorry, but let me make it up to you now. If I'd had my way you'd never have left my side, but when you're older you'll understand why I wasn't allowed to keep you then. But now that I'm married to Shane, I can.'

Louise was desperate to make him understand how much she loved and wanted him but she could see from a child's perspective that she was the person who had abandoned him at birth.

'I'm going to stay here,' he said defiantly. 'The farm is *mine* now and when I'm bigger I'm going to have cows and sheep and . . . and . . .' His small bottom lip quivered and his face turned pink.

'Of *course* you are,' Louise agreed instantly. 'It's your farm, where you were brought up and you'll be able to have all the animals you want, but I was wondering, in the meanwhile, well, if you wouldn't like to come and *stay* with us in London? Just for a while? Just to see how you like it? I'm sure Aunt Tegan will keep an eye on the farm in the meanwhile, and you can come back here, whenever you want.'

Louise's mind was working fast. She'd heard he'd inherited the small holding and if farming was what he eventually wanted to do there was nothing to stop him. Meanwhile, they could bring him down here for holidays and perhaps they could afford to employ someone to manage the place until Rupert – or was it always going to be Tostig? – was older.

'What do you say? How about a visit to our home in London? We've got animals, too. A dear little dog called Bella, and a kitten called Miggy, and some birds; we might even get you a pet of your own. Would you like that?' she added rashly.

He remained silent, scuffing the ground again with his worn miniature farmer's boots.

'Could I have a puppy?' It was the first time he'd spoken to her politely.

Louise smiled and spoke robustly. 'I don't see why not.'

He looked at her warily, still suspicious. 'When would we go?'

'Whenever you like.'

'I have to fetch my things from the farm.'

'Absolutely.' Louise was so relieved at the progress she'd made that she was prepared to do anything to please him.

The next day Aunt Tegan, who had the keys to the farm house, drove them over to collect the rest of Tostig's things. It was a bleak grey stone building, with mean little windows, and a rambling collection of outbuildings, some of which were on the point of collapse. As soon as they entered by the kitchen door, Louise was shocked by the poverty of the small pokey rooms, filled with battered furniture and clutter. The ceilings were sagging and the painted walls were frosting and stained with rising damp. It was obvious that nothing had been touched since the farmer and his wife had been killed. A mouldy loaf stood on a breadboard on the kitchen table, surrounded by hundreds of mice droppings. A jug of congealed milk stank the place out.

'I'll get my things,' Tostig said, climbing up the rickety stairs to the floor above.

When he'd gone Louise turned, shocked, to her great-aunt. 'I'd no idea he'd been given to people who lived in a slum dwelling like this,' she said accusingly.

Aunt Tegan looked defensive. 'They've had a run of bad luck. The last few summers have been bad for crops, and well . . .' She shrugged her ample shoulders. 'Things have got a bit run down.'

'Run down,' Louise repeated incredulously. 'The place should be condemned. It's not much of an inheritance for poor Tostig, who wants to live here when he's grown up.'

'Oh, I don't know. It could be fixed up with a bit of money, and there are twenty acres of good land so it's worth something.'

Tostig came clattering down the stairs at that moment, clutching a battered Huntley & Palmer biscuit tin, a mud covered football, and a few dog-eared comics. Round his shoulders he'd hung an even cheaper jumper than the one he was wearing.

'Shall we find you a suitcase for your things?' Louise suggested.

He frowned. 'I can carry them.'

'But you must have . . .?' she began.

'The rest of my clothes are at Aunty Tegan's,' he replied loftily, going out to the car.

'Is that all he's got?' Louise whispered. 'Hasn't he any books? Or toys? What about his toys? Surely he has a train set or something?'

Aunt Tegan looked at her severely. 'He hasn't been spoilt like you and your sisters, you know. I always said to Liza that you were all overindulged and had no idea what the real world was like; well, now you know. And I hope you're not going to spoil a decent little boy like Tostig. He's used to having nothing. He'll play happily for hours with sticks and stones and he has his comics to read.'

'But . . .' Louise began, then stopped, once again filled with guilt. If she'd kept him when he'd been born, he'd have had a nursery filled with toys and books, the garden at Hartley to play in, and Nanny to teach him nursery rhymes. By now he'd have been at St Peter's Court Prep School, where her father had gone, getting a good education.

Rupert had been denied all that she'd taken for granted, and the feeling that she'd failed him overwhelmed her now.

The next two weeks were fraught as Louise and Shane struggled to get Tostig to accept them as his parents. He fought them every inch of the way, refusing the food put in front of him, and insisting on wearing his worn and grubby clothes, especially his jumpers which his ma had bought him. Louise wasn't even allowed to wash them.

The London traffic terrified him as did the crowded streets. Shane bought him some small toy cars which came in match boxes, a skipping rope, and a train set with a circular track, but he refused to play with them, spending his time instead kicking around their little back garden, or re-reading his beloved comics. Louise bought him some books recommended for his age group, but he tossed them aside and she began to despair of ever getting through to him.

Then every night there was the Battle of the Bath. It seemed he'd never been in a conventional bath in his life. He'd been used to sitting in an old tin tub which his da had set before the kitchen range every Saturday night, and his ma had filled with buckets of warm water.

When Louise led him into the bathroom on the first night and she turned on the taps he screamed and yelled, refusing to get into the water. Then he chucked away the bar of Imperial Leather soap on the rack, and demanded carbolic soap because it smelled 'clean'. Somehow she managed to persuade him to wash himself, but then came a nightly tantrum as he wanted to sleep in his vest and pants instead of the new striped pyjamas she'd bought him.

'I'm not wearing those bloody things!' he yelled one evening, throwing them on the floor.

'Rupert, you are not to swear,' she told him severely.

'My name's not bloody Rupert!' he shouted. 'My name's Tostig! Why do you keep calling me Rupert? I hate the name! I hate it here! And I hate you! I want to go back to my farm and if you try to stop me I'll run away!'

Louise sent him to bed without his supper, and then felt stricken when a little while later she heard sobbing coming from his room.

'I can't *bear* this,' she told Shane after two exhausting weeks. 'He's so unhappy and he hates us and he hates being here, and I've tried so hard . . .' She covered her face with her hands. 'He's missing his . . . his parents,' she added with finality, because that was the truth. Rupert thought of the farmer and his wife as his parents, and merely telling him it wasn't so had made no difference. He had no sense of belonging to them, and it was obvious he wasn't even going to try.

'Come and sit down, dearest,' Shane said in concern, as he lead her over to the sitting room sofa. 'You're exhausted, that's the trouble. You've got Daisy to look after, and the house and the cooking, and it's too much to expect you to rehabilitate Rupert all on your own.'

'I feel I'm letting him down . . . that I've always let him down and it's all my fault. We even promised him a puppy and I haven't got around to getting one yet. He doesn't trust us, Shane,' she added in desperation. 'What are we going to do?'

'For a start, stop blaming yourself, Louise. It's not your fault. Why don't we take both Rupert and Daisy down to Hartley for a couple of weeks? I think he will adjust better if we're in the country and he'll have Sophia and Jonathan for company. Your family wouldn't object, would they?'

'Mummy won't approve, because it will confirm to the whole village that he's my son, but Daddy and Granny won't mind.' Her face had brightened and her eyes lit up. 'Oh, Shane, I think it's a wonderful idea. He'd love Hartley and he might be able to learn to ride Jonathan's pony.' Her smile broadened. 'You are brilliant!'

He grinned sheepishly, always embarrassed by praise. 'Then let's do it. We need the help of the whole family if Rupert is going to settle down. Poor little chap, it's not surprising that he's grieving for the couple who brought him up. But children do adjust and I believe he just needs time and lots of healthy outdoor exercise and distraction.'

'I'd really wanted to do this on our own, but he will probably adjust better with the help of the rest of the family. But I long for it to be just you and me, Shane, with Daisy and Rupert. Our own little family.'

Shane smiled at her. 'I know Louise, but you're an incurable romantic, and that's what I love about you. Because you were so thrilled to have him back you felt it was like the happy ending of a fairy story, didn't you? You know, long lost little boy reunited with his real mother, who he'd recognize at once and fall into her arms with rapturous happiness! But real life isn't like that, I'm afraid.'

She gave him a rueful smile. 'No, it's not, is it?'

He put his arms around her and hugged her. 'I'm owed some leave, so I'll take you all down, and stay for as long as I can. There is something else we should talk about, too.'

She looked at him with anxiety in every line of her face. 'What? What else is there to talk about?' she asked nervously.

'Now is the time to be honest with Rupert, and I think you should tell him about his real father. Let him understand I'm his step-father and I'll always be here to love and support him, but I think we should arrange for them to meet at some point, don't you?'

'Oh, my God!' Louise looked stunned. For a moment she felt horrified at having to face more of her past. But Shane was right. Not only should they meet, but Jack should be given access to Rupert, so they could build a father-and-son relationship.

'Don't you think we should let Rupert get used to us first? Before he meets Jack?' she asked, desperate to play for time, until she could get used to the changing sands of her life. 'I don't even know how to get hold of Jack.'

'His aunt still lives in the village, doesn't she? Why don't we go and ask her for his address when we're at Hartley?'

Louise's head was spinning. Too much was happening too fast, and she felt a sense of nervous dread at having to see Jack again. It had been so awkward when he'd turned up just before she'd married Shane, and the worst part was realizing that they no longer had anything in common. Her family had been right; marriage between them, even if they'd been older, would never have worked.

'Supposing Rupert likes him more than me?' she suddenly blurted out, jealousy mingled with fear making her voice high pitched.

'Why should he?' Shane asked in surprise.

'Because . . . Oh, God, I sound like my mother, but because Jack is the same class as the couple who adopted Rupert. He's bound to feel more comfortable with him, and even have more in common with Jack than he does with us?'

Shane looked thoughtful for a moment. 'We're going to have to put the boy's happiness before our own,' he said slowly. 'You'll have to let Jack have visiting rights, or Rupert will never forgive you. Do you think Jack will show an interest in his son?'

Louise nodded. 'I know he will. That last time he came to see me he said he wished he'd had a chance to see the baby before I gave him away. I felt dreadful about it at the time, but I did understand how he felt,' she added with honesty. She turned to look at Shane. 'You do know that it's you, and only you that I love, though, don't you? What I had with Jack was a passing fancy. I was fifteen and probably more in love with love than anything else.'

Shane grinned, the skin around his eyes crinkling at the corners. 'Weren't you also in love at the same time with Rupert Brooke and his poetry?' he teased gently. 'Hence the name of your baby?'

'Yes,' she admitted. 'I had *such* romantic notions at that age.'

Shane leaned forward and kissed her gently on the mouth. 'Don't lose all your romantic dreams, sweetheart. I want you to stay just the way you are. Try not to worry. I'm sure that once we're at Hartley things will get better with Rupert. We'll soon get him house trained,' he added jokingly.

'I hope so,' Louise said, remembering how, when they'd arrived home from Wales, he'd asked if 'the lavvy was in the backyard?' and where was the pot in his bedroom kept? His astonishment at seeing their pretty bathroom would have been comical if she hadn't found it so sad.

The lime trees that lined the drive of Hartley were tinged with gold, but there was still warmth in the sun as Shane drove them back to Louise's childhood home.

The rose pink Georgian house, decked out in the last of the climbing summer roses, stood serenely surrounded by lawns and flower beds and mature oak and elm trees. The polished windows seemed to be winking at them in the sunshine, and as always, the white front door stood open in welcome. On the warm stone steps the family dogs slumbered drowsily.

'Here we are!' Louise burst out excitedly, bouncing a gurgling Daisy on her knee. 'Look!' she said, turning to Rupert who was sitting in the back with Bella and the kitten, who was in a basket. 'Look! This is Hartley, Rupert. This is my old home, where we're going to stay.'

Rupert, looking sullen, turned his head away and ignored her. His eyes were blank, his expression listless, and his small mouth drooped with sadness.

Louise and Shane exchanged glances, and she was suddenly filled with a sense of foreboding. It wasn't only that she hoped Hartley Hall would work its magic on Rupert, as it had done on all the Granville family during two world wars and a string of personal disasters; she also hoped it would give her the strength to face her past mistakes. For letting Jack back into her life, for Rupert's sake, could prove to be the biggest mistake of all.

'You should have got a bigger dining room table, Henry,' Liza wailed with irritation. 'How am I supposed to get ten people around this one?'

'How was I to know you intended trying to give grand dinner parties when I got this flat?' Henry retorted with equal annoyance. He was desperately tired and hadn't felt well for the past few days. The problem was his workload at the bank had increased in the past year because the country was emerging from the doldrums of the late forties and Britain was on the brink of prosperity once again. Business at Hammerton's was good, but he was beginning to feel he could no longer cope with the pressure of being Chairman.

Coming back from work that evening, all he was looking forward to was a quiet supper, before the new novelty of watching the news on a television screen which he found fascinating. Then he wanted an early night.

Instead, their flat was in an uproar as hired caterers, a butler and a footman rushed around preparing for a dinner party he'd forgotten all about.

'Oh, really, Henry!' Liza scolded, 'How could you forget? We've got Lady Diana Cooper coming, the Duke and Duchess of Northumberland, Lord and Lady Mountbatten, and I've invited the Duke of Marlborough's heir, Lord Blandford, because I've persuaded Charlotte to stay in for once . . . now that *would* be a good match for her, and the . . .'

'All right, all right,' Henry protested, rubbing his forehead. 'Why are you calling them by their titles? They're our *friends*, – Dickie and Edwina Mountbatten, Diana Cooper and so on. I've told you it's fearfully common to refer to our friends by their titles. It sounds as if you're bragging to impress yourself, for God's sake!'

Liza's face fell and she turned scarlet. She simply couldn't help herself. She *knew* she was tremendously impressed by

156

titles. She still couldn't quite believe that titled people came to her dinner parties. Her only regret in life was that she didn't have one herself. She felt quite aggrieved that both Rosie and Juliet had married titled men, only for their marriages to end, so they were now just plain 'Mrs'.

'Henry, don't talk to me like that,' she whispered, so the hired staff wouldn't hear them arguing. 'The point is, how are we going to get them all round that stupid little table?'

'Why don't I go out? That would give you enough room!' he retorted, turning his back on her and walking out of the room.

She stared after him as he marched along the narrow corridor to their bedroom, appalled by his mood. What was the matter with him? He was usually so kind and only teased her in a joking way about her class obsession.

Swaying in a billowing swirl of black taffeta, and hung about with diamonds, she hurried into the tiny kitchen, where a chaotic scene met her eyes, as the caterer laid out the prepared first course of buttered shrimps with toast, while the rack of lamb roasted in the oven. There was food and dishes on every surface, and even on the floor.

'We're a bit short of space in here, madam,' the butler remarked in a slightly critical tone. Liza grieved inwardly for the loss of Parsons, and a kitchen that had been big enough to hold a drinks party for fifty people.

'That can't be helped,' she snapped crossly. 'You're going to have to put that narrow side table at one end of the dining room table, then we can easily sit ten. You'll find two more chairs in the hall.'

'Yes, madam.'

'And I'd like a glass of champagne, please. And take one to Mr Granville as well.'

'Yes, madam.'

As she swept away, skirt rustling, bracelets rattling, she distinctly heard one of the hired helps whisper, 'Who does she think she is? The Queen of Sheba?'

'What's the matter, Mummy?' Charlotte asked, coming out of her bedroom at that moment, in a pink satin Dior dress, which showed off her tiny waist.

'Nothing,' Liza sighed theatrically. 'It's just so ghastly not having one's own staff any more. These hired people really are hopeless.'

'Where's Daddy?'

'Changing . . . I hope,' Liza replied, suddenly worried. Henry couldn't have been serious, surely, when he'd said he'd go out? 'Why don't *you* take him a glass of champagne, darling?' she coaxed. 'He's a bit grumpy; he forgot we had a dinner party tonight.'

'He's so tired these days,' Charlotte said sadly. 'He works too hard.'

As Charlotte left the room, Liza walked over to the horrid little modern fireplace and looked at her reflection in the mirror which hung about it. In spite of having spent the morning at Elizabeth Arden having a facial, she looked old and strained. She touched her tightly permed hair with a manicured hand, and gave a deep sigh. She and Henry were at loggerheads these days. He was always tired, saying he wished they hadn't taken a flat in town, and she was bursting with frustration, because having returned to London at last, she longed to get back into the swing of things. Even at weekends he was bad tempered, grumbling about everything and criticising her all the time.

She took a swig of champagne, suddenly feeling nervous. What would happen if he no longer loved her? Worse, what would she do if he'd found someone else? Perhaps she should cut back on inviting people to the flat. But then, if you didn't entertain, you didn't get asked out. She downed the rest of her champagne, decided she must act merrily for the benefit of the guests and promptly ordered her glass to be refilled.

To her intense relief Henry appeared looking suave and immaculately groomed in his dinner jacket, just before the first guests arrived. No one, enveloped in the warmth of his welcome and charm, would have guessed that half an hour before he'd been in a foul mood.

'How is Rosie?' Lady Diana Cooper asked Liza, as they sipped their drinks and nibbled from a platter of canapés the footmen was handing around. 'It seems only the other day I came to her coming-out ball in that divine house you had in Green Street.'

'She's still in Monte Carlo,' Liza replied cryptically, as if it were a section of Alcatraz. 'I don't know when, or if, she'll return to England.'

Lady Diana lowered her voice diplomatically. 'Is she going to marry this chap she ran off with? What's his name?'

'Baron Philibert Guerin. His aunt is Lady Fulsham. Henry used to know her late husband, but Salton doesn't want a divorce so I don't know what's going to happen.'

Lady Diana pursed her beautiful lips and her forget-me-not blue eyes were penetrating. 'Duff and I used to know the Guerin family. Penniless, you know, my dear. Quite penniless.'

Liza leaned closer, whispering now. 'Philibert is Lady Fulsham's heir. I hear her husband left her a packet.'

At that moment the Northumberlands and the Mountbattens arrived and Liza switched into hostess mode, fluttered from guest to guest, delighting in her role of society hostess once again.

'Louise will be there when we get home, won't she?' Henry remarked with pleasure as he drove them down to Hartley the next afternoon.

'Yes.' Liza had come down to earth with a bump when she'd woken up, the euphoria she'd felt the night before, vanished like the bubbles in champagne.

'I'm longing to see Rupert.'

'I gather he's completely wild,' Liza retorted drily. 'I dread to think what characteristics he's inherited.'

'He's still Louise's child.' Henry's tone was suddenly cold.

'But he's been brought up by a farmer and his wife. Aunt Tegan might at least have put him with a better family than that.'

Henry spoke sarcastically. 'I imagine she didn't think she'd ever have to face your wrath that he was with working-class people.'

'That's a horrid thing to say,' Liza complained. 'I don't understand you, Henry. I would have thought you'd want the very best for your children, but there's Charlotte, throwing her chances away by being a model. And Amanda, burying herself at university, not caring how she looks; what's going to become of her? Rosie made the mistake of marrying that American and now her behaviour is causing a scandal! Now the whole village is going to know this boy is Louise's child. It's a disaster! Her reputation, which I was so careful to guard, will now be in shreds.' She sighed deeply. 'Sometimes I wonder why I bother. You never give me any support.'

159

Henry was silent for a few moments, his eyes fixed on the road ahead. Then he spoke. 'Surely you've also got something bad to say about Juliet?' he enquired.

She flashed him an angry look. 'Oh, your beloved Juliet! She can't do *anything* wrong in your eyes, can she?'

He ignored the jibe, but pressed down harder on the accelerator as if he wanted to punish the engine. 'I'm afraid you're disappointed with the life I've given you,' he said at last, his tone even.

'I just think that we haven't reached our potential and neither have the girls,' she replied sulkily.

'Of course that depends on what one's aims are? Money, power or position are the three most common ambitions but there is one other; happiness. As long as our children find happiness, I think that's the most important thing of all.'

'But happiness depends on getting what you want.'

He glanced at her discontented profile. 'I'm not sure, Liza, that you'd recognize happiness if it swamped you, because you'd always be looking over the fence, wondering if the next field isn't greener.'

'That's not true!' she exclaimed, enraged. 'Other people have children who make brilliant marriages and do well for themselves, so why haven't our girls done better? Only Juliet married a man who seemed to have everything; a dukedom, a castle and half of Scotland, and an enormous fortune, and . . .'

'It turned out to be a sham of a marriage because he was homosexual,' Henry cut in bluntly, 'and it was you who wanted that marriage more than anything. You filled Juliet and Rosie's heads with a great deal of nonsense and I think they felt compelled to follow *your* dreams and ambitions.'

She turned on him indignantly. 'Henry! I only wanted the best for them, what's wrong with that?'

'Marrying what you call "brilliantly" isn't necessarily "for the best". It certainly doesn't always lead to happiness.'

'It did for me,' she retorted quickly, then stopped, her bottom lip quivering. 'At least it used to, but all you do is pick fault with me these days. What's wrong? Why aren't we happy any more?' she added tearfully. 'I still love you. All I want is for us to be happy.'

Relenting for a moment, he reached out and laid his left hand over hers, steering the car with his other hand. 'We can be happy again, if you'd just calm down,' he explained. 'Liza, I can't go on working as hard as I'm doing *and* socialize every night and at weekends, too.'

'Then don't work so hard,' she said stupidly.

'I'm trying to recoup the enormous financial losses I incurred during the war. I lost thousands of pounds in foreign investments and no matter how hard I work I'll never be able to rebuild my fortune. But I can make sure you and the girls are all right, and that Hartley remains standing for the next generation.'

Liza dabbed her eyes with a tiny lace edged handkerchief. 'Oh, don't let's have this morbid conversation. I simply can't bear it.'

'Facts are facts, and I'm sixty-one, my dear,' he told her flatly. 'Most of my friends have already retired, and I will as soon as I feel I can, but meanwhile, let's lead a quieter life, for God's sake.'

Subdued, Liza remained silent, letting the shock of realizing how old Henry was, sink in. Why was she so surprised? She was fifty-four after all, but the difference was that she didn't feel it. If someone had asked her how old she was and not given her time to think, she'd have said she was forty, maybe forty-one.

The most ghastly thing of all, she reflected, was the knowledge that she'd got as far in life as she was ever going to get, and from now on it was going to be a downward path all the way.

Henry might not mind, but she resented the fact bitterly.

# Eleven

'My giddy Aunt!' Amanda exclaimed looking out of the library window at Rupert, who was in the paddock with Sophia and Jonathan, feeding carrots and apples to the ponies. 'He's the image of Jack, isn't he?'

She'd driven over from Oxford to have Sunday lunch at Hartley and found the whole family, with the exception of Rosie, gathered together for the weekend.

Liza winced at Amanda's enthusiasm. 'He is good looking,' she admitted grudgingly, 'but he's a holy terror. He refuses to do anything he's told and he hates having a bath and—'

'Oh, for goodness sake, Ma, he's only nine and he's been brought up in the wilds of Wales, what do you expect? Little Lord Fauntleroy?'

'He's also just lost the couple he looked upon as parents,' Juliet pointed out loyally. She and Daniel had been very taken with Rupert, and saw him as a frightened little boy with a lot of spirit who merely needed to be tamed. 'Give him time. He'll settle eventually and I think Louise and Shane are doing a wonderful job.'

Louise smiled at her gratefully. 'I'm glad he's getting on so well with Sophia and Johnnie, and of course he adores animals.'

'I hear you've given him a puppy! Clever you.'

'Remember how you gave me Bella, when I was practically suicidal?' Louise recalled.

Juliet nodded. 'What did you get Rupert?'

'A Norfolk terrier bitch called Bridie. She's only two months old and adorable.'

'I hope she's in the gun room, Louise?' her mother fretted. 'I don't want her making a mess everywhere.'

Louise and Juliet exchanged looks.

'Let's go into the garden,' Juliet said firmly. 'All the dogs can come with us.'

162

Amanda and Louise with Daisy followed her out of the room, leaving Liza sitting by the smouldering fire. Wearing warm coats and headscarves, they walked with the dogs to the paddock.

'It's a dreadful thing to say,' Louise remarked when they were out of earshot of the house, 'but it would be so much more peaceful if Mama wasn't here, wouldn't it? If it was just Daddy and Granny and us? We'd all have such a laugh, wouldn't we?'

Amanda adjusted the glasses on her nose. 'Why do you think I hardly ever come home? I can't get away during the week when Mum's in town, and at weekends she's always here.'

'I don't know why she bothers,' Juliet remarked. 'She's always hated Hartley.'

Louise let out a little groan. 'How can anyone hate Hartley, for goodness sake! It's the best place in the world to be. I'd live here and so would Shane if it wasn't for his work.'

'So would I,' Amanda agreed, 'although when I eventually become an MP I'll have to get a seat in the Midlands and live up there. I don't imagine there'll be any support for a Labour candidate in this part of the world.'

'You're still set on a life in politics?' Juliet asked, half in admiration and half in amusement. She'd always thought her sister would outgrow her burning desire to represent the under-privileged and create a utopia where everyone was equal.

'What else?' Amanda retorted stoutly. 'Sorry girls, and nothing personal, but I couldn't live the shallow life you two live, where your world begins and ends with husbands and babies, and what to wear and whose party to go to!'

'I don't lead that sort of life.' Louise laughed. 'And Shane is doing one of the most worthwhile jobs there are.'

Amanda looked kindly at her, but she spoke bluntly. 'It would be more worthwhile if he treated his patients without charging, though, wouldn't it? The government should pay for people to have all the medical care they need. Do you realize there are thousands of people in this country who are ill, or even dying, but they're too poor to afford to see a doctor!'

'There is talk of a national health system that will do just that,' Louise ventured mildly.

'Talk, talk, talk,' Amanda rattled on. 'Never mind, there's another general election next year. Mr Attlee is bound to get in again and then the Labour Party can really get to grips with things.'

'Having fun, Rupert?' Louise called out when they reached the fencing round the paddock.

He turned his back on her with a dismissive gesture and patted the neck of Jonathan's brown gelding.

'Do you want a leg-up?' Amanda asked briskly in her loud voice.

Louise said quickly, 'Oh, I don't think so, not without a saddle. He's never ridden before.' Daisy clambered up the fence on her strong little legs to get a better look.

'He can use my saddle,' Jonathan offered politely.

'It'll soon be time for lunch,' Juliet pointed out, thinking how different the cousins looked. Jonathan, who'd become Lord Padmore on the death of his father, was a typical product of an old-fashioned nanny. Although he was eleven, he looked much younger with a peaches and cream English complexion, neatly brushed hair, and Rosie's blue eyes. Dressed in a brown tweed suit and polished brogues, he was a miniature edition of Henry.

Rupert, on the other hand, looked more like a ruffian with his unruly locks, tanned skin from living an outdoor life, and knowing watchful eyes.

'He's a beautiful child,' Juliet whispered to Louise. 'Jack had the same colouring, didn't he?'

'Has the same colouring,' Louise corrected her. 'He may be coming over this weekend to meet Rupert.'

Juliet clutched her sister's arm in amazement. 'No! Really? You never said . . . Oh, my God! Does Mama know?'

'Know what?' Amanda butted in, turning to look at them.

'Hush,' Louise warned in a low voice. 'Rupert doesn't know it yet, but Jack may be coming to see him today or tomorrow.'

'Crikey! Why didn't you say?' boomed Amanda in astonishment.

'Because I don't want him to be disappointed if Jack doesn't turn up. His aunt said she'd try and get hold of him, but she couldn't promise.'

Juliet shook her head slowly. 'I can't believe it. Do you realize, Louise, that this is the most momentous . . . not to say romantic thing that could have happened?'

Amanda snorted. 'Really, Jules, you read too many trashy novels.'

'No, I don't!'

'There's nothing in the least romantic about it,' Louise pointed out. 'It's nerve-wracking. In fact, I'm terrified.'

Amanda straightened her shoulders in her baggy tweed jacket. 'Terrified? What of?'

'Everything. Rupert hasn't accepted me as his mother yet. What's he going to feel towards Shane, who he at least respects, if his own father turns up? And supposing Rupert likes Jack more than me? What shall I do then? What if Jack wants to look after him permanently? I could lose Rupert all over again.'

'Calm down and stop twittering on, for goodness sake,' Amanda said bluntly. 'Why cross your bridges before you come to them?'

Juliet put an arm around Louise's shoulders. 'I can understand exactly how you feel, darling. But try not to worry, and the great thing is, don't let Rupert get worried and upset.'

'I know.'

Sophia came up to the fence, her pony following her like an affectionate dog. 'What are you talking about?' she asked suspiciously. She was a lanky twelve year old now, with Rosie's discontented mouth and her late father's pale grey eyes. 'Were you talking about Mummy?' she demanded in a rude voice.

'Not at all,' Juliet said calmly, giving her a look. 'We were actually saying how nice it is for Rupert to have come back to us all.'

'He's no good at anything, though,' Sophia said disdainfully. 'He doesn't know how to play tennis or ride, and he can't swim, or play cards or . . .'

'That's because he hasn't been as lucky as you and Jonathan,' Juliet said firmly. She had the strangest feeling that her prickly relationship with Rosie was repeating itself with Sophia. 'I don't think you realize what a wonderful life you lead. You've always had the best of everything and up until now Rupert has been deprived of the things you take for granted.'

Sophia gave a scoffing grunt. 'What? The best of everything? My father was killed when I was small, and now my mother's run off with a frog and we don't know when we'll see her again. I don't call *that* the best of everything.'

'There are some children in this country who have *nothing*!' Amanda declared, weighing in heavily. 'They live in squalor, with not enough to eat! You live in the lap of luxury without even appreciating it.'

'So do you,' Sophia retorted, sounding so like Rosie in a debate that Juliet nearly laughed out loud.

'Never mind,' Louise said peaceably, 'from now on Rupert's going to have everything he needs so his life will be as happy as we can make it.'

Rupert suddenly turned swiftly and came bounding across the grass to where they stood by the fence.

His face was flushed and he spoke angrily. 'You won't make me happy if you don't let me go back to my farm! I hate it here. I hate Sophia and Johnnie; they're stuck-up toffee-nosed *buggers*!'

There was a stunned silence. Then Louise spoke. 'Please do not swear, Rupert.'

He did an affected little jig, mimicking her voice. '"*Please* do not swear, Roo-pert!" Me name's *Tostig*! How many times do I have to tell you that?' Then he turned and flounced off, kicking tufts of grass with his little boots as he went.

Sophia gazed after him. She looked deeply impressed.

Juliet, Amanda and Louise stared at each other, their mouths open.

'What are buggers?' Daisy asked plaintively from her perch on the top of the fence.

'Some one who's silly,' Louise said swiftly, 'but it's a very rude thing to say. Now come along, let's go in to lunch, or Granny will wonder what's happened to us.'

As they walked back to the house with the four children and the dogs trailing behind them, they met Henry, who was on his way to meet them.

'Louise darling,' he said, 'Would you like to come to the study? On your own,' he added carefully.

She started to shake and he took her arm gently.

'Daddy, shall I bring . . .?'

'Not yet. Juliet can tell Rupert to get ready for lunch.'

'Is Shane . . .?'

'In the drawing room with the others, but he knows,' Henry whispered, leading the way into the house.

Amanda raised her thick eyebrows knowingly and Juliet said softly, 'I'd give anything to be a fly on the library wall at this moment.'

Jack was sitting awkwardly on the library sofa, holding his brown felt trilby with both hands, between his knees. When Henry and Louise entered the room, he jumped to his feet as if he'd had an electric shock.

'I'll leave you two now,' Henry said. 'There are drinks on the tray; help yourselves.' Then he left the room and quietly shut the door behind him.

Louise regarded Jack with her customary open and honest gaze and thought how much he'd aged, even since their meeting just before she'd married Shane.

Jack, looking at her with a kind of wonder, was amazed at how she'd fined down since she'd been the fifteen-year-old school girl he'd first fallen in love with. She was slim now and womanly, with rounded breasts and an expression of warm serenity.

'You all right then?' he asked diffidently.

'Yes.' She smiled.

Oh, how he remembered that sweet smile that had so captivated him all those years ago. 'So you got the boy back?'

Louise nodded. 'Sit down, Jack. What would you like to drink?'

'I'm OK. Where is he now?' he asked eagerly, still clutching his hat.

'Getting ready for lunch. I didn't tell him about you, in case you couldn't come and I didn't want him to be disappointed.'

Jack's eyes looked flat with disappointment, and Louise noticed the soft peachy down of his upper lip and cheeks when he'd been a boy had turned to fair bristles.

'Is he all right?'

Louise hesitated. 'He's fine, but the loss of the couple he thought were his parents has made him very hostile towards me. Don't be upset if he's hostile towards you too, when you see him. It's me he blames for abandoning him when he was born and Shane and I are having to go very carefully, until he adjusts to us all.'

'Doesn't he ask about me, then?' There was a spark of hope in Jack's eyes now.

'He doesn't ask about anything in his new life. I don't even know if it's occurred to him that he *has* a real father. We've made it plain Shane's his step-father and it was Shane who suggested we should contact you, so that Rupert can come to terms with how he came to be born.' Louise's voice wobbled dangerously. 'And why he's come back to us.'

'It ain't "us" though, is it? It's you and your 'usband and the whole bloomin' Granville family. That's who 'e's come back to.'

Louise studied the carpet at her feet, a blush rising to her cheeks. 'I know, Jack. I know. It's a terribly difficult situation, but I think we have to think about Rupert's happiness before we think about ourselves.'

'Fair enough.'

'I don't want the poor little boy to be made more confused than he already is.' Briefly she outlined his childhood in a poverty-stricken farmhouse, and how he hadn't even had any toys to play with.

'When we brought him back to London with us, he had an old football, some comics and a battered biscuit tin, containing his "treasures" as he called them; a shell, some unusual stones –' she was crying openly now, wiping her cheeks with the back of her hand – and a tiny wooden dog his da had carved with a pen knife.'

'Don't take on so, Lou,' Jake said gruffly. 'It ain't your fault.'

She fished a handkerchief out of her skirt pocket and blew her nose.

'Sorry,' she murmured apologetically. 'I love him so much and it's so upsetting that he doesn't want to have anything to do with me.'

'Are you livin' down here again, then?'

'No, we live in London, but Shane and I thought he might settle better if we stayed here for a bit. He's got Rosie's children to play with and Granny's so good with children. Where do you live now?'

'Stepney. I wanted to get back to the East End after the war, and me dad's out of prison now, so I'm livin' with 'im. I'm getting good wages as a plumber now, in a big firm. So . . . when can I see our boy?'

The word 'our' was like a knife plunging into Louise's

heart. Not that she had any romantic feelings for Jack, but it was the sadness of the whole mess she'd made by falling so hopelessly in love when she'd been young. And now although Rupert would get to know them, they'd never be there for him as parents who lived together, as a family unit.

'I'll fetch him now,' she said, rising. 'And Jack . . .'

'Yup?'

'If all goes well, will you be able to see him regularly? Shane says it's important we don't break promises to him and we stick to any arrangement that's made.'

'You can count on me, Lou,' he replied stoutly.

Rupert was in the drawing room sitting beside Lady Anne, who was showing him a book filled with engravings of wild animals. Liza, Henry and Shane were talking to Juliet and Amanda, while Sophia and Jonathan were trying to find the right pieces for a big jigsaw which was spread out on a card table.

'Rupert, I want you to come and meet someone,' Louise said brightly, though her hands were shaking.

He scowled at her. 'I don't want to.'

Lady Anne beamed at him. 'You never know, it might be a lovely surprise!'

'I want to go on looking at the pictures of animals,' he said rebelliously.

'I promise we'll look at it again this afternoon,' she whispered. 'Anyway, we have to stop for lunch and we're having beef and roast potatoes.'

Rupert got reluctantly to his feet and walked slowly towards Louise. Lady Anne mouthed 'good luck' to her granddaughter, and everyone in the room turned to smile encouragingly at Louise.

'Who are we going to see?' Rupert asked in a small voice as they crossed the big square hall.

Louise paused and laid a gentle hand on his bony shoulder. 'You know that everyone has a mother and a father?'

His expression was impassive.

'And you know that I'm your real mother? Well, now you're going to meet your real father. He's come to see you.'

A tiny flicker of anxiety showed in his eyes. 'What's going to happen to Shane then?'

She tightened her grip reassuringly. 'Shane will always be with us, whatever happens. He loves you and he'll always look after both of us.'

'And Daisy?'

'Of course.' To her amazement Rupert let her slide her hand down his arm until she held his hand. 'Let's go and meet your dad.'

'How are you doin', then, mate?' Jack asked, jumping up from the sofa again, when they entered the room.

Rupert looked at him cautiously.

Jack shot Louise an anxious look. 'So wot 'ave you bin doin' with yourself?' he continued.

Rupert gazed down at his boots, from which he refused to be parted. 'Nothing much.'

'Why don't we have a drink before lunch?' Louise suggested going over to the drinks tray. 'Rupert, you'd like orange squash, wouldn't you? What would you like, Jack?'

'I'll 'ave a beer.'

Beer was not one of her father's drinks. 'I'll be back in a sec,' she said, rushing to the kitchen. Warwick drank beer and there were sure to be some bottles of it in the larder.

When she returned to the library, Rupert was standing by the sofa, watching Jack open and shut the various parts of his penknife.

'With this 'ere bit you can open bottles, and this is a corkscrew . . .'

Rupert looked up at Louise. 'Can I have one of these?' he demanded.

Louise hesitated, the different sized blades looked fearsome and she was just about to tell him he could have one when he was older, when Jack spoke.

''Ere mate, you keep this one.'

It was the first time Louise had seen Rupert's face light up and he actually smiled into the face of his father. 'Don't you want it?'

Jack chuckled, giving the boy a playful little punch on the shoulder. 'I can get myself another one. Let's call it a present to celebrate you an' me meetin' for the first time, eh? How about that?'

Watching them together, Louise saw how, just for a moment, Jack looked young and happy again, just as he'd done when she'd first known him.

'Your mum tells me you've got a puppy? Can I see him?'

'Why don't you both come and have lunch first?' Louise suggested. 'Then Rupert can show you Bridie, and you could both take her out in the garden.'

Jack looked up at Louise. 'Are you sure your family want me to stay for me dinner?'

Her gaze was direct. 'They're expecting you,' she said firmly.

'Blimey! Is it the war that's changed things, or wot?'

'It's the joy of having Rupert back that's changed things,' she replied. 'And definitely for the better, too.'

Jack was seated next to Rupert and Amanda, who immediately took him under her wing, thinking of him as an example of a decent young man who hadn't been given a chance because of snobbery.

'You can do anything you like with your life,' she told him boldly. 'You're obviously intelligent so why don't you study for something? Or you could start your own business? Why be employed by a capitalist who pockets the profits and keeps you on a low wage, when you could make yourself a small fortune?'

Rupert listened to them talking with fascination. Finally he spoke. 'Dad, you must come and stay with me, on my farm one day.'

Everyone around the table paused with bated breath. He'd actually called Jack 'Dad'.

His father laughingly accepted the invitation while Louise sat quite still, torn between happiness at the breakthrough, and at the same time a feeling of deep hurt. In half an hour Rupert had accepted Jack as his father, yet he still rejected her as his mother and refused to let her get close.

Fighting back tears of jealousy, she struggled through the rest of lunch, letting everyone else do the talking. It was a relief when they finally rose from the table and went their separate ways; Lady Anne to rest and listen to the wireless in her sitting room, Liza and Henry to read the newspapers in the conservatory, while Juliet and Daniel took Tristan out for a walk in the garden. Meanwhile Amanda shooed Sophia and Jonathan into the garden. 'I'm going to change,' she told them, 'then I'll give you two a good thrashing on the tennis court.'

Louise gathered up Daisy in her arms, although she was now quite heavy and carried her up the stairs. 'Why don't I

take you to the nursery for your afternoon nap, my darling?'
she suggested, 'then we can play with your dolls' house before
tea?'

When she came downstairs again a few minutes later, Shane
was waiting for her in the hall. He'd been watching her with
deep compassion throughout lunch, knowing how much pain
she was suffering. Now he opened his arms to her and without
saying a word, held her close.

'What am I going to do?' she asked him despondently. 'I
don't think Rupert is ever going to like me.'

'It'll be all right, sweetheart,' Shane promised. 'Give him
time. Right now I think he takes to men more than women.
He might see it as a sign of weakness and maybe he's afraid
of being a mummy's boy. We don't know what sort of a relationship he had with his adopted mother, do we? Try and be
patient, and I'm sure you'll win him around in time. So far,
you've done brilliantly. We haven't had a tantrum for two days
and the Battle of the Bath seems to have ended, too,' he added
jokingly, to lighten the atmosphere.

Louise gave him a wistful smile. 'Jack's going to be a good
father, isn't he?'

'That's probably because he's not trying.'

'And I'm trying too hard,' she observed quietly.

Louise and Shane brought Rupert and Daisy back to London
a week later, but if she'd hoped being at Hartley would bring
about a change in Rupert's attitude towards her, she was sorely
disappointed. Within hours he was being off-hand and dis-
obedient and when she told him she was looking at suitable
day schools to send him to, he threatened to run away again,
back to the farm.

Punishing him by sending him to his room had no effect,
and as he didn't play with the toys Shane had bought him, it
was pointless taking them away from him. Only Bridie brought
out a gentle and affectionate side to his character, and he
insisted on feeding her and brushing her coat every day, and
training her to fetch back the balls he threw for her in the
small back garden.

Every night, Louise left Bridie to sleep in her basket in the
kitchen, which Rupert didn't like but grudgingly accepted.
Then one night, when Shane was on duty at St Stephen's,

Louise checked on the children after she'd had her bath. Daisy, now sleeping in a 'big girl's bed', as she called it, was fast asleep, her little hands clutching her teddy bear. Then Louise put her head round Rupert's door. Two little bright eyes looked at her, and two small silky ears were pricked up. Peering into the darkness, she saw Rupert's tanned arms encircling Bridie's body as he held her fast to his chest.

Louise crept away, not having the heart to disturb them. Hadn't she slept with Bella on the pillow beside her, to console her when she'd been forced to give Rupert away?

Two days later, Louise was upstairs making the beds when she heard fearful screams from the kitchen.

'Mum . . .! *Mum* . . .!'

She flew down the stairs. In the kitchen Rupert was holding Daisy upside down by her legs.

'Quick, Mum, she's choking on a grape!' Rupert yelled, shaking the little girl. 'She's going a funny colour . . .'

Louise grabbed Daisy from him and thumped her hard on the back.

Nothing happened except for the horrible gasping noises Daisy was making.

'Dial 999 for an ambulance,' Louise shouted, draping the child over her left arm and thumping her again between her shoulder blades.

Rupert dashed into the hall where the telephone stood on a shelf on the wall.

'Help,' she heard him scream, 'my little sister's choking, she's dying . . .' His voice ended in a sob.

At that moment the grape came shooting out of Daisy's mouth and she started wailing.

Louise sank to her knees, weak with shock and relief, clutching her small daughter as if she could never bear to let her go. 'She's all right, Rupert,' she shouted. 'She's OK. Tell them she's OK.'

A moment later Rupert came stumbling back into the room, his face pinched and bleached white. He flung his arms around Louise's neck.

'Oh. Mum! I thought she was going to die,' he sobbed. 'What would we have done if she'd died?'

Louise put her arm around his wiry little frame and held him close, the tears pouring down her cheeks. In the past few minutes she could have lost her daughter, but she'd also gained her son, her first born, at last.

There was an air of hushed respect in the lobby of the Hôtel de Paris as people spoke in low voices, and the staff looked subdued and mournful. 'What's happened?' one of the restaurant waiters asked one of his colleagues. He'd just come on duty and the sombre atmosphere had the chill of a church vault.

'You haven't heard? Old Lady Fulsham died in her sleep last night.'

'*Mon Dieu*! Does Monsieur le Baron know?'

'*Certainement!*'

'He'll be rich now!'

The gossip in the staff quarters was rife, but in the suite on the third floor, Rosie sat in stunned silence, hardly able to take in what had happened. Only yesterday . . . Only last night . . .! She was filled with disbelief. Surely, at any moment the telephone by their bed would ring, and Lady Fulsham's light voice, speaking in perfect English, would be gayly suggesting they join her for lunch.

'I have *such* an interesting guest I'd love you to meet,' she'd announce, and that guest might be Winston Churchill, John Cocteau, or her beloved Somerset Maugham. Rosie stared at the silent phone, refusing to believe she'd never hear the old lady's voice again.

This was her first experience of death since Charles had been killed, but that had been different because it happened during the Blitz. But here, in this sunny paradise, where life was so perfect and where she'd come to believe that nothing awful could happen, death didn't seem possible.

She gave a little frightened sob. If she felt this badly about Philibert's aunt, how was she going to feel when Granny died? She blew her nose and wished Philibert would come back to their suite, but he'd rushed off 'to attend to matters' as soon as the dawn call from one of her personal staff had told him what had happened.

That had been two hours ago and she felt lonely and upset, not knowing what to do. Should she go down to Lady Fulsham's suite? What was the protocol of such an occasion? What could she do? Rosie realized with horror that she didn't even have a black dress in her holiday wardrobe.

174

Philibert had been busy since he'd been given the news, calling her doctors, then the local undertaker, and then, as was customary in a hotel, arranging for her body to be taken out of the building by the back way, to avoid upsetting hotel guests. Then he'd phoned her lawyer.

The funeral was held five days later at St Nicolas Cathédrale on the Rue Colonel Bellando Del Castro, and it seemed as if every member of both the French and English aristocracy, living or staying on the Riviera, had come to pay their last respects. Prince Rainier was among the many friends who came to mourn her passing, because she'd become a local figure of substance and elegance.

Feeling overwhelmed and awkward because she was afraid everyone would stare at her and think of her as a scarlet woman, Rosie insisted on sitting in a pew behind Philibert.

'I'm still married,' she pointed out when he protested, 'and we're living together. It was all right meeting your aunt's friends as a mere girlfriend, but on an occasion like this, it wouldn't be seemly.'

Philibert shrugged, not answering. Calmly and unemotionally he gave the eulogy, praising his 'beloved aunt' for 'her spirit of joy that encompassed all who met her', and 'her great kindness and generosity'.

Rosie watched him, admiring his eloquence and the handsome figure he made as he bravely faced the large congregation. His parents were dead and his aunt had been his only living relative.

Now he was alone in the world. Except for her. Rosie felt her heart swell with love as she sat in the cathedral, and an almost maternal adoration made her vow to make him happy for the rest of his life.

The next morning Philibert told her he had to see the lawyer about his aunt's affairs. Privately, she longed to know how much money he'd been left. Certainly a large fortune, but she couldn't very well ask and so she smiled sympathetically and agreed to meet him for lunch in the hotel restaurant at one o'clock. Nothing was going to mar her deep happiness, and although she missed Lady Fulsham, it was nice to know that they'd be able to buy a villa right away, and set up home properly.

At one o'clock, as Rosie waited patiently at their usual table for Philibert, she saw the head waiter coming towards her with a silver salver in his hand.

'*Une lettre pour vous, madame,*' he said politely.

Rosie took the envelope, recognizing Philibert's handwriting. '*Merci bien,*' she replied, smiling. Then she eagerly tore open the envelope and unfolded his letter, which had been written on the headed paper of a law firm.

A few moments later she rushed out of the restaurant, her hand over her mouth, as she hurried through the crowded foyer, where guests were enjoying an aperitif before luncheon. Pushing past people, she stepped into the lift and pressed the third-floor button. One look around their suite confirmed with heart-stabbing shock, that what he'd written was true.

She sank on to the bed, feeling as if the ground had been cut away from beneath her feet, leaving her stranded. This couldn't be happening, she thought, her body ice cold with shock.

Moaning softly, she read the letter again, thankful his hurried scrawl was at least in English.

> Rosie, ma chérie,
>
>   My aunt's lawyer has informed me that she died bankrupt. There is nothing left, except some jewellery and heavy debts. It's all gone on gambling. Every franc of it. I loved you enough to marry you if we'd been rich. But not like this. You would hate to be poor as much as the thought fills me with dread. She owes the hotel thousands of francs for her suites and for ours. Also the restaurant. By the time you get this note I shall be on the yacht of an old friend, heading for the Greek islands. There is nothing else I can do. Thank you for the generosity of your love.
>
>   Always, Philibert.

'The rat! The rat!' Rosie sobbed. 'Oh, my God, what shall I do?'

She lay on the bed, locked in the grip of panic. How could he have abandoned her like this? What was she supposed to do?

Distraught and heartbroken, she read his letter again and

again. It was too much to take in. It was a shock to hear Lady Fulsham had gambled away all her money, but it was unbelievable that Philibert had run away, leaving her alone to face the music. Feeling sick and dazed, she rose from the bed shaking and trembling, deciding the only thing she could do was to telephone home, and get her father to wire her enough money to return to England. She reached for the phone, and just as the hotel operator answered she noticed an envelope had been slipped under her door.

She ripped open the envelope, and then sank to her knees, overwhelmed with horror.

It was from the General Manager of the hotel. In it he informed her that Baron Guerin had stated that she would be settling the bill for their suite, before she followed him to Paris where they'd taken an apartment which, including meals and drinks ordered from room service, now amounted to—

Rosie gave a scream when she saw the row of noughts. Not very good at working out how many francs there were to the pound, she never the less realized that she and Philibert had run up a bill of thousands of pounds. But hadn't Lady Fulsham invited them to stay 'as her guests'?

Her mind worked quickly. There was no way she could pay this bill, and no way she could wait to receive money from England, even if her father could get round the temporary law about taking money out of the country.

Feeling too sick to eat, she decided to wait until the morning before doing anything. She got into bed and lay awake most of the night, dropping off occasionally only to awaken with a panic-stricken start, wondering if she'd had the most terrible nightmare, then realizing with plunging despair that she hadn't.

Early the next morning she ordered breakfast as usual, then she got dressed in her best white linen suit, with her beige high-heeled shoes and handbag. With care she put on her make-up, brushed her blonde hair until it shone, and then tied a jaunty red and white scarf around her neck.

As she handed in the room keys at the reception desk she said, 'If anyone wants me I'll be back in an hour or so.'

'Certainement, madame.'

Then she walked slowly and nonchalantly across the foyer

and out through the main glass doors of the Hôtel de Paris and into the brilliant sunshine beyond.

Hartley Hall slumbered quietly in the late autumn sunlight, the surrounding trees tinged with gold, while the garden prepared itself to lie fallow through the coming winter. It was mid afternoon and Lady Anne was resting peacefully in her sitting room. Shortly, Warwick would hobble in with her cup of tea and two digestive biscuits.

She loved this hour. It gave her a sense of achievement to have got through another day. She was beginning to feel her age now, and her joints hurt when she moved. She also became more easily tired although she refused to admit it. Reserving her strength for the weekends when Henry and Liza returned from London was what mattered to her.

Sometimes, Juliet and Louise came with their husbands and all their children, like homing birds to the nest. Even Daniel's two daughters and his son also joined them on occasions.

At these moments Hartley once again became a place filled with activity and laughter.

With eyes affected by cataracts Lady Anne gazed through the window at her beloved garden as though through frosted glass. Not that her semi-blindness mattered. She knew every plant and shrub, and every tree and bush as if it were an old friend.

What would we all have done, she reflected suddenly, if we hadn't had Hartley? Where would we have gone to seek peace and comfort? Where would we have found the shelter to lick our wounds and gather enough strength to carry on?

Hartley was the heart and soul of the family, a bastion that protected them all, in war and in peace from the evils of the world and she for one loved every stick and stone of it. Hartley would be her final resting place, too. In her will she'd asked for her ashes to be scattered in the silver birch copse she'd planted herself at the far end of the lawn, when she'd come here as a bride.

At that moment she heard a vehicle coming up the gravel drive.

It stopped by the front door and curious to see who was visiting her on a weekday afternoon, she went into the hall. The front door of Hartley was never locked during the day, and as she waited to see who would come through it, the figure of a dishevelled young woman in a dirty, crumpled white suit came hurtling towards her, flinging her arms around Lady Anne's neck.

'*Rosie*!' she exclaimed, shocked. 'What on earth are you doing here? My God, what's happened to you?'

Rosie's face was ravaged with grief and disappointment. 'Oh, Granny!' she sobbed. 'I'm so unhappy, and I only had enough money to get the train to Paris, and then I had to change trains to get to Calais . . .'

Her voice trailed off and she looked as if she was going to faint from exhaustion and hunger.

'Come and sit down,' her grandmother commanded, leading her into the drawing room.

Lady Anne had been very angry when Rosie had left Salton to take up with some French gigolo, and appalled that she seemed to care so little for her children that she could leave them indefinitely at Hartley while she went gadding about in the Riviera. But looking at Rosie now, she felt a sense of pity. She looked unwashed and unkempt, and there were dark shadows under her eyes. For the first time, even her spirit seemed broken.

Settling Rosie on the sofa, Lady Anne ordered tea right away before sitting down in a high chair opposite her. 'Now tell me what happened?'

'I've come straight from Dover,' Rosie began and then she burst into tears again.

'Dover? What were you doing in Dover? I thought you were in Monte Carlo?'

'I was, but I had to get out of the hotel, and I only had enough money to get a train to Paris, and then another one to Calais,' she repeated, looking down at her fingers which were nervously twisting a damp handkerchief round and round into a tight ball. 'I was able to cash a cheque when I landed in Dover, and I got a taxi to bring me here, but . . . but . . .' The wreckage of her affair with Philibert and the beautiful future she'd planned with him now lay in tatters. She sat hunched up in her chair, shaking her head, unable to say anything more.

Lady Anne watched her closely, waiting until she was ready to talk. They drank cups of tea in silence – Rosie thirstily as

179

if had been ages since she'd drunk anything – as the sun dipped below the horizon and the light faded. Only then did Rosie, in a small hesitant voice, begin to talk.

'I loved him so much, and I thought he loved me too,' she said eventually, explaining briefly what had happened. 'I still can't bear to think I'll never see him again. We were going to get a villa near Cap Ferrat, and get married as soon as I was divorced.'

'You thought he was rich?' her grandmother asked carefully.

'Yes. Well, not as rich as his aunt, of course, but I thought he had enough money of his own, but now I know she was paying for everything. All the restaurants we went to, his clothes . . . everything. Every single thing.' Her voice, bitter with disappointment, broke. 'I now realize Philibert was dependent on her, and expecting to inherit everything.'

Lady Anne's eyebrows raised a fraction. 'I see. So that's when you did a runner from the hotel?'

Rosie nodded. 'I was terrified, actually, in case they twigged, and tried to stop me.' She reached for her beige leather handbag. 'All my jewellery's in here. And my compact and lipstick. I had to leave all my clothes and make-up behind,' she added, her tone deep with regret.

'So you're returning to London tomorrow, are you? To talk to Salton?'

Her granddaughter looked horrified. 'Oh, I don't want to see him again. I can't face him, anyway. My marriage is over. I shall never love anyone but Philibert.' She saw the expression in Lady Anne's eyes. 'Don't look at me like that, Granny. You've no idea . . . Philibert and I were meant for each other. He's all I've ever wanted in a man. He's so handsome and kind and loving, and such a wonderful person to be with. I don't know how I'm going to live without him,' she continued passionately. 'We were in love and so happy together,' she wept. 'There's no one else like him.'

'Where is he now, my dear?'

Rosie blushed through her misery. 'He's cruising around the Greek Islands on someone's yacht,' she replied shamefacedly. She wished she could have said something noble like 'he's seeing to Lady Fulsham's affairs' or 'trying to make money to cover her debts'.

'So what are your plans, Rosie?' Lady Anne asked reasonably. 'As you know, Jonathan's at St Peter's Court and will be home for half term in two weeks, but Sophia will be back at any moment from Tormead.' She consulted her diamond wrist watch. 'She went to tea with the Dickensons after school. Nanny will be fetching her now.'

Rosie leaned back against the cushions, utterly drained and washed out with grief and exhaustion. 'I don't know what I'm going to do,' she murmured faintly, closing her eyes. 'All I want to do is sleep. Sleep forever and never wake up.'

Lady Anne spoke briskly. 'Why don't you go upstairs, have a nice hot bath and get into bed? When Sophia gets home I'll tell her you're back, but you're not well and you shouldn't be disturbed. I'll have some supper sent up to you on a tray.'

'I couldn't eat a thing. I feel sick.' She covered her face with her hands.

'That's because you probably haven't had a proper meal for the past twenty-four hours. Now, come along, my dear, you don't want Sophia to find you like this. They've both missed you very much so you're going to have to do a lot of explaining when you feel stronger, but in the meantime, go and have a rest.'

Feeling like a child again whose misery was self-inflicted and therefore deserving no sympathy, Rosie dragged herself to her feet and, clutching her precious handbag under her arm, half staggered across the room to the door. She stopped and turned to her grandmother.

'You've no idea how happy I was,' she said piteously. 'The whole thing . . . it was the life I always wanted.'

# Twelve

'Rosie, you're going to have to do *something*,' Henry told her, a tinge of impatience in his voice. 'You've been back for nearly three months, and you can't go on lounging around the place, letting other people take care of your children, while you contribute nothing to the household.'

'You don't understand, Daddy.' Steeped in apathy and filled with anguish mixed with guilt and self-pity, Rosie lay on the drawing room sofa, gazing up at her father as if she hoped he'd work some miracle.

Henry stared back at her, shocked by how she'd let herself go. Her face – once so pretty and fresh, now looked pale and gaunt – was devoid of any make-up. And judging by her lank and greasy hair it was obvious she hadn't washed it recently. He was at his wits end, wondering what to do with her. She'd barely left the house since her return to Hartley, and the local doctor had told him she was suffering from depression. He'd even suggested Rosie be admitted to a special nursing home for treatment.

When Liza heard that, she was appalled. The stigma of going into a 'loony bin' would stick fast to the whole family and Rosie would be forever labelled the daughter who was a 'nut case'.

Henry himself was doubtful at the idea; one heard such awful tales of people having shock treatment, but if Rosie didn't buck up soon something drastic would have to be done.

'What *can* I do?' she asked miserably. 'I can't go back to London because since Salton's sold the house I've nowhere to go?'

Salton had also returned permanently to Washington, having given Rosie a generous divorce settlement of five thousand pounds.

'You could buy a three bedroom flat in Kensington for

182

under two thousand pounds, or rent one, as I've done in Princes Court for between two and three hundred pounds a year,' Henry pointed out, 'and you still have your dress allowance. I wish I could give you more, but I can't. You should be able to live modestly on the interest from what's left over when you've got yourself a place.'

But Rosie hadn't the heart or the will to do anything. She was poorer now than when she'd first been married to Charles, but because she'd been nineteen her family had rallied around her then and supported her financially throughout the war. She'd lived at Hartley in great comfort, considering what a dreadful state the country was in, and Juliet had invited her to stay with her in Park Lane when she wanted to be in town.

Why had it all gone so wrong? Rosie kept asking herself, knowing the full answer but unable to admit it, even to herself. Salton had been good and kind. He'd bought her a nice house and then an even bigger and nicer one. He was very generous with housekeeping money and he paid for her to have daily servants, and of course Nanny. But Salton had been dull. He didn't excite her in bed and he didn't interest her out of it. Her life as Mrs Salton Webb had been barren and tedious.

That is until she'd met Philibert. Now she felt overwhelmed with grief at the loss of his love, the loss of *excitement* in her life and the loss of the beautiful life she'd had. She missed the opulent splendour of the Hôtel de Paris as if it had been a person, someone who cared for her and cherished her all the time. She missed the extravagant restaurants she'd been taken to. She missed the yacht and the vintage Rolls Royce; and she missed the sunny days and warm balmy nights in a place where it never seemed to rain.

'I wish I was dead!' she burst out in fury. 'Now I've got *nothing*!'

Henry looked concerned. 'You mustn't talk like that, Rosie. You've got Sophia and Jonathan to think about. They need you, for goodness sake. You can come here for weekends, but you should go to London, get yourself a flat, and make something of your life.'

Rosie didn't even bother answering him. It took too much effort to speak, far less think about the future. If only something magical could happen, like Philibert finding his aunt had left him, hidden away, a vast fortune after all, so that he would come back to fetch her.

She closed her eyes, submerging herself in playing this blissful daydream over and over again in her mind, which helped to shut out the ugly truth.

Juliet felt a certain sympathy for Rosie. She could recall how deeply depressed she'd felt when the war had ended, and she'd thought she'd never see Daniel or be happy again. Perhaps, she reflected, it was time she put her anger at Rosie behind her, life was too short to harbour grudges.

'I have an idea,' she told her father, when he phoned to express his concern about her sister. 'Give me a couple of days, and I might be able to fix up something that will jolt Rosie out of the doldrums.'

That following weekend she and Daniel with Tristan, drove down to Hartley.

'You should be a director of 'Universal Aunts' you know,' Daniel teased her. 'You have a knack of fixing everyone's problems, don't you?'

She grinned at him. 'Now that I've none of my own, it's easy. The biggest problem is going to be getting Rosie to agree. You know how obstinate she can be.'

When they arrived, Hartley was vibrant with life. Louise and Shane, with Rupert and Daisy, had arrived for the weekend, as well as Amanda, Charlotte and Henry's sister, Candida, with her husband Andrew Pemberton. As it was half term Sophia and Jonathan were also there, running around helping to lay the table for lunch.

'This is a real family party,' Juliet said, kissing her parents and Lady Anne. 'Where's Rosie?' she added, looking around.

Liza cast her eyes to heaven. 'Up in her room. Says she doesn't feel very well.'

'I'll go and see her.' She bundled Tristan into Charlotte's arms. 'Look after him, will you, darling?'

Charlotte, newly crowned the Face of 1950 by *Vogue*, cuddled her nephew. 'I'll take him out to the garden,' she said. 'Are you coming, Amanda?'

'Not likely,' Amanda retorted crossly. 'You know I can't stand kids.'

'You're just miffed because you think the Conservatives will win the election,' Charlotte pointed out.

Amanda looked huffy. 'It's got nothing to do with that. I just don't care for children, and Tristan looks as if he's wet himself! Ugh!' She wrinkled her nose. 'God, kids are so disgusting.'

While Charlotte took Tristan up to the nursery to be changed, Juliet hurried up the stairs to Rosie's bedroom.

Knocking briskly on the door, she marched in without waiting for an answer.

Rosie was sitting on the side of the bed, doing up her shoe laces. 'What are you doing here?' She looked at Juliet resentfully. No doubt her sister had come to crow about her happy marriage and her lovely son and the expected baby, and what a wonderful life she had.

'I've come expressly to sort out your life,' Juliet retorted cheerfully, 'and before you start screaming at me, admit things couldn't be worse than they are at the moment?'

Rosie averted her face, not answering.

'Right then. First of all, I've found you a sublime furnished flat in Holland Park, with a nice drawing room and dining room and three bedrooms, and the rent is only three hundred and fifty pounds a year, and secondly, as you love socializing and going to parties, I've managed to get the *perfect* job for you. You won't be paid a great deal but the perks are worth hundreds of pounds a year and you'll *love* it!' Juliet added forcefully.

'What is it?' Rosie looked at her suspiciously. What did Juliet consider to be the perfect job for her? She had no qualifications. She couldn't do shorthand and typing. She was hopeless at arithmetic, so that ruled out even being a shop assistant, because she wouldn't be able to work out how much change to give customers. Surely it couldn't be something as lowly as a companion to an old lady, or someone's house-keeper?

'I don't need a job,' she said defensively. 'I'll have enough to live on with Salton's settlement.'

'Providing you stay down here and let the rest of the family support you!' Juliet scoffed. She could hardly contain her excitement now at the thought of seeing Rosie's expression when she told her what she'd arranged through her contacts.

'Well, what is it?' Rosie asked sulkily.

'You're not going to believe this, but you're the new social columnist on *Society Magazine*.'

Rosie looked at her, not understanding for a moment. 'What does that mean?'

'It means, you idiot, that you'll get invited to all the best parties and you keep a diary, describing who was there, and what they wore and what it was like and your article comes out in the magazine every month . . . you know, for God's sake! Like the social columns in *Tatler* and in the *Bystander* and *Sketch*! God knows they've all written about *us* for the past twenty years! It's something you can do in your sleep, because you know the whole social scene and you know everyone. That's why they're taking you on. I know the editor and he jumped at the idea. The journalist they've got at the moment doesn't know anyone, so she turns up at the grandest events, with a notepad and pencil, asking all guests for their names.'

Rosie's expression gradually changed from sullen to bewildered and finally to ecstatic as it dawned on her that her life wasn't over, after all.

'Really? Truly? Oh, my God! I can't believe it. They've actually said they want me?'

Juliet nodded, smiling that at last she'd done something that met with Rosie's approval. 'You'll get paid fifteen pounds a month, but no expenses. So you'll have to buy your own clothes and pay for your taxis. But you'll never have to eat at home again!'

'And I'll get to go to everything? Just like I did before the war? Have you told Mummy?' She sounded like a child who'd been sent an invitation to a party after all, just when she'd thought she was out in the cold.

'I haven't told anyone,' Juliet assured her. 'They want you to start in two weeks' time, so you'd better move into your new flat as soon as Sophia and Jonathan go back to school. Here are the keys,' she added lightly, dropping them on to the bed, 'and the first month's rent has been paid.'

'Oh, thank you, Juliet.' For once, Rosie spoke to her in a humble voice. 'I really am grateful, you know. This has literally saved my life. And I'm dreadfully sorry about what I did – you know, when those red roses arrived. I was a complete cow and I felt terrible when I realized I'd nearly ruined your marriage.'

Juliet chuckled. 'There's no need to overdramatize, my dear,' she said lightly. 'Daniel and I will expect a mention in your column at least twice a year!'

Henry looked down the dining room table with quiet satisfaction and a deep sense of contentment. It was Saturday evening, early autumn, and the family were gathered together within the sheltering embrace of his beloved Hartley. The table was laid with decorative Sèvre chinaware, and in the centre a bowl of winter heliotrope and red berried Cotoneaster glowed like jewels. Silver candlesticks and crystal wine glasses sparkled, reflecting in the polished mahogany, and the soft luminance of candle light seemed to take them all back to hundreds of years ago, when Hartley had been built.

His mother, as usual, sat on his right, as upright and elegant as she'd been in her seventies, although she picked at her food and drank very little wine. Liza, facing him from the other end of the table, seemed to have calmed down these days. She'd promised they wouldn't go to so many parties and she'd kept her word, although he could see that beneath her cheerfulness lay a layer of frustration. Liza was a woman who would never realize she'd reached her goal in life and therein lay her great disappointment. Perhaps, Henry reflected quietly, getting to where she wanted to go had been more fun than actually arriving. She was laughing and joking with Daniel and he was playing up to her, using his charm to make her feel good about herself. Daniel was clever like that. Women adored him for it, and none more than his favourite daughter, Juliet, who was radiantly pregnant again, her eyes sparkling with happiness.

Smiling to himself, filled with love for his family, he glanced at Rosie, looking more content than she'd looked in a long while, now that she had an interesting job in London. He hoped, in time, she'd find someone to replace Philibert, but it wasn't going to happen in the immediate future. This time her heart had truly been broken, because she'd lost more than the man; she'd also lost being a part of an enchanted world in a magical setting. That was a total bereavement that could not be replaced.

His eyes moved on to Amanda and Charlotte, still on the threshold of life, and going in utterly opposite directions. Would they both succeed? Amanda in politics and Charlotte as a model? Would they find love and fulfilment?

And without doubt the greatest of those is love, Henry thought, on this family evening which seemed to have acquired a special quality.

Why was he summing up, as if the page was coming to an end, how they'd all faired along the way? he asked himself suddenly. There were Louise and Shane, happy together, and so gratified that Rupert had accepted them as his parents and Daisy as his half-sister, and Jack as his real father who he saw every month. That was a happy ending to their story, wasn't it?

There was even a happy ending for his sister Candida, too. No longer a widow, bringing up two children and having to manage her large Hampshire place on her own, but contentedly married to Andrew Pemberton, who she'd met during the war when she'd worked in the Cabinet Office.

Henry sipped his claret, seeing the family clearly now, as if he'd been looking at a large painting depicting them all. The next line of Granville blood lay asleep upstairs in the old nursery where he and his children had slept when they were small. The Granvilles would go on, and Hartley would continue to be their shelter for generations to come.

He raised his glass. 'I think we should drink a toast,' he announced.

They all turned to look at him in surprise.

'What are we celebrating, old boy?' Candida asked, jovially, as she seized her own glass.

'The family,' Henry said quietly. 'Here's to us! The Granvilles!'

They all raised their glasses, and murmured, 'The Granvilles.' The words echoed around the old panelled dining room like a toast from the past itself.

The next morning, when one of the daily charwomen from the village took Henry Granville's early morning cup of tea up to his dressing room, where he'd slept on his own for the past few years, she found him lying as stiff and cold as one of the effigies in the local church.

Henry had died in his sleep, with a slight smile on his lips at the age of sixty-three.

The nightmare of that Sunday morning would stay with them all forever. Liza had started shrieking, 'No! Oh God! No!' when the charwoman had come rushing into her room to impart the shocking news.

Awakened by the commotion, the sisters came out of their rooms, gathering on the landing, whispering fearfully, 'What's happened?' to each other. Then Liza, crying hysterically, opened her bedroom door and blurted out, 'Daddy's dead,' before sinking to her knees where she stayed, unable to rise.

They all looked at each other, aghast and disbelieving, then one of them, nobody could remember who afterwards, asked, 'Who's going to tell Granny?'

Juliet was the first to turn her numbed emotions to practical use, as she'd done as a nurse during the Blitz.

'I'll go and tell Candida; I think she should be the one to tell Granny,' she said, heading off down the corridor to the wing of the house where Granny and Candida and her husband were sleeping.

Juliet paused outside her aunt's room, breathing deeply to steady herself, wishing with all her heart that she wasn't the one who had to tell them. She tapped softly on the door.

There was silence and just as she was about to knock again, Candida opened the door quietly.

'Andrew's still sleeping. What is it, my dear?' Then she paused, seeing the expression on Juliet's face. Her plump hands with their flashing rings flew to her mouth. 'Is it Mother?' she whispered, suddenly alert, as she looked across the landing at Lady Anne's bedroom door.

Juliet shook her head slowly. 'I'm afraid it's Daddy.'

Candida's blue eyes, so like Henry's, widened in disbelief. '*Henry*?' she breathed incredulously. A moment later she was bundling down the corridor in the direction of his room, her bulky body encased in a flowered flannel nightdress, her bare feet soundless on the dark red carpet.

'Henry?' Juliet heard Candida's voice boom as she charged past all the others on the landing, and rushed into his room. Then there was silence, and as Juliet walked slowly back along the corridor she could hear her aunt murmuring

189

woefully, 'Oh, my dear old boy. How could this have happened to you?'

Looking back months later, Juliet wondered how they'd all got through the weeks that followed her father's death. Somehow, mostly in silence, life had taken on an unreal quality as if they were all clockwork creatures, going through the motions of dealing with a death in the family. There was the announcement in *The Times* and the *Telegraph* to see to, while they awaited the result of the autopsy. There was the village church to book for a small private funeral, as they'd decided to hold a memorial service in London at a later date, and there were the hundreds and hundreds of letters of sympathy to be dealt with.

But it was Henry's obituaries in the newspapers that meant the most to Liza, for they publicly honoured the man she'd been married to for over thirty years.

During this fraught time it seemed as if everyone had slotted themselves into appropriate roles without being asked to. Candida never left her mother's side since the moment when Lady Anne had collapsed when she'd been given the news. Then Louise took charge of all the grandchildren along with Rupert and Daisy, while Rosie stuck by Liza, sleeping in her room at night, and helping her choose a new wardrobe of black clothes to wear for the next twelve months.

Amanda booked the caterers for the wake which was held at Hartley after the service, and Charlotte organized the flowers for the church.

Juliet, with Daniel's help, had the hardest job of all and that was to select the prayers and music for the service. She remembered her father's favourite hymns, whilst wondering how she was going to get through the day they buried him, and she asked Daniel to give the eulogy.

At last they received the result of the autopsy. Henry had died in his sleep from a heart attack, and Juliet had the strangest feeling that he'd had a premonition the previous evening when he'd suddenly proposed they drink a toast to the Granvilles.

The family doctor suggested it had been caused 'because Henry always worked too hard', and as he spoke he noticed that Liza was avoiding eye contact with any of the family.

\*   \*   \*

There was now an engraved headstone where Henry lay next to his father.

HENRY FORTESCUE GRANVILLE
1888–1951

Rupert visited the graveyard every time he stayed at Hartley.

'Grandpa would have appreciated your visits,' Louise told him, the first time she found him there.

'He *does* like it,' Rupert said, surprised she didn't realize that. 'When my first dog died,' he continued, his voice still carrying a soft Welsh lilt, 'I thought it was the end of the world. We were the same age, Drogo and me. Eight. It seemed too soon for a little chap like him to go, but we buried him under a yew tree on the farm and I used to go and talk to him every day. Then it didn't seem like he'd gone forever. That's why I come here; to talk to Grandpa.'

Louise wept when he had finished speaking. Wept for him in his loss as well as for her own bereavement. She also cried for the little dog that lay in the cold earth under a yew tree, then wondered – how could one weep for a dog she had never known? But weep she did because he'd been a part of Rupert's life when she hadn't been there to comfort him.

Gradually things went back to normal although they all knew life would never be the same again without Henry.

In his will he'd left everything to Liza.

'Everything?' Rosie asked in surprise. Lady Anne and Candida had looked surprised, too.

Mr Jones, the elderly lawyer, who had driven down from London to Hartley, explained. 'I suggested a long time ago to Mr Granville that he should make a new will, but he obviously kept putting it off,' he added, shaking his head regretfully.

'What's wrong with this one?' Amanda asked bluntly. She looked pale and blotchy as she pushed her glasses higher up her nose with her forefinger. Never pretty, she now looked positively plain, with her fair hair cut short, and her baggy grey jumper and skirt more suited to a forty year old.

Mr Jones peered at her through his own spectacles,

wondering for a moment if she was one of the family. 'There's nothing actually *wrong* with it,' he replied defensively, 'it's just that he made it in 1914, when he was newly married and off to war. I don't believe he thought he'd ever come back from the Front. He certainly had no idea that he would one day have children.'

'Does it matter?' Juliet enquired. She was thinking that probably the two witnesses to his signature might no longer be alive and this might prove a technical problem.

'Why should it matter?' Rosie demanded. 'Eventually everything will be split five ways, so what difference does it make?' Under the circumstances she couldn't very well add, 'when Mummy dies.'

'But why didn't he make a new will?' Candida asked.

Mr Jones looked fussed, and smoothed his wispy white hair with a knotty hand. 'Every time I told him he should make a new will, for all your sakes,' he said, flashing a quick look at Liza, 'he made some excuse. Said he would do it later. In fact, I believe he was very superstitious about it. He once told me that having made a will in 1914, and then having survived the Great War, he didn't want to tempt fate by making another one,' he added, as if to absolve himself from any blame in the matter.

'Well, that's fine,' Juliet pointed out reasonably. 'God knows, he gave us all everything he could when he was alive, and none of us are exactly on the breadline, so I don't see a problem.'

Liza leaned forward as if to reassure her daughters. 'You'll still have your dress allowances, because Daddy set up a trust-fund for that, and the trustees will continue to pay it directly into your bank accounts every month.'

'Exactly,' Juliet replied, casting Louise a brief glance. No one in the family knew that for the past few years, she'd passed on her allowance to Louise who needed the money far more than she did.

'So be it,' Lady Anne said calmly, rising from her armchair. 'Thank you for coming all this way to see us, Mr Jones,' she said and reached out to shake his hand. 'I suppose we'll have the dreaded valuers here, to tell us how much we'll have to pay the taxman in death duties?'

'I'm afraid that's inevitable,' he replied, bowing over their clasped hands. 'Death and the tax man are always with us.' His dry attempt at a joke fell flat as he met Lady Anne's cool eyes. 'You have a beautiful place here. At least Hartley Hall is safe for future generations.'

'I should hope so,' she said graciously, as she turned to leave the room followed by Candida.

# Part Four

# The Legacy

# 1952–1954

# Thirteen

Candida spoke to her mother with her usual cheerful conviction.

'You're coming to stay with me for a while, Mama. You need a change. This place is too full of memories for you to bear on your own.'

It was five months since Henry's death, and two days ago King George VI had died, also in his sleep, bringing back with savage rawness their own personal anguish. Candida had driven to Hartley immediately, realizing how hard the news would hit her mother.

'I'm all right, my dear,' Lady Anne assured her, but her hands trembled, and she suddenly looked very small.

'They say time is a great healer, and I'm not sure how true that is, but one's just got to get on with it.'

'Certainly, but not on your own,' Candida expostulated. 'Why isn't Liza here, to look after you? She seems to spend all her time in London these days.'

'I have enough people to look after me, far too many sometimes,' her mother responded mildly.

'But the others? Rosie? Juliet? Louise? Why aren't they here more often? It really is too bad, leaving you in this great house, all on your own,' Candida scolded crossly.

'My dear, they've all got their own lives to lead. Juliet and Louise have husbands and houses to look after, not to mention children. And Rosie has to work very hard on her magazine column.'

'I'm sure. Going to five parties a night must be a great strain,' Candida snorted. 'I'm sorry, Mama, but I'm worried about you.'

'At least one of them comes down at the weekend, and it's lovely to see all the children,' Lady Anne assured her. 'I can't get over what a wonderful job Louise has done with Rupert, and Juliet's step-children are really delightful and so polite. It's not all gloom and doom, Candida. Of course the King's death is a terrible blow, and poor Princess Elizabeth. What a terrible shock for her to find that not only has her father died, but she's suddenly become Queen at the age of twenty-five and with two small children! But it does make one realize that we're not alone in the world, with our grief.'

'I know, Mama. Listen, why don't you come and stay with Andrew and me, until the weather's better?' She glanced out of the window of her mother's sitting room at the muddy bleakness of an English garden in February. 'Come back here when the daffodils and tulips come out? When you can walk in the garden and the cherry blossom's in bloom? I'm sure the family will be down a lot more when the weather improves, meanwhile my house is cosy, and we can take trips into Winchester and do a little shopping, and you know how Andrew loves talking to you!'

Lady Anne hesitated. She certainly wasn't happy at Hartley these days. She kept thinking she heard Henry coming in the front door from the garden, or walking across the tiled hall floor. One night she awoke and thought she heard him walking along the corridor past her bedroom.

She'd even opened her mouth to call out 'Henry?' before remembering that her beloved only son would never come to her call again.

'Perhaps you're right, my dear,' she said, her lips tightly compressed in an effort to control her emotions. 'Just until the spring, then,' she added, as if to prove Hartley was her home and she'd always return.

'Capital!' Candida boomed. 'I'll telephone Andrew with the good news, and then we'll get Nanny to pack for you. You can be tucked up in front of a roaring log fire by this evening, with a glass of your favourite claret; how about that?'

Lady Anne smiled. 'You're very good to me, darling.'

'What else are daughters for? Now, do you want your knitting? Are you reading something at the moment you want to take with you?' Practical as always, Candida gave various instructions to the staff, before putting through a call to Liza in London.

'I'm taking Mother home with me, to Hampshire,' she

informed her sister-in-law sturdily. 'It's not good for her to be alone here.'

Liza, on her way to a society wedding which was going ahead in spite of the King's death, though the reception afterwards had been cancelled, felt thrown and wrong footed.

'Does she *want* to stay with you?' she asked almost accusingly.

'Why shouldn't she?' Candida thundered.

'I mean . . . she never leaves Hartley. I'd have brought her up to the flat here, if I'd known she wanted to get away.'

'Living opposite Harrods is not among Mother's priorities in life. She's agreed to stay with me until the weather improves, and then she'll return home.'

'She never gave me the impression she wanted to get away,' Liza remarked defensively. 'In fact she's been very brave about Henry's death. I thought she wanted peace and quiet.'

'She needs taking out of herself, Liza. Friends and neighbours are always dropping in to see us where we live and to meet new people will help to jolly her along a bit. At the moment she's living with her memories and it's not healthy. Anyway, I thought I'd let you know,' Candida concluded firmly.

'Thank you,' Liza replied frostily as she hung up. How she hated it when Candida made her feel inadequate. For the past thirty-nine years her damned sister-in-law had made her feel middle-class, uneducated and shallow. Now she was making her look selfish, too, by coming to London during the week to see her friends and go to a few small and discreet gatherings. She was acutely aware it would not be seemly to socialize too openly so soon after Henry's death, but surely she wasn't expected to remain at Hartley, which these days was like an old-people's home. It was the most depressing place in the world. Even the garden lay like a muddy barren wilderness under a permanently grey sky.

Deeply etched on her mind was the ghastly memory of living permanently at Hartley during the war. Especially in the winter. Fuel rationing meant the house was freezing, and she had to wear her mink coat indoors, and cardigans and woollen socks in bed; even hot water bottles were impossible to get hold of because rubber came from Burma. Decent food was scarce and so was drink, and the worst thing of all was only being allowed one bath a week, and that only six inches deep!

Liza shuddered as she recalled those dreadful days, and wondered how she'd survived them at all.

It was time to leave for the wedding, so she put on her little black hat with a veil and a pair of diamond earrings to brighten the deadening effect of black, which had never suited her. Lastly, she slung her silver fox fur over one shoulder to add a little touch of glamour.

It was a pity, she thought, as she hailed a passing taxi outside Princes Court, that the reception had been cancelled. Right and proper, of course, in view of the King's death, but nevertheless a shame. It would have been very pleasant to have a glass of champagne and meet a few friends.

Rosie felt that the glorious days of being a debutante had returned. Of course she was seventeen years older now. No longer a girl but a twice married woman with a ten-year-old daughter and a twelve-year-old son. But she was enjoying herself more than she could have imagined. Juliet had been right when she'd said being a diary columnist on *Society Magazine* would be right up her street!

She reckoned she was the prettiest and most stylish of all the social columnists, too. Jennifer from *Tatler* was a fierce matron who refused to mingle with the other columnists on rival social magazines and the first time she bumped into Rosie at a ball, she put her nose in the air and refused to sit at the same table because she 'never mixed with the press'.

I'll give her press! Rosie thought, especially when she found out that when she'd been a debutante, Jennifer as she styled herself, had only been a dame at Eton.

The best part of it all was that she was only required to go to the magazine's office once a month, to hand in her copy. With a telephone, some *Society* headed writing paper for her acceptance to invitations and following thank-you letters, which she wrote after every party, and a second-hand typewriter, at which she stabbed with two fingers, she could work from home.

As soon as word got around that the former Rosie Granville was *Society*'s new columnist, the invitations started pouring in.

'Just like the old days, Mummy,' she told Liza enthusiastically. 'And I can choose which parties to write up, and which don't pass muster.'

Liza went a pale shade of green with envy. Rosie's mantel-piece was laden with stiff white engraved cards; and Liza was jealous of all the people she must be meeting. The grand houses she was going to. And the lavish parties she was attending. It was almost more than her mother could bear.

'I also get asked to film premieres and first nights, and they send me two tickets; would you like to come with me some-times?' Rosie suggested.

'I'm sure you'd rather take someone your own age,' Liza protested, half-heartedly.

'No, I'd love you to come.' She riffled through a stack of mail on her desk, 'I think I've got some tickets here.'

Liza leaned forward, trying to read the invitations to see who they were from.

'Here we are!' Rosie flourished a white envelope. 'How about coming with me to the first night of *South Pacific* star-ring Mary Martin? It's at the Theatre Royal Drury Lane, and *everyone* will be there.'

Feeling as if she were gratefully accepting crumbs from the rich man's table, Liza accepted with alacrity. Of course an invitation to a ball at Blenheim Palace would have been better, but she had to remember she was still in mourning.

Rosie continued, 'We might also go to a Chopin Recital by Malcuzynski at the Royal Albert Hall. These tickets are for the Grand Tier and cost twenty-one shillings each, so it ought to be good.'

'Sounds lovely, darling.'

They were sitting in Rosie's new flat in Holland Park, and although it wasn't Mayfair or even Knightsbridge, it was a quiet elegant area, with some beautiful Edwardian white stucco houses. It had been quite tastefully decorated and furnished by the owners, and Liza's discerning eye spotted some very nice antique pieces and a few charming landscape paintings. It would certainly do for Rosie for the time being, Liza having no doubts that her daughter was yet to make the perfect match to a man with money, and hopefully a title too. Her opportun-ities were boundless now that she was going about so much, even if only as a social journalist.

The Princes Court flat, Liza decided, was really too small for comfort. How could one give style and character to a series of square box-like rooms in a modern red brick block of flats? How could she show off her talent for creating rooms that make guests gasp with delight when they entered? Now that new fabrics from France were becoming available for the first time since before the war, and bright rich colours had become fashionable, how she longed to do up a place for herself in London, so that she could eventually start entertaining properly again?

The idea took hold and grew. She decided to pop into Harrods on her way home and have another look at the exquisite curtain material she'd seen there last week. It was very Buckingham Palace.

Nearby, at the Queen's Gate Private Clinic, Juliet bit down hard on her thumb to control her desire to groan, as increasing waves of pain swept through her body. Although this was her third baby, giving birth never seemed to get any easier, and she'd lain here for what seemed like hours, and still she hadn't gone into labour. Mr Snyder, her gynaecologist, kept dropping into her room to see her, and question her progress from the midwife who was massaging her back.

'Not long now, Juliet,' he told her cheerfully, 'and then you'll really have to do some hard work!'

She tried to grin back but the agony of another birth pang took her breath away.

Daniel had insisted that this time she go to the private clinic, instead of St Georges's Hospital. 'I can visit you at any time, and stay with you all day if you like, instead of adhering to visiting hours,' he assured her. 'They have excellent room service, too!'

'You don't want to be present at the birth, though,' Juliet said firmly.

'I will if Mr Snyder would allow it, but he won't, will he?'

She shook her head. 'He says fathers get terribly in the way. You wait at home with Tristan, darling, and we'll let you know when the baby arrives.'

Lying on her back now, wondering how much more pain she could endure, she was thankful Daniel wasn't with her. She'd have hated him to see her like this, with her hands gripping the iron bedstead above her head, her legs inelegantly akimbo and sweat pouring down her swollen body, as she pushed until she was purple in the face.

'Come on, *push* . . .!' Mr Snyder commanded. 'You're nearly there.'

Juliet grabbed the air and gas mask and held it over her nose and mouth as she gave another almighty push.

'Good! Come on, Juliet. Push!'

Just when she thought she couldn't bear another second and that she was being ripped apart, she was rewarded by the sound of a tiny wail.

'You've got a beautiful daughter!' she heard the midwife exclaim. A moment or two later, the baby, wrapped in white sheeting, was placed in Juliet's arms.

She looked down adoringly into the baby's little pink face which was dominated by dark eyes. Thick silky black hair covered her tiny head.

Juliet started laughing. 'She's the spit and image of her father, just like Tristan,' she crowed delightedly. 'Oh, my precious little girl. Wait until your daddy sees you.'

'Your daddy thinks you're beautiful,' she heard a strong deep voice speaking from the doorway of her room.

A moment later Daniel was by her side, his arms encircling both of them, as he kissed the baby's head, and then turning to Juliet, gave her a long lingering kiss.

'Well done, my darling.'

'I didn't know you were here,' she said, weak with exhaustion but wallowing in her new found happiness.

'I've been sitting in the corridor for the past couple of hours. I couldn't bear to be at home, thinking of you all on your own here.'

Juliet looked down at the baby. 'She's just like you, isn't she?'

Daniel chuckled. 'Poor kid! But she'll get over it.'

'Would you like to wait outside, Mr Lawrence,' the midwife told him cheerfully. 'Just while we tidy up in here? Then you can come back and sit with your wife.'

When Daniel returned an hour later he was carrying an enormous bouquet of white roses in one hand, and a bottle of champagne in the other.

Juliet was by now sitting up in bed, her hair brushed and red lipstick enhancing her mouth.

'You're incorrigible, sweetheart,' he said, kissing her again. 'Where's the diamond necklace and the drop earrings?'

Juliet smiled lazily. 'I believe in keeping up appearances, and when the most handsome man in London comes to visit me, I want to look my best.'

Although she'd spoken jokingly, Daniel was moved by her words.

'You've no idea how much I love you,' he said, his voice rough with emotion. He kissed her deeply, lovingly, running his hand over her soft pulpy stomach. 'I can't wait to take you home with me.'

'I can't wait to get home.' She gave a soft little sigh. 'I wish I could go to sleep now, and wake up beside you in our silver bed.'

'You will, sweetheart, soon.'

Later, Daniel tiptoed away, as Juliet lay fast asleep. When he arrived back at the house, Dudley was doing one of his hovering-by-the-flowers-in-the-hall acts. He looked up as anxiously as if he were a part of the family.

'A little girl, Dudley,' Daniel said, grinning. 'A beautiful little girl with dark hair and eyes.'

'And madam? How is madam?'

Daniel's expression softened. He'd hated Dudley always being around when he'd first married Juliet. He was even jealous that she seemed to depend on him so much, almost as if he were her friend and confidant. But over the past few years he'd come to like and respect the rather eccentric butler, with his little garden-gnome face. His loyalty to Juliet and his discretion as he went about his business were qualities Daniel now admired.

'She's fine, thank you, Dudley. Already looking forward to coming home. Why don't we drink a toast to the new baby? Open a bottle of Crystal, will you? And bring it up to the drawing room with a couple of glasses.'

Flushing with delight, Dudley scuttled off to the wine cellar.

Daniel poured the chilled champagne into the glasses, the sparkling beads shimmering up to the edge of the rims.

'Here's to my daughter!' Daniel said, raising his glass.

'Your daughter!' Dudley exclaimed, his button eyes blazing with excitement. 'Have you and madam chosen a name for her, sir?'

'Yes, we have.' Daniel seated himself in an easy chair by the fireplace. 'She's to be called Cathryn.'

'Cathryn.' The butler, remaining standing, repeated the name softly. 'That's a beautiful name, sir. I'm sure Master Tristan will be very thrilled to have a little companion.'

'Yes, I think he will.' Daniel looked at his watch. 'What time is dinner, Dudley?'

'Eight o'clock, if that's convenient, sir.'

'Perfect. It'll give me time to have a bath first, and then telephone everyone in the family, to tell them the good news.'

Daniel tried Liza's number a second time, but there was still no answer. Although it was Tuesday it struck him she might be spending an extended weekend at Hartley so he dialled the Guildford number, knowing she'd be furious if she found out she hadn't been immediately informed of the baby's birth.

One of the daily cleaners from the village answered the phone.

'Hello?'

'Is Mrs Granville there? I'd like to speak to her, please.'

'Who's that?' the woman asked cautiously.

'Mr Lawrence.'

There was a long silence on the line, almost as if the cleaner was listening to someone's instructions. Eventually she spoke. 'Mrs Granville isn't here.' Her tone was final, curt.

'Is she in London, then?' Daniel inquired.

'I couldn't say. Sorry I can't help.' There was a click and she hung up.

'Well . . .!' Daniel said aloud as he replaced the receiver. If Liza cursed him for not telling her of Cathryn's arrival, he'd at least be able to say he'd done his best.

He'd sat down to dinner a few minutes later when the phone rang. Dudley answered it and then came into the dining room to tell Daniel it was Mrs Lawrence on the phone.

Frowning, he jumped to his feet and grabbed the receiver in the hall. 'Juliet?' he said anxiously.

'Hello, darling.'

'Is everything all right?'

'Yes, fine. I just had a call from my mother.'

Relief washed over Daniel like a warm comforting wave. For a ghastly moment he'd thought there was something wrong with the baby.

'I've been trying to get hold of her all evening,' he explained.

'Really? She rang to say she had a premonition I'd had the baby, and was ringing to check. I told her we'd had a little girl . . .'

'Why didn't she ring here?' Daniel asked puzzled. 'Why did she ring the clinic? No one knew you'd been admitted yesterday.'

'I don't know.' Juliet sounded tired. 'Anyway, I thought I'd let you know, so you can cross her off your list of people to ring.'

'Thank you, sweetheart. Now get a good night's sleep and I'll see you first thing in the morning.'

Once they'd said a lingering goodbye, Daniel returned to the dining room, wondering what Liza was up to. He was certain she must be at Hartley, and she'd told the cleaner who'd answered the phone to say she wasn't there. But why? She knew Juliet's baby was imminent and she'd probably guessed he was calling to say the baby had arrived, but she didn't want him to know she was at Hartley.

He felt disturbed and uneasy, although common sense told him he was making a fuss over nothing. Why shouldn't Liza still be at Hartley during the week? As if to prove a point, although he didn't know why, he dialled the Princes Court number once more. There was still no answer. He shrugged, and after drinking a night cap before the crackling drawing-room fire, he went to bed.

It was none of his business what Liza did, and he soon fell asleep, thinking how wonderful it was going to be when, in ten days time, Juliet lay close by his side once more, her breath fanning his cheek, her slim limbs entangled with his.

# Fourteen

Daniel's heart tripped and missed a beat and he felt the blood drain from his face. He'd immediately recognized the photograph when he'd opened his copy of the *Financial Times* as he travelled to work one spring morning. As he scanned the accompanying article a sense of disbelief swamped his senses.

Suddenly he instinctively knew what Liza had been doing down at Hartley, on the night Cathryn had been born two months ago. She never normally stayed in the country during the week unless she had a very good reason. Now he knew what it was.

The print danced before his eyes as he read the short piece a second time and tried to digest the appalling consequences.

> Capital Assets Ltd, one of the largest property developers in the south of England, have purchased Hartley Hall and the surrounding thirty-five acres of land near Guildford, for £60,000. Formerly the home of wealthy banker, Henry Granville, who died last year, the Georgian building will be converted into luxury flats. Capital Assets Ltd also plan to build a hundred and fifty small houses on the land, to help meet the demand for housing, which has been acute since the end of the war.

As if in a trance, Daniel got off the tube, and once in the street, hailed a taxi to take him back to Park Lane.

The worst realization that occurred to him was that according to Henry's will, Liza had done nothing legally wrong. Hartley had been left to her in its entirety, but none of them for one moment had suspected that she would do this. In fact the whole family had taken it for granted that the five sisters would inherit the family home eventually.

And what about Lady Anne? Who was due to return to her home of nearly seventy years, within a few weeks, for a surprise party that Louise and the others were planning?

'Jesus Christ,' Daniel murmured under his breath as the taxi rattled up Buckingham Palace Road towards Hyde Park Corner. This was morally speaking the greatest betrayal of trust he'd ever come across. Liza might not have liked Hartley herself, but she knew and had always known that her daughters adored the place. It was their spiritual home, their refuge in times of trouble, their shelter in war and peace, and their retreat when hearts were broken and death cast its shadow over them.

'Oh, God!' he said aloud, covering his face with his hands. Who knew about this so far? Were other newspapers covering the story in their financial or property sections?

Grabbing his bowler hat and rolled umbrella, he got out of the taxi and rushed up the front steps of their house. He must get to Juliet before someone else broke the news to her.

Juliet, slender once more after Cathryn's birth, and wearing an exquisite black suit, was discussing the arrangements for a forthcoming dinner party with Dudley, when Daniel burst into the drawing room.

'Darling! What are you doing back here?' Juliet greeted him with delight. 'You've come at just the right moment. Dudley needs to know which wine you'd like to serve with the saddle of lamb, on Thursday evening?' Then she paused, seeing his pale face. 'What's the matter?' she asked, rising quickly.

'Dudley . . .?' Daniel turned to look at the butler.

'Of course, sir, madam.' He turned away diplomatically and left the room on silent feet.

Juliet looked anguished. 'What is it? Not Granny . . .?'

'No, no,' he assured her, taking her arm and leading her back to the sofa. 'I read something in the FT just now, and it's the most terribly bad news.'

'Has the Market crashed?'

He shook his head, bracing himself. 'I'm not sure it isn't worse than that.' He decided to give it to her straight. 'I'm afraid Hartley's been sold. To a property developing company, for sixty thousand pounds . . .'

'What are you talking about?' she asked incredulously. 'Hartley's the family home. It *can't* be sold.'

He withdrew from his pocket the relevant sheet of the pink newspaper. 'Here are the details,' he said heavily. 'I'm afraid it's a done deal.'

She held the paper with shaking hands, mouthing the text as she read the article before gazing with tear filled eyes at the photograph of her beloved home.

'But *who* sold it?' she asked, in anguish. '*How* can it have been sold? It belongs to all of us.'

Daniel remained silent, letting her reach the obvious conclusion herself.

Suddenly she looked at him sharply and there was no need for words.

'Mama?' she said aghast. 'No, Daniel. She couldn't have sold it over our heads! She'd never do that.'

He bit his bottom lip, not wanting to be the one to point the finger of accusation at a mother-in-law he'd never liked, because he knew in her heart that Liza had never thought he was good enough for Juliet.

'Why don't you ring the lawyer, who came down to Hartley after the funeral to read your father's will? He must know what's happened.'

'I will. What was he called?' She rose and hurried over to her desk where the white telephone stood. 'What was his name?'

'Mr Jones, of Jones, Kidd and Elmwood.'

She dialled directory enquiries, and a moment later was scribbling down the address and telephone number.

When she got through, having told him who she was, she asked him outright; 'Do you know if my mother has sold Hartley Hall?'

There was a stunned silence. '*Sold* Hartley Hall?' he echoed in a shocked voice. 'I'm afraid I've had no dealings with Mrs Granville for some time, Mrs Lawrence. Not since the death duties were agreed with the Inland Revenue and your late father's affairs wound up . . . are you *sure* it has been sold?'

'There's only one Hartley Hall in Surrey, and the sale has been reported in today's *Financial Times*.' Juliet's voice was tight with misery.

'It might be a good idea to check on the accuracy of the story with the editor?' Mr Jones suggested.

'What I want to know is –' Juliet spoke painfully – 'has

my mother the legal right to sell . . . to sell the house?' Her voice caught.

'I will study the will again, but if my memory serves me right, Mr Granville left everything to her, in entirety. As you know, I tried to persuade him to make a new will, on several occasions, but—'

'I know. I know. But does that mean she's legally *able* to sell . . .'

There was a long pause. When he spoke he sounded like a very old, very tired man. 'I'm afraid it does,' he said unhappily.

'Mummy was never happy at Hartley; she's never liked being in the country,' Rosie pointed out, almost sympathetically.

Juliet and Louise glared at her in fury. The sisters, with the exception of Charlotte, who was being photographed for *Harper's Bazaar* in Paris, had got together at Park Lane the next morning, Juliet having summoned them for an urgent meeting.

'That's not the point,' said Juliet. 'It's obvious Daddy trusted her to pass it on to all of us, just as we were going to pass it on to our children. She's betrayed that trust.'

'That's right,' Louise agreed, sadly. 'How could she have done such a thing? I wish Charlotte was here because she lives with Mummy and she must have known what was going on.'

'I doubt it,' Amanda scoffed. 'Charlotte's such an idiot she wouldn't know if the ground was cut from under her feet, leaving her hanging in space.'

Rosie spoke plaintively. 'It is sad, but Mummy's been lonely since Daddy died, and perhaps it all became too much for her. You know how much she loves London.'

'For God's sake . . .!' Juliet exploded. 'What about Granny? Was *she* consulted? No doubt she was lonely, too, without Daddy being there every weekend, but she'd never have sanctioned *selling* Hartley in a million years.'

'Do we know if it's actually been sold? Have the contracts been signed?' Louise asked, trying desperately to cling on to a vestige of hope that it might not be too late to save the place.

Juliet nodded. 'My own lawyer spent most of yesterday

getting to the bottom of it. Apparently contracts were exchanged last week and Mummy has promised Capital Assets Limited to vacate the house in six weeks time.'

'So soon?' Rosie looked thoughtful. 'I wonder what's going to happen to everything?'

Louise looked shaken. 'Six weeks! Shane and I were there only last weekend, with Rupert and Daisy, making plans for the surprise party we were going to organize for Granny.' She stopped abruptly, her fingertips pressed to her mouth for a moment. 'My God, Rupert had a premonition months ago that Granny would never return to Hartley, and I thought it meant she'd die whilst staying with Candida. Never in a million years did I think it would be Hartley that would go!'

'Do you think Mummy's going to sell the contents as well?' Rosie asked.

'Why all this interest in the contents?' Juliet snapped.

Rosie blushed. 'Well, there's so much stuff,' she said lamely. 'All the furniture and silver, dozens of paintings, God knows how much it's all worth . . . what's going to be done with everything?'

'Hoping to grab what you can for yourself?' Amanda asked cynically. 'You're in a small furnished flat, dear. Not an annex of Buckingham Palace. Mother will probably flog everything at Sotheby's or Christie's. Anyway, the days of families like ours, with great houses to keep up, are past. If Mother hadn't sold Hartley, we'd all have been forced to, eventually.'

'Why?' Louise demanded angrily. 'If we'd all pulled together we could have kept Hartley going? Perhaps it would have meant selling some of the land, but we'd never have sold the house, would we, Juliet?'

Juliet stood up and reaching for the cigarette box, placed a black sobranie in her jade holder. Walking restlessly around the drawing room as she lit it, she finally went and stood with her back to the fireplace.

'Do you know the most goddamn awful aspect of the whole thing, apart from Mama's betrayal?' she asked.

The others looked at her in silence.

'If Mama had told me she hated Hartley and wanted to get rid of it, I'd have raised the money and bought it myself just to keep it in the family, for all of us to share. Even if it had meant selling this house. Daniel would have helped me. I'd never have let it go – not even to a nice family and certainly never to a property developer,' she added despairingly.

'No, you wouldn't,' Amanda said accusingly. 'You'd have wanted to be the Lady of the Manor, like you are in this house. You'd have patronized the poor people in the village, and opened the garden for Conservative fêtes, and become even grander than you are now.'

White with rage, Juliet turned on her. 'How dare you talk to me like that? You're so busy trying to be a fully paid-up member of the Labour Party that you've become ashamed of your own background, which is far worse.'

'Shut up, you two,' Louise intervened. 'This is not getting us anywhere. Where's Mummy now? Has anybody spoken to her since we found out about Hartley?'

'Yes,' Rosie agreed. 'Here we are, saying dreadful things about her behind her back and we haven't even heard her side of the story.'

Juliet sat down beside Louise on the sofa again. The atmosphere in the room was bristling with animosity and tension.

'Right now Mama is in Paris with Charlotte,' Juliet said calmly, 'and I for one can't wait to hear what she has to say. All I know is she's utterly betrayed Daddy's trust, after all he did for her and for all of us, and she also went behind Granny's back, and frankly, I'm going to find it very hard to forgive her.'

Louise twisted her hands nervously. 'Does Granny know yet?'

Juliet shook her head. 'Candida is saying nothing at the moment, until we've talked to Mama. It's going to break Granny's heart, especially the thought of a hundred and fifty houses being built on the wonderful garden it took her sixty years to create.'

Amanda sniffed loudly, and crossed her legs which were encased in unbecoming brown lisle stockings that wrinkled around the ankles.

'Typical! Bloody typical!' she exclaimed. 'Forget the homeless! Forget those who have no where to go because their houses were bombed. Forget the people who can't afford to buy a garden shed, just so long as the rose garden remains unscathed, and the lavender borders flourish! You lot make me sick,' she continued. 'All you think about is your privileges as a member of the upper classes. A hundred and fifty families are going to be housed because of this scheme, and a lot more can get flats in the main house.'

Juliet looked at her scathingly. 'Amanda, are you as stupid as you sound? These houses will be sold to well-to-do middle-class people, not *given* to the poor. Don't you know that Surrey and Sussex have become known as the "stockbroker belt" because they're a quick train ride from the city? Capital Assets will make a fortune, selling each house when it's built for a very profitable sum.' She paused. 'And the poor will still be homeless.'

Amanda grunted with annoyance. 'Well, *we* didn't need to have such an ostentatious place. You and Louise have already got houses, and I'll soon be getting my own flat. It's obscene for one family to own so many properties when there are others without a roof over their heads.'

'When are Mummy and Charlotte coming back?' Louise asked Juliet, ignoring Amanda's tirade.

'According to Charlotte's agent, not for a couple of days,' Juliet replied. 'Shall I arrange for her to come here? And invite Mama, too, so we can talk to her?'

Rosie gave a little gasp. 'Oh, poor Mummy! We can't do that. It would be dreadful for her, like walking into a trap.'

'As opposed to her selling us down the river?' Juliet retorted. 'I'm sure Mama can stand up for herself. We just want to know why, not to mention *how*, she could have sold Hartley behind our backs.'

The following evening, as Juliet and Daniel dined alone, she turned to him with a troubled expression.

'This is going to drive the family apart,' she said. 'All sorts of issues have emerged between us, far deeper than I'd expected.'

Daniel looked across the polished table at her exquisite face, her skin looked luminous in the candlelight and her blonde hair gleamed, but her aquamarine eyes were dull with despair.

'What kind of issues, darling?'

'I honestly believed that beneath the skin we were all basic-ally like-minded. Now, apart from Louise, I realize I hardly know Amanda, and as for Rosie, she is much more like my mother than I thought. Whatever the outcome of losing Hartley, we're never going to be a united group again. The Granville sisters are a thing of the past. It's going to be Louise and me; we've always been close. Rosie is going to side with Mama every inch of the way. She's always been a mummy's girl. And apart from that I have a horrible feeling that now that my mother has pocketed sixty thousand pounds, Rosie may be hoping she'll get to see a bit of that money.'

Daniel nodded in understanding. Rosie hated being poor and living in a rented furnished flat, and Liza would be certain to help her financially.

'And Amanda?' he asked, his full mouth forming a little quirky smile.

'I think she's almost glad Hartley's gone,' Juliet said flatly. 'I imagine coming from a semi-stately home has done nothing for her credibility in the circle she moves in at Oxford. She'd probably be happier if we all lived in council houses.'

'Well, there's nothing you can do to stop Amanda waving the Red Flag.' Daniel chuckled. 'I just wonder how her convictions would stand up if your mother were to offer to give her a couple of thousand pounds? Now, what about Charlotte? How do you think she'll take the news?'

Looking thoughtful, Juliet sipped her glass of Burgundy. 'I don't know. I'm beginning to wonder if I actually know my family at all. I never thought Mama would betray us like this. I never thought Rosie would side with her, either. And I never realized Amanda was actually embarrassed at being a Granville. As for Charlotte, I think she's so wrapped up in modelling and she's finding her life so exciting, it may not register at first.'

'So you're meeting your mother the day after tomorrow?'

'I've asked her to lunch, and to bring Charlotte. Amanda can't make it which is perhaps just as well; her political views are irrelevant, anyway. Rosie and Louise are coming and –' she gave him a little wry smile – 'I can't tell you how much I'm dreading it. Fancy having to accuse our own mother of stealing our inheritance from right under our noses?'

'I'll be here if you want me to be.'

She stretched out her slender arm, and gripped his hand. 'You're so sweet, my darling, and thank you, but this is Granville business, and I have a feeling it is going to be very unpleasant.'

Daniel groaned in sympathy. 'If only your father had made a new will then none of this would have happened. I still can't understand why he didn't. He was a banker, for God's sake. He understood about money and property and trust funds. He must have advised hundreds of people over the years about keeping their affairs in order, and although he didn't expect to die when he did, I was shocked to find he hadn't made a will since 1914. It's ludicrous!'

'I never knew he was so superstitious, like Mr Jones said.'

'On the other hand,' Daniel continued, glancing at Juliet's sad profile, 'he trusted your mother. He'd never have expected her to do this. He probably felt there was no need to state in his will that Hartley was left to her for her life-time only, after which it would automatically have gone to her children.'

'God, I'm dreading having to face her with this. Why am I the one to feel nervous and embarrassed, Daniel?' She turned to him, her face perplexed. 'For some absurd reason I feel as if *I* am the guilty one.'

'That's because you're embarrassed *for* her, sweetheart. It's never easy when a close member of the family betrays you like this. I'm sure she'll be very ashamed of herself when it all comes out.'

Sitting very upright at her dressing table, Liza studied her reflection in the mirror, as she got ready to go to lunch with Juliet. She'd spent the morning at Elizabeth Arden's beauty salon in Bond Street, having her hair arranged into tight blonde curls around her ears. They had also done her make-up, which was pale, with a hint of blue eye-shadow and a bright red lipstick. Wearing her new cerise Norman Hartnell dress and matching coat, all she needed now was her pearls, and the stylish hat she'd picked up from Madam Vernier's salon. It was small and had a coquettish cerise ostrich feather that curved downwards, framing her face on one side.

'That'll do,' she thought with satisfaction, picking up her cream kid gloves and black crocodile handbag.

'Are you ready, darling?' she called down the corridor, towards Charlotte's bedroom.

'Just coming, Mummy.' A minute later she came hurrying out of her room, in a pale grey coat over a flower patterned dress. Hatted and gloved like her mother, they got into the lift together.

'Is Juliet giving a luncheon party?' she asked, checking her own make-up in the mirrored walls.

'I don't know whether there'll be anyone else there, or not,' Liza replied, frowning slightly. 'She just said "come to lunch and bring Charlotte", so I'm not sure.'

'You're looking very smart,' Charlotte pointed out. 'Are you going on anywhere afterwards?'

'I may be. I think we should get somewhere bigger to live, don't you? The flat's awfully cramped.'

'Cramped?' Charlotte tucked her grey clutch handbag under her arm, as they scanned the heavy traffic in Brompton Road for a free taxi. 'No, I don't think so. After all, there's only the two of us now, isn't there?' she added dolefully. 'If anything I think we should get a smaller place. Somewhere really cosy.'

Cosy was not what Liza had in mind. 'I don't agree,' she said decisively. 'Ah, here's a taxi.' She raised her hand and a black cab swerved and stopped by the kerb. 'Ninety-nine Park Lane,' she told the driver grandly.

Charlotte looked curiously at Liza's profile as they headed for Hyde Park Corner. The change in her mother since her father's death was astonishing. At first she'd been shocked and tearful like the rest of them. She'd spent a lot of time going on about her own future, asking anyone who would listen, what was she going to do now, without Henry? How was she going to manage on her own? She even went so far as to wonder if anyone would invite a single woman, like her, to dinner parties any more? She wailed that her life was over and all she had to look forward to was to being buried in the country.

Then suddenly, as if someone had pressed a switch, she became strong and confident.

Charlotte, the only sister still living at home, watched this transformation with relief. Liza no longer appeared to feel sorry for herself. In fact her manner had become quite ebullient, almost as if she'd been released from some burden.

Of course when Granny went to stay with Candida, Charlotte reflected, Hartley must have been quite a lonely place for Mummy to be on her own, especially in the middle of winter, so it was not surprising that she'd been staying for longer and longer periods in town.

Nevertheless, it was as if Liza was enjoying some kind of strange freedom, almost as if she was able to do as she liked for the first time.

In truth, Liza *had* gained in confidence since Henry's death, because for the first time in her life she'd realized there was no one there to make her feel vulgar or inferior. No longer did she feel inadequate. And however sweet, kind and supportive Lady Anne had always been towards her, the charming manners did not always hide the fact her mother-in-law was also being slightly patronizing. Lady Anne would have liked an aristocratic wife for her son, someone who 'spoke the same language' as she was wont to say about like-minded people; someone who knew that wearing diamonds in the morning was not done, and that any show of ostentation was crass. Someone who wasn't impressed by people who had titles, and who was comfortable whether they were talking to the Queen of England or the local road sweeper. Someone who wasn't a snob, or a social climber.

And Liza knew in her heart she was all of those things. She'd loved Henry very much when they'd first married and she'd marvelled at her good fortune in meeting him when she was a paid companion to his aunt. She was nineteen, the daughter of a seamstress and a teacher, with hardly any money. She'd been pretty, sweet and dizzy, the Great War had started and Henry had fallen madly in love with her.

Like the story of Cinderella, Henry had been her Prince Charming and she'd worshipped him.

Things underwent a change when, in 1920, they'd moved from Hartley to London and he'd joined Hammerton's Bank. She'd been put on her mettle from the start, having to socialize with him and his old school friends and act the part of a sophisticated society lady.

Lady Anne had presented her at Court and she was expected to hold her own among the highest in the land. Not that she didn't want to succeed. She wanted to so badly, because she loved the grand life Henry was giving her, that she went all out to impress.

Perhaps that had been her downfall, she reflected now, as the taxi drew up outside Juliet's house. She'd tried too hard, now she was determined only to please herself, and by doing what she'd done, she felt she'd evened the score, though her own children weren't going to like it.

All that mattered to her now was that no one was ever going to be allowed to belittle her again.

They were gathered in the black, white and silver drawing room. Juliet rose and stepped forward when Dudley showed Liza and Charlotte into the room.

'Dudley, I'll ring when we want lunch,' Juliet told him briefly.

He nodded in silent understanding and left, closing the door behind him.

'Hello, darlings,' Liza said, her voice ice brittle. She gave a tight smile, more like a puppet's grimace, as she glanced at Rosie and Louise, who sat, pale and rigid.

'A drink, Mama?' Juliet offered her politely. 'Gin and tonic?'

'Thank you. That would be lovely.' Liza looked awkwardly around the room, as if she was a visitor who had never seen it before.

'Charlotte, help yourself to a drink, and take a perch,' Juliet told her sister.

'Are we celebrating something?' Charlotte asked, bewildered. 'It's not an anniversary of anything, is it?'

Juliet gave a wintry smile. 'You don't know then, sweetheart?'

Charlotte stared back at her, anxiously. 'Know what?'

There was silence. Everyone looked at each other and then they all looked at Liza.

'I haven't had time to tell anyone,' Liza snapped pettishly. 'But you've all obviously heard on the grapevine that Hartley has been sold.'

Charlotte uttered a sharp cry. '*Sold?* Hartley? How can it be sold?'

Juliet gave an exaggerated shrug. 'Ask your dear mother. She was the one who went behind all our backs and sold it to a property developing company for sixty thousand pounds. They're going to turn the house into flats, and build a hundred and fifty houses in the grounds.'

'I don't understand!' Charlotte burst into tears. 'It's our *home*. What about Granny? Where's she going to go?'

Louise jumped up and put her arms around her younger

sister. 'We're all cut up about it, but there's nothing we can do. The sale's gone through. It's too late,' she explained gently.

'Mummy, how could you . . .?' Charlotte sobbed, covering her face with her hands.

'Obviously very easily,' Juliet interjected.

'Now listen to me, and stop being so hysterical.' Liza raised her voice angrily. 'You've all taken Hartley for granted, since you were small. You treat it like a hotel and you always have. None of say "can we come and stay?" You just turn up, willy-nilly, with your husbands and children and friends sometimes, expecting to be fed and looked after, and I'm telling you now, I'm *sick* of it! Don't you realize how much work it involves having the house full? Someone has to change the beds and see to the laundry, someone has to do the catering and cooking . . .'

'And not once, since I've been born, has it been *you*,' Juliet pointed out with equal anger. 'There's no good you pretending to have slaved away, taking care of us all, while you ran Hartley single handed. In fact, you used to gripe because Granny still lived there, organizing everything, so you had no say in the matter.'

Liza was white with fury, her mouth a narrow scarlet curve of rage. 'I never *said* I had to see to everything personally, but since your father died, and Granny's gone to Candida's, the house has become an intolerable burden.'

'Oh, poor Mummy!' Rosie exclaimed, going over to Liza, and hugging her. 'We've been so selfish. Of course it must have been terrible for you, all alone and having to cope with everything without Daddy.' She turned to Juliet accusingly. 'Stop being so utterly beastly to Mummy. You know she hates being buried in the country. Why didn't you tell me, Mummy? We could all have gone to stay with you in turn, so you wouldn't have been so lonely.'

'What?' demanded Juliet. 'And then be accused of using the place like a hotel? Stop being an idiot, Rosie. The house didn't have to be *sold*.' She swung round to glare at Liza, just as she'd done as a defiant debutante. 'Why didn't you close it down until Granny went back? Have you any idea what this will do to her? Have you any idea what it is doing to all of *us*? Daddy would have been heartbroken if he'd known that the minute he died, a property developer was going to wreck the house and turn the land into a housing estate.'

She rubbed her forehead as if her head hurt before continuing. 'Daddy was a part of Hartley,' she continued, 'and Hartley was a part of Daddy. He worked so hard to keep the place, to maintain the old building, to replant the orchard, to help Granny design a larger rose garden. In one fell swoop you've destroyed the Granville legacy, and I, for one, will never forgive you,' she ended with finality.

Liza put on a bored expression, as if she were an actress in a Noel Coward play. 'How you dramatize everything, Juliet. You all live in London, and that's your choice, so . . . go somewhere else at the weekend if you crave the countryside that much.'

'You don't understand, Mother,' Louise said, with quiet firmness. 'We live in London because of work. Shane's career as a doctor, Daniel's at MI5, Rosie's new job on *Society*, Charlotte's modelling career . . . but Hartley has always been home. What you've done has been unbelievably thoughtless and selfish. Were there money difficulties after Daddy died and you had to pay the death duties?'

'Money has nothing what so ever to do with it,' Liza said airily. Although she knew she was cornered and morally in the wrong, and no one except Rosie was going to forgive her, thirty-nine years of having to mind her Ps and Qs had ended, and that made her new found freedom a heady experience. I don't care what they say, a voice in her head kept repeating, as she watched her boats burning.

'So you're going to live in Princes Court?' Louise asked.

'Certainly not. It's much too small.' Liza turned to Charlotte. 'I said that to you earlier today, didn't I? We're quite cramped in those boxy little rooms. I'm moving, quite soon actually, and I expect you to come with me, darling. You're far too young to be living on your own.'

Rosie, who'd drawn up her chair next to her mother, looked intrigued.

'Where are you moving to, Mummy?'

Liza's moment of supreme triumph had arrived. She was about to announce that she was going to do what she'd wanted to do, from the day their Green Street house had been bombed.

'I've bought a very nice house in Cadogan Square,' she said calmly. 'Mayfair is passé now; there are too many commercial properties; Knightsbridge is the best residential area in which to live.'

Juliet looked stunned. 'Those houses are enormous,' she exclaimed, 'some are even bigger than this house . . .' Her voice trailed away, knowing exactly what was on her mother's mind. Liza had always been torn between pride and jealousy as far as she'd been concerned; thrilled that Juliet had married a duke, yet jealous that she herself didn't have a title. Proud that Cameron had bought Juliet the most beautiful house in Park Lane, but jealous that she and Henry lived in a block of flats because he refused to buy another London house.

'Cadogan Square,' Charlotte echoed, adding in the understatement of the day, 'it won't be very cosy, will it?'

'Those houses have ten or twelve bedrooms!' Louise pointed out incredulously. 'What on earth are you going to do with a house that size?'

Rosie brightened, having a vision of herself moving in with Mummy and Charlotte, and Sophia and Jonathan, too, in the school holidays. Perhaps they could create Green Street all over again? There was all the furniture from Hartley, as well as the stuff Daddy had put in storage at the beginning of the war; she became flushed with excitement at the prospect of what might happen. A Knightsbridge address would be so much more suitable for a society columnist than Holland Park.

'Mummy, that's so thrilling! When do you move in?' Rosie gushed.

Juliet's eyes narrowed. Rosie was so desperately transparent that surely even Liza wouldn't fall for it?

'When it's been redecorated,' Liza replied catching Juliet's eye. 'And in case you think I'm running off with the Granville money,' she continued, her voice suddenly bitter, 'I've already made a will, leaving the house and the contents to you all, to be split five ways, so don't go accusing me of squandering your inheritance.'

'It's never been about the bloody money.' Juliet's voice was weary. 'It's been about selling the family home we all loved so much, it's been about betraying Daddy and Granny, and it's been about going behind our backs and not telling us what you were planning. *I'd* have bought Hartley from you, for the rest of us to share, if I'd known what you were doing.'

'What *you* don't seem to realize,' Liza reposted plaintively, 'is that Hartley represented everything I hate about the aristocracy and their basic way of life. I was consistently shown up as a middle-class urbanite. I don't hunt, or fish, and I loathed following the guns. I don't even play tennis. I hate country clothes and country pursuits, like walking the dogs. God!' She leaned back in her chair and closed her eyes, revealing a flicker of honesty about herself that she'd spent nearly forty years trying to hide. 'I did it for your father's sake,' she continued heavily, 'and I did it because it was expected of me. But I was never happy at Hartley. However I promised your father we'd base ourselves there when the war ended and we did. I don't have to keep that promise any longer now.'

For the first time she took a sip of the gin and tonic, only the faint tremble of her hand betrayed her nerves.

The murmur of the traffic in Park Lane, like the sound of a restless sea shore, was the only thing that broke the silence.

'Is there no way we can get Hartley back?' Charlotte asked eventually in a small voice.

Juliet lit another cigarette and drew deeply on it. 'I've tried.'

'And?'

'They wouldn't budge. They're sitting on a gold mine and they know it.'

Louise sighed heavily. 'Then that's that.' She rose lethargically to her feet. 'Juliet, do you mind if I leave? I don't think I could sit through lunch, making polite conversation.'

Juliet nodded in understanding. 'Run along, darling.'

'I think *we* should leave, Charlotte,' Liza said, raising her chin. 'Nothing is to be gained by staying here.'

Charlotte looked obstinate. 'I want to stay and talk to Juliet.'

Liza rose and placed her glass carefully on a side table. 'As you wish.'

'I'll come with you, Mummy,' Rosie jumped in immediately. 'Let me take you to lunch at the Berkeley. You've had a horrid morning.' She looked at Juliet. 'I think it's despicable the way you invited Mummy to lunch, then let everyone gang up on her like this.'

'Then why are *you* here?' Juliet asked with sarcastic surprise. 'You agreed we should all get together today and have it out with Mama.'

'I didn't know you were going to handle everything in such a hurtful way, though,' Rosie said huffily.

'You're just trying to curry favour because you want to move into this smart London house with Mama! Bored with slumming it in the flat I found for you in Holland Park, are you?'

Rosie flushed with embarrassment. 'Of course I'm not. The thought never crossed my mind.'

'Rosie, don't lie to me,' Juliet scoffed. 'I know you too well. You'll always put yourself first, no matter what. Can't you *see* what a treacherous thing Mama has done? She's gone behind our backs over this whole matter. Surely even *you* can't condone that!'

'Daddy left everything to Mummy. She could do what she liked with Hartley. She hasn't done anything illegal, so stop accusing her of swindling us, because she hasn't,' Rosie shrieked heatedly, her eyes brimming with tears of anger.

Liza spoke imperiously. 'Will you please stop talking about me as if I wasn't here. Rosie is right. I was left everything. I was perfectly within my rights to sell Hartley. My lawyer has assured me of that. I'm sorry you're disappointed, but there it is. It's my turn now to enjoy my life, especially,' she added looking at Juliet, 'since it's the only thing you've ever done, so there's no need for you to take the high ground.'

'I've never suggested you'd done anything illegal,' Juliet said coldly. 'I merely think that selling Hartley secretly is morally corrupt.'

'You're a bitch, Juliet!' Rosie stormed. 'Who are you to talk of morality, with all the lovers you've had?'

The two sisters stood glaring at each other with hostility. Positions had been taken up in the last few minutes; they were now on opposite sides of the fence in this family dispute. But then Juliet had always been on Henry's side over everything, while Rosie had seen things from her mother's point of view. But this was the most serious rift that had occurred between them and the chasm that was now splitting their relationship asunder related to an issue of morality, and that went much deeper than filial jealousy or mere rivalry.

As Liza turned to leave, she stopped and looked back at Juliet.

'Where's Amanda? Didn't she want to stab me in the back, too?'

'Now who's being dramatic, Mama?'

'I just wondered what her feelings were?'

'Oh, come on, Mummy, let's get out of here,' Rosie urged. 'You know what Amanda's like. If she saw an opportunity to feed the starving masses, she'd cut off her own right hand.'

# Fifteen

It was the summer of 1953, and the whole country was galvanized into welcoming a New Elizabethan Age, under the spell of the breathtakingly young and lovely girl who was to be crowned their new queen.

Street parties up and down the country were being organized, miles of red, white and blue bunting festooned every building, and were strung across main roads coupled with golden crowns. Millions of Union Jacks fluttered from flagpoles. After almost fourteen years of war and the resulting austerity and hardship, people embraced this great new beginning for Britain with understandable enthusiasm. The atmosphere of hope and expectation for the future of the country was almost palpable, felt amongst those who were of the highest rank down to the lowest.

Would this be as great an age as that of Elizabeth I, the pundits asked?

'The fact that she's twenty-six and beautiful, married to a handsome man, and they have a son and heir and a pretty daughter, makes her the most romantic woman in modern history,' Juliet opined to Daniel. 'Poor old Queen Victoria, eat your heart out! I think this *is* a new beginning for the country. It's the shot in the arm we all need to celebrate that the dark years are behind us.'

Daniel went out and bought their first television set, which was neatly housed in a mahogany cabinet with double doors so it resembled a piece of furniture when it was switched off, and Juliet decided to hold a small lunch party on 2nd June. Their guests could watch the Coronation ceremony on the black and white screen whilst helping themselves to a buffet that Dudley was going to set up at one end of the large drawing room before Juliet and Daniel went out to the Coronation Ball that evening.

'It'll be like our own little private cinema,' Juliet said in delight, as she requested more chairs to be arranged in front of the screen. 'We'll see everything this way, because they've placed hundreds of television cameras all over the place.' Then she paused, remembering. 'My God, how technology has advanced since the last Coronation! Rosie and I went with Nanny to see the King and Queen come out on the Palace balcony. We had to go to the cinema to watch Pathé News to see the actual event on film.'

'Who are you inviting to this extravaganza?' Daniel teased curiously.

'Sara, Susan and Leo, of course,' she told him sweetly. 'They might like to stay with us for a few days, so you can show them all the decorations.'

Daniel smiled, grateful for the way she always made his children welcome. 'I don't think they've ever seen television.'

'I thought we'd also have Louise, Shane, Rupert and Daisy. I'll invite Amanda but it's not exactly her thing. Charlotte might like to come, though my mother may have other plans for her.'

He paused, looking at Juliet questioningly. 'What about Rosie? And your mother, too, for that matter?'

Juliet's expression hardened. 'I haven't talked to either of them for months and I don't intend to start now. That last time was the final straw.'

She'd been unable to rid herself of the memory of their last day at Hartley, before Liza moved out. Large removal vans were parked outside, while Mrs Dobbs and Warwick, now both elderly, watched the proceedings through tear blurred eyes. Then Candida had arrived, towing a horse box in which to put Lady Anne's personal belongings from her bedroom and sitting room. As soon as she'd seen her mother's two old retainers, she immediately offered them jobs at her own house, their sole duty being to attend to Lady Anne's needs.

'You can live in very nice quarters in a converted barn, next to the main house,' Candida told them, pretending not to notice the tears pouring down their weathered cheeks. 'It'll be a godsend for Mother to have her own people to look after her,' she added cheerfully.

'Thank you, madam,' Warwick blurted out. 'Mrs Granville didn't want our services any more, and me and Betty were wondering what was to become of us.'

'Good heavens, Warwick,' Camilla said ebulliently, 'I was only fifteen when you came to work for Mother; you're both part of the family now. Pack your bags, and you can both come in the car with me this evening.'

'That's what I call a *real* lady,' Warwick murmured, as Candida stormed off to have words with her sister-in-law.

If it hadn't been for the concerted efforts of Candida, together with Juliet, Louise, and even Amanda, Liza would have whipped all the most valuable stuff up to her new house in London, and allowed the rest to be thrown out, or sent to the local auction house.

'It's scandalous,' Amanda had growled, when faced with the two thousand books in Henry's precious library which Liza had said 'could be left for who ever wants them. Books gather dust.'

Liza's other constant cry was 'Well, I don't want it,' whenever one of her daughters asked what was happening to such and such an item. With ruthless thoroughness she selected for herself exactly what she did want; the Louis XV beech wood chairs, the Louis XVI gilded chairs, the gilt ormolu mounted writing tables, the nineteenth century Aubusson and Savonnerie styled tapestry carpets, the eighteenth century dining table and chairs, paintings by Munnings, Boudin and Millais, and a score of other artists, as well as all the china, glass and silver.

Juliet looked with longing at her father's desk and his tilting captain's chair in which he always sat when he was writing letters. 'Does anyone want these?' she asked in a small voice.

'Well, I don't,' Liza and Rosie said in unison.

'You have them,' Louise said softly. 'He'd have liked that.'

Candida, who'd already tackled Liza over her treatment of Mrs Dobbs and Warwick, having told her, 'Most people treat their dogs better than you treat the servants!' now rounded on her not caring deeply enough about Henry's personal possessions, like his books, his silver ink-well, and the framed photographs of his late father and Lady Anne, which always stood on his desk.

'Liza, I think the girls should have first choice of everything, from what after all was their home. You're doing them out of Henry's legacy.'

Liza turned an ugly shade of red. 'You seem to forget Henry left everything to *me*.'

'Only because he thought he was going to die in the trenches, my dear,' Candida retorted scathingly. 'Believe me, your treacherous behaviour must be causing Henry to spin like a *top* in his grave. He'd be utterly ashamed of you.'

'I won't have you talking to me like that in my own house!' Liza flared.

'You mean in Capital Assets' house,' Candida countered swiftly. 'All this has nearly killed Mother. It's been the last straw after Henry's death.' Her shoulders sagged, in keeping with her large sagging body, yet she was still supremely dignified and regal. 'All Mother had to look forward to was returning here to watch her garden come alive again in the spring, instead of which it's about to be turned into a building site,' she added bitingly.

Rosie burst loudly into tears, like a child. 'You're making it worse by talking like that, Candida,' she wept. 'And stop having a go at Mummy. She wasn't happy here, and she deserves a little happiness, now.'

'Judging by the size of the removal vans she's ordered, she's helping herself to quite a lot of happiness,' Candida scorned, 'but don't worry your pretty little head about it, Rosie. Your Mummy will see that you're all right.'

Amanda dragged Juliet away from the ugly scene that had developed. She spoke earnestly. 'Listen, I wouldn't mind having some of Dad's books, but I've nowhere to put them right now. I'm getting myself a job and a flat when I leave Oxford, but could you look after some of them for me in the meantime?' Her eyes, blinking behind her glasses, were red rimmed and she looked washed out and miserable because she was suffering from conflicting emotions. She'd loved her father in particular because he'd encouraged her to be 'different' and go to university, and she'd loved Hartley, although her political views were that no one family should indulge in such opulence, but now she'd lost him she felt as if her life had gone adrift.

Being careful not to sound sympathetic because she knew Amanda would hate that, Juliet said briskly, 'Why don't I take all the books and the furniture from the library, and look after them for the time being? Then as soon as you've got a flat, come and help yourself to what ever you want.'

Amanda looked relieved. 'Thanks a lot,' she said gruffly, before turning swiftly away.

In the end, Juliet, Louise and Amanda shared what was left in the house, because Charlotte said she didn't know what she wanted, and Rosie said nothing because she knew her mother would let her eventually have everything she wanted, anyway.

As Juliet drove away at the end of the long painful day, she turned to have a last look at Hartley. The empty house seemed to stare back at her sadly, its windows lifeless and dead, its silence haunting, as if it was reproaching them all for leaving.

All their lives Hartley had given them warmth and shelter, comfort and consolation, it had been a haven of peace and understanding, and now they were abandoning it into the greedy hands of a property developer. The very heart of Hartley was being ripped out and plundered and with it, it seemed, the heart of the Granville family. Relationships had been destroyed beyond repair, and without Henry and without Hartley, life would never be the same again, Juliet realized, as she let off the handbrake and pulled away up the long winding drive, for the last time.

'It was a really dreadful day, and I wish you'd been with me,' Juliet told Daniel.

'It happened months ago, darling. Try to forget about it. Your grandmother has settled in very well with Candida, especially as she's got Mrs Dodds and Warwick with her.' He held her close, kissing her lightly on the tip of her nose. 'As for your mother, well, what can I say?'

Juliet nodded. 'There's nothing to say. I just hope, after all the mayhem she's caused, that she's happy. From what I hear, Rosie adores living in one of the grandest houses in Cadogan Square, but then she would, wouldn't she? She's got nothing on her conscience except siding with Mama. It's the same with Charlotte. But if I was my mother, I don't think I'd be able to sleep.'

Cecil Beaton had decorated the Savoy with his usual flamboyant style for the Coronation Ball, and the guest of honour was Sir Winston Churchill. All those who hadn't been invited to the Abbey, spent the day in anticipation of the evening's revelry. Three thousand bottles of champagne had been put on ice in readiness for the celebration and it was expected to go on until the early hours.

Juliet, wearing a midnight blue chiffon evening dress by Victor Stiebel, which was draped and moulded to her body, added a diamond and sapphire tiara and earrings, and a diamond brooch shaped like a lovers' knot on the shoulder of her gown.

Daniel took in a sharp breath when he saw her. Juliet's allure never failed to astonish him, even after all these years. He was instantly reminded of their first night in Paris, when she'd been seventeen and she'd been afraid yet at the same time was longing for him to seduce her.

'You look marvellous,' he said, his rich deep voice croaking. 'I wish we were staying at home now.'

'Darling.' She came up to him and laid her hand on the shoulder of his tail coat. 'You look marvellous, too. I want to dance all night with you.'

He leaned forward, his mouth to her ear. 'You'll do more than that before the dawn breaks,' he whispered.

When they arrived they were surrounded by friends, including many people who'd been Henry's friends. Lady Diana Cooper, still a renowned beauty, took Juliet's hand.

'I'm appalled that Hartley Hall has been sold,' she whispered discreetly. 'What was your mother thinking of?'

Juliet was aware that the gossips had been hard at work for the past year, shocked by what had happened. 'It's very sad,' she agreed. 'If only Daddy had made a more recent will I'm sure things would have been different.'

'That's what is so strange.' Lady Diana's blue eyes looked searchingly into Juliet's face. 'Henry was so *organized*. It was so unlike him not to make sure his affairs were in order.'

The Rothchilds came up to Juliet and Daniel next, and then the Duchess of Argyll, who'd been in the Abbey. Then they spotted Chips Channon, who'd been a frequent guest before the war when Henry and Liza had entertained lavishly in Green Street.

More friends came to cluster round Juliet, who seemed to be at the peak of her beauty and radiance that night.

'There's a woman who's succeeded in getting everything she wants,' said Chips Channon, glancing over at her. As always, many men were attracted to her, fetching her glasses of champagne and asking her to dance, but Juliet moved slowly, never more than a few yards from Daniel, refusing to dance until later. After a while, she and Daniel took to the floor, moving as one as they swayed to the music. It was obvious to all who saw them that they were still in love and could never have enough of each other and that her smile was that of a woman utterly fulfilled and happy.

'Unlike her mother,' Chips naughtily pointed out, watching as Liza made several circuits of the ballroom, trying to find someone to talk to.

She'd earlier been heard to complain bitterly that Norman Hartnell 'had been too busy to make her a ball gown for the night because he'd been so wrapped up in making the Queen's coronation robes'. Her words were repeated amongst the guests amid gales of scornful laughter, until someone exclaimed, 'Who does she think she is?'

'All Henry's friends have shunned her since she sold Hartley Hall,' Chips continued with a wicked glint in his eyes. 'And now she's living in this great town house with two of her daughters, and I hear she's pushed to scrape together eight people for a dinner party.'

During the evening Juliet became aware of Liza, over-dressed in a gold lamé Grecian style evening dress, wearing more jewels than the new Queen, as she walked around looking lost, until she finally decided to sit down in a corner with several elderly widows where she was less conspicuous.

'Pigeons coming home to roost,' Juliet observed, realizing with fresh shock that in the past it had been her father's friends rather than her mother's, who had frequented their house, and that by selling Hartley she'd betrayed him and all he'd stood for and his friends knew this.

'Do you want to go and talk to her?' Daniel asked, reading her thoughts. He had little use for Liza himself, having always thought of her as a snobbish parvenue, but he couldn't help feeling sorry for her now.

'She's brought it all upon herself. There are a hundred things she could have done to make herself happy, even without Dads, but selling Hartley wasn't one of them,' Juliet said regret-fully. 'She'll just have to get herself some new friends, and I'm sure Rosie will help with all her new social contacts.'

The glorious night was almost over, the revellers began to drift off.

'What a day to remember,' Daniel said as they left the Savoy. They both looked up at the sky which was clear of clouds after a long and rainy day. 'Poor Queen; I hope the weather didn't spoil her day.'

'I don't suppose it did,' Juliet said, smiling, as they climbed into their car. 'Like me, she has a wonderful husband by her side, and that's the most important thing of all.'

Rosie let herself into the Cadogan Square house, having been dropped off by a group of young people who were wildly impressed to have met the social columnist of *Society*. The hall light was still on, and she was just about to go upstairs to bed when she heard a noise in the enormous drawing room, which the previous owners had used as a ballroom.

Peering round the massive mahogany door, she saw the soft glow of a silk-shaded table lamp illuminating one of the dark corners. Feeling as if she were entering the stage set of a grand opera, Rosie walked towards the lamp, her feet soundless on the thick carpeting.

'Mummy . . .?' she exclaimed with shock, as she saw a huddled figure draped in gold lamé, on one of the sofas. 'Mummy? What's the matter?'

Liza gave a ragged sob. 'I wish I was dead. It was the worst evening of my life.'

Rosie turned on some more lights, and saw her mother's face was blotchy from crying, and her mascara was streaked under her eyes. Her dress was crumpled, and her jewellery had been flung on the floor, like discarded Christmas decorations.

'What's going on?' Rosie asked, concerned.

'Nobody would talk to me,' Liza wept bitterly. 'All our old friends were there. People we'd known for years. People we used to have to dinner. They all snubbed me, or cut me dead. Can you imagine how I felt? Even Chips Channon was curt. And Juliet didn't come near me the whole evening, because she was too busy having a good time.'

'Oh, Mummy . . .' Rosie sank down onto the sofa beside Liza, and put an arm around her shoulder. 'Did you go alone? Didn't you take anyone with you?'

Liza raised her wrecked face. 'Who could I take? I wouldn't

want to go with another woman, and how can I take a man, so soon after your father's death?'

Rosie could see her mother's predicament. It was all right for her to go to parties without an escort, because she was young and attractive, and it was her job. She smiled to herself as she remembered the driver of the car who'd just dropped her off. He'd taken quite a liking to her, but so did most young men these days. It was different for her mother. She was dreadfully old; fifty-eight, nearly fifty-nine.

'It was very brave of you to go on your own,' Rosie told her soothingly. 'Perhaps, in future, you should go with a group of friends.'

'Don't you understand?' Liza demanded, rattled. 'I don't *have* any friends now your father's dead. No one wants me! I'm all alone and I don't think I can bear it.'

'You've got Charlotte and me.' Rosie paused, as if she'd just had an idea. 'Why don't we give a drinks party?'

'Who would we invite?' Her mother's voice was edged with panic.

'In my address book I've so far got about three hundred names of people I've met in the past few months. People of *all* ages,' she added, quickly. 'They're not all top drawer, few even have titles, but they're fun and interesting and I think it's time we sought pastures new.'

'Not top drawer?'

'Not top drawer,' Rosie echoed. 'But does it matter? All our marital forays into the titled nobility have been pretty disastrous. Look at Charlie? What did I get out of him, apart from a title? Look at Cameron Kincardine?'

'He was at the ball tonight, with a new wife. I saw Juliet talking to him. *Such* a pity he turned out to be – queer!'

'Then there was Philibert . . . he may have been a Baron, but where did that get *me*?' Rosie continued. 'He broke my heart, just like Alastair Slaidburn who loved me until Juliet stole him from me. I ask you, from now on I'm going for Mr Smith or Mr Brown, and as long as he's got some money, he'll do for me.'

Liza sat in silence gazing into the gloomy shadows of the room she'd planned as a setting when she entertained the *beau monde*. Silver grey watered silk curtains framed the large windows, the Aubusson tapestry from Hartley hung on one wall, and a plethora of Louis XV1 chairs and little tables holding objets d'art were skilfully arranged into 'conversation areas'. A titled lady who had fallen upon hard times came to arrange flowers twice a week, and a Spanish couple, Salvador and Josephine, acted as butler and housekeeper. It was all very different from the formal days of Green Street when Mrs Fowler had ruled supreme in the kitchen, and Parsons had run the whole household with military precision. This foreign couple didn't even understand half of what she said, and Salvador insisted on wearing a white jacket to open the front door, making him look like a third rate dentist.

But where were the friends she thought she had? What about the glittering dinner parties she'd planned? This house was supposed to have been a setting, from which she could relaunch herself into society, but the whole thing had fallen as flat as a deflated soufflé.

Rosie was also gazing into the shadowy room, which lacked vitality and resembled a room setting in Harrods' furniture department.

She'd expected to be living with Philibert in her own villa in Monte Carlo by now, where the sun was hot and the nights were balmy, where the restaurants served fantastic food and the shops stocked fashionable clothes. She'd also thought she'd be a Baroness, spending weekends on smart yachts, and bringing her children out to stay during the school holidays. Most of all, she'd expected to be made love to every night for the rest of her life.

All gone. Dreams turned to dust. She and her mother, in reality, were two disappointed women, who'd had such high hopes, but whose fantasies had come crashing down. Rosie blinked away her tears.

'I'll draw up a list and send out cards tomorrow,' she said bravely. 'Let's not make the party *too* grand, because it could frighten away some of the people I know. Let's just have a "jolly" and see what happens.'

'And don't let's have any of the family except Charlotte, that is if she's not busy, as usual,' Liza requested.

We're not talking to the rest of the family, anyway, Rosie reflected, as she made her way up to bed. She'd sided with her mother, and now she was wondering if she'd done the right thing.

# Sixteen

Louise looked up from reading the *Daily Mail*. It was late in the evening and Shane was sprawled along the old sofa in the window, relaxing after a long day in the hospital. 'It says here,' she told him, 'the price of houses is going up.'

'I know,' he replied sleepily. 'It's lucky we bought this house when we did. I couldn't afford it now.'

The small terraced house in Fulham had cost Shane three hundred pounds, for which he'd had to take out a mortgage.

'How much is it worth now?' Louise asked, as she folded the newspaper in half so she could more easily read Paul Tanfield's Diary, a gossip column about the elite.

'Fifteen hundred,' Shane replied, shutting his eyes and relaxing with satisfaction. 'One day it will be worth a couple of thousand.'

But Louise wasn't listening. She was clutching the newspaper, her expression incredulous. 'My God! No! It can't be true!' she exclaimed, an edge of panic in her voice.

Shane opened his eyes and looked over at her. 'What is it?'

'It says here . . . that Mummy's getting married again! Oh, Shane, it can't be true, can it? Surely she wouldn't want to marry anyone else after Daddy?'

He rolled off the sofa, and came over to where she sat. 'Let's see,' he said, taking the paper from her. She looked up at him in anguish.

'I can't bear it if she does,' she said, upset. 'Daddy only died a few years ago. How are we supposed to accept a stepfather so soon?'

'You can't rely on these gossip columns, sweetheart. They print all sorts of rubbish, because it sells newspapers.'

'But I've noticed Paul Tanfield's is the most accurate. Every story is usually true.'

Shane scanned the column.

Out and about on the town these days is Mrs Liza Granville, 59, widow of banker, Henry Granville, who is being escorted by constant companion Lord Rotherhithe, 72, a Labour life peer and an old friend of ex-Prime Minister, Mr Clement Attlee. A source close to the couple says they are about to tie the knot. Mrs Granville, who was left Hartley Hall by her late husband, sold it in order to buy herself a Knightsbridge house, in which the couple are expected to live after they marry.

There was a long silence as Shane continued to gaze thoughtfully at the newsprint. 'The first thing you'd better do is find out if it's true,' he said at last.

'I don't want to have to talk to Mummy,' Louise said quickly. 'I wonder if Juliet knows anything?'

'You'd have heard from Juliet, if she had.'

At that moment Rupert swung into the room in his striped pyjamas. He was tall and strong looking for a boy of thirteen, and he was disarmingly like his father. Every time Louise looked at him, it struck her with a gentle blow of shock that Jack had only been two years older than Rupert, when she'd fallen in love with him.

'What's up?' he asked immediately when he saw Louise's face.

'You should be asleep, old boy,' Shane said good humouredly.

'I'm hungry. I came down to make myself a sandwich. Mum, what's wrong?' Sensitive and fiercely protective of his mother, it had been Rupert who had offered to give her his little farm in Wales, when he'd heard Hartley had been sold, so she'd still have somewhere to go in the country.

Louise wiped her eyes. 'The newspaper says Granny's getting married again.'

His young face registered astonishment. 'She's a bit old for that, isn't she?'

Shane said with a grin, 'It's not Mummy's grandmother, it's Liza.'

236

'I know. That's what I mean. She's a bit old to marry; she must be nearly sixty!'

'Oh, ancient!' Shane agreed.

'I'm going to ring up Juliet,' Louise announced, going to the telephone in the hall. 'I must find out if she knows anything.'

'Are you joking?' was Juliet's incredulous reaction. 'God in heaven! What is she thinking of? Not that Mama hasn't always been a law unto herself, and she's always wanted a title, hasn't she? Listen, I'm going to ring Charlotte. Let's hope that absurd little Spaniard who calls himself a butler answers the phone, although it's quite late, isn't it? I'm going to pretend I'm a fashion editor and I need to contact Charlotte urgently. If she knows it's me ringing, she might refuse to talk to me.'

'Will you let me know what she says?'

An hour later, although it was nearly midnight, Juliet drove herself to Fulham, parked the car outside Louise's home, and hurrying up the front path, rang the bell.

'Charlotte's told me everything,' she announced, when Louise opened the door.

'Come in. I've just made some tea,' Louise whispered. 'Shane's gone to bed because he's exhausted.'

A few minutes later, curled up on either end of the sofa with their cups of tea, the sisters looked at each other, remembering past occasions in their lives when they'd supported each other in times of crisis.

'So it's true then?' Louise asked hollowly.

Juliet nodded. 'You know that Mama has been snubbed by all Daddy's old friends since she sold Hartley? Well, after the Coronation Ball last year, Rosie came home to find Mama quite hysterical because she had no friends. Everyone had deserted her, and she'd bought that great house for entertaining.'

'Were we too hard on her?' Louise asked guiltily.

'Mama is a great survivor. Don't forget that. She could have handled leaving Hartley very differently,' Juliet said firmly. 'Anyway, the point is Rosie meets lots of people and goes to dozens of parties a year, and the people who invite her are the people who love to be written up in *Society*.'

'Yes?' said Louise, not completely understanding.

'Well, she actually thought Mama might get on with them more than she did with Daddy's friends, because they'd have a similar background to her.'

Louise covered her face with her hands. 'Oh, God, we're being terrible snobs, aren't we?'

'Make no mistake, Rosie's a terrible snob, too. But she was right! Absolutely spot on. She gave a series of drinks parties in that Cadogan Square house that is a cross between a mausoleum and the stage set for *Cosi Fan Tutte* and in no time at all, Mama had a host of new friends! Really nice, interesting people, who just didn't happen to be aristocratic.'

There was dread in Louise's voice. 'And . . .?'

'And one of them was Herbert Brown, a timber merchant who was born near the Rotherhithe docks in the East End, from whence he took the name when Attlee made him a life peer. According to Charlotte he's a widower, with no children, and she described him as reminding her of a Father Christmas figure. You know, big and jolly and always cheerful,' Juliet added dryly.

They looked at each other, remembering Henry. Tall, slim and elegant, with the fine features of his mother Lady Anne, and the charm and manners to go with it.

'And Mummy *likes* him?' Louise said wonderingly.

Juliet's manner was business like. 'They're both lonely. They have a lot in common like going to the cinema, eating in good restaurants, and being gregarious. He's apparently very rich, so he won't be sponging on Mama. And she's got the house of his dreams . . .? What more can they expect at their age?'

Louise nodded slowly. 'I do mind, though. Don't you?'

'Yes, of course I do. Terribly. No one could ever begin to take Dads' place, but he'll always belong to *us*, won't he? No one can take that away from us. We had the most marvellous father,' Juliet's voice wobbled dangerously, 'but at least we won't need to feel guilty about Mama. It's her life, and you and I are lucky to be happily married so I suppose we shouldn't begrudge her a little happiness.' She blinked rapidly and reached for a handkerchief in her handbag.

'What about Rosie and Charlotte? Are they going to be turfed out of Cadogan Square?'

'Apparently not, though Charlotte wants to get a flat of her own soon, Rosie wants to stay. That's no surprise, is it?'

'Does Amanda know?'

'Only if she's read today's newspaper. I imagine she will thoroughly approve. A member of the Labour Party in the family.' Juliet raised her eyes to heaven, 'Oh yes, she'll approve, all right.'

Louise spoke thoughtfully. 'She worshipped Daddy, though. He might have had different political views, but she thought the world of him because he had an open mind and treated everyone the same. Our mother marrying a Labour supporter might just take the wind out of her sails. Amanda loves being controversial and different from the rest of us. Now she's going to be rather overshadowed by a Labour peer in the family, isn't she?'

Juliet chuckled. 'I'd better phone her tomorrow and break the news gently.'

'Do you suppose they're going to have a church wedding?' Louise asked, appalled at the thought. 'Honestly, if they are I'm not going. In fact, I'm not going wherever it's held. It will bring back all my grief at losing Daddy; there's no way I can watch Mummy marrying someone else.'

'I hadn't thought that far ahead,' Juliet replied soberly, 'but I don't think I could bear it, either.'

'Perhaps they'll opt for a quiet registry office thingy?'

Juliet gave a deep sigh. 'Oh, God, if only Dads hadn't died. And Hartley was still ours. How happy we'd all still be.'

Having received a phone call from Juliet, Candida told her mother what had happened the next day.

'Those poor girls,' Lady Anne said quietly, herself beyond hurt, beyond pain, and resigned to the vicissitudes of life.

'Damned hard on them,' Candida agreed. 'Juliet sounded quite cut up and apparently Amanda is distraught at the very thought of anyone stepping into her father's shoes.'

'But this man won't, will he? No one could take over where Henry left off. I'm just thankful all the girls are grown-up now, and have their own lives.' Lady Anne sighed. 'Poor Liza. You can't blame her, I suppose, for wanting companionship.'

'I don't blame her at all. I was a lonely widow myself at one point, but Marcus had been dead for fifteen years before

I married Andrew, and I'd made sure Marina and Sebastian knew him and liked him before I even *considered* accepting his proposal. For Henry's daughters to find out from a gossip column that their mother was getting hitched again is dreadful,' she added heatedly.

Rosie phoned Juliet later that day. 'I gather you've heard the news?' she began, obviously excited. 'Mummy wondered if you and Daniel would like to come for drinks next Tuesday? It's time we all got together so you can meet Herbert.'

'Jesus, Rosie! Do you really expect us to be thrilled by this?' Juliet exploded. 'Without a word of warning, without even meeting this man, we're supposed to welcome him into our midst as our future step-father? Why has Mama sprung this on us all? Does she really expect us to jump for joy?'

'There's more to coming for a drink than that. Mummy really wants to see you, Louise and Amanda. It's important you come on Tuesday.'

'What's so important about it, Rosie?'

'It just *is*.' She sounded evasive. 'Please come, Juliet, and make sure the others come, too.'

With reluctance Juliet agreed. 'But don't let Mama think we're pleased to have this man foisted on us,' she added. 'It changes nothing. We'll never forgive her for selling Hartley behind our backs.'

But by Tuesday evening Juliet had decided that there was no point in their being nasty to Herbert Rotherhithe. She told the others, 'This is not his fault, so we must treat him in a civilized way. After all, he's done nothing wrong except wanting to marry Mama.'

Amanda looked mutinous and said nothing, but Louise nodded in agreement. 'We obviously can't be rude, but I do hope he's nice.'

To their surprise, Liza had decided not to hold the drinks party in the enormous ballroom-cum-drawing room, but in what Henry would have called 'the snug,' a pretty sitting-room, decorated with magnolia walls and rose patterned chintz curtains and covers. There was a charming casualness about the room, which had books, newspapers and magazines strewn about, and a television set in one corner. At a glance Juliet was sure that Herbert Rotherhithe had influenced Liza's taste when redecorating this room because she'd previously had it stuffed with a lot of gilt furniture and draped satin curtains.

Rosie and Charlotte were standing with their mother in front of the fireplace when Salvador showed them into the room. There was no sign of Herbert.

'Hello, darlings,' Liza said, coming forward to greet them.

'Mama,' Juliet said formally.

Louise and Amanda murmured their 'Hellos', while Daniel and Shane smiled politely as they returned Liza's greeting.

They all noticed that their mother looked different. Quieter, less desperate to please, and as if she'd found an inner peace. Even her appearance was softer and she wore a neat little black dress, with two strands of graduated pearls around her neck and simple pearl earrings.

Salvador offered glasses of champagne, and when everyone had been served, Liza quietly signalled for him to leave the room.

Juliet and Louise flashed warning glances at each other, preparing themselves for a showdown.

'Why don't we all sit?' Liza suggested, perching herself on the arm of a large comfortable looking chair. 'Herbert will be joining us presently,' she began, 'and I very much hope you're all going to like him. He's a dear man, very kind, and he has no intention of trying to become a step-father. He met Daddy several times during the war and he liked and respected him enormously.' She faltered and for a moment it looked as if she was going to cry, but then she rallied and her voice was strong.

'I desperately wanted you all to come here this evening, for another reason.' She looked at them all, her five daughters and two sons-in-law. Then she drew a deep breath and spoke. 'I wanted you all here so I could apologize to you all, from the bottom of my heart, for getting rid of Hartley. It was a dreadful, unforgivable thing for me to do, and looking back, it was also a very stupid thing to do. I read somewhere that people often make hasty and irrecoverable decisions when one has been bereaved, but that is not an excuse for what I did.'

Juliet, Rosie, Louise, Amanda and Charlotte continued to look back at her, hardly able to believe their ears, but a voice in Juliet's head kept saying; But why did you?

241

Daniel and Shane sat very still, aware that this was possibly the bravest thing Liza had ever done in her life.

'I know how terribly upset you all were, and I don't blame you,' Liza continued contritely. 'It is something I will regret for the rest of my life. Hartley was the family home, Granny's home, and perhaps that was part of my trouble. Your father died so suddenly and so tragically, that I became desperate to get away from Hartley and all its memories.

'I should have talked to you all about it, and told you how cut-off and lonely I felt, stuck in the country in that great house. And I should have consulted Granny; all I can say is I felt panic stricken at the idea of Hartley, which seemed to be hanging like a mill stone around my neck for the rest of my life. Especially as none of you were in a position to actually live there full time and run the place, so when I was approached by a company that wanted to buy it, I said "yes". I can't tell you how sorry I am, and I only hope that in time you will forgive me, but that is something I don't take for granted. Getting to know Herbert has made me see things so differently, and I've learned . . . perhaps too late in life . . . what really matters.'

Her eyes were brimming now and her once pretty face had turned blotchy.

Rosie went and put her arms around her. 'Don't get upset, Mummy. We all make mistakes . . . God knows, I've made enough in my time.'

Juliet glanced at Daniel. He gave her a look of loving understanding, as if to say, the choice is yours, and I'll support you whatever you do.

Rosie and Charlotte had already forgiven their mother, but Juliet realized that if Louise and Amanda were to do the same, it would only be because she'd led the way. But could she forgive Liza? What really held Juliet back was that her mother had betrayed Henry's trust.

The silence in the room lengthened, deepened. Someone was going to have to say something soon or the moment of reconciliation would pass forever. What was Hartley, she asked herself, except a house made of bricks and mortar, wood and stone, and a million treasured memories that no one could take away from them? Was it worth the family being split down the middle because it had been sold over their heads?

Sister against sister? Daughters against their mother? No one could take away what Hartley had meant to them all, any more than the memory of their father could be erased from their minds. Even more importantly it struck Juliet that Henry would have been deeply distressed if he knew they'd fallen out with their mother because of it.

'Never let the sun go down on your anger,' was one of his favourite sayings.

Juliet rose to her feet, watched by her four sisters with anxious expressions. Then she went over to her mother and kissed her on both cheeks.

'We've been stupid to let it come between us all,' she said softly. 'Of course we forgive you, Mama. I did some crazy things myself when I thought I'd lost Daniel forever. We should all have stayed closer to you, instead of being so wrapped up in our own lives when Dads died.'

A moment later all the sisters were hugging Liza and each other, crying and laughing at the same time, with a mixture of sadness at what they'd all lost and a sense of relief that they'd all come together again.

At that moment the door opened and a tall rotund man with a mass of white hair and twinkling eyes set in a chubby pink face stood smiling at them all as if he looked pleased with the way things had turned out.

'This is Herbert,' Liza announced unnecessarily, and a wave of mild hysteria made the sisters giggle.

'I could be the new butler!' Herbert quipped. 'How can you be sure?'

He grabbed Louise's glass. 'A top-up, madam?' he asked with a flourish.

Then he shook hands with everyone, before joining Liza in front of the fireplace.

'Have you told everyone our immediate plans, dear heart?' he asked her gently, looking into her face with affection.

Liza dabbed her eyes for the last time. 'We're slipping away on December 1st, which is only a month away, to get married privately in a registry office, then we're flying straight to New York, where I've never been but Herbert says is marvellous, for a month long visit. Candida has invited you all for Christmas, hasn't she?'

Juliet nodded. 'God knows how she's going to fit us all in,

what with the children and the dogs, but she insists there's masses of room, and it'll give Granny a lift if we're all around.'

Liza looked sober for a moment. 'Poor Granny,' she murmured softly. 'She'll probably never want to set eyes on me again, but give her my love, won't you. And tell her I'm dreadfully, dreadfully sorry?'

'Granny has a great ability to forgive,' Rosie pointed out. 'Remember when Gaston turned up one Sunday when we were having lunch? To be presented with your late husband's love child must take a hell of a lot of grit.'

'I'm hoping to make the great lady's acquaintance one of these days,' Herbert remarked. 'Liza has told me a great deal about her. She obviously belongs to the old school of good manners and British backbone.'

Everyone started talking again, glasses of champagne were topped up and Liza said, 'I hope you can all stay for supper?' She caught Rosie's eye and smiled. 'Nothing grand. Just cold meat and salad, and Josephine has made a trifle.'

Rosie winked back in approval. Meanwhile everyone noticed that Amanda, glasses perched on her nose, hair scraped back behind her ears, was asking Herbert Rotherhithe all about Mr Attlee, and what was he doing these days to wrench power back from Churchill and the Conservative Party?

Daniel moved close to Juliet's side, and planted a quick kiss on her cheek. 'That was magnificent, darling. I know it couldn't have been easy, and I'm so proud of you.'

She looked up at him, smiling. 'I doubt if I could have done it without you,' she whispered back, 'because you give me a sense of perspective. I know now, thanks to you, what's really important.'


It was December 18th, and before packing to go to Candida's house for Christmas, Juliet decided to sort out some of the books and furniture she'd been storing from her father's study, in her attic. It had been agreed she should keep his desk and chair for herself, and they had been installed in her writing room, but there were tables, chests, dozens of boxes of books, and a beautiful glass-fronted bookcase.

Amanda, who'd graduated with honours in economics, had started a job in the Labour Party headquarters, thanks to an introduction from Herbert, and she'd already found herself a flat. In the new year she'd promised Juliet she'd come and choose what she'd like from the items saved from Hartley.

In the meantime, dressed in an old pair of slacks and a headscarf, Juliet worked in the dusty space by the light of a hanging electric bulb, sorting out the boxes of papers. Henry seemed to have kept every receipt, bank statement, tax return, insurance policy and household bill that he'd ever incurred. She hardly knew where to start; was there any point in keeping any of it? Who needed a 1933 receipt for the Rolls Royce he'd bought? Or a 1941 request from the local council to take in evacuees?

After a couple of hours she felt hot, sticky and dirty. Perhaps she should just bundle everything back into the boxes and leave it all? The only interest in all this stuff lay in the low cost of living before the war, and how different it was in 1954. She glanced at the list of staff wages when they'd lived in Green Street. A butler, cook, three parlour maids, two scullery maids, a chauffeur, nanny and nursery maid, and Miss Astley, Liza's lady's maid, had cost Henry just over one thousand pounds a year in wages. Nowadays, Juliet's staff wages in Park Lane for Dudley, a cook and three dailies was double that!

She was just about to close the last box and call it a day when a document slid out from between a stack of business correspondence. She unfolded it and sitting on a wooden crate, spread it on her lap and started to read it.

An hour later Dudley came up to the attic to offer her a cup of tea and found her in the same position, with the document still on her lap. She gazed out of the skylight at the passing clouds, with a strange expression.

He cleared his throat. 'Everything all right, madam? I wondered if you'd like me to bring you up a tea tray?' He looked at her still profile.

'Madam?' he asked urgently. 'Are you all right, madam?'

As he stepped forward with a look of concern, Juliet turned to look at him as if he were a complete stranger. Then she blinked, and heaved herself heavily to her feet.

'Madam . . .? Is there anything I can get you, madam?'

She stretched wearily, holding the document in her hand. 'Nothing at the moment, thank you.' She was automatically polite. 'I'm going to have a bath. Maybe tea ... or a drink, later. I'll let you know.'

She turned and walked slowly down the stairs to her bedroom on the first floor. Shedding her dirty clothes, she ran a hot bath and poured a generous amount of scented bath salts into the water. She felt as tired and as battered as she'd done when she'd come off duty, after a night out with the ambulance unit during the Blitz. Who could she tell what she'd discovered amongst Henry's old papers in the attic, apart from Daniel?

Should she tell anyone? Wasn't it better to let sleeping dogs lie?

She lay full length in the six-foot-long cast iron bath, her eyes closed, letting the perfumed water soothe her aching limbs. The point was, if she didn't tell anyone, it was going to be an agonizing burden to carry over Christmas with all the family gathered together.

Would she be able to smile and act naturally for the four long days of their stay, whilst hiding the existence of the document she'd found?

Or would Granny and Candida, both sharp-eyed and intuitive, spot there was something wrong about her demeanour?

Candida and Andrew, always perfect hosts, were in the hall to greet everyone when they arrived on Christmas Eve.

Their charming house was warm with blazing fires in all the rooms, and a nine-foot tree stood in the curve of the staircase in the hall, decorated with artificial snow and silver baubles. Underneath, an ever growing stack of presents was piling up. All the lights in the house were on, and sprigs of holly rested on top of picture frames and doorways, tied with red ribbon.

'Well, with all the kids here, I thought we'd jolly well better decorate the house,' Candida said when Juliet congratulated her on how lovely everything looked.

'Is there anything I can do to help?' Juliet asked, determined to hide her feelings. If the family were to know what she'd discovered, the repercussions would be terrible.

'Dear girl,' Candida replied, 'we're as organized as it's possible to be with nearly twenty people staying in the house! Andrew's in charge of drinks, someone else, thank heavens, is doing all the cooking, otherwise we're all just going to have

246

to muck in,' she added cheerfully. 'Ah, here's Louise! My goodness, how Rupert's grown!' With that she bustled off to greet them as they clambered out of their car in the drive.

Juliet and her children went to the drawing room to see her grandmother, who was sitting by the fire.

'My darling girl, it's so good to see you,' Lady Anne greeted her, kissing Juliet on both cheeks. 'And Tristan and Cathryn, too! What a treat to have you all here. Cathryn, you're growing into a big girl!'

'And I'm beginning to feel my age!' Juliet joked.

Cathryn had inherited her father's dark eyes and hair and Juliet's exquisite features.

'What a little beauty,' Lady Anne whispered in delight. 'Now come along, and tell me all your news, Juliet.'

Rosie and Charlotte arrived next, bearing extravagant presents for everyone, and more luggage than anyone else.

'When is Amanda arriving?' Candida asked. She worried about the girl, because she was always the odd-one-out in the family, and easily forgotten amid the glamour and good looks of the others.

Louise grinned. 'She's arriving later this evening. Herbert has lent her his brand new Austin Sheerline whilst he and Mummy are in New York and she's driving herself down after some political meeting she had to attend, in Battersea.'

'Well . . .!' Lady Anne clapped her hands and laughed. 'That girl's going to go far. I'm so glad Lord Rotherhithe has taken her under his wing. Henry would have been very pleased.'

Rosie giggled. 'It certainly pays to know people in high places, doesn't it? You'll see quite a change in Amanda, Granny.'

'I see what you mean,' her grandmother whispered a couple of hours later, as she watched Amanda talking to Andrew Pemberton. Amanda had had her hair cut short in quite a fashionable style, and she was wearing a very neat dark green tweed suit, and black shoes with a slight heel. She had a pair of fashionable glasses, and she was even wearing a very small amount of make-up.

'She's realized that even Labour politicians have to look good,' Rosie whispered back. 'Not showy, but good. We went on a shopping spree when she got her new job, and it's quite a transformation, isn't it?'

'I'm so pleased for her. And I gather you're going to continue living at Cadogan Square, Rosie?'

'Yes. Mummy's had the top two floors converted into a flat for me and the children. Sophia is nearly seventeen, you know, and Jonathan's fifteen.'

'How the time flies,' Lady Anne remarked, looking at them as they sat chatting to Rupert. 'What does it mean to Jonathan to have inherited his father's title?'

'I think he tries to live it down at the moment,' Rosie admitted. 'To be Lord this or Lord that isn't what they call very 'cool' these days. Anyway, so many of the boys at Eton have titles; it doesn't mean as much as it used to.'

'Except perhaps to your mother?' Lady Anne suggested slyly. 'Now she's Lady Rotherhithe it's only natural she should be pleased.'

Rosie shook her head. 'Mummy's changed. I think she'd have married Herbert even if he'd still been Mr Brown.'

Christmas day dawned clear and sunny, more like a spring day than a midwinter one. All the young ones were up early, opening their stockings, although little Cathryn was the only one who still believed in Father Christmas.

After church, the family congregated in the hall where Andrew had set up a punchbowl of *glühwein*, which he poured into glasses with a ladle. The aroma of the mulled wine and cinnamon was warm and heady, mingling with the scent of applewood burning in the fireplaces.

'Just what one needs after church,' Amanda observed, taking a swig of the warm drink. 'God, I'm starving! When's lunch?'

In the dining room, festooned with paper chains and bunches of balloons, Candida had set up a long festive looking table for Christmas lunch. Candles and crackers, bowls of chocolates and fudge, little antique carved angels and small branches of greenery had been arranged in charmingly haphazard fashion on the table, and with 'help from the village' as she always described the local charladies, everyone was quickly served with turkey and ham, half a dozen different vegetables, cranberry sauce, bread sauce and gravy.

'My dear Candida, you've done us proud,' Andrew said approvingly, as he filled up Lady Anne's wine glass.

The chatter around the table was lively and animated, and

as always, Candida kept the party atmosphere going with her robust remarks and ready laughter. And all the while Juliet was thinking, My God, if they knew! When the main course was eventually cleared, the lights were dimmed, and the Christmas pudding, enveloped in the blue flames of burning brandy, was ceremoniously carried into the dining room.

'Hurrah!' Candida bellowed, clapping her hands, amid a chorus of approval from everyone.

Seven-year old Tristan, sitting between Juliet and Daniel on cushions to raise him up to the right level, shrieked with excitement. 'Has it got sixpences in it?' he squawked. 'Can I get a lucky sixpence?'

'It's got so much money in it, it weighs a ton!' Candida joked. 'There's a sixpence for everyone here! So if you get two, give one to your neighbour!'

When they were all served, and the brandy butter had been handed around, Andrew took the opportunity of getting to his feet, while all the children prodded and poked with their spoons in search of pieces of silver.

'Firstly, Candida and I would like to welcome you all, and say how truly delighted we are that you've decided to abandon your magnificent town residences to spend the festive season in our humble dwelling.'

Amid the laughter, Candida smiled at him encouragingly. He was a shy, quiet man, and she knew she overshadowed him in her jolly boisterous way, but he never seemed to mind.

'I'd like to propose a toast,' he continued, raising his glass of wine, 'A toast to those we have loved who are no longer with us, and a toast to the young ones who represent the future, but most of all, a toast to us, the grown-ups. May we never again be pulled asunder by strife and discord!'

Everyone rose to their feet, including Tristan who stood wobbling slightly on his chair, as they all drank a toast to the Granville family.

'May God bless the Granvilles!' Candida added, 'and I hope you'll all come again next year!'

Andrew pretended to stagger with horror, much to the amusement of the young ones. He mopped his brow with a silk handkerchief and swayed in his chair. 'If the family gets much larger we'll have to build a wing on to the house,' he said with a mock groan.

It was four o'clock when lunch ended, and just as they were about to get up from the table, the telephone rang.

'Get that, dear girl, will you?' Candida asked Rosie, who was nearest to the door. 'Tell whoever it is that we've all gone out!'

Rosie returned a few minutes later flushed with pleasure. 'That was Mummy, ringing us all the way from New York! Imagine! I could hear her quite clearly, too. She just wanted to wish everyone a very happy Christmas. It's only eleven o'clock in the morning there, and they've just had breakfast in their suite at the Plaza Hotel!' she added, as if that sounded like the most exciting thing in the world to be doing.

'That was very thoughtful of her to telephone,' Lady Anne said generously. 'I hope you told her we all send our love back to her?'

'Yes, I did, Granny.' Rosie hugged Sophia. 'Wasn't that exciting, darling? Granny phoning us from America? She'll be back in the New Year and she says we must all get together soon.'

'I can never, ever, tell them now,' Juliet told Daniel that night, as they got ready to go to bed. She was sitting at the dressing table, taking off her diamond and emerald earrings and placing them in her jewel box. 'It would wreck everything, just when we've all got together. As soon as I heard Andrew's toast about the family not being torn asunder again, I knew, no matter what, I had to keep this secret to myself for the rest of my life.'

Daniel came up and stood close behind her, his hands resting on her shoulders. 'That's a great burden for you, darling. Do you wish you'd never found out? It's so hard for you knowing what *might* have been. And you'll always have doubts now, won't you?'

'You mean wondering if my mother knew all along?'

Daniel nodded. 'From the beginning I thought it was inconceivable that a banker of your father's calibre should only leave a will he'd made so many years ago.' He sighed in frustration. 'None of you queried it when your mother said that Mr Jones was your father's solicitor, either.'

'Frankly, we were all in such shock and so grief stricken that if she'd said the man in the moon was Dads' lawyer, none of us would have queried it. Anyway, he *had* been Dads' lawyer. That I know because I faintly remember him from when I was a child.'

As she spoke, she lifted off the shallow top compartment of her jewel box, which held rings and earrings, and took from beneath it the document she'd found among Henry's papers.

'He did admit he hadn't had any contact with your father for ten or twelve years,' Daniel said thoughtfully.

'Which is probably true. This will,' she continued, unfolding the stiff white paper, 'was made almost ten years ago. In 1945. Just after the war ended. According to the letter attached to the will, Dads had moved to a legal firm called Cartwright and Soames by then.'

'And in the will he doesn't leave everything to your mother?'

'He left her everything for *life*,' Juliet corrected him, 'and on her death, he requested Hartley was to be passed on to the five of us, and kept as a family home.' Her voice dropped so low Daniel could hardly hear her.

She put the will back in her jewel box, and carefully replaced the top compartment. Daniel watched her reflection in the triple dressing table mirror, and saw how her delicately featured face was drawn with pain and regret.

'Oh God, sweetheart. I'm so sorry,' he burst out, his voice deep and ragged. 'What a tragedy you didn't know about this. I wonder why the lawyers – what were they called . . .? – didn't contact your mother when Henry died? They must have seen the announcement of his death, not to mention all his obituaries?'

'Maybe they did,' she murmured.

He looked horrified. 'So you *really* think . . .?'

Juliet looked up at him, her eyes clouded with doubt. 'I don't *know*, Daniel. I'll never know, now. For the rest of my life I'll be wondering . . . but how can I ask Mama? And what good would that do? It would only cause an even worse rift in the family, just when we've patched things up. In fact it would be the end of the family. Daddy would never have wanted that to happen.' She gave a deep sigh. 'Hartley's gone. Nothing can be done to get it back. All that's important now is that we stay close as a family, and support each other.'

Daniel looked deeply into her eyes. 'Can you bear to live

with this secret? And how are you going to face your mother, for the rest of your life with these doubts in your head?'

'I can do anything,' she said firmly, 'as long as I have you by my side. People are so much more important than places. And after all, Hartley was only a place, wasn't it?' she added, speaking with more conviction than she felt.